Christmas Magic

Written by five artists of extraordinary talent, these very special, newly written stories celebrate the simple joys and traditions of Christmas—with each heartwarming tale evoking its own unique style and flavor. In Gayle Buck's "Old Acquaintances," the magic of Christmas is remembered in a story of love and longing, while in "A Gift of Fortune," Anita Mills writes of the snowbound reunion of two unlikely lovers. Both Edith Layton's "The Duke's Progress" and Mary Balogh's "The Star of Bethlehem" are moving stories of holiday sadness, hope, and the renewal of spirit. And "The Kissing Bough" by Patricia Rice is a bittersweet tale of love and reconciliation. These are stories to warm your heart with the romance, generosities, and joys of the season—holiday tales that can be read and enjoyed year after year.

A REGENCY CHRISTMAS

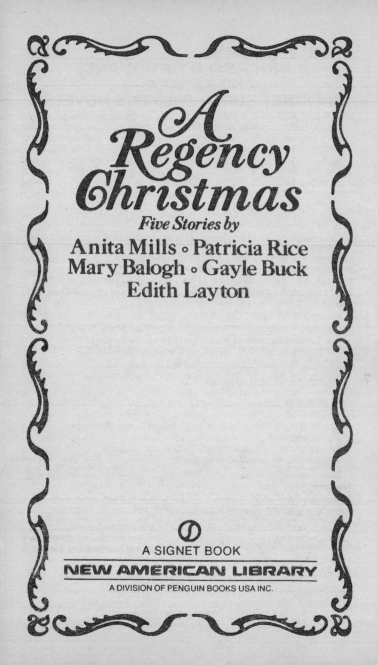

A Regency Christmas

Five Stories by

Anita Mills ∘ Patricia Rice
Mary Balogh ∘ Gayle Buck
Edith Layton

Ⓞ
A SIGNET BOOK

NEW AMERICAN LIBRARY
A DIVISION OF PENGUIN BOOKS USA INC.

SIGNET, SIGNET CLASSIC, MENTOR, ONYX, PLUME,
MERIDIAN and NAL BOOKS are published by New American
Library, a division of Penguin Books USA Inc., 1633 Broadway,
New York, New York 10019

First Printing, November, 1989

1 2 3 4 5 6 7 8 9

PRINTED IN THE UNITED STATES OF AMERICA

Contents

Old Acquaintances

by

Gayle Buck

The well-sprung carriage rocked in a soothing rhythm. She was perfectly comfortable. She had a brick to warm her feet and a heavy lap rug tucked snugly over her legs. In her hands, she held a favorite book. And she was returning home to Elmswood Hall for the remainder of the holidays. She should have been content.

But Miss Judith Grantham was restive. She finally admitted it to herself when her eyes drifted away from the page of her book for the hundredth time since starting on her journey. Not one to fling herself after a lost cause, Judith lay aside the book and gave herself over to the changing landscape outside the glazed window.

Snowflakes flashed past the glass, winking in the late afternoon sunlight like so many bits of shiny tinsel. The white fields and hedgcrows were marked by tall pristine drifts. It was an enchanting prospect, but Miss Grantham was not in the least appreciative.

She sighed, wondering what had gotten into her. She should be anticipating getting home to Elmswood, but instead her spirits sank ever lower as the carriage closed the distance to her destination. She knew the reason, of course. It was the same at the end of every visit to her sister's sprawling home, when she swore, amid the loud protests of her nieces and nephews, that she would be glad of the peace at Elmswood. But the truth was that she missed the companionship and confidences of her sister, her brother-in-law's quiet wit, and the numerous progeny who dragged on her hands, demanding her attention, and who generally besieged one whom they called the best of aunts.

Judith knew herself to be fortunate. She enjoyed the adoration of her sister's family and was a welcome and frequent visitor. She was the possessor of a fair estate, unentailed and bequeathed by her mother upon her birth, with the added benefit of an adequate income that had been settled on her through the terms of her father's will.

Though she hardly gave a thought to it, she knew that she was considered to be a young woman of uncommon good looks. She was of a willowy height that lent grace and proportion to a deep bosom and curved hips. Her eyes were dark smoke gray that could lighten either with amusement or anger. Her hair was dark and curling, her winged brows well-marked, her nose straight, and her mouth delectably full. In fact, there was but one flaw attached to Miss Judith Grantham and that had to do with her past.

When Miss Grantham had been brought out for her first Season, she had become an instant success. The gentlemen raved in admiration of the "English Tea Rose," as she was immediately dubbed, and though there were ladies who experienced twinges of envy, little was said against Miss Grantham because her kindness of manner quickly won over even some of the haughtiest of dames.

Miss Grantham had therefore enjoyed exceptional popularity. When her engagement to Sir Peregrine Ashford was announced, it was touted as a very satisfactory ending to a spectacular career, for Sir Peregrine was himself as popular with the gentlemen as he was with the ladies.

But that had been five years ago, before Judith had

jilted Sir Peregrine, for reasons still unknown beyond
the parties involved, and she had earned for herself a
reputation. At four-and-twenty, Miss Grantham was
still considered a beauty but quite beyond the marriageable age. She might still have been seriously
courted if there had been a gentleman audacious
enough to brave both Grantham's reputation and the
aura of mystery that clung to her. For there always
seemed to lurk a faint hint of amusement in her eyes,
as though she viewed the world from a vantage point
not given to others. The distance in her gaze put off
even the most obtuse of gentlemen, who uncomfortably suspected that they were the object of Miss Grantham's amusement. So Miss Grantham was looked
upon as an unattainable beauty, certainly worthy of
admiration but never to be approached.

Judith was well aware of what was said of her and
it amused her to encourage the speculation because for
the most part the life she led perfectly suited her. It
was only in rare moments such as this, when she had
left the warmth and cheer of her sister's home, that she
was not quite content with her lot. After the bustle,
Elmswood seemed particularly echoing during the remainder of the Christmas holidays, but Judith always
made a point of returning to Elmswood so that she
could uphold her role on Boxing Day, the first week-
day after Christmas, when by tradition she handed out
a Christmas gift box to each member of her household.

Of course, it was pleasant to be mistress of her own
household and her staff did decorate Elmswood in the
traditional manner with holly and fir, and roaring fires
provided welcoming heat in every room. But it was
not as though she would be sharing the warmth with
anyone else, she thought with a touch of melancholy.

Judith realized that she was fast sinking into a
maudlin self-pity and she gave herself a thorough mental shaking. She detested self-pity in others and it appalled her that she could come close to indulging in it

herself. "Enough of that, my girl," she said firmly.
She could have had that other well enough, but she
had chosen against it. Actually, she had had no true
regrets for her decision. It had been the right one at
the time. But once in a while the thought crept up on
her to wonder what her life might have been if she had
married.

For the briefest of moments her thoughts touched on
Sir Peregrine Ashford. After she had jilted him, it had
been a very long time before she had been able to
think of him without feeling a constriction in her
throat. But in five years Judith had learned that time
had a way of softening certain memories and she no
longer felt that flash of pain. Sir Peregrine had been
the most attractive gentleman that she had ever known.
As surrounded as she had been by gentlemen, she had
still been attracted to Sir Peregrine upon first sighting
his broad shoulders and the crisp curling hair that
touched his collar. When he had turned his head and
his incredible piercing blue eyes met hers, Judith had
literally felt her heart take flight.

A reminiscent smile played about her mouth and her
eyes held a certain light. She and Sir Peregrine had
been quite a match, complimenting one another in
every way. Except one, Judith remembered. Her smile
faded a little as her thoughts carried her into the past.
It had been an unfortunate happening, but certainly
her eyes had been irrevocably opened to the truth. And
she had never been one to shirk the truth once it was
borne in upon her.

The carriage slowed, distracting Judith from her
somber thoughts. She leaned closer to the window and
realized that the vehicle was actually stopping. Judith
unlatched the window and put out her head. "Edward,
why have we stopped?" she called out. The cold
frosted her breath.

The driver was climbing down from the box, having
snubbed his reins. "A mail coach has overturned and

the road is blocked, miss. It looks to be a bad accident.''

Judith snapped shut the window. She did not wait for the carriage door to be opened, but unlatched it herself and stepped down. Snow crunched under her boots. She felt the immediate impact of the icy air against her face, but fortunately she was attired in a warm pelisse and a heavy traveling dress and the cold did not penetrate to any great degree.

"Miss, ye'll catch your death," objected Edward.

"Nonsense, I shall do no such thing," said Judith firmly. Nevertheless, she was glad of her muff and thrust her hands deeper into its warmth. "I wish to see for myself the damage and whether anyone has been hurt." The coachman was long inured to his mistress's firmness of purpose and without further protest he helpfully placed a hand under her elbow when it appeared that she might slip on a particularly bad patch of ice as they walked around to the front of the team of horses.

Judith was appalled at the sight that met her eyes. The mail coach was on its side in a drift, baggage had been flung in every direction, and the frightened horses were tangled in the traces. The passengers were seated on whatever was at hand, or standing in the snow, depending upon their inclinations. Most appeared simply bruised and shaken, but here and there was the unmistakable show of blood. "My word," said Judith inadequately.

"I'll just go help the coachman untangle his cattle, miss," said Edward.

"Of course, Edward, pray do whatever you can," said Judith. She looked about again at the passengers, some of whom appeared to be haranguing a lanky young gentleman who was sunk down on a portmanteau and holding his head in his hands. It was clear from the shrill accusations that the young gentleman had been the one at fault for the accident, having taken over the driver's whip and setting the mail coach at a dangerous pace over the frozen road. Dismissing those vigorously scolding individuals as probably undesirous of her help, Judith approached a woeful-looking gentleman who held a handkerchief to his brow. "Sir, I see that you are injured. Is there something that I might do?" she asked.

The gentleman grimaced as he glanced up at her. "A bit of flying glass, it was. I thank you kindly, my lady, but it is naught more than a scratch. Perhaps you might see to the young lady there, who I suspicion was quite shook up. She ended on the bottom when we was all thrown about," he said.

Judith looked around, surprised. She had not before noticed the young woman who stood somewhat separate from the others, perhaps because a light flurry of snow had blurred the outline of her pale gray pelisse. But now that Judith's attention had been drawn to her, she could discern the weary droop in the slight figure.

Judith went over immediately. "My dear ma'am, may I be of assistance? Have you been hurt?" The young woman lifted her head and Judith was struck at once by the budding loveliness of her heart-shaped countenance. Judith's compassion was fully aroused by the paper white of the girl's face and the pathetic look in her black-fringed china-blue eyes. The schoolgirl—for of such an age she judged her to be—had wrapped her arms about herself and it was plain that she was freezing cold. Judith held out her gloved hand. "Come with me at once. You must not stay out in this weather. You are not dressed for it."

The girl automatically took Judith's hand but she held back, objecting faintly. "My-my portmanteau and-and bandbox. What shall I do?"

"I shall have my coachman gather them up for you. Are these the ones?" asked Judith, pointing at the meager baggage at the girl's feet. At her nod, Judith called out to her servant, who was returning from helping the mail coach's driver. "Edward, pray put these up. I shall be taking this young lady to the next posting house."

"Aye, miss. And I have promised to take word of the accident, so it would be best if we was to get on, Miss Judith," said Edward.

Judith nodded. "Very well. Come, child, let us climb up into the carriage. You shall be warmer in a trice, I promise you." With that she led her unexpected guest to her carriage and opened the door for her. The girl climbed in somewhat stiffly and Judith followed, closing the door behind her. She sat down and turned her head to smile at the girl, who had sunk down on the seat with almost an air of dejection. Judith took note of the girl's expression but did not comment on it. Instead, she said bracingly, "I was just wishing for company. We shall share the lap rug. There you are, tucked in as snug as you please. You must take my muff, for I at least have gloves. And there is a brick to our feet. What more could one wish?"

The girl burst into tears.

"My dear! What have I said? I certainly never meant to offend you," said Judith, taken aback.

"No, no! You have been so kind—so good!" stammered the girl, tears slipping swiftly down her cheeks. She opened her reticule and frantically searched in it, at last bringing out a small handkerchief. She made an obvious effort to choke back her tears. She blew her nose, which Judith noticed with a touch of envy was not pinkened in the slightest by the violent exercise.

Judith reached out and captured one of the girl's agitated hands. Even through her glove she could feel that the slender fingers were chilled. "Child, you are safe with me. I am Miss Judith Grantham of Elmswood Hall. It is easily seen that you are out of water. Whatever possessed you to travel by mail coach? I am

persuaded that your family never countenanced it,"
she said quietly.

The girl threw a scared glance at her. "I do not
know what you mean. I frequently travel by mail
coach. It-it is perfectly comfortable for one of my station."

Judith put up her brows. There was the veriest hint
of a smile in her eyes. "And what is your station,
miss?"

The girl threw up her chin and challenged the older
woman with a bold stare. "Why, I am a lady's maid,
to be sure."

Judith could not help but laugh. She pressed the
girl's fingers before releasing her hand. "Dear girl, a
lady's maid is never so young, nor so pretty, as you.
Nor would one be attired in such an elegantly cut pelisse. And pray do not tell me it is your mistress's cast-
off, for I shall not believe you. Your manner and your
attire both proclaim you to be gently born, so you
must not attempt to pull the wool over my eyes, if you
please."

The girl cast a glance down at her gray pelisse and,
apparently realizing that it was futile to deny the truth
of Miss Grantham's observation, she sighed. Her
china-blue eyes bravely met Judith's gaze. "Since you
have found me out, I shall not try to hoodwink you,
ma'am. I am running away from my guardian, who is
a detestable beast. And though I do appreciate your
kindness in carrying me to the next posting house, I
hope that you do not feel compelled to persuade me
to change my mind. I am quite determined never to
return to my cousin's domination."

Judith was silent a moment. "I see. Pray, what is
your name?"

The girl hesitated briefly and then she shrugged. "I
doubt that it signifies, for I shall not see you again. I
am Cecily Brown. I hope that you are not too offended

that I do not divulge my direction as well, but you must see that simply would not do.''

The name meant nothing to Judith and she was disappointed. If by remote chance she had heard of the girl's family, as a family acquaintance she might have been able to offer the hospitality of Elmswood Hall and perhaps provided a neutral ground upon which the girl and her guardian could thrash out their differences. As it was, she knew that she could do little but offer the girl some food for thought. ''Cecily, have you perfectly thought out what you are attempting? I know nothing of your circumstances, but surely your guardian would not wish you to disappear without some assurance of your continued well-being. And pray, how do you intend to live? Do you have relatives or friends who would be willing to take you in?''

Cecily shook her head. ''I have no one but my cousin. And as for him, I think that he will be heartily glad that I am gone. He never wished to have me cast on him, you see, and that is why he came up with his horrid notion to marry me to the first gentleman that he found acceptable.'' Her bosom rose as deep indignation overcame her. ''Miss Grantham, the gentleman is twice my age and he is bald and he smokes a cigar, which I cannot at all abide! I shall not marry him, I shall not!''

There was a hint of hysteria in her voice that Judith was quick to note. ''The gentleman in question is not clamoring for your hand at this moment, so you may rest easy for a while yet,'' she said with deliberate callousness.

After a stunned moment, Cecily unwillingly laughed. ''I am sorry, Miss Grantham! I never meant to treat you to a turn of drama. Only it is all so idiotic. Why, I have not even been brought out. I think it frightfully unfair of Per—of my cousin. I should so like to go to London.'' She ended on such a wistful note that it touched the older woman's heart.

Judith shook her head. It would not do to become too sympathetic. Cecily's story struck such chords of understanding within her and it was an effort to recall that there was another side. The overbearing guardian may have had his reasons. There, it is plain whose side I have aligned myself with, thought Judith with exasperation. Overbearing, indeed! And he very likely wears a corset and helps himself too liberally to snuff, she thought whimsically. Aloud, she said, "Cecily, in all conscience I must ask you to reconsider your ill-considered flight. I would feel responsible if something untoward should happen to you once I have set you down."

"Of course I appreciate your sentiments, Miss Grantham. But truly, I am quite capable of caring for myself. I have had the splendid notion to enter service, you see, and so I shall do very well," said Cecily with bright confidence, her beautiful eyes shining from beneath the longest black lashes that Judith had ever seen on a female.

"Oh, my dear," she said helplessly, her gaze traveling from Cecily's lovely fresh face to her slender figure and back again. She took a breath. "I am sorry to inform you of it, Cecily, but no one is likely to hire anyone quite so pretty as you are. Except perhaps just the sort of gentleman that you are so adamant against marrying. And I fear that it will not be the gentleman's cigar smoke that you would find particularly objectionable, but his attempts to—to steal a kiss." She felt herself entirely inadequate at relaying the realities of the world to a young girl such as Cecily and she waited somewhat uncomfortably for her companion's inevitable query for enlightenment.

But Cecily's expression was not one of confusion. She looked surprised, then thoughtful. "Once, as a small child, I surprised Papa with one of the maids. I suppose that is the sort of thing you mean. No, I should not care for that. Perhaps I shall become a mantua maker instead.''

Judith was taken aback. ''Cecily, do I perfectly understand what you are saying about your father?''

''Oh yes. Before Papa died, he was a bit of a rake. And though I do not know precisely, I suppose it meant he was quite fond of maids,'' said Cecily with an innocent and inquiring glance.

Judith sat back against the seat, her breath quite knocked out of her. ''Indeed, I suppose so,'' she said weakly, clearing her throat. When Cecily turned her head away to glance out of the carriage window, where the day could be seen as fast growing dim, Judith studied her profile with a mixture of astonishment and bewildered estimation. She was fast coming to realize that Cecily Brown was not an ordinary miss. Cecily presented the appearance of a schoolgirl, naive and trusting, and yet Judith had seen depths of character and experience that belonged to someone several years older.

Her determination not to fall in with her guardian's wishes was perhaps nothing much out of the common way, but coupled as it was to her ability to act upon her decisions made Cecily unusual indeed, thought Judith, remembering a young girl who had not had the same courage of her convictions. As for Cecily's casual reference to her father's peccadillo and her acceptance of it, Judith thought she was never more shocked in her life. She herself had known nothing of the opposite sex until her engagement. Her cheeks flushed warmly at her unbidden memories and she hastily returned her thoughts to Cecily.

Despite herself and knowing that she should not become involved more than she already was, Judith turned over in her mind what Cecily had said of her situation. There had to be something she could do to aid the girl in establishing herself happily. Judith felt that she must make some sort of effort in Cecily's behalf, or she would always wonder what had happened to the girl.

The carriage slowed and stopped. Judith put down the window as her coachman came up to it. Snow swirled briefly with a gust of cold wind. "What is toward, Edward?"she asked.

"We have come to the posting house, miss," said the coachman. He threw a look at the dusk sky. "I mislike the weather, Miss Judith. The wind is sharpening a bit and the snow is heavier."

Judith made a quick decision. "I shall step down with Miss Brown for a quick cup of tea while you report the accident to the innkeeper, Edward. Then we shall go on as quickly as possible to reach Elmswood before nightfall."

She and Cecily walked into the inn. The innkeeper's wife recognized Judith and she expressed surprise to see her. "Miss Grantham, it is a pleasure, I am sure. It is that rare that you honor us with your company, what with Elmswood so close and all. What may I do for you?" she said.

Judith looked about the coffee room, which was nearly deserted at that hour, and decided against bespeaking a private parlor. "I think that we shall have a strong cup of tea, and perhaps a light repast for my young friend," she said.

Cecily looked alarmed. "Really, I do not wish supper. I feel as though I could not swallow a bite. It is rather warm in here, is it not?"

Judith stared at her, frowning. The coffee room was warmed by the fire in the grate, but it was not so warm that Cecily should become flushed by the heat. She hoped the girl was not becoming ill. "We shall have just the tea, then."

"Certainly, miss. It is shaping up to be a bad storm tonight. I know that you ladies will be wishful to get on to Elmswood, so I will bring the tea straight away," said the innkeeper's wife.

"Oh, but I shall not be going with Miss Grantham. I wish to bespeak a room for the night so that I may catch the mail coach in the morning," said Cecily.

The innkeeper's wife looked at her in dismay. "I am sorry, miss, but we haven't a room to spare. What with the weather and all, wc'vc had more than our share of travelers who have decided to stay until first light. If you was a gentleman, I might see if there was someone who would not mind sharing his room with a stranger. But as it is, I haven't even a closet for a decent young lady."

Cecily stared at the woman, speechless. She did not seem to know what to do. Judith took matters into her own hands. "My dear child, you must certainly come home with me."

"But I cannot impose on you further, Miss Grantham. You have already been so kind," said Cecily.

"Nonsense. It will be you who will be doing me the favor. Elmswood is very quiet this Christmas. Indeed, I would not mind it in the least if half a dozen more personages chose to become marooned on my doorstep. It would make for quite a jolly little party, don't you think?" asked Judith in a reassuring way. Cecily responded to Judith's jest, though her smile wavered a little.

The innkeeper's wife saw that the matter was settled and she nodded in satisfaction. She bustled off at once for the promised tea and she was soon back, saying that she always kept a hot pot handy. Judith declined sugar but accepted milk for her tea. She saw that Cecily was fond of a very sweetened tea and it almost made her teeth hurt to watch the girl sip at the resulting syrup.

Before the ladies had quite finished their cups of tea, Edward the coachman came up to inform Judith that the innkeeper had promised to send out help to the stranded mail coach passengers. "The snow is becoming that heavy, miss, that I think it best that we get on as quick as we can," he said, casting an anxious glance at his mistress's cup.

"We shall go at once. Miss Brown will be accompanying us after all, Edward. I hope that you have not set down her baggage," said Judith, rising from the table. Cecily immediately leaped up, not wishing to delay their departure and thus be any more of a burden to her benefactress.

"No, miss. That is to say, I will put it back in the carriage this instant," said Edward.

Judith nodded and walked out of the coffee room to find the innkeeper's wife so that she could pay the bill. With the woman's good wishes ringing on the air, the carriage bound for Elmswood Hall once more turned onto the icy road. Snow swirled about its dark moving shape, then it was gone into the dusk.

The welcoming light and warmth of Elmswood Hall were all that Judith had hoped. The scent of fir and pine and warm wax wafted out the open door, drawing the travelers inside. Judith was glad to step into the hall and hear the butler's welcome. "I am happy to be home, Withers. This young lady is Miss Cecily Brown. The coach she was on had an unfortunate accident and so I have offered the hospitality of Elmswood to her. Pray see that a room is prepared for her," she said, beginning to draw off her gloves.

"At once, Miss Grantham," said Withers, motioning for a footman to take up the portmanteau and bandbox that had been brought in from the carriage. "I took the liberty of setting up a cold collation in the drawing room in anticipation of your arrival and I shall bring in tea in a quarter hour."

"Bless you, Withers. That will be just time enough to change from this damp travel dress," said Judith, bestowing a grateful smile on him. She turned to Cecily and took her hands in her own. Again she noticed how cold the girl's slender fingers were. "The footman will show you the way to your room. I shall meet with you again in the drawing room for supper in a few minutes.''

Cecily smiled her acquiescence and then followed the footman carrying her baggage up the stairway that occupied one side of the entry hall. Her weariness was underscored by the droop of her slim shoulders. She was in no mind to demur at whatever was proposed, only wishing for rest. Through the fog that had settled over her, she noticed the festive loops of holly and fir that decorated the graceful lift of stairs. Her wavering spirits were comforted by the cheery sight. She was safe here, she thought gratefully, and stifled a yawn.

Judith watched her guest ascend, a tiny frown between her winged brows. She pulled her gloves through her fingers without being conscious of it. The butler was thoroughly familiar with Miss Grantham's moods and he observed this sign of perturbation with interest. He wondered what there was about Miss Brown that should prove disquieting to Miss Grantham. ''Miss Grantham, will there be anything else?'' he asked quietly.

Judith was startled out of her thoughts. ''No, not at the moment, Withers,'' she said. She walked to the stairs and swiftly went up them and thence to her bedroom. Her maid, whom she had sent off earlier in a separate carriage with all of her baggage, had arrived some time before her and was waiting to help her out of the heavy travel dress. In moments, Judith was freshly attired in a long-sleeved merino gown of a soft dove gray that enhanced the smoky shade of her eyes. Her hair, freed at last of the confines of her bonnet, had been brushed into soft waves.

Judith went downstairs, thinking to join Cecily. Instead, she discovered a small group of strangers who were loosely clustered about her butler in the entry hall and besieging him with loud statements. Judith paused on the last step, her hand resting on the banister, surprised. The woman in the group spied Judith and surged forward. "You must be Miss Grantham, then. I was just telling this fudsy-faced butler of yours that you had left word at the posting house that any who could not find a bed there would be welcomed at Elmswood Hall," she said firmly.

Withers rolled his eyes in appeal as one of the gentlemen asserted that what the woman had said was so. Judith was entirely taken aback and for a long second she was speechless. Though she was unaware of it, her very immobility and the exquisite austerity of her dress lent her an air of command. The woman dropped back a pace and the others quietened, waiting.

Judith realized that she was the object of all eyes. She focused on the woman in front of her. "Who might you be, ma'am?" she asked quietly, trying to make sense of the happening.

The woman flushed, thinking that she was being gently reprimanded for her own curt greeting. "I am Mrs. Nickleby, and that gentleman is Mr. Nickleby. We were on our way to our son's house when the mail coach was overturned by his young lordship, who, as I made certain to tell him, should have known better when anyone could tell he was tipsy as a wheelbarrow."

"Aye, his lordship was singing at the top of his lungs for some time before. All of us inside of the coach heard him as plain as a pikestaff. Very pretty it was, too," said the gentleman who had been pointed out as Mr. Nickleby. He belatedly made a bow in Judith's direction.

Judith's gaze traveled on to study the face of his young lordship, who had flushed when he came under discussion but whose dignity was such that he would not offer a word in his own defense. "Lord Baltor. Your servant, ma'am," he said, making a creditable bow despite the obvious headache that he sported. The slight gentleman who stood next to Lord Baltor, and who up to that point had not addressed anyone but the butler, also bowed to Judith and mumbled something incoherent that she took as a pleasantry of some sort.

"Miss Grantham, these persons say that according to the innkeeper's wife, you graciously opened Elmswood Hall to unfortunate travelers," said Withers in a wooden voice.

Judith was puzzled for only a moment before she recalled her jesting remark to Cecily about wishing for a handful of marooned guests. Looking at the motley foursome in the hall, Judith thought wryly that her offhand wish had just been granted. Certainly she could not turn them away since the inn was full. But surely there had been one or two other passengers on the ditched mail coach, she thought, when she did not see the gentleman of the bleeding brow. "Is this all of you?" she asked.

Her question seemed to relieve the tension of those who looked at her. "Aye, Miss Grantham. The others were able to double up in the rooms or bed down in the coffee room in front of the fire," said Mr. Nickleby.

"But that was not for me, as I told Mr. Nickleby," said Mrs. Nickleby. "I said that since a lady had been so gracious as to open her home, it would be fairly rude not to give her ladyship the satisfaction of helping those less fortunate than herself."

"I appreciate your kind thought, Mrs. Nickleby," said Judith, a decided gleam in her fine eyes. Before her unlooked-for guests could realize that she viewed their advent on her doorstep with amusement, she gestured toward the drawing room. "A cold collation and tea is served in the drawing room. I assume that you must all be famished after such an arduous day and I invite you to make free. I shall have rooms prepared for you in the meantime."

"There now, Henry. Did I not tell you that we would not make fools of ourselves?" asked Mrs. Nickleby complacently, leading the way into the drawing room. Her husband's reply was lost as he followed his spouse. The slight gentleman, rubbing his hands together in obvious anticipation, lost little time in ducking after the Nicklebys. Lord Baltor alone hesitated, his lip unconsciously caught between his teeth as he looked uncertainly at his hostess.

Judith smiled serenely at his lordship. "I shall not keep you from supper, Lord Baltor." He flushed again and went with a hasty step into the drawing room.

The butler could scarcely contain himself. "You are never sitting down with that lot, Miss Grantham!"

"Oh, I don't know. It might be rather diverting. I have never dined with tradespeople before," said Judith. She had divined in one glance that the Nicklebys were of the rising middle class.

"Cits, and likely thieves to boot," said Withers sweepingly.

Judith laughed. "You have forgotten poor Lord Baltor. Really, Withers, it would be frightfully rude to abandon my unexpected guests because they chance not to run in the same circles as I do. Has Miss Brown come down yet?"

The butler shook his head. "The maid who was sent in to Miss Brown found her asleep on top of the bed, still in her travel dress. She thought she should not wake the young miss."

"Quite right. I could see that the poor girl was dead on her feet. I shall look in on her later to see that she is comfortable," said Judith, nodding. With every expectation of being entertained, she went into the drawing room.

It always pleased Judith to see her home done up for the holiday season, and in particular the drawing room. Garlands of bay, fir, rosemary, and pine twigs offset by red silk bows looped across the mantel and several branches of candles burned with cheery light. From the ceiling hung the traditional kissing bough of fragrant greenery adorned with candles, red apples, rosettes of colored paper, and various ornaments. A bunch of gray-green mistletoe laden with white berries was at its center. All in all, the scene was a decidedly cozy one, what with the addition of her unexpected houseguests to complete the atmosphere of seasonal cheer, Judith thought.

Her guests had taken her at her word and had helped themselves to the cold meats and cheeses and bread that had been meant for her own supper. Mr. and Mrs. Nickleby had established themselves well in front of the fireplace where they could be certain of feeling the heat. The slight gentleman, who had not yet introduced himself, Judith remembered, had taken up a place a little separate from the others, apparently preferring to stand in the shadows by the curtained windows and holding his heaped plate in his hands. Lord Baltor sat on the settee, obviously ill at ease and with only a meager cup of tea. Mrs. Nickleby was recommending in almost a maternal fashion that he should eat at least a crust of bread. "For I know for a fact that one does not sleep half as well on an empty belly, your lordship," she said authoritatively, carrying a generous portion of lavishly buttered bread to her mouth.

"Quite right, pet," said Mr. Nickleby, nodding.

Upon catching sight of Judith, Lord Baltor leaped up from his seat with an expression almost of relief. "Miss Grantham!" he uttered.

Judith went forward, an easy smile on her face. "I trust all is to satisfaction," she said with an encompassing glance about her guests.

"Indeed it is, miss," said Mr. Nickleby. He was making inroads on a heavily loaded plate and he barely glanced up. Mrs. Nickleby, her mouth full, satisfied herself with a vigorous nod and a wave of what remained of her thick slab of bread. The slight gentleman nodded deferentially, but he did not vouchsafe a syllable.

Judith turned her smile on Lord Baltor. Without seeming to stare, she took notice of his reddened eyes and haggard face. "Pray do join me in getting a plate, my lord. I am persuaded you must be at least as famished as I."

Lord Baltor turned a shade green at the thought of putting food into his queasy stomach. "No, I think not at the moment. I-I prefer the tea, thank you."

"Then you must have a refill. Allow me to pour it for you," said Judith, turning to the sideboard and the tea pot. Lord Baltor followed her, voicing disjointed phrases of thanks. Judith responded soothingly as she poured tea for his lordship and for herself. She sipped at her cup and then asked in a lowered voice, "My lord, you appear a trifle pale. May I offer you a headache powder before you retire tonight?"

Lord Baltor flushed. "You are most kind, Miss Grantham." He summoned up a wavering smile and met her curious gaze frankly. "It was only a bit of a lark, you know. I never intended—that is to say, the coach swung too wide in the turn and before I knew it, we were all flung into the drift."

Judith did not comment on the young gentleman's obvious state of inebriation at the time, but instead asked, "Where are you bound, my lord?"

He seemed relieved that she did not pursue the cause of the accident. "I was supposed to visit with friends the entire break between terms, but I am going home for the remainder of the holiday. It is to be a surprise to my aunt, who is all the family I have in the world. She is a wonderful old lady."

"I am certain that she shall be most happy to see you," said Judith. She was on the point of saying something further, but her attention was claimed by Mrs. Nickleby, who proposed that a card game be got up as the evening was still young. Judith thought there was a point at which even she drew the line. "Thank you, but you must not count on me, ma'am. It has been a rather fatiguing day, as I am persuaded you must understand, having traveled also. I shall say good night to you all now, and my butler will show you up to your rooms whenever you are ready."

"Well, that is as strong a hint as I ever heard," said Mrs. Nickleby, somewhat affronted.

"I am persuaded Miss Grantham meant nothing by it, so kind as she has been, dear wife," said Mr. Nickleby, setting aside an emptied plate with a replete sigh. He cracked a huge yawn. "Truth to tell, pet, I am that ready for a soft bed myself."

Mrs. Nickleby's expression softened. "Of course, Mr. Nickleby. Anyone can see that you are dead on your feet." The couple made their good nights to the company and went out of the drawing room, Mrs. Nickleby exclaiming all the while that she hoped the bed was not too soft or her back would suffer. "And one cannot tell what one may find in a strange place. I shall myself inspect the freshness of the sheets. You know what is said of these great houses, Mr. Nickleby. The rooms are done up and then left for months on end without airing."

Judith and Lord Baltor exchanged speaking glances. A soft cough claimed their attention and they both glanced with surprise at the slight gentleman, who had been so unassuming as to have been forgotten. "Begging your pardon, miss, but I was wishful of thanking you for a fine supper," he said.

"You are most welcome, Mr.—? I am sorry, but I do not know your name," said Judith.

There was almost an imperceptible hesitation before the slight gentleman bowed. "I am John Smith, at your service, miss."

Judith's gray eyes lit with amusement. It was obvious that the slight gentleman had chosen to offer to her a pseudonym and she wondered for what reason. He appeared a most harmless sort. "Of course, Mr. Smith. We shall undoubtedly visit again on the morrow, if this weather has anything to say of the matter. Normally one cannot hear the wind so plainly in this room."

"Indeed, miss," said Mr. Smith. He bowed again and left the drawing room.

Lord Baltor offered his arm. "I would count it an honor to be allowed to escort you, Miss Grantham," he said formally.

Judith inclined her head, again amused. Despite his lordship's wearying day and the persistent headache, he was no less mannered than his birth would allow him to be. She accepted his escort and they left the drawing room together, to separate at the head of the stairs where Judith left him to the guidance of a footman and went on to her own bedroom. It had been an interesting end to what had begun as a rather depressing day. Judith, who was reminded by the rumble in her stomach that she had not eaten anything while downstairs, requested that a cup of broth and a sandwich be brought to her room. Not even the enticement of a supper would have persuaded her to remain in the drawing room and in peril of being roped into a card game with Mrs. Nickleby, who was surely one of the most vulgar individuals she had ever met.

Judith was never at her best in the morning, yet she detested remaining late abed. It was therefore her custom to take breakfast alone in the breakfast room, in blessed quiet with a large pot of coffee at her elbow and the view through the French windows of Elmswood's snow-covered lawn to soothe her jaundiced eyes. The servants had long since become aware of her distaste for speech in the morning and they always served her with silent efficiency before leaving her to her sluggish thoughts. Judith appreciated and even looked forward to this golden hour when she could literally waken slowly to the rest of the world.

With guests in the house, her usual routine would be next to impossible to maintain. Judith did not think that she could bring herself to face the voluble Mrs. Nickleby over the breakfast table. But she could not remain in her bedroom either, for to do so would make her feel unnecessarily claustrophobic. She hoped that by going down to breakfast at a particularly early hour she would be less likely to run into any of her assorted guests and would still be able to enjoy her usual solitary beginning to the day.

She did not bargain on someone being before her in the breakfast room, and especially not the gentleman she found. At sight of him, she stopped dead in her tracks. The hawkish features and the broad-shouldered, lithe body were all too familiar to her. An incoherent sound escaped her.

Sir Peregrine Ashford was in a foul temper. The day before he had spent hours out in the freezing weather chasing down a foolish chit of a girl. He had thought when he reached the posting house that his pursuit had finally come to an end, but the intelligence that the young lady had been taken up by Miss Grantham had sent him once more out into the heavy swirling snow. When he had at last caught up with his prey, he had been obliged to bang on the door of a private residence at the ungodly hour of midnight and demand admittance, which had been granted to him with astonished dismay. He had risen early after an indifferent sleep, determined to quit Elmswood Hall as swiftly as possible and get on with his business. But he had been informed somewhat unhappily by the butler that the house was snowbound. Sir Peregrine had not accepted the news with equanimity.

He felt that the situation could not be worse, until he looked up from his breakfast and met the startled gaze of the woman who had once jilted him. His smile was sardonic. He had been prepared for this encounter, though perhaps it had come earlier than he had anticipated. "Good morning, Miss Grantham. I trust that you slept well," he said with the manner of a perfect guest. But he did not rise to offer his hostess a chair, instead leaning back a little in his own so that he could survey her better.

Judith had gone rather white, but she managed to nod coolly at him. She approached the table and seated herself. It took all her fortitude not to allow how shaken she was by this totally unexpected encounter to show. "Sir Peregrine, this is quite a surprise. I had no notion of your arrival," she said, and knew instantly how inane and inadequate were the words. Questions tumbled through her still sleep-fogged mind. She knew that she must get hold of herself, and quickly. Desperately, she looked about and she seized gratefully upon the coffee pot.

"Meaning that if you had known you would have given orders to bar the door against me, leaving me to freeze slowly on the steps," said Sir Peregrine.

Judith could not stop the faintest tremor of her hand as she poured steaming coffee into her cup. Anger at herself for the slight betrayal steadied her nerves. She cast an irritated glance at her companion. "How idiotic! Of course I would not have. Though if you mean to rip up at me this early in the morning, I shall probably wish that I had had the opportunity," she said.

Sir Peregrine smiled, though with little amusement. "You have always been quick to take fire, Judith."

"And you, sir, have always had the singular knack of setting up my back," said Judith swiftly. All her hopes of a quiet easing into the day had vanished with Sir Peregrine's unexpected presence, and that did nothing to improve her overall mood. She eyed him in a decidedly unfriendly way. "Why have you come to Elmswood? I do not mind telling you, it is an unpleasant shock to discover you at the breakfast table." She was still thinking of her lost solitude and therefore his reaction caught her by surprise.

"Thank you, ma'am! I had long ago been brought to realize that you held me in contempt, but I was not aware of those feelings of revulsion that you have obviously harbored," said Sir Peregrine. His piercing blue eyes were bright and hard.

Judith flushed, realizing belatedly how uncivil she had sounded. She had always prided herself on treating others as kindly as she herself would like to be treated. No matter what history lay between herself and Sir Peregrine, it did not give her license to insult him unnecessarily. "I am sorry. I was unforgivably rude. My excuse must be that I am not at my best in the morning. I am not usually so prickly after I have had my coffee," she said.

Sir Peregrine stared at her. After a long moment he allowed a fleeting grin to cross his face. "I have overset your hopes of a solitary breakfast, have I? If it will ease your disgruntlement in any measure, I was not best pleased to have my own breakfast interrupted. I detest making conversation so early in the day."

"And so do I," said Judith. He laughed and turned his attention to his unfinished plate, obviously with the intention of suspending communication until they were both ready to resume it. Judith helped herself to eggs and ham and then set to with relish, finding that she had quite an appetite after her light repast the night before. She finished eating and began her second cup of coffee in the ensuing silence. Over the cup's rim she watched Sir Peregrine begin on a second helping of steak and kidneys. Finally, she sighed. "It is of no use, Perry. I still wish to know why you have come to Elmswood. You cannot have a sudden uncontrollable desire for my company." She meant the last to be a light touch of humor, but when she looked into his suddenly frowning eyes, it occurred to her that it would not be such a bad thing if he had come with the object of seeking her out.

Sir Peregrine was apparently not subject to the same wistful thought. "Believe me, nothing short of necessity would have brought me to Elmswood Hall. I was informed at the posting house that you arrived there with a young lady who was subsequently persuaded to come on with you here. I believe that you are harboring my ward, Miss Grantham."

Judith, who had flinched at Sir Peregrine's blunt disclaimer, now looked at him in stupefaction. "You!? You are the beastly, overbearing cousin that that poor girl is fleeing? I cannot credit it."

"Indeed, can you not?" Sir Peregrine's smile was grim. "I am certain that Cecily has spun a fine tale for you, but do not allow her to play too strongly on your sympathies. She is too young to know what she is about, besides possessing a decided turn for the dramatic. I have had little ease of mind since succeeding to her guardianship. If the truth be known, I would as lief wash my hands of the business."

Judith had listened to him with increasing stiffness. Everything he said seemed to confirm Cecily's assertions. "I am persuaded that you do not mean that. Surely you are not grown so callous that you have forgotten what dreams one may hold at age seventeen! Of course the girl is high-spirited and romantic. What young girl is not?"

"I was never a dreamy youth, even in my salad days. And you, dear Judith, did not allow romantic fancy to turn *your* head. Indeed, far from it. I doubt there was ever a more prosaic young lady in all of England," said Sir Peregrine with irony.

Judith bit back the impulsive retort she was about to utter. It would not do to cut up at Sir Peregrine over the past, not if she was to discover how best to aid Cecily out of her predicament. She took a deep breath to calm herself, though Sir Peregrine's unfair observation stung. "Cecily is still a child, I grant you, but there is a hint of fortitude, of determination, about her that is appealing. My interest was caught by her story of an unwanted suitor and an overbearing guardian. However, I certainly do not approve of the course of action she has taken, and I hope that while you are here, Sir Peregrine, you and Cecily may iron out some of your differences."

"Your concern is misplaced and misguided, ma'am. I think that I know better how to deal with Cecily than would a stranger," said Sir Peregrine coolly.

Judith lost her temper. "Indeed, and see what has come of your handling of her! She was fleeing from you in a common mail coach, intending to solicit a position as a lady's maid. I do not pretend to understand the desperation of a gently born girl who feels compelled to such a course, but I do think that if you had had an ounce of common sense you would have attempted to sound out her feelings before—"

"My God, do you think that I have not tried reason? But it is akin to addressing a whirligig. My precious ward had tumbled headlong into love not fewer than six times in two years. The last was the dancing master at her boarding school, who, I am given to understand, thought it might be lucrative to encourage the simpering adoration of an heiress," said Sir Peregrine. He gave a short bark of laughter. "Cecily was not best pleased to learn that her inamorata chose a purse of silver and flight over the less charming prospect of enduring penury with her."

The years rushed over Judith, an echo of long-ago hurt. "How odd that you should choose the same means to direct Cecily's destiny," she said with a brittle smile. Her gray eyes had lightened almost to transparency, so great was her fury.

Sir Peregrine was taken aback by the sudden blaze of passion in her expression. He was given no opportunity to question her oblique statement, however, as the breakfast room door opened and the Nicklebys entered.

At sight of Judith, Mr. Nickleby smiled and nodded. "There you are, Mrs. Nickleby. Did I not tell you that early hours are kept in the country? We have almost missed breakfast with our kind hostess. Your servant, Miss Grantham. Sir," said Mr. Nickleby, making a courtly bow to the two sitting silent at the table. If he had been a sensitive man he would have been struck by the electric tension in the room, but as it was he never noticed the flush of temper in Miss Grantham's face or the coldness of the gentleman's expression.

He held a chair for Mrs. Nickleby, who seated herself with a sniff of disapproval. "I cannot for the life of me understand why some insist on breakfast at the crack of dawn, and then it must be kippers and eggs. So heavy and unhealthy for one, I am persuaded. I myself take only chocolate and toast. Mr. Nickleby, I do not see any chocolate. It must be an oversight, surely. Pray pull the bell and have a pot brought." She glanced across the table and her brows rose. "Miss Grantham, you are not leaving us, surely?"

Judith, who had arisen from her seat, paused momentarily. Her eyes glittered. "Mrs. Nickleby, allow me to make known to you Sir Peregrine Ashford, who arrived some time in the night. I am persuaded that he will be spellbound by the story of your unlucky trip on the mail coach. Pray do excuse me, but I have a hundred and one items to see to this morning," she said. She swept out of the breakfast room, deriving a certain satisfaction at leaving Sir Peregrine to the Nicklebys and their unceasing conversation this early in the day. She hoped that it would give him a fine case of indigestion.

Judith went upstairs at once. She knocked at Cecily's door and, at her soft invitation, entered the bedroom. Cecily was sitting before the cheval glass while a maid put the finishing touches to the heavy curls that had been swept back and were held away from her face by a bright pink riband. The result was not unlike a soft dark cloud framing Cecily's huge eyes and heart-shaped face. Judith thought that she had never seen a more beautiful girl.

Cecily leaped up at once when she saw her hostess in the glass. She held out her hands. "Miss Grantham! I do apologize for falling asleep last night when I was to join you. It was just that I was so sleepy and I thought that I would close my eyes for only a moment. When I awakened, it was morning! I was never so mortified."

Judith pressed Cecily's fingers briefly before letting go her hands. Laughing, she said, "Never mind, dear girl. I shan't eat you."

"How well I know that! You have been all that is kind," said Cecily, looking at her with gratitude.

Judith sighed. She gestured for the maid to go and when they were alone, she said, "Cecily, I must tell you that Sir Peregrine is here."

The normal color was driven from the girl's cheeks, leaving a hectic patch high on each rounded cheek. "Here! But he cannot be. However did he find me so quickly? Oh, Miss Grantham! I beg of you, do not allow him to take me away. I shall be so desperately unhappy. You have no notion what he is like when he is angered!"

"Oh, don't I just?" uttered Judith under her breath. The whole encounter with Sir Peregrine had left her seething, and she was not at all repentant that she had saddled him with the Nicklebys. She saw that Cecily was looking questioningly at her and she pushed aside her own perturbation to answer. "My dear girl, I have no right to keep you from your guardian, if such he is."

Cecily took a step backward and regarded Judith

with a look of betrayal. "I had thought of you as my friend," she said.

"And I trust that I am still." Judith saw that Cecily was regarding her with the old wariness and she said urgently, "Cecily, you must see that I have no choice in this. Why, Sir Peregrine would have every right to call in a constable if I were to deny you to him. You shall simply have to meet with him."

"No, no! I cannot. He has such a *cutting* way about him, you see. He makes me feel so awkward and inadequate that I become tangled in knots whenever I try to speak to him," said Cecily.

Judith felt sympathy for the young girl's plight. She also had once been too reticent and shy to express herself well. And that inability had cost her dear. "If you wish it, I shall go with you when you meet with Sir Peregrine. I shan't allow anyone underneath my roof to be browbeaten, I promise you."

Cecily shook her head quickly. "Miss Grantham, I beg of you, if you will not shelter me from my cousin, at least lend me a chaise. I shall be gone in a trice and I will send your carriage back the instant that I have found a mail coach to London. Just give me an hour or two before telling Sir Peregrine that I am gone."

"It is out of the question. Even if I were inclined to do anything so absurd, it would not serve you. We are all snowbound and likely to be for the remainder of the day," said Judith. She watched as Cecily flew to the window and lifted the curtain. She was not entirely amused by the girl's bitten-off exclamation and the stomping of one dainty foot. Nevertheless, she kept her voice gentle. "Cecily, you really have no choice but to speak to Sir Peregrine. Perhaps this is just the opportunity you have needed to set things right between the two of you, since you both are forced to remain at Elmswood for the time being."

Cecily turned swiftly. She was flushed. "Nothing

could persuade me to step foot into the same room with Sir Peregrine. I shall remain upstairs.''

Judith experienced a feeling of disappointment. ''I am sorry for that, Cecily. I had thought you possessed more courage. But I see now that I was mistaken.'' She turned and left the bedroom, leaving Cecily to stare after her in astonishment and gathering gudgeon.

Judith slowly made her way downstairs, her brows knit. She did not know what to do about the standoff between Cecily and Sir Peregrine. But fortunately it was not her problem and she could easily wash her hands of it, she told herself, though without much success. However much Cecily had behaved in just the sort of dramatic, childish fashion that Sir Peregrine had said to expect of her, Judith could not but wonder if there was not more substance to the girl. Her own initial impression could not be entirely incorrect.

Judith had reached the bottom of the stairs before she recalled her other guests. She hesitated, not wanting to walk in on the Nicklebys or for that matter Sir Peregrine Ashford. She had had quite enough of high drama and absurdity for one morning. Indeed, she had the unmistakable beginnings of the headache. What she required was quiet and a chance to order her thoughts, she told herself.

Withers had seen Judith descend the stairs and his sympathy was aroused by her worried frown. He had heard through the servants' grapevine that Miss Grantham had been up to see Miss Brown. Obviously, her visit to that young lady had not gone well. He stepped forward. ''Is there anything you wish, miss?''

Judith smiled, a rueful light in her eyes. ''There is, actually. Where may I be private from my various assorted guests, Withers?''

The butler's expression reflected his complete understanding. ''The library, miss. I have not seen anyone enter that particular room, though some persons have taken it upon themselves to inspect the premises," he said in censorious tones.

Judith laughed, before recalling that she did not want to be found. She glanced about hastily. "Why is it that I feel a fugitive in my own home? Withers, I should like a lemon water and a headache powder in the library, please."

"Very good, miss," said Withers.

Judith entered the library and closed the door behind her with sigh. She turned to seek one of the wing chairs before the grate, behind which crackled a welcoming fire. She was just seating herself when out of the corner of her eye she caught a flicker of movement. Judith turned her head, but finding nothing out of the ordinary in the curtained window or the shelves of books, she put back her head and closed her eyes. It was as she began dozing off that she heard a whisper of sound. Judith started up, her eyes flying wide.

Mr. Smith stood awkwardly in the midst of the carpet, a vaguely furtive look on his face. "Begging your pardon, miss. It weren't my intention to startle you."

Judith's heart was racing. She swallowed. "Where did you come from, Mr. Smith?" she asked sharply.

Mr. Smith's expression became sheepish. "I was perusing the titles, as it were, when you came in, miss. I saw immediately that you had not seen me and I was about to bring myself to your attention when you sat down all tired-like and closed your eyes. Not wishing to disturb you, miss, I thought I would tiptoe away and leave you to it," he said.

It was more than Judith had ever heard the gentleman utter at any one time and definitely more than she wanted to hear at that moment. She put her hand to her head. "Mr. Smith, I appreciate your consideration. However, do keep in mind that on any given day I for one would prefer to be civilly disturbed rather than half frightened out of my wits."

The library door opened and Withers entered, a silver tray in his hand. He paused when he saw that his mistress was not alone as he had expected. Mr. Smith seized his moment. "I shall remember it, miss. I perceive that you have called for refreshment and so I will be running along now." He sidled past the butler and whisked himself out of the door, without seeming in any great hurry but yet moving with speed.

Withers looked around at his mistress. "That is a very odd gentleman, if you'll pardon my saying so, Miss Grantham."

"Indeed he is," said Judith, reflecting that Mr. Smith was not the only guest whose behavior was extraordinary. She shook her head on a sigh. "I do not know what I have done to deserve all of this."

Withers made a commiserating noise. He set the tray with its glass of lemon water and the packet of powder on an occasional table and straightened up. "Is there anything else that you require, miss?"

"No, Withers, that will be all, thank you," said Judith.

The butler left her alone, closing the door softly behind him, and relayed quietly to the footmen that Miss Grantham was not to be disturbed. Any persons found near the library were to be firmly steered away and if anyone was to inquire after Miss Grantham, they were to be given the reply that she was consulting with the housekeeper. That should do it, thought Withers with satisfaction.

But he did not take into account that Miss Grantham's nature was fairly well known to one particular gentleman, who snorted with derision when he was given the housekeeper excuse and with very little reflection hit upon the library as the most likely place that Miss Grantham would secrete herself. Sir Peregrine marched toward the closed door, brushing aside all efforts by a conscientious footman to turn him away, and thrust open the door.

Judith looked up from the book in her hands, startled. During an hour and a half of blessed solitude, her nerves had steadied and her headache had dissipated almost to nonexistence. It was therefore an unpleasant shock to see Sir Peregrine standing so aggressively in the doorway, his expression both grim and triumphant. The question of Cecily's well-being, which had receded proportionately with the interest that she had found in her book, came rushing back to the fore. "Bother," said Judith under her breath. She summoned a polite smile to her lips. "Sir Peregrine. How . . . nice."

He laughed at her intonation and came forward. "Quite so. But you should have known that I was not to be hoodwinked so easily, Miss Grantham. Your estimable housekeeper hardly needs such strict guidance as your footman tried to persuade me into believing."

The footman in question hovered anxiously about the open door. Judith, who realized at once that her household had been attempting to shield her, gave a reassuring nod to him. "You may go, Henry. I shall speak to Sir Peregrine." The footman reached for the brass knob and closed the door.

Sir Peregrine walked to the mantel and leaned his shoulder against it, not bothering to move aside the fir and holly that decorated it. The scent from the bruised greenery became pungent on the air. "Kind of you to grant me an audience, ma'am," he said with irony.

Judith marked her place in the book and closed it. "What may I do for you, Sir Peregrine?"

Sir Peregrine came away from the mantel and seated himself in the wing chair opposite her, crossing one knee over the other. His booted toe swung gently. "I first wish to convey an apology, Miss Grantham. I realized after your precipitate exit from the breakfast room this morning that I was perhaps harsher in my speech with you than I had any right to be. I hope that we may begin again, and with greater civility.

Judith was silent a moment. Her eyes were unreadable. "Of course, Sir Peregrine. I certainly will not cast aside such a handsome apology."

"You revenged yourself upon me finely, you know," said Sir Peregrine reflectively. "I never in my life wish to hear a single word more regarding mail coaches and their attendant discomforts and dangers."

That brought a laugh from Judith. Her eyes sparkled, having lost their shuttered look. "I suppose I should apologize for that. It was very bad of me, I fear."

Sir Peregrine agreed with the faintest of grins. "But you were always one for pranks, were you not? It was one of your most likeable qualities."

The easy smile was wiped from Judith's face and her expression became notably cooler. "What is it you wished to speak to me about, Sir Peregrine?"

Sir Peregrine mentally cursed himself for the misstep. He had wanted to disarm her and sweep away the barrier that she had erected between them so that his task of persuading her to his viewpoint would be easier. Now the barrier was firmly entrenched and he thought that there would be little use in gentle, logical persuasion. He decided on a frontal assault. "Miss Grantham, once more you have anticipated me. I think that you may guess what I wish to address, and that is your obvious hampering of my efforts of establish an understanding with my ward, Miss Cecily Brown."

"I?! You mistake, sir. I have done nothing to *hamper* you, as you put it. Quite the contrary, in fact," said Judith.

"Come, Miss Grantham! I have sent word up to Cecily twice that I awaited her and both times she sent back a refusal to see me. I know well where your sympathies lie and also your disapproval of my intentions for my ward's future. Surely you do not intend to deny that you have brought influence upon Cecily," said Sir Peregrine with impatience.

Judith stared at him with distinct coldness. "My

dear sir, your opinion of my character is most gratifying, to be sure. You accuse me of harboring your
ward, recommending to her that she have nothing
whatsoever to do with you, and generally flying in the
face of all that is honorable and lawful!'' She rose
quickly to her feet, the book sliding unheeded from
her lap to the carpet. Her heated emotion had brought
becoming color into her cheeks. ''I do not blame Cecily in the least for refusing to deal with you, for you
are too clothheaded to entertain the least understanding of anyone but you!'' She spun on her heel, intending to leave his presence.

But Sir Peregrine, having leaped to his feet, caught
hold of her arm and turned her ungently about. Her
angry gaze met his hard blue eyes. ''Judith!''

''Unhand me this instant!'' exclaimed Judith. She
tried to pull free of his grasp, but his fingers only
tightened on her arm. The situation was intolerable.
Furious, she slapped his face with every ounce of her
strength.

''Damn you, Judith!'' he exclaimed. His hands slid
up to her shoulders and he gave her a quick, hard
shake. They stared at one another then, tension crackling between them. Sir Peregrine found that he could
not look away from her eyes or her whitened face. The
years had rolled back for him and he no longer remembered his ward. All he was aware of was the breath
coming quickly from between Judith's half-parted lips,
the feel of her slender bones under his hands.

The spell was broken by a knock on the library door.

Sir Peregrine slowly loosened his fingers from her
shoulders. Judith stepped back, her eyes still on his
face. Sir Peregrine turned away to the mantel, as
though he had been contemplating the fire for several
minutes. Judith took a shuddering breath. She was unutterably shaken. A second knock sounded and she
found her voice. ''Enter!''

The door opened and Withers stepped inside, his

expression giving nothing away, but when he spoke
there was a thread of anxiety in his voice. His eyes
went from his mistress to Sir Peregrine's broad shoulders, and back again. "Miss Grantham, I am sorry to
intrude, but there is a problem that Cook would like
to consult with you about."

"Yes, I shall come immediately," said Judith. She
was immeasurably relieved that she was not to be faced
with dealing with the tumult of emotions she was feeling at just that moment. She went quickly out of the
library. Sir Peregrine did not look around at her exit.

Judith dealt with the minor culinary emergency,
smoothing Cook's affront at having her kitchen in-
vaded by Mrs. Nickleby and being told in lofty tones
that her pudding was off. "I ask you, miss! My pudding had never been off and so I told that noseybody
to her face, *which* she did not care for, you may be
sure of that!"

"No, Cook, I am certain that she did not," said
Judith with a sigh, sensing that she would have further
calming to do whenever she should meet Mrs. Nickleby. And that would undoubtedly be at luncheon, she
realized. She wondered dismally what had happened
to the dull quiet that she was used to whenever she
returned to Elmswood from one of her visits.

When Judith left the kitchen she went directly upstairs and ordered a bath. She told her maid that under
no circumstances did she want to be disturbed until it
was time to dress for luncheon. The maid was astonished that her mistress would shut herself up when
there were guests in the house and she was not behind
in mentioning it in the servants' hall when she went
down to request hot water to be brought up.

After several sympathetic observations and sighs, it
was the consensus of the household that Miss Grantham's holiday was not quite what it should be, what
with vulgar tradespeople running tame in the house, a

suspicious shadow of a man snooping about, and a runaway heiress kicking up a dust. Not to mention the disturbing presence of the gentleman who had once broken Miss Grantham's heart.

Perhaps fortunately, Judith was unaware that she was the prime topic of conversation belowstairs. She took her time in her bath. She had much to think about, primarily of how a certain gentleman made her feel whenever he looked at her. Since she had jilted Sir Peregrine five years before, they had met one another on numerous occasions at London functions to which they had both been invited. She had always been able to prepare herself for those moments, only to be expected since she and Sir Peregrine were members of the same social circle. Those fleeting meetings had always been made easier by the tacit understanding of their peers that Miss Grantham and Sir Peregrine Ashford were never to be seated together at dinner or left without other partners during a ballroom dance.

She had come to rely on that distance to preserve herself from pain, Judith realized. When she had come so unexpectedly upon Sir Peregrine at her own breakfast table, she had come close to fainting away from the shock. Their relationship had undeniably not improved through that distancing. They had immediately cut up at one another in such a horrid manner that Judith could only wonder what had become of their social breeding.

But the worst moments had been those in the library. When Sir Peregrine had taken hold of her, time was flung aside as though it did not exist, and she had felt everything for him that she had felt for him before. He infuriated her, teased her, made her love him. And that was the crux of the matter, thought Judith bleakly. She had been fooling herself for a very long time. She did still love him. In those moments when her gaze was locked with his, she had seen something stir in his piercing eyes. She had sensed the precipice yawn-

ing before them, and had welcomed it. Then Withers's
knock had come and the moment had been lost.

Judith sighed. She was not certain whether she ought
to be glad for it or regret that Sir Peregrine had not
kissed her. However, at this point it was all rather
academic. The snow would let up and Sir Peregrine
would bundle Cecily into his carriage and be off with
never a backward look.

It was a thoroughly depressing thought. Judith decided that she had wallowed long enough, both in her
unproductive thoughts and in her bath. She toweled
dry and pulled the bell rope to summon her maid. It
was time to dress for luncheon. Actually, it might be
a welcome diversion to sit down with her disparate
guests.

An hour later, Judith wondered how she could have
harbored such a hopeful thought. Before she had even
entered the dining room, Mrs. Nickleby had latched
onto her sleeve and proceeded to bend her ear regarding her cook's attitude.

"Insufferable, Miss Grantham, I assure you! The
woman positively *threatened* to throw me out of the
kitchen on my ear. Why, I was never more surprised
in my life, when all I had done was to offer a bit of
well-meant advice," said Mrs. Nickleby.

"That you have a talent for, pet," said Mr. Nickleby.

Judith glanced at the man, wondering if he was deliberately stoking the fire of his wife's wrath, but Mr.
Nickleby's expression was as pleasant and complacent
as usual. She returned her attention to Mrs. Nickleby
and once more attempted to bring reason into play.
"Mrs. Nickleby, surely you must understand that the
kitchen is Cook's domain. I am certain that there is an
area in your life you must care greatly for and that it
would give you pain to have someone, perhaps less
knowledgeable than—"

"Less knowledgeable! Begging your pardon, Miss

Grantham, but I am a superb cook," uttered Mrs. Nickleby. She looked to her husband for confirmation and he willingly gave it, patting his ample waistline in testimony. "That you are, pet," he said.

Judith glanced about helplessly. At this rate, none of them would ever get to the table, she thought. And she could not simply withdraw from Mrs. Nickleby. The outrageous woman actually had hold of a bit of her sleeve, thought Judith in annoyance.

Judith's glance met that of Lord Baltor, and he comprehended the situation. He promptly stepped forward and his action edged Mrs. Nickleby back a half-step so that she was forced to drop her hand from Judith's sleeve. "Miss Grantham, allow me the privilege of escorting you into luncheon," he said, offering his arm to Judith.

She placed her fingers on his elbow and thanked him with a dazzling smile. Over her shoulder, she said composedly, "Do join Lord Baltor and me, Mrs. Nickleby. We are to have a delightful current pudding for dessert."

"Well!" exclaimed Mrs. Nickleby. "And here I have just been saying that the pudding is not fit to be spooned up."

Her spouse patted her reassuringly on the shoulder. "Never mind, pet. The Quality abide by their own rules," he said.

Mrs. Nickleby took his arm and lowered her voice to an octave that she mistakenly thought private. "I shall never be more glad of anything than to shake the dust of this house from my feet, Mr. Nickleby. I have never been subjected to ruder treatment. And as for the help! Why, what do you think? I discovered one of the maids going through the pockets of my best cloak. She excused herself by saying that she was looking for an extra button to sew on in place of one that has fallen off. I hope that I know better than to believe that tale! No one looks for work, now do they, Mr. Nickleby?''

"It is unfortunately true, pet," said Mr. Nickleby with a sigh. "Haven't I pointed out for years that very same thing in the clothier business?"

The Nicklebys' conversation carried them all into the dining room. Judith pretended not to hear. She was determined that the luncheon was to be a pleasant interlude. She quietly thanked Lord Baltor when he seated her and she was not unpleased that he took the chair beside her. She noticed when the slight gentleman slipped into place on her other side and she nodded pleasantly to him, not in any anxiety that she would offend if she did not verbally greet him. She had become used to Mr. Smith's quietude and she knew that her task of conversing with her table partners would be greatly reduced since Mr. Smith never put himself forward into any conversation.

While the Nicklebys seated themselves opposite, she leaned over toward Lord Baltor and said in a low voice, "I am unutterably relieved to have you for my partner at table, my lord. You have no notion how I shook at the thought of Mr. Nickleby, and just beyond him his good wife.''

For the first time since Judith had met Lord Baltor, she saw an uninhibited smile on his face. "I consider it an equal protection, ma'am," he said.

Judith laughed, almost surprised by the dry witticism. She had gathered that, sober, Lord Baltor was much too serious for his years. It pleased her that his lordship was capable of charm without first imbibing from a bottle. "I hope that I am to hear a rendition of a carol from you during your stay here at Elmswood. I, too, enjoy singing," said Judith, smiling.

Even as Lord Baltor flushed at her gentle teasing, his grin widened. All at once he looked his young years. "If you will but join me, Miss Grantham, I will endeavor to lift the ceiling," he said.

"I shall hold you to that, my lord," said Judith. She had wondered at Sir Peregrine's absence and now she sensed rather than saw him enter the dining room. She turned her head. He had paused in the doorway, sweeping the table with a glance and taking note that the only available place was beside Mrs. Nickleby. When his eyes met Judith's, her own sparked to amusement at his thinly veiled dismay. "Do pray join us, Sir Peregrine," she said, at her politest.

"Aye, do so," said Mrs. Nickleby, diverted from a running commentary on the centerpiece and those dishes that she could see on the sideboard by craning her neck. She smiled amiably and gestured at the place beside her. "There is ample elbow room, as you can see, Sir Peregrine."

"Thank you, Mrs. Nickleby. You are most kind," said Sir Peregrine hollowly.

With Sir Peregrine's sacrifice on the altar of good manners, Judith's spirits took an upturn for the better. The butler bent down to whisper in her ear that Miss Brown would not be joining the company for luncheon, preferring a tray in her bedroom. "Why does that not surprise me?" murmured Judith, not allowing herself to be in the least upset. She did, however, make a mental note to visit Cecily later in the afternoon.

The girl simply had to be brought to an understanding of her responsibilities, for nothing in the world would persuade Judith to go through another private interview with Sir Peregrine. She glanced down the table as the soup was served. Predictably, Mrs. Nickleby was addressing herself to anyone who was unfortunate enough to be within range. Judith smiled at Sir Peregrine's pained expression. She much preferred seeing that gentleman in public. It was so much kinder to her spirits, especially if he was to act as a buffer against Mrs. Nickleby's volubleness.

After luncheon, the company dispersed with various announced plans for passing the afternoon. Sir Peregrine and Lord Baltor discovered a mutual interest in billiards and went off to take a crack at the balls. Mr. Nickleby voiced a half-wish to join them, an aspiration quashed by his wife who scolded him for succumbing to what would surely become a gambling match. "For we all have heard what goes on in those clubs of the Quality," she said. He apologized for even thinking of indulging himself in such an evil and instead joined Mr. Smith in the library, each lying in an easy chair with a newspaper spread over his face that soon rose with rhythmic regularity. Mrs. Nickleby looked to Miss Grantham for what she termed a comfortable coze, but that lady firmly excused herself and took herself upstairs to visit with her recalcitrant guest.

In the hall Judith met the maid who was looking after Cecily. Noticing the still-laden luncheon tray in the woman's hands, Judith stopped her. "Hasn't Miss Brown any appetite?" she asked.

The maid shook her head. "The miss nibbled on naught but a cracker or two, Miss Grantham. And she took nothing but tea and dry toast for breakfast," she said.

Judith quietly thanked the maidservant and walked on. Her brows had become knit by a small frown. Cecily had not had anything substantial to eat since before she had met her. Judith thought that was something else that must be addressed. She simply could not have the girl becoming ill, not with Sir Peregrine convinced that she was capable of contriving any sort of ruse to keep his ward from him.

Cecily granted Judith's entrance to the bedroom with a show of reluctance. "For I know why you have come, Miss Grantham. And I have not changed my mind by so much as a hair," she said. There was a spot of color high on her cheekbones as though she was flustered, but her eyes appeared bright with obstinance.

It was not a promising beginning, but Judith was

highly motivated to persuade the girl to at least a compromise. She seated herself in a wing chair in front of the grate, glancing up at the young girl as she did so. "Pray sit down, Cecily," she said quietly.

After a moment's hesitation, Cecily did as she was bid and perched on the edge of an accompanying chair. She folded her hands in her lap and her lashes dropped over the expression in her eyes.

Judith was not fooled into thinking that the girl was in any fashion cowed. She was beginning to see what Sir Peregrine had referred to when he had said that he had had difficulty in reaching Cecily. Judith did not speak immediately, allowing her silence to work on the girl while she ordered her thoughts. Cecily was beginning to cast up quick curious glances when Judith at last addressed her. "Cecily, I perfectly understand the reasons behind your reluctance in meeting with Sir Peregrine. He has undoubtedly treated you with a great deal of unfairness," she said.

Cecily looked full at her, surprise mirrored in her extraordinarily fringed, china-blue eyes. "I-I do not know what to say, Miss Grantham."

Judith held up her hand. "Pray allow me to finish. I have had occasion to converse with Sir Peregrine and certainly he is not the . . . easiest personage to deal with. However, I do believe that you must think of your best interests."

"My best interests?" faltered Cecily.

Judith nodded. "Quite so. Sir Peregrine is not likely to change his mind without good reason. I think that you have gained his attention by running away, but now you must capitalize on your position."

"Whatever are you talking about, Miss Grantham?" asked Cecily, bewildered. Her eyes suddenly widened. "Oh! Do you mean that I should threaten him?"

Judith shook her head, allowing a smile to flit over her face. "Not precisely that, no. But certainly you must make it plain that the same determination that

led you to run off will also lead you to cause him
distress whenever a decision regarding your future is
made without first consulting your opinion of the matter. And you must persuade Sir Peregrine of this without showing your fear of him.''

''I am not precisely *frightened* of Perry,'' said Cecily haltingly.

''Then you do agree to meet with him while at
Elmswood,'' said Judith. She watched as first astonishment, then comprehension flooded Cecily's expression.

''Oh! Of all the infamous tricks!'' exclaimed Cecily.

''I am sorry to have had to trick you, Cecily, but I
really felt that you gave me little choice in the matter,'' said Judith gently. ''You see, if I allowed you to
remain closeted away, then Sir Peregrine would almost
certainly decide to come up himself and drag you from
the bedroom. I do not think in that instance that he
would be open to anything that you might have to say.''

Cecily stared at her thoughtfully. ''You speak as
though you know Sir Peregrine very well,'' she said.

Judith stood up. ''I shall expect you to come down
and join us all for dinner this evening, Cecily. And in
the meantime I shall have a cup of broth sent up to
you, for you are looking too pale.'' She turned to leave
the bedroom, but she paused with her hand on the
doorknob to glance back with the faintest lifting of her
winged brows. ''You know, I am so glad that my first
impression of you was correct. I had thought you a
determined and bright young woman. You have quite
restored my faith in you.''

Once more Cecily was left to stare after her, this
time with much more food for thought, not the least
of which was her hostess's declining to reply to her
observation pertaining to Sir Peregrine.

Once downstairs Judith busied herself in preparation
for the traditional observance of Boxing Day. When

her household had assembled, she handed out the gift boxes, taking a moment to address a personal word to each servant. It was a ceremony much enjoyed by all, including Judith. As always, she was glad that she had made the effort to return to Elmswood in time to uphold this particular tradition.

The boxing took longer than she had anticipated and she had to rush back upstairs to change in time for dinner. In the cheerful atmosphere generated by the boxing, she had forgotten the uncertain prospect before her in the dining room. There would likely be tension between Cecily and Sir Peregrine, as well as the usual reluctance of anyone to share table with Mrs. Nickleby, and she did not particularly look forward to the evening.

Judith had dreaded the half hour before dinner when all of her guests could be expected to assemble in the drawing room. But it went easier than she had expected, principally because the Nicklebys did not immediately appear. She was talking quietly with Lord Baltor and Sir Peregrine when Cecily came hesitantly through the door.

Judith knew that Cecily had entered when Lord Baltor's eyes flew wide and a stunned expression settled on his face. She rose and went toward the girl. "Cecily, my dear child," she said, holding out her hands. Cecily grasped her fingers with almost a desperate grip and Judith looked searchingly at her. The girl appeared strained and her eyes were overbright. Judith smiled reassuringly. "I shall stay right beside you," she murmured. Cecily cast up a grateful glance and allowed herself to be drawn toward the gentlemen.

Lord Baltor had leaped to his feet. His eyes had never left Cecily's face. His thoughts tumbled incoherently, but one remained crystal clear: He had never seen a more beautiful vision. When Judith brought

Cecily up to him and introduced her, Lord Baltor accepted Cecily's hand almost with reverence. "Your servant, Miss Brown," he said in a strangled voice.

Cecily was not unused to admiration and she forgot her nervousness for a moment. She looked up at Lord Baltor with her wide innocent gaze. "I am so very glad to make your acquaintance, my lord," she said softly. She was quite taken with the manner in which Lord Baltor kissed her fingers and she was smiling as she reclaimed her hand.

But when she met the glance of her guardian, her smile faltered and a scared look entered her eyes. "Good-good evening, cousin," she stammered.

Sir Peregrine looked at her somewhat grimly. "You have led me a fine chase, Cecily. I hope that you are aware of the folly of your actions."

Cecily looked ready to sink into the carpet. Judith came to her support. "You shall be much better able to discuss these private matters at another time," she said firmly.

Sir Peregrine threw a piercing glance at Judith, who awaited his reaction with lifted brows. He seemed to reconsider whatever comment that he was on the point of making and instead nodded. "Miss Grantham for once is right. We shall speak after dinner, Cecily."

Lord Baltor had listened to the interchange with a gathering frown. He understood little but that somehow Sir Peregrine was related to this glorious creature and that she was frightened of his displeasure. When Lord Baltor looked into Cecily's piteous and lovely face, he was seized by a strong feeling of chivalry. He knew that he would do anything in his power to protect her from distress. "I hope that you will do me the honor of joining me at dinner," he said, addressing Cecily as though she was the only other individual in the room.

She nodded with a shy smile, soft color rising in her face. "You are most kind, my lord," she said, and

placed her hand trustingly in his. The young couple
drifted toward the settee, their heads inclined toward
one another as they softly conversed.

Judith looked on with astonishment. Surely she was
not witnessing what she thought she was. It actually
appeared to her that Cecily and Lord Baltor had fallen
in love on the instant. When she glanced toward Sir
Peregrine, she was annoyed to find that he had been
waiting for her to do so, a faintly superior smile on
his face. "You needn't look so smug, Perry," she said,
unconsciously falling into her old habit of address.

Sir Peregrine noticed it, but he did not let on.
"Needn't I? One so rarely is handed an opportunity
to be able to point out one's infallibility. I did mention, did I not, that Cecily had been in love half a
dozen times in two years? I was certain that I had. Do
pray correct me if I am mistaken."

Judith surrendered the point with a laugh. "Oh, I
would not dare to counter your memory, sir."

"Would you not, Judith?" Sir Peregrine spoke quietly and there was a strangely intent look in his blue
eyes.

Judith felt her heart turn over in her breast. "I-I
think not," she said with an odd breathlessness.

Mr. Smith and the Nicklebys came into the drawing
room and Judith greeted their appearance almost with
relief. She hid a shudder at Mrs. Nickleby's appearance. That lady had attired herself in a rich purple
robe, a feathered velvet turban, and a ruby necklace
that was matched by large rubies in her ears. An ad-
ditional deep red stone flashed on the finger of one
hand. The colors clashed hideously, thought Judith,
but nothing of her opinion appeared on her pleasant
countenance. "Here are the others. Pray excuse me,
Sir Peregrine. There you are, Mr. and Mrs. Nickleby.
And Mr. Smith, too! I see that Withers is ready for
us. Shall we all go to dinner?"

She was surprised when her elbow was taken in a

firm grasp. In her ear was Sir Peregrine's civil voice. "I shall claim our fair hostess's company this evening, I believe." Judith looked up. She was quite unprepared for his cool smile or the challenge in his keen eyes.

"That is only proper, I am sure. You look a fine couple, too," said Mr. Nickleby approvingly. He did not appear to notice the slightest stiffening of Judith's frame. He held his arm out for his wife. "As splendid as you appear this evening in those shiny baubles, pet, I would not give you up if the Queen herself wished me to escort her."

Mrs. Nickleby tossed her head, pleased. The black feather in her turban waved above her deep-set eyes. "Why, Mr. Nickleby, I never!" For once she seemed to be content with the utterance of a mere phrase.

Judith and Sir Peregrine preceded the others into the dining room. They were followed by Lord Baltor and Cecily and the Nicklebys, with Mr. Smith bringing up the rear. When all were seated, only Mr. Smith was without a dinner companion, but Judith did not think that he minded in the least. He had tucked his napkin into his collar and rubbed his hands together over the first course of mince pies, barley soup, and a choice of vegetables. Her glance traveled about the table. Mrs. Nickleby was supplying her spouse with an opinion on the entrées of roast beef and the customary seasoned Christmas goose to which the gentleman was paying but half an ear, and no one else was giving even a semblance of polite attention.

Dusk fell at an early hour in the winter and the dining room had been lit with several branches of candles, which shed a soft glow over the faces of those present. Lord Baltor's and Cecily's shared glances and shining faces made the candlelight seem rather redundant, thought Judith. She could only feel misgivings about Cecily's obvious attraction to Lord Baltor. Not that his lordship was other than a pleasant young man,

but his latest infatuation could only damage Cecily's
case in Sir Peregrine's eyes.

"A penny for them."

Judith glanced around. Sir Peregrine's expression
was quizzical. She shook her head and a fleeting smile
crossed her face. "I was only reflecting on the ca-
prices of human nature."

"Ah." Sir Peregrine's keen eyes immediately sought
out his ward and Lord Baltor. He swung his glance
back to the lovely lady at his side. And she was very
lovely, he acknowledged silently, his eyes traveling
slowly from her smooth-skinned face to the exquisite
figure that was set off nicely by a close-cut velvet
gown. He cocked his dark brow, his devastatingly keen
gaze once more meeting her gray eyes. "Do I detect
a hint of regret for opportunities lost, Judith?"

Judith had colored faintly under his scrutiny. Now
she sucked in her breath in startled surprise. Her eyes
flashed at his audacity. "I am sure I do not know what
you mean, Sir Peregrine," she said loftily.

Across the table, despite her absorption with Lord
Baltor, Cecily had caught a portion of their quiet exchange. Her curiosity had been aroused earlier by Miss
Grantham's obvious knowledge of Sir Peregrine's nature and now she had heard him address Miss Grantham by her given name. "Why, cousin, I did not know
that you and Miss Grantham knew one another so
well," she said in surprise.

Judith's eyes flew to meet Sir Peregrine's. He regarded her for an infinitesimal pause before he replied,
"We are . . . old acquaintances." He gave his ward
no chance to pursue the matter, as she seemed inclined to do, but at once asked Lord Baltor whether
he enjoyed shooting. Cecily's attention was immediately diverted as she listened spellbound to her new-
found love expound on the types of sport one might
find in his part of the country. Judith was able to re-

spond to a sally from Mr. Nickleby with all appearances of composure.

She gradually relaxed as dinner progressed. It went far better than she had dared hope, there being no rash words between Sir Peregrine and Cecily and even few complaints from Mrs. Nickleby. Indeed, Cecily seemed in her best manners, thought Judith, approving of the subdued civility that the girl showed to her guardian and the rest. At least Sir Peregrine could not say that Cecily's head had been so turned by Lord Baltor's attentions that she had behaved in too forward a fashion.

When at last the ladies left the gentlemen to their wine and repaired to the drawing room, she was actually beginning to believe that the interview between Cecily and Sir Peregrine would also go off well.

"Miss Grantham, I do not feel at all the thing," said Cecily faintly.

Judith turned to look at her and she became instantly alarmed. The girl's eyes had become fever-bright and there were hectic patches of color in her cheeks. "My dear!" Judith laid a cool hand across Cecily's brow and her heart plunged. The girl was burning to the touch. "You must be gotten to bed instantly. I shall myself take you up to your room. Only wait one moment so that I may ring for something for the fever to be brought for you."

Mrs. Nickleby regarded Cecily's drooping figure in some alarm. She drew back her skirts from possible contamination. "Fever! I do hope that it is not catching. My dear Miss Brown, surely you could have shown more consideration for the rest of us and stayed up in your room if you were ill."

"I am sorry. I thought at first it was only my nerves that made me feel so peculiar," said Cecily. She sat down abruptly on a chair. Her flushed face had gone stark white.

Judith stared at Mrs. Nickleby with acute dislike.

"Madam, I doubt that any fever would dare take residence in one of your constitution," she said. Mrs. Nickleby opened and closed her mouth, astonished and confused by the biting setdown. Judith tugged vigorously on the bell rope. The door to the drawing room was opened instantly by a footman. "John, Miss Brown has been taken ill. Ask Mrs. Wyssop to make up something for her fever. I shall myself help Miss Brown upstairs to her room." The footman bowed and hurried off on his errand.

Judith put her arm about Cecily's narrow shoulders and helped her rise from the chair. The girl swayed and Judith steadied her. "There you are, child. I shall not let you fall," she said gently.

Cecily threw a grateful glance up at her face. "You are unfailingly kind," she murmured. Judith admonished her not to speak but to concentrate on making her way up the stairs.

When Judith returned from settling Cecily comfortably in bed, she discovered that the gentlemen had taken up residence in the drawing room and that they had been informed by Mrs. Nickleby of Miss Brown's surprising collapse. Sir Peregrine looked over at Judith, his visage a bit sardonic. "Protecting her to the last, are you?" he asked.

Judith's already frayed temper flared. She said coldly, "I do not know what you mean, Sir Peregrine." She turned her shoulder on him then and smiled encouragingly at Lord Baltor, who inquired rather anxiously of Miss Brown. "Miss Brown has apparently contracted a fever from becoming chilled yesterday, but I daresay that she will presently be much better."

Lord Baltor was struck with remorse. "It is my fault," he said hollowly.

"Indeed it was, your lordship. A heavier-handed whipster I hope never to see! It is a wonder any of us escaped with nothing worse than a few bumps after being tossed hurley-burley into the snow," said Mrs. Nickleby with a decisive nod. She embarked on an involved recital of the accident to the mail coach and her thoughts on the matter.

Judith could not stifle an impatient exclamation. Sir Peregrine had the audacity to laugh. Pointedly ignoring him, Judith pinned a smile to her lips and set herself to endure what was left of what had been for the most part a trying day.

After a moment she heard someone whistling "Good King Wenceslaus." She turned her head in relief. "Mr. Smith, what a truly happy notion," she said. The gentleman addressed broke off in mid-note, disconcerted and faintly alarmed. But Judith was no longer looking at him. "Lord Baltor, let us do as you once suggested and lift the ceiling with a few Christmas carols." She seated herself at the pianoforte, the top of which was covered with an arrangement of laurel, bay, and rosemary that filled the air with spicy scent.

Lord Baltor was completely amenable to the suggestion, especially as it served to distract Mrs. Nickleby from her droning recital. "I am at your service, Miss Grantham," he said, positioning himself behind her shoulder.

A carol was quickly agreed upon and they lifted their voices in song. Sir Peregrine came to lean against the pianoforte and added a pleasant baritone. After a small hesitation, the remaining three joined in the singing. When it was done, Judith began playing another familiar old tune and this time the caroling was more resonant.

An hour had passed in the pleasant exercise when the butler entered the drawing room with a long taper. With some ceremony he lighted the kissing-bough candles, which had been lit for the first time on Christmas Eve and would be again each night of the twelve days of Christmas. As each wick caught, the appearance of the yellow flame was greeted with claps and good humor.

The company broke up soon afterward and good nights were exchanged. With a quiet request, Sir Peregrine delayed Judith's exit from the drawing room and he closed the door behind the others. Judith raised her brows in inquiry. She was astonished and obscurely pleased that Sir Peregrine's expression was exceptionally friendly. She thought that her own expression must reflect the same amicability that had been induced in them all by the caroling.

Sir Peregrine advanced toward her. "I wished to apologize for my manners earlier in the evening. It was ill-conceived of me to accuse you of spiriting away Cecily under pretense of malaise," he said.

Judith was still affected by the surprising pleasantness of the evening and she discovered that his apology put her in complete charity with him. "I have quite forgotten it," she said with her easy smile.

Sir Peregrine carried her hand to his lips. "You are gracious, Judith." He retained hold of her fingers. There was a decided twinkle in his extraordinary blue eyes. "You do realize that we are standing beneath the kissing bough," he said.

Judith cast a disconcerted look up at the crown-shaped kissing bough and the mistletoe suspended from its center. She laughed. "So we are. Rest easy, sir. I do not subscribe to all of the Christmas traditions," she said reassuringly.

Sir Peregrine smiled. "But I do." He took her into his arms and kissed her slowly and thoroughly.

Judith's thoughts tilted and tumbled into confusion.

Sir Peregrine released her. There was a curious expression in his eyes. "Merry Christmas, Judith," he said softly, and he left the drawing room.

Judith remained standing where he had left her for several seconds before she left the drawing room and made her way upstairs to her bedroom.

* * *

The two days following were marked by weak sunshine and the rising hopes of various members of the household that the snow had at last run its course. When the man who regularly delivered meat from the village butcher appeared at the servants' entrance, it was felt that Elmswood Hall would soon be back to normal. "That noseybody is as good as gone," said Cook with satisfaction, and she began to plan a special menu to celebrate the happy event.

Miss Grantham would willingly have echoed her cook's sentiments. She heard the announcement about the weather with welcome relief, Withers having chosen to deliver it himself to the entire company when they were assembled for luncheon. "That is wonderful, indeed," she said. She turned an inquiring gaze in the direction of her guests, her winged brows lifted. "Perhaps I may send a message to the posting house?"

"That would be fine for Mrs. Nickleby and myself. We should be getting on with our visit to our boy," said Mr. Nickleby. He tucked in the last bite of a meat pie. After eyeing the port wine trifle on the sideboard a moment, he regretfully decided against it. He had eaten well and he did not think that he could swallow another mouthful.

Mrs. Nickleby's lips opened as she prepared herself to deliver a comment. Ruthlessly, Judith passed over her to address Mr. Smith. "And you, sir?" she asked, her smile appearing again.

Compared to the Nicklebys, Mr. Smith had been a paragon of a guest even though more than once his roaming about the house had served to give a fright to the maids when they had come upon him in unexpected places. She herself had discovered him again in the library and she had felt an initial surprise, for she had not thought he looked the sort who would enjoy books. But she had reminded herself that appearances could be deceiving. Thereafter she had made a point of commenting on some story or other that she had found of interest and Mr. Smith had seemed to appreciate her efforts because his eyes had crinkled up with a quiet humor that she had found endearing.

"Aye, miss. And I will be thanking you kindly," said Mr. Smith.

Judith nodded, appreciating his quiet manners—quite unlike some she could think of, who had not once uttered a gracious word, she thought. She turned her gaze on Lord Baltor, who was looking unhappy. "Why, is there something wrong, my lord?" she asked.

Lord Baltor hesitated a moment, vacillating. At last he took his courage in his hands. "The thing of it is, Miss Grantham, that I do not feel that I can take my leave just yet. I mean to say, it was my doing that caused Miss Brown to fall ill. I would not feel right to leave Elmswood without knowing—"

"You refine to much on it, Baltor," said Sir Peregrine impatiently.

Judith glanced at Sir Peregrine. She smiled warmly on Lord Baltor. "Your sentiments do you credit, my lord. Certainly, you may remain at Elmswood for as long as you would like. However, I do not wish you to sacrifice your time with your aunt. Did you not say previously that you were on your way to visit with her?"

"Oh, but she has no notion that I was coming. It was to be a surprise, so I daresay that a day or two more will make little difference," said Lord Baltor ingenuously.

"Quite," said Judith, not daring to glance at Sir Peregrine. She could sense that he was deriving much the same amusement as she was from Lord Baltor's artlessness. It was passing strange that she and Sir Peregrine could be so alike in some ways and yet set one another's backs up so readily, she thought. "Well, that is settled. I think that we shall all be glad to get on with our individual plans for the holiday, though I must say it has been quite an experience to have all of you here at Elmswood. I do not think that I shall ever quite forget it," she said with an encompassing smile.

"Quite," murmured Sir Peregrine.

Judith ignored the thread of irony in his voice. She glanced at him in a determinedly friendly fashion. "Sir Peregrine, I know that you in particular have chafed at your enforced stay at Elmswood. But like Lord Baltor, I assure you of continued hospitality until Miss Brown is well enough to travel. Perhaps you would like to visit with your ward later today? Though I have not talked with Cecily, I think that a visit from you might underscore your concern for her well-being."

Her suggestion was couched with all the trappings of the solicitude of the polite hostess, but the gentleman to whom she addressed it was well able to gather a more pointed meaning to it. It was but another skirmish line in their ongoing battle.

"An excellent suggestion, Miss Grantham," said Sir Peregrine in appreciation. "I shall certainly do so." He smiled at her and he was surprised by the answering spark of merriment in her eyes. He realized that she also derived a certain enjoyment from the repartee between them. They had scarcely spoken more than a few sentences to each other in five years and it seemed that they were equally determined to make up for that oversight. In particular, he recalled how right she had felt in his arms under the kissing bough. He could not for the life of him see where that could possibly lead since the past still hung there, unalterable and unpalatable. At the thought, his smile faded and a distinct chill entered his eyes. Luncheon was done with for all intents and purposes and he excused himself to the company.

Judith had seen the instant that Sir Peregrine's expression changed. His manner had gone cold of a sudden and the warmth in his eyes had become shuttered.

It unsettled her. She had assumed after he had kissed
her that their differences were on the way to being
mended. However, she was not particularly sorry when
he left the dining room. She thought that if there was
anything that she was sorry for, it was that Sir Peregrine would be remaining at Elmswood yet a while.
His uncertain moods made the atmosphere distinctly
uncomfortable.

That afternoon, shortly before the dinner hour, a
commotion was raised abovestairs in a flurry of furious voices. Judith, who had been reading in the library, left her book in the chair and hurried out into
the entry hall. The altercation was rapidly becoming
louder and attracted the notice of all within earshot.
Sir Peregrine and Lord Baltor emerged from the billiards room, Sir Peregrine exclaiming, "What the
devil?" The footmen and a maid or two left their various tasks to step into the entry hall and Mr. Smith
appeared from somewhere. They all stood in the hall,
their faces raised in the direction of the balcony where
the ruckus was originating.

Mrs. Nickleby hove into sight and marched down
the stairs in full sail, her high accusing voice rising
above the scared protestations of a slight maid, hauled
along by Mr. Nickleby, who recommended the girl to
keep her mouth closed or she would accuse herself all
the deeper. Mrs. Nickleby spied her hostess below.
She seemed to swell. "Miss Grantham! I do not know
what kind of household you find acceptable, but believe me, I would be ashamed to employ such persons
as this wanton *thief!* A fine thing! As your guest, I
expected much better. Indeed I did, ma'am!" The
Nicklebys and their captive came swiftly down the
stairs, Mrs. Nickleby never letting up in her loud di-
atribe. Mr. Nickleby punctuated his wife's unrelenting
scold by nods and occasional utterances of agreement.

Judith raised her voice. "Mrs. Nickleby! Pray calm

yourself, madam. I cannot make any sense of this at all." She might as well have tried to quell a storm.

Sir Peregrine was not so helpless. He said in his direct way, "Mr. Nickleby, if you do not have the decency to shut your wife up, then I shall be forced to do so." His level gaze was hard.

Mr. Nickleby apparently took him at his word. He let go of the maid and shook his wife's arm. The maid scuttled quickly behind Withers, who had come into the hall, and peeped fearfully out around him at the Nicklebys. "That's enough now, pet. We have Miss Grantham's undivided attention, of a certainty."

"So I should hope!" exclaimed Mrs. Nickleby. She pointed a shaking finger at the maid, who squeaked in fright. "That is the one! That is the thief. She denies it, but she has taken my rubies!"

"I never, Miss Grantham! I couldn't have done such a thing," said the maid, practically in tears.

"Miss Grantham, I assure you that no one under my command is capable of what this . . . lady suggests," said Withers, not demeaning himself by even so much as a glance in Mrs. Nickleby's direction.

Judith nodded her awareness of the butler's patent outrage. "Mrs. Nickleby, perhaps if you could tell me why you believe that your rubies have been stolen, then perhaps we may come to some sort of conclusion," she said calmly.

"My rubies are missing and that little hussy stole them," said Mrs. Nickleby. "All that talk of replacing a button on my cloak! Phah! She was but learning where my jewel case was kept, weren't you, missy?"

Pandemonium broke loose. The maid again squeaked her innocence. Withers raised his voice, his indignation plain. "Miss Grantham, I must take leave to observe—" Mrs. Nickleby roared her disbelief, reiterating her accusations.

"That is quite enough!" Judith's voice cracked through the air. Instantly the hall fell quiet, various pairs of eyes fixing on her face with surprise or approval, depending upon their owners.

"Good girl," murmured Sir Peregrine under his breath. He entirely approved of the tide of rose in Miss Grantham's face and the manner in which her gray eyes flashed.

Judith looked at Mr. Nickleby and said coldly, "Since your wife appears quite incapable of expressing herself with any degree of control, I should like to hear the tale from you. If you please, Mr. Nickleby!"

Mr. Nickleby was nothing loath. "It is as my good wife has been saying, Miss Grantham. The ruby necklace and earrings are gone, as well as the ring, and a pretty penny I paid for them, too. That maid there has been serving Mrs. Nickleby since we come. She had the opportunity. And it did seem suspicious at the time that she claimed to want to replace a button on Mrs. Nickleby's cloak without being told. Why, I ask you, what servant offers to do the extra thing? No, as I told Mrs. Nickleby, that maid has done the deed. She was but throwing dust in our eyes, being so helpful."

"On the contrary. Those I employ anticipate the needs of myself and of my guests. If that is not what you are used to, I am sorry for it; but certainly that does not give you leave to wantonly accuse any member of my staff of thievery or falsehood," said Judith with distaste. "If your rubies are missing as you say, they have probably only been misplaced and will certainly turn up in time."

"Did I not tell you, Mr. Nickleby? Did I not say that the servant was but an extension of the mistress's own lax nature? I would not be a bit surprised to learn that Miss Grantham is every bit as larcenous as that wretched maid!" exclaimed Mrs. Nickleby.

There were several indrawn breaths among the fascinated audience and all eyes flew to Judith's face. She stood quite still, her face white and expressionless.

Only her glittering eyes, which had paled almost to silver, gave away her cold rage. "Mr. Nickleby, your wife has worn out my hospitality. I shall appreciate your departure within a quarter hour. A carriage will be readied immediately to carry you to the posting house."

Mr. Nickleby found himself making a bow and he straightened up hastily, annoyed with himself that he had been intimidated by Miss Grantham's lofty air. "There is still a question of my good wife's jewels, Miss Grantham," he said.

Judith looked at the gentleman for such a long moment that he became restive. She said thinly, "I am so anxious to have you out of my home that I shall happily pay whatever the wretched stones are worth."

"There! If that is not an admission of guilt I have never heard one," said Mrs. Nickleby. "Tell her that I shall have my rubies, Mr. Nickleby."

Mr. Nickleby paid his spouse no attention. A shrewd look had entered his eyes. "The stones came dear enough, but I shall be satisfied with five hundred pounds for the set," he said.

Sir Peregrine gave a short, sharp laugh. "My dear sir, you shall catch cold at this game. I shall not stand by tamely and allow Miss Grantham to be shamelessly fleeced. You'll take a hundred pounds and count yourself fortunate that I do not throw you and your wife out on your collective ears."

Mr. Nickleby nodded. "Done, sir." Mrs. Nickleby was outraged, and made her feelings known in no uncertain terms.

Judith thought she must get away from the awful woman or she would not be able to retain control over her temper. She turned on her heel and walked swiftly toward the stairs.

"But what of my rubies?" shrilled Mrs. Nickleby, surging after her.

Judith paused, her hand on the balustrade, and looked down at her from the advantage of the first step. "My dear madam, you are fortunate that one of my extremely larcenous nature does not strip you of the petticoats that you stand in!" she uttered. Without a backward glance she went swiftly up the stairs.

Judith took refuge in her private sitting room, done in pale lime silk and cherry wood that gave it a warm effect. She paced about the pretty room, giving full rein to her fury for several minutes. A servant timidly knocked to inquire if she would be joining the gentlemen downstairs for dinner or if she wished to be served dinner in her room, to both of which she gave an emphatic negative but added that she would like tea. By the time that the servant brought in the tea and a selection of biscuits, she had calmed considerably and she was even able to swallow a few bites of biscuit. When her maid quietly entered to relay a request from Sir Peregrine that he be allowed to wait on her, Judith was able to view the prospect of once more playing hostess with equanimity. Judith indicated that she would see him and seated herself in front of the fire.

When Sir Peregrine strolled into the sitting room, he was struck immediately by her air of unruffled composure. He said humorously, "My word, I thought to find you rending the draperies at the least."

Judith laughed at such a fitting description of her recent state. "I hope that I am too old for such dramatics, though I will admit to a strong desire to strangle a certain vulgar female."

"If I had known, I most certainly would have delayed the Nicklebys' departure for such an admirable inclination. But unfortunately, I myself saw them off more than an hour past," said Sir Peregrine. He suddenly grinned at her. "You were magnificent, Judith."

Judith flushed and pressed her palms against the heat

of her cheeks. "Oh dear! My wretched temper. I so very nearly disgraced myself."

"True, but in such a noble cause. However, Mr. Smith was apparently so overawed that he preferred to share a carriage with a hysterical Mrs. Nickleby and her increasingly short-tempered spouse rather than overstay his own welcome," said Sir Peregrine.

Judith felt thoroughly ashamed of herself. "That poor unassuming little man. I grew rather fond of him." She gestured at the small table beside her chair, upon which sat the teapot. "I usually have tea at this hour, as you see. Pray won't you join me, Sir Peregrine?"

"Thank you, I should like that, I think," said Sir Peregrine. He seated himself opposite and idly watched as she poured. He declined sugar or milk and took the cup from her hand. "By the by, I have visited Cecily. I do not think that I shall tear her from Elmswood just yet. She appears on the mend, but I shall not risk bringing on a relapse of her fever by traveling in this weather."

"I am happy to hear that your good sense prevails," said Judith with a touch of soft irony.

Sir Peregrine's eyes lighted with laughter even as he acknowledged her thrust. "I am not so lost to a proper sense of my responsibility as to risk my ward's health, whatever thoughts you may have had on the matter."

"Why sir, I would not dream of interfering," said Judith with bland innocence.

"Quite," said Sir Peregrine dryly. "I noticed, however, that Cecily is becoming restless at her enforced inactivity and I have given permission for Lord Baltor to visit with her. He seems willing enough to wait on her, while I harbor no such inclinations. You will say next that I am shirking my duty not to dance to whatever tune Cecily wishes to pipe."

"Not that, no," said Judith hesitantly. "But do you think it wise to throw Cecily and Lord Baltor together in such a fashion? They were so taken with one another, after all.''

Sir Peregrine brushed such considerations aside. "Cecily will be madly in love with the fellow for six weeks and then she will quite literally forget his lordship's name. Believe me, I have seen the pattern before. She'll take no hurt from proximity with Lord Baltor. As for his lordship, one always makes a recovery from one's first calf love.''

"You are cynical, sir," said Judith, smiling at him over the rim of her cup. Sir Peregrine returned her smile and bowed from the waist in acknowledgment of her observation. She was aware that several seconds had ticked by and she marveled at the unusual ease of their companionship. She spoke her thoughts. "Do you know, I believe this is the first time that we have managed a civil conversation of any length between us? It is . . . pleasant.''

"We did not often use our times together to such advantage," said Sir Peregrine in agreement.

"No. We were engaged more in seeking out one another's weaknesses. Those are not particularly good memories," said Judith quietly, her eyes contemplating the fire.

"It is odd, but I do recall a few good moments," said Sir Peregrine softly.

Judith's eyes flew to his and what she saw in his expression made the color rise in her face. "Perhaps there were some," she acknowledged. "But the quarrels between us overwhelmed any sort of lasting affection.'' She was silent a moment before she summoned up a smile. "Actually, I am surprised to feel so much in charity with you. I do not know what has come over us. We have not ripped up one another for the better part of two days.''

Sir Peregrine studied her face. "I suppose that we have become infected by the yuletide season," he said.

"Yes, I suppose that must be it," said Judith. She

felt distinct dissatisfaction that he offered such a simple explanation. It had not been the Christmas spirit that had set her pulses racing when he kissed her. But certainly she could not have expected an acknowledgment of anything more from him.

A knock at the sitting room door heralded the entrance of Withers. Judith looked inquiringly at the butler. "Yes, Withers, what is it?"

Withers's usually expressionless countenance appeared troubled. "Miss, I have come with rather singular tidings," he said. He advanced toward her and held out his hand. In his palm was a gold band set with a large ruby.

Judith instantly recognized Mrs. Nickleby's lost ruby ring. "My word! Wherever was it found?" she asked, taking it between her fingers. The ruby flashed in the light.

"It was found in Mr. Smith's room, together with this note," said Withers. He handed a twist of paper to her.

Judith smoothed open the note. It took but a moment to scan it. Then she went into a peal of laughter. Sir Peregrine instantly demanded to be let in on the joke and she thrust the note at him. "Here, sir! Read it for yourself. I was never more amused in my life," she gasped.

Reading the note, Sir Peregrine started to laugh as well. "Our John Smith seems to have been a cunning devil. Who could have guessed that he was a thief? And an honorable one at that."

"Indeed, and I had thought that he was reading on those occasions that I found him in the library. I never dreamed that he was squirreling away odd bits of silver and Mrs. Nickleby's jewelry!" said Judith, still chuckling. She looked up at the faintly disapproving expression on Withers's face. "Come, Withers, surely you must see the humor. It is not every day that a thief leaves a token of his appreciation for the hospitality of Elmswood!'' As she spoke she held up the ruby ring.

"The hospitality was not all that John Smith admired, Miss Grantham. He appeared quite impressed when you dealt so summarily with Mrs. Nickleby. I suspect that was what persuaded him to leave your silver spoons in the library,'' said Sir Peregrine.

"I suppose that I must be flattered,'' said Judith, laughing again.

"A most singular gentleman, indeed. I shall go at once to the library and retrieve the silver,'' said Withers repressively. He nodded at the ring. "Shall I take custody of that object, ma'am?''

"Pray do,'' said Judith promptly. She handed over the ring. She shook her head as the butler left the sitting room. "I fear that it will be some time before Withers can look on this with any degree of humor. He has taken it as a personal failing that he was not able to see through Mr. Smith's mild demeanor.''

Her quiet words seemed to trigger a parallel of recognition in her companion. "We all fail to correctly divine an individual's character on occasion,'' said Sir Peregrine, all levity gone from his expression.

Judith stared at him, her heart beginning to sink. The truce between them was obviously over. "Quite true. I think we may agree on that point, Perry,'' she said coolly.

He smiled, though no amusement appeared in his eyes. "We seem to have come to another Rubicon, Judith. Being in your company these past days has forced me to acknowledge a desire to understand what happened between us. I do not think that I shall let you go until we have hammered it out.''

Judith gave the faintest of laughs. The ironic expression in her eyes was reflected in her voice. "It does seem the perfect opportunity, does it not? Perhaps this time we may even manage to preserve a semblance of civility.''

"The rules are established, then. Civility and frankness are the only limits. And as a gentleman, I must bow to your prerogative to begin," said Sir Peregrine with a wolfish grin.

Judith stopped herself from delivering a withering setdown. It would hardly forward relations if she were to immediately set up his back, and quite suddenly she wished very much to be able to hold this frightening conversation. Quite frightening, she thought, aware of her dry throat and the tenseness in her shoulders. But she would not give way to it, as she had before. There was deeply buried pain within her that had never quite healed. She knew now it never would unless she went through with this confrontation.

A long silence fell while Judith thought over and rejected a dozen questions. There was one that had always stayed at the forefront of her mind, but she did not have quite the courage to ask it. Despising herself for a coward, she said, "I have found certain contentment in my life. I have always wondered whether you did as well."

Sir Peregrine gave a short laugh. His piercing eyes derided her timid start. "I suppose one may say so. I do not lack for friends, if that is what you mean."

Judith bit her lip. She felt ready to sink, but from somewhere she found the courage to continue the dangerous game. "Have you—have you a female companion?" she asked hesitantly.

He was silent a moment. "No. I am not entangled in any sort of relationship. But surely you know that."

She shook her head. "No one ever speaks of you to me, you see." She gestured helplessly. "It was as though there was always a determination to shelter me from anything that might cause me unpleasantness. Or more likely, to ward off any possibility of my making an uncomfortable scene if I were to learn anything that I did not quite like."

Sir Peregrine regarded her steadily. "Would you have? Made a scene, I mean."

Judith laughed, though a bit shakily. "Oh, I don't know. Perhaps early on, but at this point it hardly matters, does it? We have grown inured to one another's existence and in the last few days we have proven that we are even able to be civil toward one another. That in itself is rather refreshing, do you not think?"

"I think that we were both fools," said Sir Peregrine forcibly.

Judith looked over at him in astonishment.

He got swiftly to his feet and turned to stare into the fire, presenting his hard profile to her. "Do not look at me like that, Judith. You do not know what your eyes say to me." He glanced around at her then and his mouth curved into a rueful smile. "You always had the most bewitching eyes, did I ever tell you?"

Judith clasped her fingers tightly together. She felt as though she was about to suffocate. "No, I do not think so. But then there was not much time for such words."

Sir Peregrine gave a bark of laughter. "That is surely an understatement, my girl! We fought nearly every moment that we were ever together, which was not often since we were surrounded by a constant crowd of the curious. It was a ridiculous courtship. In public we were the epitome of polite breeding, smiling and gracious to every personage who wished to congratulate us on what a splendid match we were making. It makes me ill now to recall how I allowed myself, and you, to go through that rot, when all I wanted was to speak to you alone and to make love to you. My God, Judith, why did you jilt me?"

Color flamed in her cheeks. She stared at her hands, clasped tight in her lap. Her voice came low and intense. "I discovered that you were bought for me."

Sir Peregrine swung around. "What the devil are you talking about?" he snapped.

* * *

There was a commotion at the door and it was thrust open. Cecily's voice sounded a determined note. "I do not care! I shall speak to him at once, Arthur!" She came into the sitting room on the tail of her words. Lord Baltor was close on her heels, his countenance perturbed. Cecily stopped when she saw Miss Grantham's expressionless face and her guardian's unfriendly gaze. She raised her delectably pointed chin. "Forgive my interruption, Miss Grantham. But I was told that I would find my cousin with you and I must speak to him at once," she said.

"Of course, Cecily. Pray join us, and you also, my lord," said Judith, her experience as a hostess granting her the poise she required to form a gracious reply. Her lips felt stiff as she smiled. She gestured to the settee situated near the fireplace.

Cecily shook her head. "We shall stay but a moment, I think. At least—" As her eyes went to Sir Peregrine's grim expression, her voice faltered slightly. She felt Lord Baltor's fingers on her elbow and the contact gave her courage. "Sir Peregrine, I have come to inform you that I have engaged myself to Lord Baltor. I shall therefore refuse to consider the suit of the gentleman whom you chose for me. I hope that this does not come as too great a shock to you and that you will grant us your blessing," she said in formal tones.

"You shall catch cold waiting for it," said Sir Peregrine pithily. He looked at Lord Baltor with something akin to impatience. "Come, Baltor, you do not truly wish to tie yourself to my flighty ward. She tumbles in and out of love with such regularity that I have become resigned to it. Believe me, you would do better to wait on a more steadfast maiden."

"I am aware of Cecily—Miss Brown's—past, sir. She has informed me of it herself, which but adds to my admiration," said Lord Baltor.

"I have not the stomach for this," muttered Sir Peregrine. He met Judith's gaze for a second only, because she at once turned her head away, but he was quite able to read the censure in her eyes. It gave him pause.

"Perry, I know that I have given you cause to mistrust my steadiness. So I have thought up a compromise, if you should like it," said Cecily. She clasped her hands in front of her. "I have discussed the matter with Arthur and he has agreed that my plan is reasonable."

Sir Peregrine threw a sardonic look at Lord Baltor, who met his gaze unflinchingly even though a flush rose in his boyish face. "I see. Pray continue, Cecily. I cannot deny you a hearing, I suppose," he said.

Cecily drew a breath. "I am under age, of course, so you have the right to squelch any union that I may wish until I attain my majority. I know that I have at last truly fallen in love, but I realize that I must prove that to you. So I propose that an informal understanding be recognized between myself and Lord Baltor. In the meantime, I should like to be brought out in London so that I may be exposed to positively scores of gentlemen. If I do not change my allegiance from Lord Baltor to another in the year before my majority is up, you will agree to a formal announcement of our engagement to be inserted in the *Gazette*."

There was a short silence during which Sir Peregrine studied his ward with an unreadable expression. He said finally, "You have at last succeeded in surprising me, Cecily. It seems that you have learned a bit of common sense. Your stay at Elmswood seems to have been to your advantage." He did not glance toward Judith, but he sensed her start of astonishment.

Cecily flushed with the beginnings of excitement. "Then you do agree to my compromise?"

"I think that I do," said Sir Peregrine. He glanced at Lord Baltor. "And now, my lord, you may escort my ward back to her parlor. She appears ready to faint at my easy acquiesence.''

The young couple extricated themselves from the sitting room with several exclamations of thanks. When the door was closed behind them, Judith glanced at Sir Peregrine with a faint smile. ''I am glad for Cecily,'' she said.

''At this moment I care not one jot about my ward's future,'' said Sir Peregrine. He stared frowningly at Judith. ''I believe that we left off with a positively idiotic statement regarding my motives for offering for you. Pray enlighten me further, Miss Grantham!''

Judith stiffened and something flashed in her expression. Her eyes challenged him, daring him to deny her accusation. ''You were my father's choice. After we became engaged, he congratulated himself for having struck a bargain with you, though it had cost him what he termed a tidy little sum!''

Old anger had laced her tumble of words, but now she sighed. She passed a hand over her eyes. ''He told me that I should be a grateful daughter because he had found such a splendid match for me. I knew in that instant I could never be happy with you.'' Her eyes were shadowed when she looked at him. ''I had thought you cared for me a little. It was unbearable that you had offered for me for quite different reasons. Oh, I know that marriages are still arranged and that bride's money changes hands, but I was a naive and romantic young girl and that was not what I wanted for myself.''

Sir Peregrine had been riveted by her account. He understood now why a few days previously she had been so hostile when he had mentioned bribing away one of Cecily's undesirable suitors. He expelled a deep breath. ''That is when you decided to reject my suit, then.''

Judith shook her head. ''I did not know what to do.''

"Judith, why did you not come to me? I would have told you the truth," said Sir Peregrine quietly.

"What was the truth, Perry?" she asked.

He felt bitterness spark into life, but after an instant he thrust it aside. Pride had once led him to walk away without demanding an explanation. He would not allow himself to make that same mistake again. He must keep his own end of the bargain as well as she had. "Your father approached me to arrange a match between us. I was entirely taken aback by such an arrangement being offered in this day and age. Looking back on it, I think that he must have thought my hesitation due to lack of monetary incentive. That was when he offered that damnable 'tidy little sum.' "

Sir Peregrine gave a fleeting half-smile as his eyes studied Judith's tight expression. He continued quietly, "But once I had a moment to think about you, I discovered that your father had merely anticipated my own unformed desires. I had already met you and become intrigued by you. The money that your father spoke about meant nothing to me. I was ready to set it immediately in trust for you to use as you wished. I hoped that you would pass it on to any children that we might have."

Judith's expression had altered and become vulnerable as he spoke. The last completely overset her. She covered her face with her hands. "Dear God, how could I have been so wrong?" she whispered.

"Judith." Sir Peregrine knelt beside her chair and gently pulled her hands down, to hold both clasped between his own fingers. "My very dear Judith, why did you never tell me? We could have saved one another so much anger and bitterness."

Judith's smile wavered. "You have said it yourself, Perry. We were not given much time to learn about one another. Whenever we were private, we either fought or you kissed me. I could not keep a single coherent thought in my head."

A light entered Sir Peregrine's blue eyes. "That is most interesting, Miss Grantham." He slowly leaned closer.

Judith watched him come, mesmerized. As his lips brushed hers, her lashes fluttered down. His mouth tasted wonderful and the kiss was heady as wine. The familiar swirl of melting feeling began to engulf her. Realizing it, Judith broke away. She pulled free her hands and pushed against his broad shoulders. "Perry, do not," she whispered. For several seconds she was afraid that he would reject her plea. He was still so close that she could feel the warmth of his breath on her face. But then he sighed and eased away from her.

"You are right, Judith. We have still too much that lies between us," said Sir Peregrine. He rose to his feet and moved deliberately to stand at the mantel so that there was distance between them. "You have said that it was the discovery that your father had offered money to me that decided you against my suit. But I seem to recall quite a different explanation that you gave to me. It sounded a pack of nonsense designed to insult me. But what so deeply enraged me, and what I have carried from that day to this, was your assertion that you feared me."

Judith sighed and shook her head. "I tried to explain feelings that I did not myself understand. What I did understand was that I was frightened. You see, I did not really know you and what my father said had shaken my faith in what I thought I knew. I was frightened and I had no one to ask for counsel. All my life I had never been able to withstand my father's will on any occasion, accepting his decisions for my future even when I was caused unhappiness. But my marriage to you—"

She looked at Sir Peregrine somberly. "I would be giving my life into what had become the hands of a complete stranger. I tried to talk to my father, but he paid me not the least heed. He patted me on the head and recommended that I turn my thoughts to my trousseau. My father wished our marriage to take place just as he had planned, but as the date approached my fear of the unknown became stronger than my awe of him. I did not consult with my father before I saw you that day. He was . . . disappointed.'' She could not keep the hurt out of her voice. She had been a frightened young girl sorely in need of support and comfort, but that was not what she had received.

When Sir Peregrine recalled that her father had been a burly gentleman possessed of a supreme confidence in his own opinion, he thought that Judith had surely understated the man's reaction. All these years he had harbored an erroneous conclusion. His estimation of her mettle had been sadly wanting, he thought. "I know that your father must have made your life very difficult," he said quietly.

Judith brushed it aside. "It is unimportant now." She smiled at him wearily. "You must think me a perfect fool, I know."

Sir Peregrine shook his head. "On the contrary. That is what I thought then, but now I can only salute your courage. You flew in the face of all that you were taught to revere in order to preserve your integrity. I, on the other hand, behaved with as little common sense as I have credited Cecily with. I was so blinded by my own pride and anger that I scarcely listened to what you tried so inexpertly to convey to me."

The emotional intensity of the past several minutes was proving to be a terrible strain. Judith felt that she simply had to place the situation back into proper perspective or she feared that she would burst into tears. "I shall ring for sackcloth and ashes if you wish," she said.

For an instant he was completely taken aback. Then he grinned and there was fondness in his eyes as he looked at her. "You are the most obliging hostess of my acquaintance, I must say. Thank you, but I believe that I will do very well without." He straightened up from his leaning posture against the mantel. Lifting her hand, he carried it to his lips. "Good night, Miss Grantham."

Judith smiled up at him tremulously. "Good night, Sir Peregrine." She watched him go to the sitting room door. She had never asked him whether he still loved her, she thought. But perhaps it was just as well. She was not certain that she really wished to hear the answer.

Sir Peregrine opened the door, but he did not go through immediately. Judith stood up. She felt that she had never been more tired in her life. It was difficult to recall that the tail end of yuletide holidays were normally the quietest days of the year for her. "Was there anything else, Sir Peregrine?" she asked.

"I do not think that I can allow you to dwindle into an old maid," he said reflectively.

Judith gasped in outrage, quick color flying into her face. "I beg your pardon!"

Sir Peregrine came toward her, his expression unreadable. When he was within touching distance of her, he said, "I have been haunted these past five years, I thought, by my hatred for what you had done. But that was merely hiding the truth from myself. Judith, when I think of the years stretching ahead without you beside me, I find it a very dull and empty vision. I fear that I am still very much in love with you."

Her outrage over his outrageous announcement faded away. On a sigh, Judith walked into his arms, which folded tight about her. She caught hold of his lapel. "That is just what I wished to hear, my old and enduring love."

Sir Peregrine put a hand under her chin and raised her face. His bright, piercing eyes laughed at her. "I mean to kiss you, you know."

"Pray do so," breathed Judith.

He took her at her word.

The Duke's Progress

by

Edith Layton

Thin sleet dashed down sporadically, like course salt being sprinkled by an overzealous chef, covering over the pavements with an icy dust. Lowering clouds promised more compliments of the season. But this was London, it was December, and so even though pedestrians slipped and carriages crawled along the slick causeways, no one cursed the weather, and not a few of the sufferers on foot or in coaches hoped for the sleet to turn to snow, not rain. Because Christmas was coming and there was nothing like an old-fashioned holiday. And so sentiment killed complaints at birth, as Londoners tiptoed and bounced and slithered about their ice-encrusted city. 'Twas the season, after all.

The sweepers weren't making much headway against the successive waves of falling ice pellets, and neither were those who were trying to negotiate the treacherous streets. And so the idling fops, dandies, and sportive gentlemen at ease at their stations in the bay window of their select club were enjoying themselves mightily as they watched their fellow Londoners making cakes of themselves on the icy pavement outside. They were betting on when the falls would occur, roaring with laughter at the more comical of them, and quite beside themselves at the way some of their own distinguished colleagues were unwittingly capering.

Their jeering comments took neither rank nor sex of the victims into account, and they were as overcome with mirth at the sight of a housemaid falling on her rump as they were at how some of their own set obeyed gravity this winter's day. In fact, they deemed the plight of their own acquaintances even funnier, watching some step daintily as opera dancers before they fell, seeing others, who'd spied their snickering friends in the window, trying to ignore the situation by taking their usual long strides and so eventually taking even longer slides down to their inevitable pratfalls.

They weren't respectful of age, either, and when they caught sight of a tall, erect gentleman in a many-tiered greatcoat, his hair beneath his top hat grayer than the ice he trod, they immediately began to lay bets on how long it would take him to be toppled, and some of the less charitable among them on how many bones the old fellow would break as he hit the ground. They watched him with growing anticipation as the wagers went astronomically high, because incredibly enough, he was approaching rapidly and without mishap. The slender gray-haired gentleman was taking one Hessian-booted step after another down windy St. James Street as sure-footedly as a mountain goat, as gracefully as if it were a May morning. The wagers flew higher, surely such luck as the old codger was having couldn't last. But he walked on, unhampered. Then, as he approached their lookout post, he shot them a glance from eyes grayer than the sleet which then again veiled his austere features. Some of them groaned at that, some sighed, some looked abashed, but recognizing him, they all canceled their wagers and looked about for more profitable game.

And yet the glance they'd got hadn't been malicious or threatening. It had been brimming with mirthful awareness of the situation. Which was worse to his would-be tormenters. Because after the gentleman entered the club and gave his hat and coat to a footman,

it could clearly be seen that it was a serene and youthful face beneath that thick crop of deceptively silver
hair. And the tight-fitting, fashionable clothes revealed the form and figure of an extremely fit gentleman who was not above thirty winters. No, it hadn't
been his age, rank, or dignity that had immediately
canceled all bets, and accounted for his fellow club
members' slightly apprehensive expressions now. It
was that quietly amused and chilling smile he wore
that dismayed them. That, and the fact that Cyril
Hampton, Duke of Austell, was known for a wit that
was keener than the ice that dripped from his greatcoat
and a tongue sharper than the north wind that drove
the storm.

He didn't join the others at the window, which relieved most of them, although they'd invited him to
share in their sport. After a desultory wave of one
long, thin hand, he instead took a comfortable leather
chair near to the fireplace just as an old fellow might,
which being a supremely ironic and satirical gesture
in itself, caused many faces at the bow window to
flush with embarrassment.

"I, at least, didn't place a wager on how soon you'd
take a spill," a medium-sized gentleman with a crop
of light curls announced as he dropped into an adjoin-
ing chair.

"Recognized me from afar, did you?" the duke
asked lightly.

"No, pockets to let," the other gentleman reported
blithely. "Just paid Harrison and McTeague. The mill
last week, picked the loser there—and then lost out on
the Honorable Miss Martin. She jilted Palmer on the
fifth, you remember," he supplied helpfully. "I said
she'd keep him on the string until the twelfth. Said it
fifty pounds' worth," he grieved.

"Females have always been your downfall," the
duke commiserated with much insincerity as the curly-
haired gentleman sighed his agreement.

"Just so, and if you're being ironical," the sufferer reminded him, "it don't matter. I ain't in the petticoat line, as you know, and so I don't understand them in the least."

". . . Precisely why he's friends with him," another gentleman standing nearby commented overloudly to his friend, as they dried their dampened coattails by the fire. "Austell can be ironic as he pleases, and Beverly never feels the sting. I doubt he understands three out of four words Austell speaks."

Before the other man could caution his friend to lower his voice, the duke cut in sweetly, his melodic tenor tones carrying as well as any professional singer's, "Rather say, sir, that like he who grasps the nettle firmly and doesn't get stung, Bev here is never hurt because he's brave enough to confront danger directly. It's those who shy away who graze against the thorns and are pierced."

A stillness fell over the entire room. The gentleman by the fireplace flushed more than the heat of the fire could account for, as his companion laid a cautionary hand on his sleeve. He hesitated, and the tension in the room abated. Gentlemen who took up such challenges as the Duke of Austell had just instantly, if obliquely, issued, took them up at once. The hesitation meant that the gentleman had remembered other sharp and killing things the duke was renowned for, aside from his tongue. He was an excellent swordsman, a crack shot, and famous for how well he displayed at Gentleman Jackson's boxing salon. Unless a new way was found to duel, a man would be well-advised to take anything but umbrage from the duke's comments. This gentleman took his time, which meant he'd wisely decided not to take the insult.

"Just so," he eventually murmured grudgingly, in agreement, before he added, because a man had to have some spine, "Lord Beverly is to be congratulated, then, for his bravery if not his taste . . . in po-

sies, that is," he explained as another silence fell,
". . . nettles, after all," he said, and then grew still,
belatedly worried about the result of his meager, re-
flective spurt of daring.

"Indeed," the duke said equitably enough, "there's
no accounting for some tastes."

The subject was allowed to drop, and the room returned to normal. Lord Beverly looked at his friend
approvingly, but the duke only sighed. He'd taken the
fellow's retraction in the spirit it was offered, just as
he took his last feeble display of spirit. No man should
be made to crawl, after all. Nor was he eager to fight,
however well he did it, but a challenge would have at
least allievated the boredom. That was precisely why
he was friends with Lord Beverly. It was true that Bev
didn't understand half the things he said, but then,
neither did most of the people he was acquainted with.
At least Bev had the best of human attributes, "a good
heart," and most of the time he was, at least, amusing.

"And so," Lord Beverly asked, as though he'd been
speaking all the while, "where are you going for
Christmas?"

The duke looked up at that, genuine surprise on his
face. Bev often spoke in non sequiturs, but this sudden
introduction of a topic he'd not thought of challenged
him more than the foolish fellow by the fire had. And
filled him with more cold dread too, he realized. So
of course, he spoke up instantly, saying idly, "I haven't
thought about it. Is it really that time of year again? It
seemed just yesterday that I bumped into Father
Christmas on the stair."

"As if you didn't know," Lord Beverly replied.
"Probably got an invitation to every house party in
the country. Like me. And I'm just a fribble, and I
know it. But hostesses can always use an extra male,
so I've been asked everywhere too. Much good it will
do," he said gloomily, "because m'sister wants me at

home, family duty and all, and fun be damned. Family duty, ha! Wants to trot out a dozen marriageable chits for me, as if I didn't know it. And here I've got an invitation to Lyonshall, my old friend Morgan's place. Earl of Auden, you know him,'' he added helpfully.

"Yes,'' the duke answered, smiling, "and know he's fairly newly wedded too. Do you enjoy being fifth wheel on the chariot, Bev dear?''

The curly-haired gentleman looked blank.

"Oh,'' he said at last, his color slightly heightened. "But makes no matter. I know the bride too. Wouldn't have asked me if they didn't want me,'' he argued before he subsided, conceding, "I suppose you've the right of it. Still, I'd have preferred visiting them even if I had to pass half the time staring at the ceiling pretending I didn't hear the cooing. They're best friends of mine, and—Christmas, after all. Instead, I have to go home,'' he said moodily as a schoolboy. "And you? Are you going home too?'' he asked suddenly, his thoughts veering, as always.

The duke's normally impassive face grew colder.

"Hardly,'' he said.

He was a handsome enough fellow when he smiled, Lord Beverly thought, with those straight, even features and those slanting gray eyes. But when he pokered up like this, his thin silver brows the darkest thing on white skin grown blanched as marble, his finely chiseled face about as expressive as that stone itself, he looked positively threatening, even to an old friend. And so he told him, forgetting, as he did—as he'd wanted to—that it had been a bad question with only one possible answer. Because everyone knew Austell detested his stepfather, pitied his mother for her poor judgment in marrying him, and realizing how that misguided lady insisted on championing the boor she'd wed, stayed as far from his family home as possible. The dower house where the duchess and her gigolo husband dwelt was a mile from the manor. But since being in the same county with the pair was too much for any of the duchess's children, it was no surprise that it would take more than Christmas—it would take the duke's stepfather's funeral to bring him home again.

"But as you say," the duke said equitably enough now, "since I've enough invitations to read until the New Year ends, I haven't decided where I'll be as yet."

"Best make up your mind," Lord Beverly warned. "Fast away the old year passes, and all that. The street's swarming with beggars, fell over three—'pon my word, don't laugh, I did, literally—on the way here. Cost me every cent of spare change I had. Hard to ignore a chap you've just landed on," he grumbled. "And the price of mistletoe's rising; all the ladybirds are cooing at Rundel's windows—the devil's got all his finest bracelets out on display—Christmas is almost upon us."

The duke laughed. "You make it sound like a ravening wolf," he said, and then sobered. "But then, in a way it is, I suppose," he said thoughtfully. "It's the one time of year one's supposed to be with the ones one loves . . ." He paused. It was only when he noticed the suddenly sober look in his friend's eye that he went on, on a laugh, "Which presents a problem to most of the gentlemen we know. After all, with all the holly and mistletoe, caroling and gourmandizing, kiddies and nursery pantomimes, between the mince pie and having the neighbors in for wassail, it must be difficult for a family man to find time to slip away from home and hearth to visit his mistress. Especially if he goes to his country estates."

"Which is why there's all these house parties, enough room in those drafty old piles for a fellow's wife, mistress, and her mother, I should think," Lord Beverly said at once, speaking more warmly than he was wont to do, discussing matters he'd little interest in, all to get his friend's mind off those things which seemed to be tripping him and hurting him as his stroll through the dangerous streets never had or could.

"Welcome to come along with me to m'sister's," Lord Beverly added, without much hope of agreement, and so wasn't surprised when his friend answered, "Find someone else to hold your hand, Bev. Your nephew's worse than all five of mine combined. I'll be visiting some of mine in town—the rest are safely snugged away at their home in the north . . . which reminds me," he mused, "I'd best remember to send Louis—my sister Emily's oldest—a chess set. All the letters I have from him hint so strongly for one that I wouldn't be surprised to find the little rogue's already sent me the bill."

Lord Beverly heard his friend chuckle. "Gad!" he said with some wonder, "Listen to you! You sound just like a doting old bachelor uncle! Ninety if you're a day. Time to have your own, I'd think."

The duke seemed discomposed for a moment, and then, in the voice his enemies so detested and even his friends were wary of, he said, "Why, so I would, my dear, if you could show me how to have them legitimately without tying myself for life. Exactly as you've done, I presume?"

"I'm not in the petticoat line, myself," Lord Beverly reiterated uneasily. "Which isn't to say I won't be someday. I'll wed if only to cut my nephew out of the succession. But since we're speaking of it, I suppose you'll be going to the Edgecombes' houseparty then? In Buckinghamshire? Well, I thought you were considering the Incomparable. Everybody else is."

The duke didn't bother to mention that they hadn't been speaking of it, or ask which Incomparable his friend meant. Bev's thought progressions had a logic only unto their own selves, and there was only one new Incomparable beauty each Season.

"Everyone else is considering her? Or considering me considering her?" he asked instead, before he said,

"Yes, Miss Edgecombe is everything desireable, true. But I don't know if I'm ready for everything desirable yet. Still," he sighed resignedly, "it's likely I'll go. After Christmas Day. I've Randall's boy coming to town before the holiday, and I thought I ought to do the pretty with him first."

There was nothing in his voice as he said the last to make Lord Beverly look up, but precisely because there was so much of nothing in it, he did. He'd known Randall Thomas, the brave officer who'd fallen at Waterloo the previous year, too, if not as well as his friend had done. But the only way he could cope with sorrow was to flee it. Before he could think of how to do that, the duke went on, "But after that, I've been asked to the Incomparable's house party, a houseparty in Sussex with last year's Incomparable, and another in Hampshire with a young person I've been promised is to be next year's Incomparable. Not to mention being invited to a score of Christmas dinners here in town with all the runners-up. Odd, I hadn't noticed how decorative the female youth of England has become. Still, so everyone says—something in the water supply that year, possibly?"

Lord Beverly groaned. His friend was succumbing to another mood. He damned himself for bringing up the topic of prospective wives. And Christmas. Talk of brides and holidays seemed to be bringing out the worst in him. And that, as his friend knew too well, could be very bad indeed. He looked around for something to divert the duke, saw a new arrival coming through the door, and hailed him with gratitude.

The gentleman that joined them was a great favorite of everyone at the club's, and his entrance caused some desertion of the bow window, leaving that outpost to a clutch of only the most rabid gamesters. The Viscount Talwin was a great raconteur and after he'd been prompted and primed with a glass of fine brandy, he took a seat near the duke and soon had a circle of listeners laughing at his latest tales of the *ton*.

". . . and then the gentleman—no, he *shall* remain nameless," the viscount insisted as he went on, "went to visit his bit 'o muslin—a young creature up to the mark in everything, I might add—in expectation of receiving the Christmas present that she'd promised him in her note. A thing, as she'd writ, 'of rare beauty, and greater worth.' Well, what could he do but reciprocate? He'd a necklace of rubies and diamonds in his pocket, and was fair trembling that it mightn't be good enough. Never do to look no-account in front of one's doxie—especially since he suspected she was deceiving him with two of his best friends, and wouldn't want to look clutch-fisted to them either.

"Her maid let him in, the lights were low, he crept to her boudoir as he was bade, nervous as a cat about what she was going to give him for Christmas. Well, it was a problem. If it was worth that much, he'd want it to be something he could flaunt without his wife's being the wiser, and yet something that could make his friends expire from envy.

" 'Come in!' she caroled, from the general direction of the bed.

"He did. To find his mistress stark, staring naked save for a huge length of wide red ribbon, which she'd used to do herself up, with a bow tied under her lovely I won't say what! 'Happy Christmas!' she cried. Truth! Truth! It happened only yesterday night, and cost him a king's ransom!" the viscount insisted as they all laughed.

"Truth indeed!" another gentleman said indignantly as he arose from his chair. "Damned unfaithful wench!"

"Peace, my lord," the viscount said, as the others roared with merriment. "It's never the same lady. I know your—ah—little friend, and it's never she."

"No, no, it's not," another gentleman put in, with

an embarrassed look, "for I was enchanted to find myself the recipient of just such a gift this morning, and I know your *cher ami* is not mine. And it was a pink ribbon mine used," he added sadly, as the other men laughed.

"Oho," one of the gentlemen said, "Seems like the demireps of London are on to a good thing. Giving nothing and getting something for it."

"The demireps, and a great many others," the Duke of Austell commented. "But isn't that the way of Christmas? Especially when you receive something from a dependent? Only more of the usual, done up in gay ribbons to look like a gift, when it's only always something you've yourself already paid, and dearly, for."

"Remind me to invite you to my next Christmas party," the viscount said dryly as all the gentlemen fell silent, pondering the duke's words.

"You already have, thank you. But sorry, I can't attend," the duke answered sweetly.

"I'm sorry for it," the viscount answered, and he was. Austell's wit might be lethal, but it was fair. He observed the same rules of conduct in public that a prizefighter did, never using his talent against those weaker or younger or unable to defend themselves. Most of all, the viscount thought, the duke never spoke without provocation, and knew when not to, even when provoked. Impatient with fools because he was so clever, suspicious of his fellow man and woman because he'd been catered to and flattered unmercifully since he'd come into his estate and honors, at the same prematurely young age that he'd gotten his distinctive silver hair, he took tribute as his due and duly disregarded it. Wealthy and elevated in the *ton* as he was, he'd not hesitated to work for his country in diverse ways during the recent wars, traveling the Continent and risking danger as he did. And he'd been invaluable, not only because he saw beneath the surface, but because beneath his own icy surface, those who knew him knew how much he cared.

Some thought Austell too high in the instep, but the wily viscount knew better. Nine and twenty, going on sixty in his good sense, yet daring as a boy; as high in principles as he was in rank, yet willing to bend to any situation. That odd combination of silver locks and youthful face was very like the man himself, in his attractive, deceptive contradictions. In all, he was, as most men with enough convictions to make great enemies were, an even better friend to have than a foe. And that, his one-time employer, the spymaster viscount thought on a reminiscent smile, was saying a great deal.

"I'm sorry to take my leave now," the duke said, rising gracefully, "but as I've been repeatedly fore-warned of Christmas's imminent appearance, and can already feel its mince-scented breath hot on my neck, I think I'd be best advised to take myself off and armor myself for its arrival. There are diverse shops to visit and monstrous debts to incur in the spirit of the season. So good day, gentlemen, and God rest ye merry," he said on a bow.

"What? Shopping? In this weather?" one of his audience cried, amazed.

"What weather?" asked the duke, blandly.

That bit of arrogance caused many gentlemen to lose large sums as they crowded at the bow window hoping to see him stumble. But he made his way down the street like a man gliding on invisible skates, until he was lost to their sight, swallowed up by the gloom of the lowering afternoon.

It was good to have a plan for the day, these days it was as important to the Duke of Austell as having a menu before dinner. That way, even the blandest of-fering could be taken with equanimity, knowing other treats beckoned after it was swallowed down. So, the duke thought as he strolled out from his townhouse the next morning, reviewing his mental agenda, he'd get the chores of Christmas out of the way before it came. This morning he'd complete his shopping for things his secretary couldn't buy for him, so as to be able to present his secretary and household staff with those gifts before Christmas, since he might be off to a house party then. Then he'd lay other offerings of the season at his next stop, his sister's house; then, after lunch at his club, he'd pay a visit to Miss Clarissa Dunbar, the latest light-minded and light-moraled young woman to enjoy his keeping. He'd a gift sure to delight her, because it was her favorite thing: expensive. After that pleasurable interlude, he'd return home to dress for the night and take something far less valuable to his latest flirt, the Incomparable Miss Edgecombe. Because something valuable would betoken something more than best wishes of the season, and even though she was the Toast of the Season, he wasn't yet sure that he wanted to give her what she most wanted from him this Christmas: his name.

The streets of London were always crowded, but the weather had cleared and this morning it seemed that the many people who thronged the avenues were dressed in brighter colors and wore pleasanter expressions than he could recall having seen in a long while. But it was only fitting. The interminable wars seemed to be truly over at last, the sun was out, street musicians played Christmas tunes to do with hope, and joy, and perfect love and peace. Everywhere, there was color and variety that defied the calendar. Even the humblest grocers' shops displayed bounty for the oncoming holiday: impossibly fat fowls, bright red beef, tender white lamb, berries and nuts and fruits, and things that were green and growing against all reason of the real season.

In the district where the duke paused to browse, the foods displayed were those that were select and savory, but however delectable, the rare treats were just that—those that could be lived without. Similarly, the elegant shop windows were filled with things that glittered and shone; things of great price and little purpose. His eyes were caught and dazzled by items of magical beauty, seemingly imbued with an Arabian Night's mysticism and wonder. Imported and ancient, or newly devised and exquisitely executed, the windows displayed silken and satin things, gold and silver thingamabobs of uncertain function, or no function at all. Or common objects made remarkably uncommon: plain things flowered, simple things painstakingly embroidered, everyday things lavished with adornments until it seemed a waste to use them every day—who would dare to use a musical snuffbox? What lady's foot merited a true glass slipper fashioned of finest blown crystal? And nail scissors made of baroque chased gold—whose toenails but a sultan's should they address? It was a bazaar of the luxurious and unnecessary, and yet such was their appeal that even to a traveled gentleman such as himself, every foolish trinket seemed to be just what the duke had never known he'd always wanted.

But today wasn't for himself, although the fever to buy was upon him. He'd a great many things to purchase, and a great many people to gift. Suddenly the expectation of the effort of selecting, acquiring, and then giving of gifts gave him an unexpected feeling, and he paused on the pavements to ponder it. Yes. It was definitely a thrill of pure pleasure such as he hadn't felt in years. He was home, unoccupied, and alone in London at this season for the first time in a long time. Christmas was coming, and he found himself greeting it as he hadn't done in years: with a full and anticipatory heart.

The tall, lean, gray-haired gentleman was a shopkeeper's delight. His secretary, Pritchard, would appreciate that calfskin wallet initialed in gold—yes, it would be a nice touch to give him his Christmas bonus in it. His London housekeeper should love the fine tooled leather belt for her chatelaine keys—no, no, that intricately seedpearled and enameled brooch, instead. Totally useless except for decoration, but who had given Mrs. Raines a useless gaud for years, if not in the whole of her virtuous, hardworking life? A snuffbox for Alec, the butler? No, let it remain his secret vice. That handsome ivory-handled walking stick instead. Yes.

Too soon the gifts had been bought, wrapped, and sent back to his house—for a gentleman never *carried* anything but his quizzing glass and walking stick. All Christmas presents purchased, since Pritchard had ordered the dozens of others for the staff on all of the duke's farflung estates, as well as those for his family and friends . . . yet the duke was loathe to get on with the rest of his day. The shops drew him as if he were a brainless dandy with a full purse on his first day in town. But after all, he thought, it had been so long since he'd experienced leisure at this season. And after all, as he didn't wish to think, there was in this business of buying to please others some of the joy and warmth he'd missed at this season in all the years since his sisters had wed and he himself had fled his home and the idiot his mother had replaced his father with.

His attention was caught by a display in a window, and before he could think of what he was about, he'd gone into the toyshop and spoken for one of the most beautiful dolls he'd ever seen. She was French, the proprietor announced, as if in apology for her outrageous pricetag. And had sky-blue eyes and silky black hair and a pouting mouth and a magnificent set of clothes on her porcelain back.

Then the duke remembered that Pritchard had already bought his niece a perfectly charming toiletry set. But mirrors, combs, and brushes were practical, heartless things, and he'd the sudden notion of giving his niece something to remember her uncle with, something specially fine. A thing as lovely and unforgettable as this magnificent toy, whose beauty bordered on art. Imagining her glee settled it.

"She's beautiful, one of a kind, expensive, but worth it because of the pleasure she'll bring," the proprietor continued to urge, seeing that the duke paused with the magnificent doll in his hands.

"Very like many living examples of the sex that I know," the duke commented agreeably. "Very well, wrap her, please, I'll take her with me now. And for my nephew, that set of tin soldiers," he added, motioning to a mock battle set up on a countertop. "No," he decided, looking at the uniforms and suddenly seeing all the figures fallen, broken, and bloody in his mind's eye. "No," he repeated softly, "they've been too lately seen in reality to charm in tin—that set of medieval knights, instead. And for the infant, that clown music box, I think. The babe's too young to even turn his head to the music, but a pleased mama is the only gift for an infant, after all, isn't it?" he added, as the proprietor hastened to comply, scarcely listening, grinning at whatever he said for the price he was about to pay.

And though a gentleman never carried anything through the streets of town, and a nobleman certainly not, the Duke of Austell, cumbered with packages, grinning to himself at the thought that he looked like a demented, if extremely well-dressed Father Christmas, walked lightly toward his sister's house in the heart of town, his own heart unaccountably high.

"It is very beautiful, Uncle Cyril," the child said graciously, tucking the doll back into her papers in the box, "Thank you very much."

"And?" prompted her mama before the duke could answer.

The child turned questioning eyes, bluer than the

doll's, to her mama. She bit her lip and then brightened, remembering, "And Happy Christmas, Uncle," she said, almost as enormously pleased as her mama was with her cleverness.

"The proprietor at the toyshop said she was French," the duke explained, surprised to find himself deflated by the way the doll had been taken out, inspected, and then packed up again. "But you needn't worry about playing with her, I'm sure she'll take to an English girl."

"I'm sure she will," the child agreed.

"Perhaps," the duke wondered in an undervoice to his sister, "she's too old for dolls? Ten, after all."

A trill of laughter was his answer.

"Elizabeth, take your uncle upstairs to your room, and show him your dolls, will you?"

Elizabeth smiled. Genuinely, this time.

"I see," the duke drawled as he stood in his niece's bedchamber and found himself the cynosure of at least a hundred eyes: painted, enameled, glass, and beaded. The wall of dolls stared back at him.

"I think I'll put her on the third shelf, to the left," Elizabeth said officiously, bustling over to that area of her doll collection, "because she hasn't got open-and-close eyes, like the ones near the window, and she's dressed for court, like these over here, do you see?"

"Oh yes, I see." He sighed. "And I suppose instead of a name she's to be given a designation. She's to be filed under F for French, is that it? Or B for blue eyes?"

"Oh!" giggled his niece after a moment, when she understood—Uncle Cyril was always making odd jests, "No, under C for Christmas," she replied, playing along with him. And then wondered why he wasn't amused with his own game, because he only sighed.

"And I suppose your brother will put his knights next to his Armada, or on top of his Crusaders, when he gets home from the park and finds them?'' the duke asked quietly.

"Oh no," Elizabeth said on another giggle, "in his castle, of course. His silver castle, that is," she corrected herself, remembering her brother's habits, "because the others are already filled."

"I think," her uncle said as he turned to leave, "it would have been better, no matter what your mama said, to have waited until Christmas to open the presents."

"Oh no," Elizabeth said, horrified. "Because then I wouldn't have had time to notice her at all, and how could I have remembered what to put on the thank you note?"

"A problem, certainly," her uncle replied as he left.

Miss Dunbar's lodgings weren't far in distance from those of the duke's sister, but they were, by tacit mutual agreement of all concerned, leagues apart in every other respect. Gentlemen of the *ton,* married and not, often had need of female companionship of a nature only too natural to be discussed, or provided, in polite circles. Young persons such as Miss Dunbar supplied such needs when they weren't dancing at the theater or otherwise displaying their wares. They were in turn supplied by their protectors with lodgings nearby to their own, for convenience, yet far enough away for conscience's sake. The Duke of Austell was one of the few gentlemen of the *ton* who scarcely cared if the entire kingdom knew of his arrangement, but there was, in fact, little other place for him to keep Miss Dunbar. Respectability mattered in most polite neighborhoods, either of his own class or below it. And the impolite neighborhoods, where young women such as Miss Dunbar often found themselves when they grew older if they weren't exceptionally frugal and prudent, were places where no one with any sense would care to live, much less visit.

Clarissa Dunbar was neither frugal, prudent, nor especially wise, but she was lovely in her fashion, and clever enough to conceal her lack of wisdom. If the duke, in his innermost heart, disliked the idea of keeping her as though she were an appliance provided for his occasional pleasure, and so sometimes found himself disliking what he most enjoyed because of the mercenary, impersonal nature of that most personal act of all, he disliked that act with complete strangers even more. Clarissa was not as witty as Harriet Wilson, but neither was she as cruel; she wasn't as beautiful as Julia Jeffries, but she wasn't as foolish; and she was never as fashionable as Lucille LaPoire, but she wasn't as mercenary either. She was young, buxom, and merry, and the duke told himself she was original and charming. And sometimes, he almost believed it.

Now, as he waited in her front parlor, he found himself wondering what rig she was up to. Her maid had admitted him, and then instead of directing him to her room, as always, bade him wait and, suppressing a giggle, dashed away to attend to her mistress, and his. His spirits lifted. Trust Clarissa to come up with something novel, something more than the usual, although the usual would have been good enough for him today. He was oddly blue-deviled, losing himself in something as elemental as what Clarissa provided was what he was after. Lovemaking with wit to spice it and lift it from the basic squalor of such an arrangement as they had would be a more bountiful present than he'd expected, and by the time the maid finally reappeared, he was expecting something delightful. Even more so when she curtsied and simpered,

"The mistress'll see y' now, yer grace."

It was a late winter's afternoon, but the bedchamber was dim as dawn; he could just make out Clarissa's rounded form in the center of her bed. As he approached, she turned on her side, reached out, and

pulled a cord to draw the heavy draperies away from
the windows. Then she lay back again, grinning. He
stopped in his tracks, just as she'd wished.

She was completely bare, save for the huge, wide
green riband which was wrapped criss-cross around
her, tied up beneath her bottom, and resolved in a
huge bow beneath her breasts.

"Happy Christmas!" she caroled.

But then she frowned, because he didn't roar with
laughter, he simply stood and looked at her, without
so much as a glint of humor in those light gray eyes.
A moment later there was amusement there, but it was
rueful, not riotous. She pouted—every observable bit
of her. There must have been, he thought, a chill in
the room.

"I didn't think you'd be so prim, your grace," she
complained. "I thought you'd like my Christmas present to you."

"Original," he said wryly.

She had the grace to blush, everywhere.

"Oh, so you've heard," she said. "But it's all the
rage. Eva Prentice thought it up, or so she says, and
it sounded so amusing . . . everyone's doing it."

"How nice to be in the vanguard," the duke commented. "There'll be a shortage of ribands before you
know it," he observed dryly, while nevertheless he
began to shrug out of his tight-fitting jacket.

"There's truth!" she said, stroking her bow pride-
fully. "I had to fight like the devil to get this much!
Now there's only black left anywhere in the shops, and
that's hardly Christmasy, is it?"

"Hardly," he agreed, as he took the drapery pull
and dragged the curtains back across the windows, so
it would appear he couldn't see as well as he did, before he bent to her where she lay, plump, rosy, blushing, very like the other plaything he'd lately bought—
except, he noted with scrupulous fairness, her eyes
opened and closed.

He gave her what she'd thought he wanted, and after, gave her what she wanted more, and to her credit, she exclaimed as prettily over the bracelet as she did over his attentions. If he thought there was more honesty in her gasps over the second gift, he was courteous enough not to mention it—or the fact that her gift to him had been an insult to him. Because she'd never understand that it was the conceit that their arrangement was different that had made it bearable to him. And he was gracious enough not to tell her he wouldn't be back when he left her, soon after. Because though he'd be generous in his farewell gift, it would be no kindness to tell her he'd decided this was to be his last farewell to her. At least, he reckoned wryly, not now, at this joyous season.

The townhouse was filled, so stuffed with guests that if another was admitted, the duke thought, someone present would have to climb out the windows to make room. The thought entertained him, and it was as well, because little else about the affair did.

"My mistake," he admitted to Lord Beverly as they stood at the sidelines and sipped punch as the other guests prodded and inched their way into the thicket of guests thronging the salon. "Our hostess, the Incomparable, asked me to a small 'do' here tonight, and like an ass, I believed her."

Lord Beverly looked puzzled, as he often did.

"What mistake?" he asked, "It's small enough, only four musicians, they haven't opened the ballroom, I suppose there's not even a dinner on tap."

"In case you hadn't noticed, there isn't any air, either," the duke commented. Looking for his hostess and not seeing her, he asked, "Bev, do me a favor. If you ever see her tonight, pay my respects, and say that like a good wife, I'd a headache and had to say good night before the fun began."

But no sooner had the duke begun to edge his way

to the door than he heard a clear and merry voice call
to him, and turning, found the Incomparable herself
at his elbow, her eyes twinkling up at him almost as
much as all the brilliants that were sewn on her white
gown did in the candlelight.

"Fie, sir!" she cried, "stealing away so soon? Why
you haven't had a dance with me yet!"

"Not surprising," he answered, looking down into
her clear blue eyes with amusement, "since I could
scarcely ask you to twirl on a tabletop with me."

She tapped him with her fan. It was a bold gesture
for so young a chit, but she was Society's darling this
Season and could do anything, within reason, and be
forgiven it. It was just that impudent air that had attracted him when he'd first seen her a few weeks ago.
It was that insouciance that made him call on her again,
and accounted for his presence yet again tonight. Blue-
eyed blond little ladies with engaging dimples were
delightful stuff, but fairly commonplace. Most maidens her age interested him about as much as his niece
did in conversation, and if they were socially correct
maidens, had little else to offer him. He was only a
decade older than the misses making their debuts, but
in the common run of things, felt it as a century. But
so far, at least, he'd found this Incomparable to be
uncommon.

Still, he was nine and twenty, and unwed, because
he was as careful of where he gave his heart as where
he gave his word. And that, unfashionably enough,
was his goal: to marry where his heart lay, and he was
wealthy enough to be that eccentric. He knew he was
considered a great catch, but didn't care to be caught
so much as enticed, or want to be captured so much
as captivated. He'd many women friends, and many
lovers, but never any who'd been enough of both. He
sought a kindred spirit, a matching wit, a companion
as much as a coquette. Most of all, he wished to be
cared for as deeply as he was prepared to care. He'd

always thought he'd know at once if he met the right female, but he hadn't, not even a long while after "at once." For some reason, it had never happened. The Incomparable had certainly caught his attention, though. He'd seen the charming little rogue a total of six times, never entirely alone, or even partially alone for longer than the correct half hour call or interminable country dance. He was intrigued, and his bachelorhood weighed heavily upon him, especially tonight. But it was early days, he reminded himself as he smiled down at her, although the rest of the days he could foresee looked bright.

"Papa's going to open the ballroom in a moment," she said merrily. "The decorations are so fine we wanted it to be a surprise."

"Ah, drama," the duke said, nodding, as greatly bold, his hostess asked, tossing her fair head back to look him in the eyes, "And shall you have the first waltz with me?"

He didn't hesitate. His training as a foreign agent stood him in good stead, as ever.

"Ah, too much drama for me," he said with mirth he didn't feel. "Your other suitors would be at me with challenges to appear at dawn. And I'm such a late sleeper. Not to mention what Papa would say. My dear, only your papa, or your fiancé, should have that honor."

"I know," she said.

Not so uncommon, after all, he thought, with as much sorrow as shock. But he did cast aside his intention of leaving and engage to have the second waltz with her.

When the ballroom doors were flung open, the company could see the boughs of holly and sheafs of pine draped everywhere about the room. Mistletoe hung from the great chandelier and huge yule logs blazed in both fireplaces. The tables were garnished with evergreens and weighted with punchbowls hissing with hot crabapples.

As the duke bowed before his hostess before the second waltz, she, saucy to the last, said with only a trace of chagrin to belie her twinkling eyes, "We rushed the season a little, I suppose, but isn't it delightful?"

"Delightful," he agreed.

They spun about the room gracefully, the tall, serene, gray-haired gentleman and the lovely, lively little blond lady, and not a few romantics sighed, even as some of the unwed young ladies and ardent young gentlemen hissed as much as the crabapples did at the sight of them together.

But, "In another moment it would have looked like wrestling, not waltzing," the duke murmured when Lord Beverly trailed after him to the anteroom after the dance was done to ask why he was leaving so early.

"You've no idea how exhausting it is to waltz around a room avoiding the chandelier as if it dripped henbane, not mistletoe," the duke said softly. "Especially when your partner is determined to steer you beneath it," he added as he put on his hat.

And muttering something about "Papa's with rings and preachers at the ready," he marched off into the night, less in love with the season than ever, and slightly bilious from the scent of pine.

The Duke of Austell's study was stocked with such esoteric treasures it looked like an Aladdin's cave only to a connoisseur. The faded rose color, intricately designed carpet beneath his slippers was comfortable enough to the feet, but would catch the eye, and then the breath, only of someone able to recognize its age and rarity. Similarly, the bit of statue on his mantel— the athlete sadly lacking a nose—would look as no-account as Lord Beverly once proclaimed it to anyone who didn't know how greatly daring it was for the duke to have it out in plain sight, not covered by glass or protected by a museum guard. Just as the jolly Dutch gent in the painting over the mantel, the landscape mounted by the window, the etchings near the door, the various knickknacks, the vase atop the bookcase, not to mention the contents of the overflowing bookshelves, would help present a picture of a comfortable well-lived-in library to most; a glittering hoard only to a select few astute others.

But now, as he sat in his favorite chair and sipped brandy, the Duke of Austell looked at the room filled with accumulated treasures and felt like a dragon he'd once read about in an old nursery tale: like an ancient and antiquated hermit creature gloating over his solitary treasure, which was actually useless to him because he'd love for nothing else in his scaly and hardened old heart.

All the objects were things he'd badly wanted in his time. Now that he had them, they did give him pleasure. Yet now, too, it seemed not half enough pleasure to show for his almost thirty years on the planet. Reasonable, he thought on a sigh, staring into the fire— and inevitable, he realized at length. It was the season, of course. A new year was approaching, and no matter how caricaturists delighted in personifying them, they were never innocent infants. No, new years were accountants: dry and demanding, bustling in armed with ledgers and papers, sums and statements of losses, projected earnings, and reminders of accounts long past due. Just as Christmas, he thought, rising and going to his desk, arrived with nursery rhymes in its mouth and childhood in its eyes.

That must have been why he found himself searching for his oldest, chiefest treasure in his desk drawer. Finding it immediately, although he hadn't brought it to light in years, he carried it to the firelight and inspected it as he turned it round and round in his long, slim fingers. It wasn't worth much really—only more to him, he realized suddenly, than any other object in the room.

Randall. It was that—the recent thought of his best and boyhood companion—that had made him unearth it. For it was Randall's grandfather who'd brought it back from his travels on the Continent that long-ago season. One for each boy, for such faithful companions should have identical gifts for Christmas, Randall's grandfather had said. It had been a wondrous thing then, not the least wonder of it was that he still had it, almost four and twenty Christmases later.

It was an apple-sized thick glass globe mounted on a stout wood pedestal, and in it, a scene of Christmas. Within its glass walls it housed a minute winding road that ran through a tiny, perfect town, where a team of little horses pulled a miniature sleigh peopled by a man, a woman, and two even more infinitesimally detailed children. And when he turned the globe upside down, a swirling blizzard was created in the glass.

When he'd been young, he'd gazed into the globe for hours—then he could almost hear the sleighbells, the shushing of the runners rushing over the snow, and the laughter—he could have sworn he'd heard the laughter then. Because the little figures wore such jolly smiles it was hard to remember they were painted on to last through their eternal winter. The tiny gentleman was fair as ice, the little smiling lady had honey-brown tresses beneath her gay bonnet, the merry children were swathed in winter clothing. When he'd been a boy he'd imagined himself one of the children. Now, as the snow fell again, settling on the driver's hat and hair, he saw that it was the gentleman who was very like him.

Everything else was changed too, the years had seen to that. The globe had a chip in the heavy glass at the top to show where a careless maid had dropped it, and myriad scratches drew a fine veil over all the scene. Well, after all, he thought, it had been packed and

moved so many times since it and he were young—
traveling with him from home to school to university
and back. Somehow, though so much else had been
lost, it had made the journey to his adulthood. Now,
too, it could be seen that the snow floated in water,
because the liquid had gotten cloudly—perhaps the
chunks of snow had bled into it, perhaps it was all
decomposing with age. The wooden mounting was
nicked and scraped; it was a wonder he could still see
the scene in all its detail, and now he wondered how
much was real and how much was memory that he
saw.

He'd studied it often enough in his youth. It had
been his talisman when he'd been sent away to school:
better to stare into it than to give way to shameful tears
beneath the covers on those first sleepless nights. And
when his father had died, and again, so soon after,
when his mama had married that oaf . . . Nevertheless, he thought, shaking off those memories, even in
placid times it had always exerted a powerful hold on
him, even when he'd grown old enough to not be able
to forget the thick glass walls holding the perfect scene
within, and himself, without.

As the duke watched the grayish snow tumble over
the tiny, silent scene in the clouded globe, he decided
that it was more than the fact that it had reminded him
of home, his friend Randall, and other comforting
things. It was that then, and always after, it seemed to
signify everything he wanted and would never have
again: security, a family, more than that—a kind of
joyous love that was Christmas itself personified. Or
so, at least, he'd thought of it then, when he'd been,
after all, so very young.

Which was odd, because he'd never had what this
globe always seemed to tell him he'd lost. His father
and mother had never been so casual with each other
as this tiny couple were, he'd no such commonality
with either sister, nor ever seen exactly such a quaint

little Tudor-styled town or driven such a sleigh—or actually, wanted to except in his imagination in those long lost lonely days.

Before that void in which he'd grown to manhood, it had been Randall and Maryellen Tanner and himself, three neighbor children with a world to explore together whenever they could steal away from the enemy—the adults who tried to bind them to propriety, to lessons, and to manners. Then, Christmas had been a pleasure almost beyond that which a child could hold, with all of them sharing all their bounty, as they did in summer, autumn, and spring. Perhaps if Maryellen had survived until adulthood, he thought . . . before he buried the thought firmly and with almost as much sorrow as he'd felt when she'd been interred, those many years ago, so long before he'd neared his majority.

He'd survived it all, all these years, just as the globe had done, only perhaps not even so well, he thought wryly: separation, schooling, the losses—of his father and so, in a sense, of his mother, and perhaps most keenly, since it was the most recent, that of his friend, Randall. But really, it was almost beyond comprehension, how such a quicksilver boy could grow so quickly into a clever young man, marry a bright-eyed girl, produce a son, and then perish so suddenly, falling in battle as swiftly as he'd raced through his bright young life. And even so, for all it still stung, Randall had had the greater losses in his brief life, even before he'd lost his own. For his devoted grandfather had gone before him, his parents long before that, his wife had gone to childbirth . . .

The duke shook his head, carried the globe back to the desk, and put it back deep in the drawer. Christmas was no time for ghosts.

Now only the boy was left. And to him. The legalities had finally ground to a halt. The distant maternal aunt had capitulated, the cousin in the colonies had signed the papers. As Randall's will stipulated: young Randall junior had been left to the Duke of Austell. He'd recently been appointed the child's guardian. And so the child, at almost eight years old, almost the same age his father had been when he'd met Cyril Hampton, later to become Duke of Austell, would finally meet him.

The boy lived somewhere in Kent, in his late maternal grandparents' house, with a full staff of servants and a governess. He'd go to boarding school as soon as his fragile health permitted, but that wouldn't be until his guardian was entirely convinced that he was sound, because the governess had written of a fragile constitution. There was no chance the duke would jeopardize this last mortal scrap of evidence that his friend had existed. The boy was to be seen by a panel of physicians when he arrived in London. That would be this very week. It would be, in fact, tomorrow. Then, if the child's health permitted, he'd escort the boy on a round of pleasure in London before he sent him home again, to be sure of his hardihood, until the autumn term began.

And then, of course, the duke thought on a grimace as he settled back in his chair, he'd be free to pursue his own round of pleasure. He'd been invited to fêtes in town and at the country homes of all his peers, all his good friends: Jason Thomas, Duke of Torquay, the Baron Daventry, the Marquess Severne, and a great many others. He'd been asked to grace noble piles as well as simple country estates this season, for if ever a man could be said to have friends, he did. But those fellows were all married, and some had children. Although he enjoyed their company and that of their wives, and was sure he'd dote on their children, he was, after all, not really the elderly gent he felt he was tonight, and would prefer a livelier holiday.

No, he'd likely pass Christmas at the Incomparable's house party in the countryside, after all. Well, he told himself savagely, as though he'd heard himself mocking, he'd been invited, many of his unwed friends and acquaintances would be there, she was very young, there was no crime in exuberance and no insult in the fact that she so obviously wanted him for her husband—perhaps it was the fault of her parents' prodding—he was getting no younger . . . he could do worse.

He drained the brandy in his glass at a gulp, frowned, and looked around for more.

What should he wait for? The girl in the glass globe?

The duke took a deep breath, decided to forego the brandy, and rose in order to go to bed. He had to be up beforetimes tomorrow. That was, if he ever got to sleep tonight. He calmed himself, telling himself he would wait and see, there was time. For now, Randall's son was expected. And Christmas was coming.

And so, for all his disappointments, his cynicism, his true knowledge and wisdom, with all that he knew and all that he didn't wish to know, still, for the first time in years, like the boy he'd been thinking of, the duke discovered he could scarcely wait for tomorrow—when a boy who was all that was left of the boy who'd been his best friend would come to visit with him for the holiday.

The carriage slowed at the top of the street as the driver looked for addresses. Miss Greer sat up straight and patted her hair. She was so excited her gloved fingers trembled as they touched her careful curls. They'd arrived at last. Within moments she'd meet Randall's guardian, the Duke of Austell. More importantly, he'd meet her. Because though she was but a governess, she was well-born, well-educated, and well-mannered. And she had dreams, as well.

For the duke, the lawyer had said, was as witty and urbane as he was wealthy and titled. And unwed. She savored the words she'd remembered so well, ". . . a fine-looking gentleman, tall and straight, gray-haired as yourself, Miss Greer. You'll like him very well, I'm sure." She believed she would. She'd never have permitted this journey if she didn't.

With Randall's guardian so distant after the tragedy of Lieutenant Thomas's death, she'd been in complete charge of the boy. It would have been simple enough to keep him at home with her for several more years; he was a thin child by nature, and the nature of doctors and guardians was to err on the side of caution where there was any question at all. And she'd kept those questions continuous because it had become a snug position, an extraordinary one, with no mistress or master to order her, with the running of the house entirely in her hands. She'd felt like her own mistress for the first time in years—more, as it was such a grand house, it was an even headier delight. And certainly, she thought righteously, it never hurt the child. But now she'd ventured to agree the boy was sound enough to take to London, at least. Because she ventured to think there might be something here for herself as well. Months of lording it over the staff hadn't given her ideas above her station, it had made her rethink it entirely. She smiled. Randall's voice recalled her to the moment.

"Miss Greer, we're here."

She tittered some reply, her expectations depriving her of speech, and was glad for the diversion of getting down from the coach and ascending the marble steps to the duke's townhouse so she could catch her breath again. The butler let them into the magnificent house, the footmen took their coats, the boy stood at her side, only a step ahead of her, as he waited, no less eagerly, for the first sight of his guardian, his father's friend, his unmet idol. When the duke appeared, Miss Greer wasn't the only one speechless.

The Duke of Austell gazed at the boy hungrily, disbelief and something very like despair shining in those odd silver eyes, until he relaxed and smiled. No, it wasn't as if Randall had returned, after all. What was gone was past, and it was better that way for all of them if they were to go on. But it was as if Randall had cleverly replicated himself, as one of his famous jests. The boy was not quite his image: he was not so dark-complected, his hair was brown, not black. But he was as small and thin, his face as unusual on a child, just as lean and long as his father's had been, as was that distinctive, unfortunate nose. And saving all, the intent eyes were as large, black, luminous, and vulnerable as he remembered, as they looked up at him with hope and glimmerings of doubt.

"Hello, Randall," the duke said easily, extending his hand as he would to an equal. "I'm very glad to meet you at last, although it feels like 'again,' for you're amazingly like your father was, you know. I can only hope you and I get along half as well, for then we'll get on very well."

It was a pretty speech, but it was a moment until Randall could answer, and Miss Greer couldn't speak at all, to save her soul. It was as if the air had been knocked out of her. She was as terrified as she was angry.

It wasn't the welcome she'd expected. The duke was as good-looking as he was gracious; a tall, upright, fine-figured gentleman, exactly as she'd been told. But although his hair was gray, just as the lawyer had promised, the smooth face beneath it was that of a man almost half her age! She felt like a woman who'd moved her king hoping to make a jump, only to find it a trap. Another king lurked at her back, her home was in dire jeopardy, the game almost up. The duke gave her a knowing, mocking look in that moment of silence and she drew in another shallow breath. He knew! But a heartbeat later, there was no hint of what she'd thought she'd seen, or rather, too many, in his uncanny silver eyes. Because at last, Randall spoke, and drew his complete attention.

"I'm happy to meet you, your grace," the boy said, but his voice was low and disappointed. He was as shocked by his guardian as his governess was, but for opposite reason. The silver hair spoke louder than the duke's words had done, and the fading dream of his father faded further.

"No, I think not. But I hope to prove you will be," the duke answered with such amusement that Randall's dark eyes flew up to meet his in sudden hope, and Miss Greer's lips tightened.

"I could wish my own lad had such a constitution!" the first physician declared.

" 'Lean and hungry look' be damned, your grace," the second physican exclaimed. "It's just these close-to-the-bone fellows that live forever. Sound as a pound—no, sounder," he snorted, since the Regent was no favorite of his, and he delighted in predicting the downfall of the nation when he wasn't listening to chests and tapping knees.

"Thin as a wraith, but a vat of cream wouldn't make him fatter or more robust. It's his constitution, and it's a good one. He'll flourish like a weed if you give him air and sunlight. It's coddling will harm him," the third physician expounded.

"Three in a row wins at naughts and crosses, so it will do for us," the duke said with satisfaction as the coach drew away from Harley Street and a morning of consultations there. "It's school in the autumn for you, my friend," and as Randall began a grin, he went on, making it grow wider, "but first, as it's a joyous season filled with delights, a tour of holiday London with me, do you think?"

"Appearances," Miss Greer said hollowly from her corner of the carriage, "are deceptive. Yes, *now* he looks stout enough, to be sure. Such was not the case a few months past. It was nursing and care that brought him to this.''

"Indeed, and I understand we're in your debt for it,'' the duke said smoothly, as Randall's brilliant smile began to fade.

"It was my pleasure as well as my duty,'' Miss Greer answered repressively before she added, "So, knowing the vagaries of fate and Randall's delicate health as I do, I urge you to pray think hard, your grace, before you risk him again by sending him off to school. Childhood is a treacherous time for such as he.''

"And thee, and me, Miss Greer,'' the duke said charmingly, "as life itself is. And I doubt the chicken pox will come his way again. So I do believe we'll risk it, don't you?'' he asked Randall.

"Oh yes, sir,'' Randall breathed, and then shot a troubled look to his governess.

"I would not advise it,'' Miss Greer said, playing her last card.

"I understand entirely,'' the duke said with great sympathy, "and would not dream of troubling you.''

Randall's long, thin face grew mournful as his new guardian went on to say amicably, "Rest assured, Miss Greer, that knowing your reservations and having a care for your peace of mind and sensibilities, I'd never ask you to be party to it. You'll have a generous settlement for the work you've done, and a brilliant recommendation for your future employers,'' he said firmly, as he called in all the cards and swept up the pot, "and all our thanks for all your tender care, eternally. Right, Randall?''

But Randall couldn't answer. He didn't have to, it was clear he was looking up at his new guardian with absolute, transcendent joy.

Astley's Amphitheatre enchanted Randall. He wasn't horse-mad, as so many boys his age were, but he was country-bred and couldn't fail to appreciate the feats of horsemanship he saw that afternoon. The only shadow over his pleasure was that he couldn't share it properly. It was more than his naturally generous spirit. For, "Betsy would love this," he whispered to the duke several times as the show went on. Since Betsy's name had been brought up often enough as their coach drove through the streets of London, every time, in fact, that Randall saw something amazing and new—which was every few moments—the duke knew very well by now that the young lady was his ward's boon companion and closest friend at home. Nor was he surprised to hear Randall confide, as the great white horse in the center ring rose up at the prodding of its gloriously beautiful rider to walk on two legs clear around the ring, "This will be something Molly will not believe!" Because the skeptical Molly was Betsy's older sister, and the two girls were the center of Master Randall's limited universe. In fact, the duke was surprised to hear himself included along with those two paragons in Master Randall's bedside prayers that night.

But as delightful and yet disturbing an episode as that was—and it was enough to keep the duke home alone, thinking, in his study, instead of out carousing as usual on a Friday night—it didn't please him half so much as walking to the Tower with his charge the next day did. Because when he passed along St. James Street with Randall in tow, he had the pleasure of answering the queries of that famous fop, Harry Fabian, who'd been sent out of his club to quiz him, as a great many familiar, interested faces appeared in the bow window to watch.

"The boy?" he answered after a moment's pause, as though surprised anyone should inquire after the child who walked at his side and was puzzled to find the boy attached to his own gloved hand when he looked down at it. "Oh. *This* boy! I'm taking him for an airing. Before I bring him home and prepare him for dinner,'' he confided.

And then there was the pleasure of seeing, through the corner of an eye, the expressions on all those faces at the bow window after Harry hurried back inside to report to them. And Randall's, of course, as he began to giggle.

"But he believed you!" Randall finally managed to say.

"Of course," the duke answered. "Well, he almost did,'' he added, looking down into those candid and revealing eyes.

"But why? Is he such a fool?'' Randall asked.

"Almost," the duke repeated. "But in this case," he said carefully, "rather say, it's because I'm known as something of an ogre—if of another kind.''

"But I saw you give coins to that beggar today, and when you met those two men just before, you asked why they hadn't asked for a donation for their charity at Christmas, and they laughed and said you'd given enough, no sense killing the golden goose, and you called *them* geese for it, and signed up for more. Ah,'' the boy paused, and then said knowingly, "I see. Just as Papa said in a letter once. He said your wit was as sharp as your tongue, but it had to be, because your heart was so tender.''

"Hush!" the duke said with a wonderful scowl. "Do you want to ruin my reputation?''

Randall giggled again, and then chattered happily as they walked to the menagerie. Where, of course, he was immediately moved to tell the duke that Betsy would be green as grass over having missed the sight of an elephant. Not to mention the fact that Molly would be taken down a peg or two to know that the lion didn't look as though he could pounce on the pigeon strutting before him, much less the small boy she'd warned about getting too close if he should be lucky enough to be taken to the Tower.

"Because they'll never see for themselves," Randall explained, when the duke couldn't help but remark that he seemed to be storing up memories for the girls as well as himself everywhere he went. "They've got four older brothers to see through school, and the vicar can hardly keep the roof over their heads as it is, Miss Greer says. Though Molly says never mind, things will come around in time for Betsy to be presented, when the time comes. As if Betsy cared," he added, chuckling knowingly, "even if Molly does. But that's only because Molly's so *correct* about those things. Some girls are," he explained helpfully.

But for all his familiarity with the fair sex, Randall made a poor job of it with the duke's niece. He was sitting by himself at the window in Elizabeth's room as she prattled over her dolls, looking every bit as lost and sad and painfully fragile as Miss Greer could have wished him to, when the duke came to collect him after his visit with his sister.

"She isn't a bit like Betsy. Or Molly," Randall allowed as they strolled home together. "She plays with dolls, and talks about nothing but them, and her dresses," he added, with disdain. "Betsy and Molly might care how they look," he explained, trying to tread the line between truth and manners, as a gentleman should, "because they always look very well. But they don't go on about it all the time. And if they play with dolls, they let them go to war sometimes," he added as the duke did his best to agree that the Misses Betsy and Molly Garland showed exquisite taste and manners.

The next day Lord Beverly joined them as they made themselves most in sight in the streets of London. The three of them traveled to one museum and another cathedral, and then after one quick look to each other revealed a wonderful mutual sympathy, they made quickly for the streets again. The weather held, so they strolled on through town to see what offered. They saw a raree show and a circus of fleas that strained the eyes as the performers did astonishingly intricate things, or so the owner of the circus said they did. It took both Randall and the duke to pull Lord Beverly away from it so they could proceed to ruin their appetites for dinner with pastries and lemonade bought in the streets where they walked. The next morning they paused at a Punch and Judy show on their way to the puppet theater, and spent the rest of a cold afternoon dodging intermittent flurries as they ran from toyshop to toyshop. They laughed, they talked, they passed the days in diversions and the evenings in recollection of laughter that spurred more.

Lord Beverly had genuine tears in his eyes as he bade them good night on the fourth night of Randall's visit.

"If I didn't have to go to m'sister's I'd never go," Bev said somewhat thickly as he presented Randall with the top he'd bought on the sly after the boy had admired it and thrust a note into the duke's hand. As Randall unwrapped and exclaimed over his gift, Bev murmured for the duke to secrete the note.

"Because it's the name and direction of that yellow-haired opera dancer I fancied," he whispered, "But you admired her at the theater last week, too. Remember? The one with the mole. Y'know," he motioned furtively, "yes, there. Well, Happy Christmas, old fellow," he said loudly as he noticed Randall glancing up at them. "There ain't a thing I wouldn't do for a friend. Ah, and thanks for the book you got me. I'm sure I'll read it some day."

There were tears of mirth in the duke's eyes as he managed to choke his profound thanks for his present, but those in Lord Beverly's were far different.

"I have to go now—Happy Christmas, fellows, and good night," was all Bev was able to say before he headed out into the night in disarray, trying to keep up his countenance, for a fellow of almost thirty years didn't weep, so much as he wanted to, as he was saying good-bye.

The duke felt genuine sympathy for his friend as his eyes rested on Randall, where the boy sat at his ease at the dinner table. His thin face was alert, for all the growing lateness of the hour, and there was still laughter glowing in his dark eyes, although his governess had already come to collect him for bed. Miss Greer was to leave in a month; no gentleman would fling her out of her employment beforetimes, and indeed, there was scarcely any reason to want to anymore. She'd been given a handsome severance, far more than she deserved, and she knew and accepted it. She'd be replaced by a tutor, the duke decided, and he himself would see to Randall's care otherwise. It would be a delight rather than a duty.

The duke sighed with relief as he gazed at his young ward. Christmas, that season that had loomed so large and ugly only days before, now lay before him like another delightful prospect.

"Poor Bev. Poor fellow. A sad Christmas, indeed. We've better plans. Far better. I'd thought," the duke said luxuriously, as he stretched his long legs beneath the table, "that we might pass Christmas Day and the entire weekend at my friend the Duke of Torquay's country house. It's not far, only an hour's ride or so. There's bound to be a great many children there, good sorts too, as he's having other guests. He's got a fabulous estate, and is the greatest of hosts. As the place is several hundred years old, it's rumored to have secret passages," he added, for a stricken look had come into Randall's eyes. "You'd like him, I do believe you would, your father did," he went on more gently as the boy lowered his head to hide his expression, though his dejection was clear to read in the line of his bowed shoulders.

"Come, cub," the duke said a moment later, "what is it?"

"It's only," Randall began, and flushed darkly before he said, in a rush, "that I'd thought I could go home."

"Oh," the duke said softly as Miss Greer drew in a hissed breath at the boy's presumption.

That, of course, settled it.

"Why, certainly, if you wish it," the duke said.

But Randall's eyes were as clear-seeing as they were vulnerable, or else it was that he was especially sensitive to pain, his own and others', just as his father had been.

"I'd love to spend the holidays with you, sir," Randall said, sincerity in his voice and face, "but Betsy and Molly, you see, we'd plans . . . and I don't want to disappoint them. . . ."

"Those girls have got above themselves," Miss Greer put in. "Of course, your guardian's wishes come first."

"A gentleman's word is his oath," the duke said coldly. "If you've made plans, lad, they must be honored. A gentleman's honor comes before all else," he added as Miss Greer subsided, as much from his words and the tone of them as from the cutting glance she got from those steel-gray eyes. She was suddenly very glad she'd soon be leaving the duke's employ.

"I think it best you get to bed, lad," the duke said more softly. "You'll have to make the long ride to Kent in the morning, since Christmas is almost upon us."

"Would you like to come home with me?" Randall asked suddenly.

"No thank you," the duke said, more sharply than he'd intended, the thought of the boy's pity staggeringly painful to him. "Never fear, I'll hold holiday for you as well as myself."

"But you'll come visit with me sometime?" Randall asked, his voice wavering a little.

"Of course I shall," his guardian answered, wishing the boy would get to bed.

"I thought you would," Randall answered with relief. "On one of your Progresses at least.

The duke raised a slender silver brow. "One of my . . . 'progresses'?" he asked.

"Yes. Molly was telling us how Queen Elizabeth used to make Progresses through the countryside, staying at one house and then the other as she traveled. She said the Queen fair beggared the Simpsons then, they had to entertain her so well. It was over three hundred years ago, and they still haven't recovered, which is why Melissa Simpson had to marry the squire. . . . Anyway," Randall said confidently, "I knew you'd find time when you made one of yours."

"Undoubtedly. Only, never fear, I don't expect such lavish treatment," the duke replied, smiling at the idea of his making a modern ducal "Progress," even as his thoughts turned to the tutor, obviously sorely needed, that he'd get for the boy.

He walked with Randall to his room, and intercepted a signal Miss Greer gave to the boy as they said good night.

"Oh," Randall said quietly, blushing. "I'd almost forgot."

He burrowed into a carpetbag by his bed and brought out a tissue-wrapped square, which he then presented to the duke with a bow.

"Happy Christmas, sir," he murmured.

The duke unwrapped the package as Miss Greer nodded approval. He unearthed a leather shape, something like a square. Opening it, he discovered the interior to be red felt, boldly and very badly stitched to the leather.

"Ah!" he said, "just what I wanted. Thank you, Randall."

"It's a pen wiper," Randall muttered, red-faced. "I made it."

"Remarkably fine," the duke said, perjuring himself with ease. "Thank you. I'll be sending your present ahead so you'll have it at Christmas," he invented rapidly, because he'd originally planned to buy the boy his gift after taking him to a few more shops so as to gauge what he wanted most. "Good night. I'll see you in the morning, before you leave."

He left Randall's room, the pen wiper in his hand, wondering if he ought to go to his mistress's, his flirt's, or a friend's house for the rest of the evening. Then he remembered his last encounter with his mistress, and why it was to have been his last one, and that his flirt had gone to the country for the holiday, just as all his best friends had done. Or were going to do.

But he could go gaming at any one of a number of amusing hells, or go to the theater, or the Opera, or to his club, or to any number of parties, or to a house of pleasure, or he could please himself by just staying at home. The world was his, he was entirely free, and as ever, there were no end of delicious choices available to him. He settled himself in his chair in his study as he debated the matter. Instead he found himself himself making an entirely different decision.

It would be the Incomparable's house party for Christmas, then. He'd be damned if he'd sit alone like this every night of Christmas week, picking and choosing between pleasures. Yes, he'd take the Incomparable's house, and then maybe her hand, and then perhaps in time he'd have a houseful of young fellows like Randall, but ones who'd wish to pass the holiday with him . . .

Bedamned to the holiday! Bedamned to Christmas, anyway, he thought, rising in agitation and going to stand in front of the fireplace. He put his arm on the mantel, and his face on his arm, and the heat from the fire matched that in his usually cool face. He'd been a fool, a great fool, and that was the worst sin his world acknowledged. And although no one but himself knew it, any more than they ever guessed at any of the emotions the fastidious, untouchable fellow most of them believed him to be experienced, he was as shamed as chagrined to realize what an idiot he'd been.

He'd pranced and capered like an organ-grinder's monkey, cavorting gracelessly to the music played: knuckles to the ground, a silly smile on his grinning face, dancing to the mad music of carols and hymns. And then he'd held out his hat and received rubbish for his efforts, or cruel rewards like heated pennies that burned his fingers when he touched them. All because he'd not missed a waltz to the music the world played at this holiday season.

A present for the butler, and one for the housekeeper, oh and never forget the second footman, he mocked himself, or the kitchen skivvy, every last undermaid, and every maid underneath you in other ways too, your grace, for your mistress is decked with holly as well, although, as usual, it's her palms that you'll see stretched out to you. And be sure to give to every charity at this holy time, too, as well as to every niece and nephew and ward, and all in the spirit of the sacred season. And smile as you do.

No, he wasn't really the monkey, he thought bitterly, he'd only looked like one. It was the organ-grinder he resembled, working at some great, cumbersome, creaking machine that squealed and croaked as he kept turning the crank alone—he, the Duke of Austell, and his great useless Christmas machine. He gave and gave, until he didn't know what else he could give; it seemed he'd given everything he owned, in time and money, heart and purse, and see what difference it made, and what he got from it.

But what had he expected, after all? Some Christmas miracle, as in children's stories? Some of the impossible peace and love they sang of endlessly at this passing season? A place in a perfect world under glass that never existed?

He'd had such hopes . . . but they were no one's fault but his own. It was the same every season, only this year he'd finally seen beneath the sham, because this year he'd had more, and different, higher hopes as well. He smiled sadly, admitting it at last. Those hopes had turned out to be like the wicked brother's jewels in an old fairy tale he and Randall had once heard: jewels that had turned to water in a day. Because he'd won a boon that had come to nothing, after all. As few men before him had done, he *had* recaptured the past. He'd looked for his friend, and found him again, just as he'd been. The jest was that he himself was no longer the same. All the joy he'd anticipated had been watered down to fatherly affection. And that, not even returned. Time had come, and gone. And be damned to it, he thought.

No more, never again, he decided with determination. He would become exactly what his face implied: cold, aloof, alone—he'd give nothing away . . . no, he thought wearily, no, not likely. Or necessary, or intelligent. There were too many people and causes he knew and admired, and it was never their fault that it wasn't enough for him. Humanity amused rather than infuriated him. He might look like a cold, old miser, he thought, but he'd too much self-knowledge and not enough spite to portray one. And he knew, all too well, that he'd a spendthrift heart, for all it had not bought him anything to comfort him tonight.

He'd been too preoccupied with his thoughts to hear the scratching at the door, but when it slowly swung open, he turned from the fire to see what disturbed his wretched reveries. The fire had dazzled his eyes, and so at first he saw the little figure in a nimbus of light, pure and blurred and blindingly bright as some heavenly visitation. Until the vision resolved itself into Randall, in a long white nightshirt, barefoot and hesitant, standing at the threshold, holding something in his hands before him.

"Please," Randall whispered, "may I come in? Before *she* discovers that I've come?"

The appeal to thwart authority tickled him as much as it might have done all those years ago, and the duke moved swiftly, before he thought. He went across the room, scooped up the boy in his arms, and closed the door, before he carried him to a chair near the fire.

"Your feet are ice," he grumbled. "Little gamecock," he added, as he swung into the chair and sat Randall on his lap and looked about for something to warm the boy's blue-tinged toes with, before he discovered he could hold both icy cold feet in one large warm hand.

"Slippers would have made more noise on the stair," Randall explained.

"Just so," the duke admitted.

"The pen wiper was *dreadful*," Randall said ruefully. "No, you see I *knew* it was. She made me make it. I can't sew," he said.

"I'd never have guessed," the duke said.

There was a silence . . . before they both snorted, and giggled, and then laughed together, before they stopped and looked up guiltily. The duke didn't have to answer to any woman on the earth, much less Miss Greer; he was of age, titled, and richer than he knew. But he seemed to have forgotten that as they sat close and spoke quietly as conspirators. It felt very right, and much better than he'd felt alone, a moment before.

"I'd have *hated* to get such a Christmas present," Randall finally went on, "and so I told her. But she insisted," he said glumly.

"Betsy said I ought to buy you another gift, a secret gift, in the village," Randall said softly, "but it's a very little village, you see, and I couldn't find anything a duke wouldn't have at least two of, and so Betsy agreed, too. Then Molly said I might give you something I already owned. Something I loved, because that would be the greatest gift anyone could get from another, after all. In that case, Betsy thought it should be Ruffles. But I didn't think you'd want a dog like him in London, would you?'' he asked a trifle anxiously. "He's very large, and not very well-trained, but he's very handsome, if you enjoy fur," he added fairly.

It was difficult to remain straight-faced at such close quarters, but the Duke of Austell was not known as a cool customer for no reason. Once he'd told a certain famously clever lady at even closer quarters that he did, indeed, admire her mind as much as her body. It was even more difficult to dissemble now, but he contrived.

"No," he said, "I don't think I would want Ruffles. I like dogs very well, but—London, after all." He felt the sigh of relief as it vibrated through the thin frame perched on his lap.

"Sometimes," the duke said thoughtfully, "what one most loves can be something someone else mightn't value as much. Next to most can do in such cases."

"*Just* what Molly said," Randall breathed with pleasure. "So, here, please, sir," he said, proffering the burden he carried. "This is really what I'd like you to have for this Christmas. I thought about it a great deal. My father's letters spoke of you a great deal, too. It isn't new, but it's very valuable—at least to me. Happy Christmas, sir," he said shyly as the duke took the parcel held between them both and unwrapped it. And then sat silent, staring at what he held.

"Ah, no, lad," he said, in a strangely muffled voice, "It's too valuable to give away, I think."

"No, please," Randall said seriously, as the duke's slender hand shook and some of the snow began to drift down in the scene in the globe. "It was my father's, and I know he'd want you to have it now too. It's great fun to look in, and dream on, he said, and so it is. It's very wonderful, isn't it?''

''Very,'' the duke agreed before he lifted Randall from his lap, only to replace him in the chair as he arose and went to his desk.

''But see,'' he said when he came back to the chair and held out the other globe, twin to the one he'd been given, ''your great-grandfather gave each of us one. Yours is in better condition,'' he said ruefully, looking from his battered, chipped, cloudy scene to the clear one in the pristine glass globe Randall held, ''but mine went with me on all of my travels. And yours has a dark-haired gentleman and a red-headed lady, very like your own parents were, my boy. Otherwise, they are the same. And as I loved to gaze into mine, so I think you ought to keep yours. So that you can always revisit that happy scene, in that altogether miraculously pretty place.''

''But sir,'' Randall said, smiling charmingly as he gazed up at the duke, whose eyes glittered silver as the falling snow in the globe in the rising and falling firelight, ''I don't need the globe to revisit that scene. I've a portrait of my mother and my father. And the village in the globe—why, aside from the smith's, whose shop burned down and was rebuilt before I was born, it's my own town, where I live. Exactly.''

The duke stood still as the night around him and stared down at the boy and the glass globe.

''Exactly?'' he asked.

The driver, a fashionable gent, sawed at his reins and pulled his horses to a skidding stop as the sleigh flew by in front of him, crossing before him before it left the main road for a lane to the side.

''Dashed—damned old fool!'' he sputtered as he rose from his seat and shook his fist at the leaden sky.

''Coming it too strong,'' his friend, another exquisitely fashionable gentleman, said. ''You was going too fast in all this snow, Jeremy, and you know it. Fellow's got a sleigh, with bells all over it. We heard them a mile back, he was going like the wind, and you should have given way long since. Quite a dasher he was with, too,'' he added, staring out longingly at the departing sleigh as it disappeared on the downside of the long hill.

"How could you tell, if he was going so fast?" the driver asked, grumbling as he sat down again.

"Never miss a stunner like that, 'less I was blind," his friend vowed as he adjusted his gloves.

"Old fool's got her," the driver mumbled as he sought to sort out the various reins clenched in his own left glove.

"May be her grandfather," his friend commented fairly.

"Maybe you're blind. He'd his arm around her. Money bags always gets fair lady, town and country," he said angrily, remembering a certain ladybird of his who'd once flown away with a certain highly placed lord.

"Mightn't be so old," his friend said fairly. "Look at Austell. Gray as a goose and he can go ten rounds with the Gentleman any day without puffing."

"Austell! Did you get a look at him?" the driver asked, wondering if that dashing lord had been the one to cut him off. If so, then it wouldn't be such an insult to his driving.

"Didn't have a glance for the gent, think I'm dicked in the nob? What, look at him when she was there?" his friend asked wonderingly. "Anyway, no one knows where Austell is. The Incomparable's mad as fire that he didn't turn up at her house. Word has it she's ready to accept anyone, for spite.''

There was a silence. The two young exquisites looked at each other.

"Right," the driver said. "Dickie won't mind if we

don't show up at his place, will he? The Incomparable lives in Buckinghamshire, don't she?''

"Still," his friend commented as the driver pulled a map from his greatcoat and perused it, "could have been Austell, couldn't it?''

"Here? In Nowhere? Be serious, will you, old chap?'' the driver sneered. "With a parcel of kiddies in the sleigh, too?''

"Kiddies?'' his friend asked blankly.

"Didn't you hear them laughing?''

Their laughter rang out over the sound of the runners shushing as the sleigh traveled over the hard-packed snow.

"I never knew what a treat this could be," the driver cried, "but I always suspected it. Good Lord!'' he said when he turned to see his companion's reaction, "I'm a beast! You must be freezing! Here, I'll slow down, the wind's beginning to cut sharply, no sense in my adding to matters. We're a ways from the village yet.''

"I'm not cold," the lady protested.

"No, you always wear a red nose to go with your scarf," the gentleman said, slowing the horses to a subdued trot as the children behind them wailed their disapproval.

"Those who complain can always walk," the gentleman offered casually, and the complaints quieted to mutters of disapproval, until the sounds of the bells on the harness drowned them out entirely.

"And your hair is coming down, too," the driver added as the lady giggled.

"Very complimentary, your grace," the lady said as she tried to tuck a strand of her honey-brown hair up under her bonnet.

"Come, let's have some fairness. You said my compliments were making you uneasy," the Duke of Austell complained. "But nothing can dim your loveliness,'' he said more gently, before, seeing her wind-blushed cheeks blush even more as she glanced away from his light, searching eyes, he relented, adding, ''and that's nothing but plain truth, Molly, my dear, so don't nag at me for it.''

The lady fell silent. She'd never met anyone like the duke in all of her twenty years, although she'd dreamed of him for almost every moment of them. As witty as he was kind, and as handsome as he was clever, she knew very well that he'd come for a visit like a Christmas angel, or any of the other miracles that supposedly could occur at this season. If country folk said that animals could talk on a Christmas eve, as on such a special evening as last night, why then, she thought, a gentleman like the duke could appear in their midst at this time of the long and rolling year as well. But the season would pass, he was all too real, and so he'd be gone soon. And so she'd enjoy every moment of this visit, and store it up to keep in her heart like a scene under glass, to warm her through each returning season. Because he'd leave soon, and she remembered it even as she reveled in his company. For there is no pleasure without the awareness of pain, she reminded herself sadly.

He glanced at her and smiled at how the wind and his words had caused her cheeks to blush; he'd never imagined such a fair complexion could achieve such a glow. It almost matched the light in her amber eyes—or so he thought when one of his nicely turned compliments wasn't causing her to shield them from his view with those incredibly long lashes of hers. But it was such fun to make the sensible Miss Molly lose all of her composure with just a word as to her loveliness.

''Molly won't shatter from the cold, your grace,'' a light voice called from the back seat. ''She's from the country, after all.''

''Brat,'' the duke said lightly, and Miss Betsy, after being soundly pinched by her best friend, Randall—or at least as soundly as he could muster while encumbered by mittens—changed her tune and cajoled, "Some more speed, please, please, sir?"

"A neat trot, then," he agreed, "as a neat compromise. Now, quiet, bratling, I've important things to say to your sister."

"Come closer," the duke said, suiting action to words as he put his hand about the lady's waist and pulled her closer to him. "It's getting colder and I don't want to shout what I have to say."

The lady caught her breath, and it had nothing to do with the cutting wind.

"Your grace . . ." she began.

"Cyril, Cyril, Cyril," the duke ordered with a show of great exasperation, "the name of my youth, and heart. Or Austell if you're going to cut up prim. Remember?"

"Yes, your gr— Cyril," she said, still holding herself stiffly upright, acutely aware of his arm about her waist. "I don't know how they go on in London, but we're coming into town now, and here, you see—holding me so. I cannot struggle, it would look dreadful," she said in a small voice, very unlike her usual clear tones, "but here, such a thing is . . . is very like a declaration," she concluded anxiously.

"So it is in London," he answered.

"Oh," she breathed.

"And so?" he asked, turning his head to look at her, and catching the way her eyes were fixed on him with a look half of trepidation, half yearning, "Will you? Shall you? May I? Can we? Please, please," he added gently, echoing her little sister's tone as she looked at the slight smile on those well-shaped lips before she tore her gaze away and saw the warmth and yearning in the soft dove gray of his eyes.

"We've only known each other a matter of days," she said, as though the words were forced from her, and they were, for she'd an active conscience.

"If you were a London chit and I'd known you for six months, I'd scarce know you better," he said, "for I'd never be alone with you except for the space of a dance, or a forbidden walk out on a balcony at a dance. We've walked and talked for hours here, in our little time . . . and I think perhaps for years, in another time. But no more of that. I'm no fortune teller, or magician." He laughed.

"As Randall's great-grandfather was," she said, remembering, and glad of the diversion to give her time to think about what his impossible request likely really meant. Because, she decided, he could never have meant what she supposed.

"Was he?" He smiled. "Much is explained. But not answered. Come now, Miss Molly, I want to marry you," he said seriously, and there was no more doubt in her mind of his intentions, although now she knew only too well what her answer must be.

"I've never been to London. I've no money at all—no dowry, scarcely enough for clothing. Please think on it, and think it over again. You can do so much better, I'd never wish to take advantage of your emotions at this emotional season," she said, although all she wanted to say was yes.

"If you'd been to London, someone else would've snapped you up long since," he said with deceptive calm, looking out at his horses. "I've enough money for both of us, I believe. And see how I've done so much better in all these years! I'm as single as you are and I've nine more years than you. I don't wish to spend the rest of them without you, thank you. I have not half the breeding and scruples that you do, my love," he added, turning to watch the expression on her lovely face, "so say yes, and instantly. I want very much to take advantage of this miraculous season."

The horses picked up speed as the driver's attention slipped from them to the look on his lady's face, and the nearness of her berry-red lips—which he, remembering her honor and vulnerability, in all honor, hadn't touched as yet, sorely tempted as he'd been from the second they'd met.

"Molly," he said, "please?"

She looked at him steadily as she answered, low.

"Sir!" Randall cried as he saw the Duke of Austell gather his friend Molly up in his arms and kiss her soundly. "Molly!" he breathed, shocked, as he saw his friend's arms go up around the duke's shoulders to hold him closely so that he could.

"Oh hush!" Betsy said, prodding him, for although the same age as her best friend, she'd already a store of woman's wisdom to her credit. She was delighted at what was transpiring in the driver's seat. "And look at the horses, she giggled, diverting him, for she wanted nothing to interfere with this moment for her sister's sake. "Just see! Hoorah! We're coming into town at wonderful speed!"

"Wretches," the duke commented when he recalled himself, releasing his lady so that he could remind the cattle who was in the driver's seat, before his lady moved as close to him as she could and he forgot everything but her again.

"Happy Christmas, love," he whispered, never taking his eyes from hers. "And thank you for the most wonderful gift of all."

"Ah no," she sighed, "thank *you.*"

"Children," the duke said over his shoulder, "it's all holiday with us. Give me congratulations, Randall, for your friend Miss Molly has given me her hand for Christmas."

"And I," Molly said in a voice shaking with emotion and dazed with delight, "have taken his."

"Oh, how shabby," Betsy said, with an admirably straight face, "when you really needed gloves."

The elegant gentleman in the coach tucked away his roadmap and picked up his whip again, satisfied. They could be at the Incomparable's house party in a day.

And if Austell still hadn't gotten there, there was a chance for lesser men, such as himself, for example, as he smugly told his companion on the driver's seat. But his friend was paying him no attention. He was staring out at the countryside around them. They were stopped on the crest of a hill. As the trees were bare, he could look down to see the village below, in a cup of the hills, as though in miniature. The sleigh that had passed them by moments before was entering the tiny town, and though distance reduced its size to insignificance, he could just make out the driver, his honey-haired lady at his side, and the two miniature children behind them, as the snow began to sift down over them.

In the winter's stillness, even from the distance between them, he could hear their laughter ringing out in the clean, cold air, even over the rhythmic cadence of the sleigh bells. He continued to watch them, enchanted, until they disappeared from his sight. He thought he could still hear their laughter after it had faded away, as he was to think for many long years after, every time he thought of Christmas Day.

The Kissing Bough

by

Patricia Rice

Diana Carrington balanced the fragrant bundle of evergreen roping in one hand and held on precariously to the ladder with the other. Holding her breath, she moved one kid slipper from the second rung to the third, then with more bravery, her other foot followed.

She had seen her father do this for years, and it had always seemed so simple. It really shouldn't be that difficult. She just needed a little practice. Only it seemed such a long way down.

By the time Elizabeth entered the main drawing room, Diana had triumphantly managed the hanging of the first loop of the garland with only one minor mishap that left several curls decidedly disheveled. The second bold swoop of greenery posed a more difficult problem. Halting in the doorway, Elizabeth held her breath as her older sister leaned daringly toward the chandelier and swung the end of the greenery in what would have been a graceful arch had their father done it.

The tangle that ensued brought an exasperated sigh from the slender, black-bedecked figure on the ladder, and Elizabeth chose that moment to announce her presence.

"Mama isn't going to approve."

Diana glanced down at Elizabeth's neat golden curls as her sister approached the ladder, and grimaced.

Both sisters wore the colors of deep mourning, but
Elizabeth's sunny coloring somehow seemed to
brighten the fine wool of her modest, high-waisted
gown. Diana felt more like a crow perched on a branch
even though her black velvet was more modishly cut
and trimmed with violet satin ribbons. Black simply
did not enhance her own drab brown coloring.

Not that it made much difference, Diana rationalized. With another abrupt tug at the recalcitrant greenery, she almost succeeded in making the second loop
match the first. "Papa would have wanted it," she said
firmly, as much to herself as to Elizabeth.

"Papa would have wanted what?" The harried voice
drifted in from the dining hall before the speaker appeared in the doorway. Upon entering the drafty drawing room, Mrs. Carrington gave a gasp of horror as
her eldest daughter swung precariously near the crystal
chandelier to fasten the greenery. "Diana, upon my
word, there are times when you are worse than the
twins. Get down from there at once, young lady. I
vow, I should think the twins nuisance enough without
you adding to their deviltry. Elizabeth, go get Goudge
and have him bring down this nonsense at once!"

"No, Mama." Diana pulled her long, firmly molded
lips into the thin line that so resembled her father's
that her mother shivered at the sight. "Papa would
have wanted to have the kissing bough just like every
other Christmas. It's a tradition, and he wouldn't want
us to break tradition."

Georgina Carrington heard the quiver in her daughter's voice and held back the urge to reach for her
handkerchief to hide the tears that had welled behind
her eyelids much too often these last few months since
her husband's death. She had to be strong for the sake
of the children, but the sight of the kissing bough going up brought back more memories than she was prepared to cope with right now.

"Diana, we're in mourning. Such decorations are inappropriate," she remonstrated without conviction.

Diana deliberately finished securing the garland without looking down at her mother's matronly figure. She wanted to cry herself, not just for the loss of her father but for all the heart-breaking losses of her twenty-two years. She had drowned her pillow with tears too many nights to count, and they had never made the pain go away. What she needed now was happiness and light, and she was determined to have it even if she must go against her mother's wishes.

"And what if Charles is allowed to come home? Do you want his first Christmas home in four years to be without candles and greenery? After all this time at war, should he be greeted with gloom?"

At this mention of her eldest child, Mrs. Carrington surrendered the argument. She had relied too much on Diana these last months, and the girl had learned too much independence. It wasn't seemly, but it was comforting, and Diana was almost beyond the age where it would matter. Besides, Diana was right in this. She could not wish Charles such a gloomy homecoming.

"Don't get your hopes up, either of you," she warned. "And don't mention it to the boys. We don't know for certain that he can make it. It's been two months since he sent the letter, and he hasn't come yet. Maybe there is some difficulty in selling out his commission, and he hasn't wanted to worry us."

Or maybe he'd had the ill fortune to be wounded or killed after writing he was coming home, thought all three of the room's occupants, but none would say the words. They had suffered one loss already these last months. To bear another would be too cruel a fate. Charles's name hadn't appeared in the casualty lists. There was still hope.

"He'll be here for Christmas if he can. Charles always loved Christmas. And who would carry in the yule log if he didn't come?" Elizabeth inserted this

defiant question into the silence that had fallen after
her mother's warning. She had been denied much because of her father's untimely death, she would not be
denied Christmas too.

The ten-year-old twins burst into the room trailing
the cold, fresh scent of the outdoors and carrying a
basket of apples from the cold cellar. Oblivious to the
solemn atmosphere in the dim drawing room, they
bounced excitedly beneath the ladder, both talking at
once.

"It's snowing, Di! Can we go sleigh riding?"

"Here's the apples, Di. Can I hang one, can I, Di,
please?"

Mrs. Carrington groaned and closed her eyes as Diana retreated down the shaky ladder with what she
assumed was every intention of allowing the twins both
their requests despite the lateness of the hour. The care
of the two rambunctious boys had been hectic enough
when there had been a man in the house to control
their antics. They would shortly reach the uncontrollable stage.

"We can't hang the apples until we tie on ribbons.
Freddie, go ask Goudge what Father used to hang
them. Frank, you need to fetch a box of candles. We
can't go sleigh riding until there's enough snow for
runners."

With a whoop, both boys ran off, content to be
keeping busy. Mrs. Carrington followed soon after,
deciding mince meat pies and a pudding might be suitable after all. Charles might come home, and it would
be dreadful to disappoint him.

Elizabeth helped her sister sort through the box of
Christmas ribbon. With a pensive glance at the sad
droop of Diana's usually laughing mouth, she asked,
"Have the Drummonds heard from Jonathan? Do you
think he and Charles are together?"

Diana stiffened, and without looking at her sister
started back to the ladder with a green and red plaid

streamer. "The Drummonds will be here tomorrow. You can ask, but I should think they would have written if they had had word."

"Fustian!" Sixteen-year-old Elizabeth expertly tied a bow in a red satin sash. "Mr. and Mrs. Drummond are so stiff-laced they read Marie's letters before she can post them. They won't allow Jonathan's name to be mentioned, but I know he writes. I just thought maybe Mrs. Drummond had said something to Mama."

Perched on the top of the ladder, Diana reached down for the bow Elizabeth handed to her. If she concentrated on her task, she could almost forget Jonathan existed. It had been four years, after all. She should be very good at pretending now. "Jonathan always was one to write. Remember when they went off to Oxford together, the only way we ever heard about Charles was when Marie brought Jonathan's letters to read to us? Maybe they have had a letter and Mr. Drummond won't let them speak of it. Mama will persuade it out of him tomorrow, if so."

The thought of Jonathan's writing his family cheered Elizabeth but only increased Diana's dismals. She had every reason to remember Jonathan's letters. Since they hadn't been formally engaged when he went away to Oxford, he could not in all propriety write to her, but somehow he had managed to smuggle a missive or two to her whenever he could. Of course, it was only the continuation of a childish game, she told herself, but at the time those letters from her brother's handsome friend had been like diamonds and gold to her. Even during the holidays Jonathan had still hidden letters in their secret cache, and she had left him flowers and favorite poems and whatever trinkets had pleased her that day. He had delighted in teasing her for her choices, but he had worn the flowers in his lapel and memorized the poems to surprise her.

She had loved him wildly then. Too wildly, she knew

now. Looking into those passionate gray eyes and
hearing his deep voice speak the words she had said
only to herself, she had fallen head over heels for Jonathan's charm despite the fact that he had never declared himself.

For the second time that evening tears threatened to
inundate Diana's eyes, and she jerked hastily on the
streamer she was wrapping around the pine boughs. A
loop started to come loose, and she grabbed for it just
as the drawing room door bounced open again, admitting the twins.

"A coach and four! A smack-dab-up-to-the-rigs
coach and four! Come see it, Diana! It's coming down
the lane now!" Both small voices exclaimed this litany
of excitement more or less in unison.

Diana steadied herself and threw an anxious look at
the tall, mullioned windows covered now in heavy maroon drapery. Charles! It had to be Charles. He was
the only one they knew mad enough to hire a coach
and four to carry him to the back of nowhere. Her
heart set up an erratic beat, but she dared not let
her hopes rise too high. If she let the boys know her
thoughts, they would be dreadfully disappointed if
their adored older brother were not the coach's occupant.

"Well, it must be some poor person out in the snow
looking for shelter for the night. Or perhaps the Drummonds are here early. Go tell Goudge we're to have
visitors while I try to finish this up. Hand me the apples, Freddie."

Diana's disinterest didn't douse the twins' excitement in the least, and even Elizabeth deserted her to
run to the windows and look out. Drawing back the
draperies, they could see the winding country lane filling with snow, the flakes white and dainty against the
velvet backdrop of the night. Within minutes the carriage lamps grew brighter and the crack of a whip and

a faint "Halloo!" echoed down the road. The twins dashed for the foyer, screaming with delight.

Determinedly, Diana continued hanging the ribbons amid the greenery. Her hopes had been smashed too thoroughly at Christmas before to allow them to rise to any heights now. She dearly wished to see her brother again, safe and sound and at home at last, but she could not bear the thought of some stranger descending from that carriage.

"Two gentlemen, Diana! I can see them climbing out!" Elizabeth reported from the window where she continued to peek discreetly from behind the draperies. "They've tall beaver hats and greatcoats and mufflers and Hessians, Di! Oh, they look very grand, just like they must in London. Oh, Diana, do you think I will ever be allowed to go to London with Marie?"

Since this complaint had been heard ever since Elizabeth had turned sixteen, Diana ignored it in favor of the description of the gentlemen. They knew few gentlemen in London, so these must be strangers come to ask the way. They would probably drive on shortly. Or perhaps Mama would ask them in for tea before turning them out again to the cold. She really ought to climb down and make herself respectable, but her heart wasn't in it. She so much wanted it to be two other gentlemen out there that she wouldn't be able to hide her disappointment.

"Oh my, Diana! I think they're a trifle foxed! One just slipped on the road, and the other is laughing and holding him up. Oh, Diana, it has to be Charles. I know it does!"

Elizabeth flew from the room, leaving Diana perched on the ladder biting back tears and praying as rapidly as she knew how.

The draft from the opening of the double front doors sent the ribbons spinning and candle flames flickering. The excited chatter of half a dozen voices glittered in the air outside the drawing room door, but still Diana kept her perch. Two gentlemen, Elizabeth had said. It couldn't be. She wouldn't believe it. Superstitiously, she remained where she was, doggedly reaching for the next apple and the next bough. If she got down, it wouldn't be them. She couldn't get down. It had to be them.

"Diana! I've brought you a Christmas present! Where in blazes are you?"

The laughing, familiar voice filled her heart with joy, and Diana turned eagerly, nearly toppling the ladder in her haste to greet her older brother.

The shadowy figure entering the room behind Charles's towering frame gave an involuntary curse as the ladder swayed.

In seconds, Diana's small waist was clasped in an elegantly clad arm with the strength of a vise before she was lifted bodily from her precarious throne. She scarcely had time to register astonishment before she was on her feet again, staring into once familiar eyes that had turned cold and forbidding since she had seen them last. She raised a hand to cover the cry of surprise coming to her lips unbidden when he suddenly dropped his arm from her waist and turned away in disgust.

The hand she raised should have worn a ring he knew by heart, but it hadn't. The knowledge hurt more than surprised, but her reaction to his appearance stabbed more bitterly than any wound he had suffered at the hands of Napoleon's army. Stiffly, Jonathan lowered his bandaged hand and, turning with the help of his walking stick, glared at the traitorous friend who had forced him here.

"I told you I shouldn't have come, Carrington. The coach can take me on to the manor. I'll be on my way, then."

"You great clodding sapskull, you terrify my sister and then expect to walk out without apology or explanation? Besides, there's no one at the manor; if you remember the letter I showed you. This is our year to do the celebrations. Take off the dratted coat and I'll find us some brandy.'' Charles's golden hair gleamed in the firelight as he threw off his hat, thoroughly enjoying the attention he was receiving as the elderly butler happily gathered up his outer garments, his mother tearfully hugged him, and his younger brothers and sister crowded around. The only thing he enjoyed more was the sight of Diana's face for that one brief second when she recognized his guest. He had been right to bring Jonathan home. Both the clothheads had gone cold and polite as they ignored each other now, but he vowed to put an end to all their dismals. He had seen enough war. Now he wanted only joy and happiness around him.

As the brandy materialized, Jonathan Drummond gripped the goblet and made a proud and formal bow to the lovely young woman who had grown from the pretty little girl he had once courted. Her soft brown curls hung in charming ringlets about a throat as graceful as any swan's. The laughter he had remembered in her wide brown eyes and on the lovely curved lips had faded, but he understood and wished only that the floor would open up and swallow him. He should never have come, not like this, perhaps not at all.

''I apologize if I frightened you, but you had no business being up there. You could have tangled your feet in the hem of that flimsy little gown and broken your neck.'' That had been the image Jonathan had seen when he had walked into the room to see the ladder tottering so dangerously. Visions of returning home just to see her die at his feet had flown through his besotted brain. After four years of war, he had seen death come too easily too many times, and he had acted instinctively.

Diana, on the other hand, reacted to his high-handed manner with an anger she did not fully understand. The chestnut hair she remembered falling down over a high, intelligent brow now tumbled over an ugly and still raw gash that should be covered with a bandage had Jonathan not been too stubborn to wear one. The arm that had so easily lifted her from the ladder sported a hand useless in its cover of white gauze, and his other hand gripped a walking stick with grim determination to keep from placing weight on a leg he obviously favored. Her irrational anger heightened even more with the discovery of each of these flaws.

"It looks to me as if I have learned to take better care of myself than you have, Mr. Drummond. And it's *my* neck, if I choose to break it, as you have so recklessly chosen to risk yours."

"Diana! Upon my word, is that any way to greet a guest? Jonathan, give me that coat and go sit yourself by the fire. Your mother will never forgive me if I let you catch a chill. Here, Goudge," Mrs. Carrington took the greatcoat so grudgingly surrendered and handed it to the servant. "Frankie, Freddie, give Charles a hug and get yourselves upstairs to Nanny. He'll still be here in the morning when you come down."

When the twins protested, Charles grabbed their elbows and steered them toward the hall and stairs, whispering something excruciatingly funny in their ears. Finding herself suddenly relieved of her nightly chore, Mrs. Carrington fluttered uncertainly about the room for a few minutes, then hurried after her sons. That left Elizabeth and Diana to entertain the wounded soldier.

Not quite understanding the tension that had erupted between her sister and the man she knew only as her best friend's prodigal brother, Elizabeth retreated to the formal etiquette of the tea table, taking her place near the tray that the maid had brought upon the appearance of guests. Diana deliberately returned to the ladder.

"Did you stop to see your family in London before

bringing Charles home?'' Elizabeth inquired politely, if somewhat nervously. Just out of the schoolroom, she was unaccustomed to dealing with elegant male strangers, particularly ones who favored brandy to tea and glared at her sister with such . . . venom? She didn't think that was the word, and she cast a quick look at Diana, now fastening the last batch of apples on the boughs.

Her sister looked prticularly pretty tonight with her cheeks all flushed from working so hard on the kissing bough and her curls all disheveled just like in the ladies' books. The black velvet gown with the lovely violet ribbons contrasted nicely with the whiteness of her throat and shoulders, and Elizabeth wished she had thought of fastening a ribbon about her neck since jewelry was forbidden. It looked quite fashionably simple, and she had the first glimmer of understanding of why Mr. Drummond kept staring at Diana.

As if just realizing the child in front of him had said something, Jonathan reluctantly tore his gaze away from the proud woman on the ladder and back to the speaker. ''My parents apparently left before us. Since they don't seem to be here yet, I suppose they chose to rest overnight while we rode on. That's their usual style. They should be here by morning, I venture to say.''

Above them, Diana gritted her teeth at this stilted speech. The Jonathan she had known had been full of life and laughter and eagerness. He had defied his father by saving his quarterly allowance until he had enough to buy his commission into the cavalry. He had gone off to war determined to defeat Napoleon and return a hero. Now here he was, wounded and ill and, judging by Charles's condition, probably half-liquored, sounding as pompous and bored as his curmudgeon father. She had half a mind to throw an apple at him as she might have done in happier times.

As if in answer to her thoughts, Charles returned

and quickly took stock of the situation. Diana sat
perched in high dudgeon upon her pedestal and Jonathan sat sulking behind the barricade of a great wing
chair. Charles briefly contemplated knocking their hard
heads together, but it was Christmas and there had to
be better ways to raise their spirits.

"Get down from there, puss. That's my job." Without preliminaries, Charles grabbed his sister's waist
and hauled her from the ladder. Then, throwing off his
long-tailed frock coat, he promptly applied his trousered legs to the flimsy ladder and nearly reached the
ceiling when he stood on the top rung. "Now give me
the rest of those apples. You would never have got this
top branch right."

"Charles!" Elizabeth gave a gasp of fright as her
brother swayed alarmingly at the top of the ladder.
"Do come down, Charles. You do not look at all safe
up there."

Jonathan had turned with wry interest to observe his
friend's assumption of the role of man of the house,
and now he, too, raised a skeptical eyebrow. "I daresay you enjoyed the innkeeper's punch a trifle too
much, Carrington. You're going to make a proper
botch of a perfectly good garland if you don't climb
down."

"I can hold my liquor as well as you, Drummond,
and you had twice as much of the grog. You just rest
there like a proper invalid and let me take care of
things. Diana, where's the mistletoe?"

"Mistletoe?" Diana stared dubiously upward at her
slightly wobbly brother. He looked remarkably handsome in his crisp white cravat and linen, and she was
thrilled to have him home again, but he was just a wee
bit too tipsy for his own well-being. "You do remember this is a house of mourning, Charles? I don't think
Mama would approve of something quite as frivolous
as mistletoe."

Her words had an instant effect. Charles stared down

at his sisters in their stiff mourning and went silent. He climbed down a few steps, then suddenly slumping over the ladder, he held his head in his hands and asked with anguish, "Do you think I can forget, Diana? Do you think for one instant of these last months I have thought of anything else but you and Mama and the children and how selfish I have been? I should have been here. I shouldn't have to be notified by letter a month after the fact. Devil take it, I left him to die alone with only women and children at his side." His voice rose as he spoke, and he pounded the trembling ladder with his fist for emphasis.

Jonathan rose quietly and reached to grasp his friend's arm to help him down. "He was proud of you, Carrington. You showed me his letters, remember? He was as proud of your accomplishments as if they had been his own. Be glad of a father like that. You could have had mine."

Diana looked up swiftly at the bitterness she had never heard before in Jonathan's voice. Even with the vicious scar across his brow he was a handsome man. His deep-set eyes could hold wells of compassion, and the heavy eyebrows could frown thunderclouds of anger when he observed injustice. The aquiline nose and distinguished cheekbones revealed his pride, however, and it was there in full force now. The years of war had worn away any forgiving softness, and the taut lines of his features now revealed the man who had once been a pampered boy. She gulped back a heartbroken sob at what had once been and was now lost.

Mrs. Carrington entered as Charles climbed down, dispelling the silence that had suddenly fallen between the young people. "I have the servants airing your rooms and warming baths for the both of you. You must be overweary. Elizabeth, it's time for you to retire. I will need your help with the twins in the morning. Diana, if you would come to the kitchen, I need your help with tomorrow's menu."

The sisters stared at their mother's renewed energy with astonishment, but hastened to comply. While Elizabeth hurriedly departed after her mother and Charles carried out the box of ornaments, Diana began gathering the scattered tea things. Jonathan lingered uncertainly in the doorway, watching her slender figure as she studiously pretended he had left with the others.

"I liked your father. I have not offered my sympathy at your loss."

Diana started at the sound of his deep, masculine voice. It had always thrilled her when he came home for the holidays and hid behind a door or wall or tree and caught her by surprise with the sound of his voice. The same thrill went through her now when she had no right to feel it.

She swung around to face him. He was not just an image in her mind any longer but a man, a soldier returned from war, a person with dreams and a life of his own. Once, she had thought that life would include her. His silence since he had departed for the war had taught her differently.

"He was ill only a brief time. Perhaps it was better that way. It just seems very . . . strange, without him." To her disgust, Diana felt her eyes filling with tears again. She so desperately wanted to be held and cosseted and told everything would be all right, but as the eldest, she had been the one to comfort the others. There had been no time for self-indulgence.

Jonathan heard the way her voice broke over the words, felt her anguish, and wished he had the power to give her the comfort that she needed. She had made her disgust of him clear from the moment he had walked into the house, however, and he had too much pride to take a second rejection. He still did not understand the first.

"Things have changed all over, Janey." He used the secret name they had chosen when they were children.

"It's a part of life and growing up. Sometimes it's for the good, sometimes it's not." He strived to keep his voice casual as he shrugged and looked around him. "This room, even. I like the painting of the hunt. That's new. But I miss the old secretary. Whatever happened to it?"

At this casual mention of the old hiding place for their childish notes and secret love letters, Diana had to turn away, unable to meet his eyes without dissolving into tears at the memories he revived. "The twins . . . The twins decided to experiment with fire with the pair of candles we kept there. The blotter they were testing—" she hiccuped on what could have been a sob or laughter—"went up in a sheet of flame, scorching the desk, not to mention their little fingers. Mama always meant to have it refinished, but she never did. I suppose it's still up in the attic somewhere."

A sudden, extremely painful thump paralyzed Jonathan's heart as he heard her words and watched the proud line of Diana's slender back as she turned away from him. It could not be. It was not possible, was it? All these years, all these confounded lonely years thinking she had rejected him . . . Could she really not have known he would never have left her without a word?

Tentatively, he probed for more information. "That must have been some time ago. They look too old for such mischief now."

Diana gave a shaky laugh and finished gathering the last of the cups. "They are only just recovering from broken bones after falling from the apple tree, but at least they have learned their lesson about fire. It's been nearly four years since they've touched a candle, since right after that Christmas when you left, as a matter of fact." She spoke more firmly now, recovering from her shock and reminding herself of her place in things.

Right after Christmas. There had been time, then. She should have found it. Jonathan sighed and made a polite bow. "Then we can all go to our beds without fear of waking up in flames. I'll leave you to your tasks, Diana. Good night."

It was when the door closed behind this cold stranger that the tears came, great wrenching sobs that had no place in her life any longer. Diana curled up on the window seat, buried her face in a pillow, and cried like the child she had once been.

Her mother had to plan the Christmas menu without her help, after all.

By the next morning Diana had completely recovered from her momentary lapse of self-pity, and no trace of last night's tears remained. Since it was the day before Christmas, she felt the occasion warranted her first break from full mourning, and she donned a lavender percale gown that pleated gracefully in back. Although it was merely a simple morning gown, the mameluke sleeves adorned with velvet ribbons and the shoulder ruffles made her feel feminine and sophisticated. She had crimped the hair about her face so it curled attractively for a change. Without thinking it, she allowed herself to feel satisified. Let Jonathan see what he had given up when he had chosen life as a soldier over her.

She was late coming down, but Charles was later. There was no sign of her brother as Diana joined her mother and sister in the dining room. Jonathan, however, had apparently overcome last night's excesses and sat sipping coffee at one end of the table. Diana noticed his untouched plate in passing, but thought nothing of it until she sat down with her own breakfast of muffins, ham, and soft-boiled egg. The minute she held her egg cup with one hand and lifted her knife to crack her egg shell with the other, she understood Jonathan's dilemma.

"Good morning, Diana," said her mother. "Will you be certain Cook doesn't double up the spices in the pudding this morning? I want to freshen the linens in the guest rooms before everyone arrives.'' Without stopping for her daughter's agreement, Mrs. Carrington smiled at their single guest. ''I hope you slept well last night, Jonathan. Your appetite didn't used to be so poor.''

''I've learned to live without, Mrs. Carrington. It will take some time to get back in the habit again.'' Jonathan's eyes were shadowed as Diana sat across from him, but he offered a smile and lifted his bandaged hand in greeting.

Diana calmly buttered her muffin, then set half on his plate. ''Then you should begin breaking bad habits now. That dreadful brew will ruin your digestion, elsewise.''

Jonathan and her family looked at her as if she had taken leave of her senses to speak so boldly, but a small smile formed at the corner of Jonathan's mouth as he accepted her muffin.

''You always did have a way with words, Diana,'' he murmured before biting hungrily into the muffin he could not have managed gracefully to butter with one hand.

''I should rather like to be thought of as a person who acts instead of talks,'' she responded tartly, breaking open her egg and neatly scooping the contents onto his plate, mashing it so he could use a fork to eat it instead of chasing the egg cup about the table. ''Words aren't very reliable.''

Developing some understanding of what was happening at the other end of the table, Mrs. Carrington wisely kept her own countenance. Distracting Elizabeth with plans for the day, she gave the other two time to settle their differences.

''It is common knowledge that actions speak louder than words,'' Jonathan replied stiffly. The egg was delicious, but he couldn't show his gratitude while she poked at still festering wounds. Diana was never one

to carry out conversations on a single level. She was
baiting him, and he didn't like it. He didn't think he
would like being treated as an invalid, either, but Diana was somehow making it very easy to accept his
limitations.

Perhaps that was because she thought of him more
as a brother than a lover, or even a rejected lover. In
all these years of puzzling over her actions, he had
never once considered that possibility, and it was a
very likely one. They had grown up together. Just because he had felt their relationship had been a special
one did not mean she thought of him as more than her
brother's friend. The likelihood depressed him even
further, and he couldn't bring himself to say thank you
when she matter-of-factly placed the cut-up sections
of ham on his plate.

Diana was relieved of the task of answering his cold
words by the startling bellow of a deep male voice
from above stairs.

"By the devil, I'll have you martyred and hung upon
the cross if you're not out of here now!"

"Charles!" Scandalized by this blasphemy, Mrs.
Carrington hastily pushed away from the table and
hurried to chastise her eldest and to assess the twins'
damage. There wasn't a doubt in anyone's minds as to
whom Charles was speaking. The only question was
what catastrophe they had wrought.

Charles didn't linger with quiet patience for help to
arrive. He appeared in the upper hall still in shirt
sleeves and stockings, one guilty twin caught by the
collar in each hand. Seeing his audience streaming
from the dining room below, he shook the rascals and
held them up for all to see.

"They're too blood—" he cut his curse off short and
rephrased the oath—"too young for catechism class!
They've made the Last Supper out of my last bottle of
wine. Where the h—" Again, he stopped to rephrase.
"Where is their d—" Throwing up his hands in dis-

gust, he released his brothers. "The army is easier. Where's their nanny? I can't get dressed with this mess stinking up the room."

Jonathan tried to smother a grin, but the sound of Diana's muffled giggles made it difficult to keep a straight face. The twins looked decidedly green around the edges as they ran to their mother for comfort, and part of the reason for Charles's dismay became a little more obvious.

"Don't worry, Charles," Diana called out sweetly. "The maids haven't forgotten how to take care of drunken little boys. I'll send someone right up."

Charles glared down at her. "See if I do you any more favors, Miss Jane."

"And when have you ever done me any?" she demanded, irked that he had used the private name only Jonathan should have known.

Charles turned his glare to the tall man standing silently just behind his sister, then growled irascibly at the noncommittal expression he found there. "Bloody damn fools. Drummond, we're going after the yule log just as soon as I get down there. No excuses." He stalked off in righteous indignation, oblivious to his mother's protests at such language.

Puzzled, Diana turned to catch Jonathan's expression, but he merely shrugged and asked, "He didn't have his cravat on yet, did he? It will be another hour before we see him again. I, for one, prefer to return to the table." And he did so, leaving Diana to stare after him with bewilderment and a shaky awareness of his physical presence that hadn't been there before.

The boy's shoulders she remembered so well had broadened into those of a man, a man accustomed to the rigors of a soldier's life. Muscular arms strained the seams of his civilian coat, and his athletic grace and masculine strength made a mockery of any injuries. Obviously, his wounds were such as not to limit a man of his stature to any great degree.

She could detect no bandages beneath the tight line of his trousers, but she suspected Jonathan's pride would prevent him from wearing any if they were at all to be avoided. She almost felt his wince of pain as he entered the dining room and reached for a chair. Were his wounds so painful that he could not relax and be himself, or had the war changed him to this cold and unrelenting stranger?

She had loved Jonathan Drummond for as long as she could remember, since she had been too little for him to notice. He had been just one of her older brother's many friends, but he had always been special. He was the only one who had spoken to her, treated her as an equal, and she had adored him. Later, when they were older, their families had shared their holidays, and there were picnics and romps and theatricals where they had just naturally paired off together, or against each other, depending on their ages or the game. Diana remembered a particular snowball fight where she managed to get him squarely in the head, and he had chased her until they both tumbled down a hill of snow, soaking themselves thoroughly. They had both caught a chill that day, but he had arranged to send her a bouquet from their greenhouse to cheer her sickroom. It was that next summer when his nonsensical notes began to take a more serious vein. The hiding place in the old secretary that had been their cache of secret jokes became a place to exchange private thoughts.

Diana watched as Jonathan returned to eating his breakfast, carefully adjusting his injured leg beneath the cloth and propping his bandaged hand upon the table, keeping his back to her. Four years couldn't have made him a total stranger. Charles had not changed that much. Why should Jonathan hate her now when he had loved her before?

She would find out. She did not know what she had done that had made him stop loving her, but she could no longer bear the suspense of wondering. He was alive and here and she would find out. That was the smallest price he would have to pay for leaving her with a heart that would not open to anyone else.

He nodded without smiling when she returned to her breakfast. Mrs. Carrington and Elizabeth had run off to direct the settling of the twins' latest disaster, so there was no one to monitor their conversation. Not that Jonathan invited conversation, Diana thought wryly as he calmly lifted his cup of coffee with his undamaged hand.

"Where did you take your injuries?" Trying her best to be as cool and sophisticated as this stranger sitting across from her, Diana added more hot water to her tea.

"In battle." Not caring to expound upon the subject over the breakfast table, Jonathan diverted the topic. "Your brother has been seeing to my welfare. That is why he was so late in returning. I don't suppose it occurred to him to write and tell you that, and unfortunately, I was not in a position to do so. I am exceedingly grateful for his care. The army surgeons would no doubt have insisted on amputation, and I would still be in some fly-infested tent if he had not come to my rescue."

Diana's eyes widened in horror as she turned her gaze to the gauze-enshrouded hand resting so casually amid the china and silver. That was his writing hand, his right hand. He could have lost it forever. The pain of that fear must have been as great as the physical pain, but he dismissed it so lightly. Determined not to let Jonathan see how he had upset her, Diana returned her gaze to rest on the raw scar of his forehead and raised one dark eyebrow quizzically.

"Amputation of the head would have been a trifle drastic, but I daresay it would have relieved any concern about the flies."

She said it with such a straight face that Jonathan nearly choked on a swallow of coffee. He had forgot-

ten her dry sense of humor, or rather, he had forgotten
its effect on him. He still felt the overwhelming urge
to retaliate in kind. He just hadn't remembered that
the need to retaliate hid a much deeper need. She was
much too beautiful in the mornings for his senses to
resist. The physical urge to gather her into his arms
and kiss that sassy mouth into submission had to be
prevented in some way.

"Your sympathy is gratifying. I shall always remember it with fondness." Collecting himself, he coldly
returned to his coffee.

"Then let me give you something else to remember
with fondness." Furious at his caculated coldness, furious with herself for caring, Diana rose precipitously
from her chair and overturned his plate and all his
carefully cut breakfast into his lap.

Without further word, she sailed from the room
trailing lavender ribbons. Who needed sophistication
when righteous anger felt so much better?

Jonathan almost smiled as he contemplated the remains of his breakfast, running down his once immaculate trousers. In some ways, Diana hadn't
changed at all, and he felt oddly relieved that the little
hoyden still remained behind all her stylish beauty.
And there certainly couldn't be any pity lingering there
if she felt free to take advantage of his temporary
handicaps. In another time and place he would have
chased after her and made her pay for her temerity,
but he was no longer that heedless boy, just as she was
no longer the pigtailed girl who would wrestle him to
the ground. Just the thought of such a combat roused
definitely unchildish desires.

With a grimace at his response to this enforced
proximity to a woman who had made it quite clear that
she held him in disfavor, Jonathan struggled from his
lonely seat and set out to find clean trousers.

Charles found him sometime later staring up the
narrow back stairs to the attics. Eyeing his melancholy

friend skeptically, he slapped a hand to Jonathan's back and steered him toward the main staircase. "The maids don't sleep up there, old fellow, if you've taken a sudden penchant for slap and tickle. It's too damn hard to heat those rooms."

Jonathan scowled. "I bloody well don't give a damn where they sleep. I owe you a great deal, Charles, and don't think I'm ungrateful, but this isn't going to work. You should have left me in London."

"To do what, may I ask? Hide from your father? Or Diana? Or both? Devil take it, Drummond, but you're a bloody great hero on the field, and a complete horse's ass on home ground. You've got the courage to stand up against the worst Boney could send you, but you haven't got the backbone to stand up to one sharp-tongued female. You're the one who has thrown his cap over a windmill for that frippery sister of mine. I could have warned you it was a foolish piece of business. Diana's a right one, but she can be mighty high in the instep when she wants to be. She's not so easy-natured as your Marie."

"Marie is a senseless chit, even if she is my sister. And I'm damned sorry you ever got near me while I was fevered. Remind me never to become ill again."

The two men clattered down the last of the stairs and into the hall where the butler waited with their greatcoats and mufflers. Unoffended by Jonathan's irascible curses, Charles grinned and shrugged into the caped coat.

"On the contrary, you should be ill more often. It's quite an enlightening experience. You're a damned close-mouthed devil, Drummond. I had no idea your passion for my sister had got so out of hand as to stoop to pet names! Come on, nodcock, let us get a log that will last into eternity. That will show them what kind of stuff we're made of."

They disappeared into the blowing cold of a white-laced winter wonderland, leaving a gaping Elizabeth hovering behind the parlor door. Jonathan and Diana? Is that why her sister had become an old maid at the age of twenty-two? Did they really have a *tendre* for each other? Or had she misunderstood Charles's words? It would be something lovely to have Marie as a sister-in-law and to be able to visit the Drummonds in London whenever she wanted. Surely Diana would invite her as often as she asked. Jonathan and Diana. Oh, yes, that would be a lovely match. And then she could come out next Season without fear of being overshadowed by her older sister.

Practically dancing up the stairs, Elizabeth set out in search of the twins.

The yule log arrived while Diana was completing the greenery in the drawing room later that afternoon. Besides the kissing bough in the center of the ceiling, she had decorated the mantel candelabra with ivy and holly and made a centerpiece of evergreen branches intertwined with ivy for the spinet. Already several small gifts dangled tantalizingly from the boughs on the ceiling, and Diana smiled as a gust of wind from the open front door sent them dancing. Her father had initiated the tradition of hanging gifts when they were very young and the kissing bough's main feature of mistletoe meant nothing to them. This year, only the gifts would be there. The mistletoe was not only perilous to reach, but inappropriate for a house of mourning. But she could not resist the gifts.

Jonathan watched her wide smile of pleasure as he and Charles carried in the enormous log meant to burn for the next twelve days. Not many houses had fireplaces large enough for the old custom, but the drawing room in the old part of Carrington House was ideal for the purpose. The enormous room had a fireplace that engulfed one wall. Dwarfed by the towering stone and timber fireplace behind her, Diana balanced precariously on the edge of a wing chair as she added another piece of ivy to her bouquet.

She leapt lightly from her unseemly perch, her dark eyes dancing with delight as she carefully inspected their beribboned presentation.

"It is lovely. I do believe it is the best log ever. It will make a splendid sight when you light it tonight. Do we have any of last year's log left to light it with?"

"How am I supposed to know? You were here, not me, but I shouldn't think Father would have forgotten to set a few pieces aside."

At this mention of their father, Diana's smile faded, and Charles regretted his hasty words. Jonathan gave him a look of disgust, and resignedly helped lower the log to the grate, an awkward business with his one good arm.

Once it was settled, Charles pulled off his gloves and circled Diana's shoulders. "I'm sorry, Di. I have been tormenting myself for weeks for not being here when you needed me. It's hard to come home and act cheerful when there's this big gaping hole that he used to fill."

Diana nodded in understanding. "I keep waiting for him to come through the door and yell for the twins and spin Mama around the room like he did when he had a good day. I miss talking to him in the evenings. I even miss his scoldings. I catch myself sounding just like him sometimes when the twins are in the briars."

Jonathan had moved quietly to the door so as not to intrude upon this family scene, but Charles caught the movement before he could escape.

"Don't bolt yet, Drummond. The greenery ain't up yet in the hall and unless you want Diana climbing up there to do it, you'd better stay here. The twins are in their best clothes and I promised Mama to keep them entertained until their keeper gets back from the village, so I'm taking them out." He ignored Diana's dubious look. "Goudge ain't much help, but he may lend a hand if you need him."

Releasing Diana's shoulder, Charles reached up to spin one of the dangling packages and grinned at his friend's stoic expression. "Or you can take the twins and I'll help Diana."

"Heaven forbid." Jonathan raised expressive eyes to the ceiling at the thought. "I'd rather face Boney himself than those two. Were we ever like that?"

Diana demurely nibbled at the end of her finger as she contemplated her older brother and his friend. "Don't I remember a time when the two of you put me in an empty barrel and sent me down Scott's Hill? And then, of course, there was the time—"

"Don't let her get started!" Charles hastily dodged a Chippendale sofa in his effort to reach the door before she could continue. "She'll make the heathens look like saints before she's through."

He was gone before either could say a word, his booted feet carrying him rapidly up the hall stairs in search of his elusive brothers. Jonathan turned a thoughtful gaze to the slim young woman now sitting at the table idly removing discolored leaves from a branch of holly. They had shared so many times together, it was hard to exclude himself from her life now. He had to remember that she was the one who had chosen to exclude him after he ran off to join the cavalry instead of staying home to court her as she deserved. Although she wore no ring, he supposed she had found someone more suitable while he was away. She had too much beauty and spirit to wither away on the vine.

"I am nearly done decorating," she lied. "You don't need to help me unless you wish. Mama's right. This is a house of mourning—I should not be so frivolous."

"I should think a little frivolity is what we all need right now. I speak for myself, of course." Jonathan grimaced as he indicated his bandaged hand. "But the twins and Elizabeth are young yet. They need things to be the way they used to be, just for a little while. It's hard on them.''

Diana raised her eyes to his, and Jonathan caught the sparkle of tears behind thick lashes. His breath lodged in his lungs, and the sudden, desperate urge to take her in his arms almost sent him fleeing in the opposite direction.

''You've changed, Johnny.'' She saw his stiffening at this boyhood name and regretted her familiarity. He was no longer a boy but a man full grown, a man she had trouble recognizing at times. The unruly chestnut hair still fell across his wounded brow, but it was the sun-darkened brow of a man who had spent years on foreign shores. What had made her think he would have any interest in a country miss such as herself? She had not even a London bronze to catch his eye or hold his attention.

''So have you,'' he reminded her. ''You're not a skinny little girl in pigtails or a bluestocking with her nose in a book or even a hoyden who can climb trees with the best of them. We all grow up.''

Diana made a vicious cut with her pruning shears at the evergreen branch she was trimming. ''I still read books and can climb trees as well as the twins. In happier times, I even know how to laugh. But not you. You look just like your father when you glare at me like that with your nose up in the air and that disapproving frown between your eyes.''

''Do I?'' To put the lie to her words, a twinkle began to gleam in those maligned features. He removed the branch she was butchering and gave a quick twist to the wire tying it to a second branch from the stack on the floor. ''Then perhaps he will find me so changed he will forgive me for my tresspasses. One can always hope. And what about you, Diana? Have you found a suitor who will read poems to you and admire your collection of antiquities?''

"Oh, they always read poems to me when they find out I like them," she answered crossly, twisting a ribbon around the roping taking shape beneath his capable fingers. Even with one hand Jonathan managed the unwieldy branches better than she. "And they mutter suitable exclamations when I show them my pieces of Roman pottery. And then they go on to talk as if I hadn't half a brain in my head or the wit to know the difference. I really don't think men are all that necessary. I can keep the books as well as my father could. He had managers to oversee his various interests. I could do that if they'd let me. But no, they must pat me on the head and tell me what a good little girl I am, and why don't I fetch them a cup of tea? Men! They are a thoroughly useless lot."

"You go too far, Janey. Would you march to war without us?"

"There wouldn't be any war without you," she answered blithely.

"You have a point there. But look at the women you know. How many of them are capable of keeping the government running?"

"About as many as there are men." Diana looked up from her ribbon-tying to find Jonathan watching her, a grin pulling at the corners of his mouth. He was leading her down the garden path, but she didn't care. She twitched his self-importance again. "Why should a woman marry when all it ensures is a lifetime of cooking and cleaning while the man carouses? Any sensible female must see that marriage isn't made in heaven but in a much more earthly place."

"Oh, I'll agree with that. If it weren't for earthly pleasures, no self-respecting male would find himself leg-shackled to a shrewish female who complains night and day and gives him no peace until he is in his grave. I am certain it is only the desire to breed heirs that keeps the custom of marriage alive. I can't remember your feeling that way before. You certainly have changed more than I imagined. It is a relief to learn that now.''

"You are not what I once thought you to be either,'' Diana responded tartly. "I can remember once when you enjoyed my company instead of calling me a shrewish female. But of course, that was when you were inclined to wager on whether the first leaf would fall from the oak or birch, and you enjoyed wrestling on the lawns with children and teasing shrewish females. That was back before you lost your sense of humor and became your father, when you knew how to laugh.''

"Ah yes, I remember that time. And didn't I used to pull hair ribbons and run away and hide them where shrewish females couldn't find them? Like this?'' And to Diana's dismay, Jonathan leaned over the table and slipped one of the ribbons from her hair, causing a tumble of thick tresses to cascade over one shoulder. Before she could grab it away, his long trousered legs carried him toward the door, his limp not hampering his swiftness to any great degree.

"Jonathan Drummond, you give that back! I haven't another to match and your family will be here any minute!'' Brushing a shower of evergreen branches from her lap, she jumped up and raced after him.

"You'll never find it!'' he cried out from the top of the stairs as Diana dashed into the hall.

"Jonathan, upon my word, I will pull every hair from your head if I catch you!'' Lifting her skirts, Diana raced up the stairway after him.

Appearing in the corridor from the kitchen with a ladle of hot punch she had meant to offer for sampling, Mrs. Carrington stared after the young couple as if they had quite taken leave of their senes. They acted as if they had already been sampling the punch. Frowning as she turned back toward the kitchen, she tasted a sip for herself. Not enough ale. Cook would need to heat some more before the Drummonds arrived.

Diana found Jonathan perched on the attic stairs with no sign of the ribbon in sight. She grinned in satisfaction and sat comfortably on the step below him. The high stickler from the drawing room now appeared more like the Jonathan she remembered, with his hair down over his forehead and a smile dancing about his lips.

"You can't hide up there anymore. Mama keeps the attic locked ever since Freddie fell asleep in one of the trunks and disappeared for hours. So now give me my ribbon."

Jonathan ignored her outstretched hand and looked contemplatively at the door that kept him from discovering the secrets of the old desk. Perhaps it was better he not know if the ring remained concealed in the hidden drawer. What could he do if it still were? Diana was a grown woman now, not the impressionable little girl he had hoped to persuade to wait for him. Besides, he had even less to offer her now than he had had before. His father most likely had disowned him, and if there were any chance his hand would not mend properly, he had few means of making a living. With neither home nor means of support, he could not renew his suit. It would be better to let old wounds heal, but in four years the one in his heart showed no sign of closing.

"I guess that eliminates a fast game of hide and seek. Shall we bob for apples next?" Jonathan pulled the crumpled ribbon from his pocket and dangled it tauntingly just out of her reach.

"You may join the twins at the apples, if you wish. Besides, hide and seek isn't any fun. You always knew my favorite hiding place, even if you pretended you didn't."

In the narrow, walled stairwell, Diana felt dangerously close to him. They must have been much smaller when they used to hide up here and talk while the others searched for them. Jonathan's tightly trousered leg now rested daringly close to her knees, and the way he leaned his elbows back on the stair behind him made her amazingly aware of the leanness of the hips resting just above hers. Yet, boldly, she continued to stare into the warmth of his gray eyes.

"I wanted to make certain I was the one to find you. I was an amazingly selfish young man, wasn't I?"

"You most certainly were," Diana answered as severely as she was able. And then, the one thing she most held against him, the one thing she had sworn never to say out loud, slipped past her lips before she could prevent it. "I'll not ever forgive you for slipping off to war without thinking to tell me first. That was the height of your selfish career."

"You don't know the half of it, my lovely Janey." Wistfully, Jonathan swung the ribbon within her reach and watched as she grabbed it to twist and bind in her straying locks. In an effort to determine just how and where she had found out about his leaving—had it been from his letter or some other source first?—he asked, "Where were you when you heard the news?"

"Sick in bed." Diana made a face of disgust. "I caught the twins' chicken pox. I was so mad at them, and then I was mad at you and Charles when I heard the news. I couldn't believe it. I must have been delirious. I was going to ride out after you and ring a proper peal over your heads. I suspect my mother gave me laudanum to keep me quiet. When I woke, Elizabeth brought me a rose on my breakfast tray, and I knew you weren't coming back. I never have been able to pry out of her where she found a rose at Christmas, but it was like receiving a funeral wreath, I guess. I just knew you weren't coming to hold my hand and make me laugh anymore."

"A rose?" The word came out more as a groan than a question. A rose. He had thought she would never miss that certain signal indicating a message waited for her when he placed it on the old desk. A rose in winter. He had been very proud of that romantic gesture. But she had never seen it on the desk and had never known he had sneaked through the window that night to place it there. How could she have known? What a stupid, childish fool he had been. The chances were very good she had never found his letter, and now it lay resting somewhere above, mouldering away with his dreams. Without thinking, Jonathan answered the question in her words. "It was warm that winter. Sometimes the potted roses keep blooming in the greenhouse."

Diana glanced sharply at him. "Your greenhouse, you mean. We don't have one."

He was saved from responding by the sound of a loud rap on the front door knocker below. They sat in silence as they listened to the doors being thrown open and cries of greeting filling the air.

"Your family," Diana whispered, throwing him a hesitant glance. Did he know his father had not mentioned his name since he left? From the bleak look on Jonathan's face she surmised he had some inkling of the situation. "I will go down and tell them you are resting. After a few cups of Mama's lambswool, your father will be much more amiable."

Jonathan offered her a crooked grin. "Maybe you haven't changed so much, after all. You always were a wicked liar."

"It will at least give you time to straighten your cravat and wash the dust smeared across your cheek," she replied tartly. "Do as you wish."

"You know what I wish, don't you?" He leaned forward suddenly and caught her shoulder before she could flounce off in a huff.

Diana felt Jonathan's breath warm against her cheek and his lips tantalizingly close to her own, and she caught her breath. She had a very good suspicion of what he wanted, but she wasn't going to let him know that, not like this, not in secrecy anymore. She stood up hastily and brushed out her lavender skirt.

"Don't mistake me for someone else, Jonathan. I haven't changed that much." She marched off without another word.

Damn! Jonathan hit his thigh with his fist as Diana hurriedly disappeared down the upstairs hall. She hadn't guessed. After all these years, she hadn't guessed where that rose came from. Or perhaps she didn't want to know. Sadly, he glanced over his shoulder at the door behind which the answer lay. After four years of thinking he had run away from her, she would not be very likely to welcome his suit now, but he was too miserable not to know.

With the air of a man who has made a decision, Jonathan rose to his feet and, brushing the dust from his trousers, started down the back stairs.

He knew the keys were kept in the kitchen. As a child, he had been allowed full run of the house, and he didn't think the routines had changed greatly. If he could just somehow slip down unnoticed and figure out which was the attic key, it wouldn't be a moment's work to run up the stairs and find the old desk. He had to know whether she had found his letter.

He chased away all the doubting thoughts about what difference the knowledge could make. Disowned by his father, disabled and without funds, he certainly couldn't repeat his offer. In that case, it would be better if the letter were safely in his pocket where it could cause no misunderstanding if someone came upon it at a later date. If it was there.

That's what he had to know. At the pain of risking the same blow of rejection he had felt when he received no reply to his letter the first time, he would know of a certainty if she had found it. If she had found it and chosen not to reply, he would at least know where he stood and could act accordingly. He could leave now and not submit himself to the torture of sharing this holiday with people who no longer wished to include him in their lives.

But Diana had not behaved as if she had cast him aside as she had her childhood. True, she was not as outgoing and lavish with her affections as she had once been, but people change. He, of all people, should know that. Once, all he had wanted was the adventure and thrill of seeing the world and fighting to save his home and country. Now, he had seen his fill of war and wanted only the security of home and family. Unfortunately, it looked very much as if neither war nor family would have him now. He had to have at least the hope of one day regaining the love he had so foolishly neglected.

One of the twins sat munching an apple on a stool near the pantry where the keys were kept, his hair mussed and his best clothes slightly awry from whatever entertainment Charles had provided. Jonathan could hear the uproar in the kitchen beyond, but none of the servants were in the back hall to observe him. Just Frankie. Or Freddie.

The boy grinned at the sight of company. "You come to snitch an apple, too? All them smells make me hungry."

Jonathan hesitated. He hadn't counted on anybody seeing him purloin the key. The explanations involved could be exceedingly messy. But he needed it now, before facing the confrontation with his father. He had to know if Diana smiled at him out of pity or if she still harbored some feeling for him. If he could just get in the damned attic . . .

"Me, too," he answered casually, easing himself around the stool for a glimpse into the pantry. The keys weren't there! "Why aren't you with Charles?" he asked desperately, looking for some way to rid himself of any witness.

"Mama said we had to come in and clean up but I

was hungry. I hate coats.'' He shrugged at the confining shoulders of his best new suit and he eyed Jonathan with caution. ''Cook said she'd cut off my hand with an ax if I touched anything in there,'' he informed him helpfully. ''Better just get an apple.''

The obstacles only made Jonathan more determined to have what he wanted. Giving the boy a level look, he said, ''Actually, your mother sent me down for a key. They used to be in there. Do you know where they are kept?''

The boy brightened. ''Mama hung them way up on the back of the door so we couldn't climb the shelves to reach them, but I can still get at them. Which one do you want?''

''Perhaps I'd better find it myself.'' With a dry lift of his eyebrows, he went behind the door to find the key board. Row after row of polished brass keys hung in neat array, if he could only decipher their order. First row, first floor? Top row, top floor? No, there were too many. Frowning, he tried to think like Mrs. Carrington. How would she arrange the keys?

The sound of voices approaching caused him to panic. How would he ever explain his way out of this one? A child might believe his story of a guest being sent to the kitchen for a key, but no one else would. He was tempted to grab a handful and run with them.

The boy solved his dilemma. Slipping around the door, he pointed helpfully to a key dangling in the shadows at the very top of the door. ''We can't get that one. It's the attic key. We wanted to see if there were any ghosts up there, but the stool isn't tall enough.''

Jonathan glanced thoughtfully down to his nemesis and savior. ''There weren't any ghosts there last time I looked, but you know that back bedroom with all the boxes and dustcovers? I thought I saw one in there before. Where's Frankie? Go get him and maybe you can see if it's still there.''

The boy's whole face lit up and he stared at Jonathan with excitement. "Do you really think so? Let's go see. How did you know I was Freddie? Even Elizabeth sometimes gets us mixed up."

The voices were coming closer and Jonathan was growing desperate. "Because you're the one who does the talking. Frankie just waits for you to come up with ideas. Go on now. I hear Goudge, and he'll probably frown about that apple."

Freddie was off and gone without further argument. Reaching with his one good arm, Jonathan just barely managed to pry the key off its hook. Pocketing it swiftly, he picked up Freddie's half-eaten apple and wandered out into the hall with it. Nodding at a suspicious Goudge, he ambled toward the back stairs, apple in hand, key in pocket. His heart thundered in his ears. Never in all those years of war had he reached such a pitch of nervous excitement. Soon, he would know.

The attic stairs were around the landing from the back stairs. All he had to do was keep on going and no one would be the wiser. Just up one more flight of stairs . . .

The twins sat perched expectantly where he and Diana had just been sitting, blocking access to the attic door. Jonathan groaned inwardly as he heard Charles shout his name somewhere nearby. Someone would no doubt come looking for him shortly and find him grubbing for ghosts with the children. He'd never really had a chance. It had been foolish to think he could sneak around a friend's house like some damned thief. He would have to place his future in the hands of fate.

Downstairs, Diana surveyed the scene of excited greetings, winter wraps, and the brisk scent of cold air in the front hall with less than complete happiness. The Drummonds had arrived from London with fashionable hats, fur-lined coats and muffs, a carriage full of trunks, and an air of sophistication that the country-bound Carrington household seldom attained. Marie, the little girl who once romped the fields on ponies with Elizabeth, was now a young lady with rosy cheeks framed by stylish auburn curls and a fur-lined bonnet as she hugged her young friend. Mrs. Drummond hadn't changed from her plump, shy self, but she seemed a trifle nervous as she shed her velvet pelisse. Glancing at the formidable frown on Mr. Drummond's brow, Diana had some idea of the tense scene that lay ahead.

"Diana! Don't you look lovely! Come here and let me see you." Mrs. Drummond held out her arms in greeting as Diana came into view on the stairs. "We saw Charles out on the drive a few minutes ago. Doesn't he look dashing? Isn't it grand to have him home at last?"

All her nervousness came pouring out in this voluble greeting, and Diana understood at once. Charles must already have told them Jonathan was here. She glanced anxiously toward the elder Drummond as she came forward to embrace his wife.

"It is such a relief. I could not have asked for a better Christmas gift," she murmured. "Jonathan is upstairs resting," she added with a hint of defiance. "It seems he was wounded and Charles would not come home without him." This she said loudly enough for Jonathan's father to hear.

He ignored the mention of his son as he allowed the near-sighted butler to help him with his cloak. Mrs. Carrington sent her daughter an anxious glance at this breach of a forbidden subject, but she continued helping old Goudge with the gathering of hats and gloves and scarves and muffs.

Mrs. Drummond clutched eagerly at this mention of her son. Taking Diana's elbow, she led her toward the drawing room, the two whispering young girls following close behind. "How is he? He has not been seriously injured, has he? Oh, tell me, Diana, for I am in a frightful state. I did not think ever to see him again.''

"His injuries are not grave, but a serious blow to his pride, I suspect. He will be down shortly, I am certain, and you will see for yourself. Come, let me pour you a cup of hot tea, and you can tell us how marvelously Marie fared in her first Season.''

"We should have come out together.'' Elizabeth pouted as they settled near the fire. "We had it all planned. I was to be the Snow Queen and she was to be the Rose. Now it is all spoiled.''

"Oh, no, it is not!'' Marie protested. "I shall be able to tell you which gentlemen are the best catches, and we can start out by favoring only the most eligible young men. It will be great fun, you will see.''

Pouring the tea for Mrs. Drummond, Diana could see her mother offering Mr. Drummond his brandy, and she hid a smile of relief. Perhaps the brandy would warm the frozen features of his face. If she were a miracle worker, her Christmas gift to Jonathan would be his father's forgiveness.

Charles and the twins had apparently hastily repaired their best attire for they joined the company now all polished and immaculate. The twins had their brown cowlicks slicked back and their short coats on. Charles had donned a formal hammer-tailed coat of chocolate brown over a gold waistcoat and fawn trousers. With his cravat starched and neatly tied and his blond hair gleaming in the candlelight, he made a striking picture, and all heads turned in his direction.

"I should like to welcome you more politely than with snowballs,'' he said genially, holding out his hand to Jonathan's father.

For the first time, he must act as man of the house, and Diana thought he played the part exceedingly well. It seemed very odd to think of her older brother as a man and not the young scoundrel who came in foxed at night and crawled through windows when his father locked him out. But he acted the host with a maturity that had not been there when he left home, and she felt a glow of pride.

"You'll have your hands full stepping into your father's place, I'll warrant," Mr. Drummond said gruffly, accepting the offered hand. "I'll lend a hand wherever you need it."

"I appreciate that, sir. Would you like Frankie or Freddie?"

Charles said it with such a straight face that the older man looked momentarily bewildered, but when the girls giggled and Mrs. Carrington gave her son a quick rap on the arm, he caught the joke and nodded. "Those young scamps will make you think twice about starting your own nursery. I can remember when you and . . ." His voice trailed off as he realized his error in almost mentioning his son, and he returned morosely to his glass of brandy.

An awkward silence fell, into which Jonathan had the misfortune to step. All eyes turned to observe his presence. He had made some attempt to brush back his unruly dark hair, but that only made the scar along his brow more evident. His navy frock coat fit his broad shoulders to perfection, but his cravat had a rakish angle created by his inability to use his right hand. The civilized cut of his silver-gray waistcoat and pantaloons did nothing to disguise the striking darkness of his visage or the bleakness of that whitely bandaged hand. Gray eyes searched the room for reaction and rested momentarily on Diana's anxious gaze.

"Do I interrupt?" he inquired with brave frivolity.

"No, do come in, Jonathan, and have a seat," said Mrs. Carrington. "I was about to send Charles for the lambswool to take the chill out of everyone's bones. Charles?" She quirked an eyebrow at her eldest son, who, responding with alacrity to this command, left the room.

"Yes, have a seat," Diana urged him. "Cook has

prepared a light supper before we go off to church, and it will be ready shortly. Mama, the twins might stay up until then, may they not? The carolers will be here soon, and I think they're old enough to behave.'' Diana shot her younger brothers a meaningful look, and they returned it with bright grins.

The normal, everyday activities of the Carrington family removed Jonathan from the center of attention, and he settled quietly into a large chair in the corner of the room where he was nearly engulfed in shadows. His attempt at disappearing from the company did not go unnoticed. Irritated with this unfeeling behavior while his mother nearly shredded her handkerchief into fragments, Diana rose to perch like some malicious angel upon the arm of his chair when no one else seemed prepared to chastise him for his rudeness.

"How good of you to join us, darling. Wouldn't you care to step over here by the fire and warm yourself? I should think you would have learned to appreciate a good fire by now.''

Since the word darling had once been an epithet they had thrown at each other when warned against calling each other impolite names, Jonathan didn't misunderstand Diana's message now. And since the yule log had not yet been lighted, she was veritably hitting him over the head with his misconduct. Instead of resenting her interference, he threw his avenging angel a grateful look for easing the awkwardness of his situation.

"You are quite right, my darling,'' he answered suavely, catching her offguard with a sudden smile. "I am behaving like a graceless savage. I shall have to practice returning to civilized ways. Did Charles find the tinder from last year's fire?''

No one missed this exchange between the couple in the corner except Charles, who had gone to find the punch. Both families were aware of the couple's method of exchanging insults, but the manner in which

Jonathan used the phrase this time brought a sudden color to Diana's cheeks and with it, the first hint that something besides friendship had developed between these two. Marie and Elizabeth watched with awe and delight as Jonathan rose and, bowing politely, appropriated Diana's arm to lead her across the room to his mother. To distract Mr. Drummond's attention from this performance, Mrs. Carrington nervously went into a monologue about the supper she had prepared. The twins, left to themselves, began to eye the kissing bough.

"Mother, you are looking fine, as usual. Shall I light the fire for you? I'm sure Charles won't mind if I relieve him of one of his many duties this evening."

Enraptured by having her son home again, Mrs. Drummond ignored her husband's furious expression and gazed up at her only boy with adoration. "It is good to have you back, Jonathan. Your letters have been the delight of my life since you've been gone."

Jonathan gave a familiarly rakish grin and glanced down at Diana, who surprisingly still clung to his arm. "Do you hear that? I haven't lost my touch. I think I shall take up writing letters for a living."

"All you have to do is find someone who will buy them," Diana replied solemnly. Then releasing his arm, she lifted the basket containing the remaining pieces of last year's log. "Shall you do the honors, sir?"

"Sir" was much more promising than "darling," and Jonathan graciously accepted. He was well aware he was goading his father into a greater fury, but he couldn't help himself. It was good to be accepted without question into this warm if however unruly family. He resented having to win the affection of his own father.

Charles entered carrying the steaming bowl of punch while Goudge managed the difficult job of drawing open the dining room doors. The twins gave a shout of joy at the heaping platters revealed, while their mother hovered anxiously over Charles's shoulder.

"You are certain you added the proper amount of cream? I would not want it to curdle. Your father always said if it was not done just the proper way . . ."

"We shall let Mr. Drummond taste it to declare whether it is proper done or not, Mama." Charles lowered the silver punch bowl to the table and graciously ladled out the first cup for their guest. "I trust I haven't forgotten all of my father's teachings."

Mr. Drummond sipped experimentally at the mixture of hot ale, spices, sugar, and eggs, and nodded his head approvingly. "Your father taught you well, young man. He would be proud of you this day."

Diana saw the pain shoot through Jonathan's face at this chance remark, and her fingers clenched in her palms at his father's heedless cruelty. The man had not said a word to his injured son, home from a war fought to protect king and country. Jonathan had spent four years bravely risking his life so that they could celebrate this Christmas in safety. His father had no right to throw all that aside to salve his injured pride.

Knowing it was not her place to interfere, well aware that she defied every stricture of proper behavior by doing so, Diana calmly turned to comment upon a remark that had not been made to her. "My father was proud of both Jonathan and Charles. Papa always said if it weren't for such men as them, Napoleon would have walked across England as he has Europe."

She said it quietly, without defiance, but the polite murmurs of conversation all across the room died as Mr. Drummond turned to meet her proud gaze.

In the candlelight her mahogany tresses shimmered in a rich halo about features as fair as fine porcelain. For the first time he realized she had grown into a striking woman instead of the young chit who once got caught in the top of his best apple tree. He couldn't scold her as he would a child, and as much as he would like, he couldn't give her a setdown. Not only would it mar the memory of his late friend's words, but she was right. He just refused to admit it out loud. He had suffered when his only son had rejected the lands and position he had carefully built to take up the life of an adventure-seeking soldier. The humiliation and suffering had not lessened with the years, but the fear of losing his only son had added to it. Still, he had a position to uphold in the eyes of the others. The boy had to be punished, even if it meant a continuation of his own suffering. The only problem was that the cold stranger who had returned seemed already lost to him, and the only one suffering from his punishment was himself. He could not say the words to show his relief that his son had returned safely.

"Your father was quite likely right, as he was in many things." That was as far as he could unbend without injuring his pride. Let the boy make of it what he would.

Charles began pouring small cups of punch for the ladies, but they scarcely heeded him as Diana now turned to glare at Jonathan. He had the fire licking at the brittle kindling beneath the log, and he rose when he first heard what he recognized as Diana's declaration of war. He wasn't surprised when she turned on him, but his father's grudging admission caught him unprepared, leaving him no defense when Diana launched her attack.

"He also said it was wrong for a son to act against his father's wishes without trying to understand his father's reasons. It is not always possible to adhere to the wishes of one you love, but if you truly love him, you would at least listen to him and consider his feelings."

Jonathan met her gaze steadily, hearing more in her words than he dared admit even to himself. Reluctantly, he tore his gaze from the passion blazing in Diana's eyes and turned to face his silent father. He had never been very good at apologizing, and he still felt himself the wronged party, but it was Christmas, and he could not abide this distance that separated him from his family. In her outspoken manner, Diana had given him the opening he could never have made for himself. He took the cup Charles shoved between his fingers, and raising it, nodded to his father.

"Your father was a wiser man than I, Diana. Perhaps it is still possible to learn from him. Charles," Jonathan caught his host's eyes and raised his cup in salute, "To fathers, past, present, and future, who must bear the ingratitude as well as the affection of their unthinking sons. May we bear the task as well when our turn comes."

Charles grinned irreverently and gave a roguish wink to the delightfully pretty miss watching from the corner. "I'll drink to that. To fatherhood."

Mr. Drummond's loud "harrumph" removed the grin from Charles's face, but as all eyes returned to the patriarch, he lifted his glass to join in the toast. "Past, present, and future—that was very well said. I'll drink to that."

It wasn't a healing of the breach, but it was a rough acknowledgment that one existed. The evening moved more swiftly and more pleasantly after that, giving time for the momentary unpleasantness to dissipate. The village musicians, who earned extra shillings at Christmas by roaming from house to house singing the ancient carols, appeared shortly after to fill the huge old drawing room with song and share the punch. Neighbors stopped by to enjoy the chorus and to exchange greetings, and the strained atmosphere of earlier disappeared in the general merriment.

The returned soldiers found themselves the center of these festivities, but above the heads of his well-wishers, Jonathan followed Diana's movements as she entertained the guests. He could not decide whether she had defended him out of affection or her usual determination to see things right. It mattered little enough. His father obviously wasn't prepared to admit his own pigheadedness and welcome his erring son home. He couldn't blame him, he supposed, but he couldn't forgive him easily, either. Had he accepted his son's decision to go off and fight as Charles's father had, he would not have had to run away in such a havey-cavey manner, leaving Diana to turn elsewhere for affection, if that was what she had done. They had both chosen their paths; there was nothing for it but to go their separate ways, it seemed. The package wrapped in his pocket had no purpose anymore. He must have been crazed even to consider it.

Catching a glimpse of Freddie eyeing the highly polished apples adorning the branches of the kissing bough, Jonathan managed a wry smile in remembrance of Christmas past. He and Charles had often connived some means of reaching those tempting apples, even though their stomachs were filled to overflowing with Christmas delicacies from the table. Judging by the front of Freddie's coat, the lad had already sampled everything on the table, but the forbidden apples always looked more delicious than what was at hand.

Successfully evading several older couples saying their farewells, Jonathan slipped up behind Freddie and whispered, "What will you give me if I help you get one?"

Freddie beamed up at his brother's friend. Charles and Jonathan were as much together in the minds of the twins as to seem equally like brothers. Without hesitation, he offered, "Me and Frankie got the mistletoe like Elizabeth said. We gave it to Charles, but we'll get you some, too, if you like." He wasn't much concerned with the adults' need for the pretty greenery that hung on the highest branches of the old walnut tree, but he understood its value in terms of trade.

Jonathan chuckled. "Is that what you scamps were

up to? I'll not send you back out in the cold. The information is sufficient payment, thank you. Climb up on my shoulders. We should be able to reach that low one there.''

Since the branches were hung so that the lowest loop just barely missed his head, Jonathan could have reached the apple for himself, but that wouldn't have been nearly as much fun for the young boy. Without thought to the crease of his coat, he hoisted Freddie into the air where he triumphantly captured the apple he had been admiring.

From her corner of the room, Diana watched this display with a peculiar wrenching feeling in the middle of her stomach. A man like Jonathan should have children of his own. He had always been patient with Marie, more so than Charles had been with his younger siblings. She could tell by the smile on his face that he was enjoying the mischief as much as Freddie. Perhaps he hadn't changed as much as she had feared. Perhaps it was only his feelings toward her that had changed. Or perhaps she had only imagined those feelings in the first place, mistakenly thinking his attentions more than those of an older brother, when all he did was play the part he played with Freddie tonight.

''Look, that package has my name on it!'' Freddie cried excitedly from his lofty perch. ''And there's one for Frankie!''

''And it will still have your name on it in the morning when you come down.'' Charles materialized beside them and lifted the imp from Jonathan's back before his friend discovered the difficulty of lowering that hefty weight with a bad knee and one hand. ''Where's Frankie? It's time you're both off to bed. The guests are starting to leave.''

Both hands filled with apples, Freddie came down reluctantly, but he turned his expectant gaze to Charles. ''Aren't you going to hang the mistletoe, Charles? Can we help you?''

Charles exchanged a laughing glance with Jonathan as his secret was revealed, and he whispered, "It can't be a kissing bough without mistletoe, can it?" To his brother, he added, "Get upstairs now and we'll see about the mistletoe later. It's a surprise, so not a word, mind you!"

They watched as Freddie located his twin and the two ran off whispering together. Then Charles followed Jonathan's gaze as it drifted back toward Diana. She and Elizabeth and Marie were conferring over something in the corner by the fire, and Charles let his gaze linger on Jonathan's younger sister. She had turned into a real beauty since they had left. He had never dreamed the difference four years could make in a thirteen-year old child. Diana, now, was a different story. She had been a pretty child like Marie when they left. She was a stunning, self-assured woman now. He glanced surreptitiously to his friend's face.

"Have you discovered yet if another has captured her fancy? I can't believe you were fool enough to go off to war without securing her pledge. If I'd known Marie would become such a diamond, I would have sought hers. Now I suppose I'll have to fight her suitors away just to get near her."

Jonathan quirked a doubting eyebrow but did not look away from the focus of his attention. "Diana was young and had only been out one Season. I couldn't ask her to wait for a man who might never come back, not any more than you can ask Marie before she's had time to test the waters. So don't lecture me, Carrington."

"Then make haste while you can, sapskull, instead of idling time like some moonling. I'd see her wed to you before any other I know."

Jonathan shot him a wry look. "You'll not ever make a proper head of the household with that attitude. You haven't inquired into my prospects. They don't look particularly bright, you realize. I haven't a feather to fly on. My father still isn't speaking to me, and with a crippled hand, I have very little use in any position.''

Charles gave him a look of disgust that spoke his opinion of these objections. "You're quite correct. You forgot to mention you haven't a wit in the old brain pan, either.'' With that frosty remark, he left to see off the remainder of their guests.

Diana was caught by surprise when she entered the dining hall some minutes later to discover the only other occupant was Jonathan. Almost everyone had left or retired upstairs to rest and freshen up before midnight services. She had hoped to help in packing the boxes of left-over food for the needy.

The cold punch had been returned to the kitchen, but he sipped at tea kept hot over the chafing dish while he sampled the moist remains of a fruit cake. At Diana's appearance, he gestured a greeting with his cup.

"I was hoping to speak with you, but you seem to be avoiding me. Have I given you cause for offense?''

Nervously, Diana glanced away. His eyes still had the ability to send her heart into a rapid flutter, although she had considered herself well past the stage of girlish palpitations. His presence made her more nervous than that of any man she knew, which was senseless. Four years could not have made that much difference in the person she had known all her life.

"I've been trying to help Mama. It's been difficult for her. Forgive me if I have neglected you.''

Jonathan winced at this coldly formal speech. "It is I who have neglected you, Diana. I wanted to thank you for what you did earlier. My father and I are much alike in some ways, as you have already thrown up in my face several times. The silence between us would never have been broken without your help.''

"I only did what I've been scolded for time enough again. It always surprises me when I'm not ordered up to my room directly anymore after one of my outbursts." Diana managed a wry smile. Despite the fact that he seemed almost a stranger—an exciting stranger, she was forced to admit—this was Jonathan, and she had never kept anything from Jonathan.

"My father and I tend to keep our grievances to ourselves. You are like a burst of fresh air between us. Perhaps that is why I have always admired you."

The tone of Jonathan's voice made Diana look up quickly, and a touch of rose colored her cheeks as she discovered the warmth in his gaze. She had not remembered it being quite like this before. Just his look and the tone of his voice sent thrills through her center. She feared the moment he tried to touch her. He would know her heart then, and she would never be able to look him in the face again. If he did not want her for wife, they could still remain friends if she did not let him see how he affected her. She must remain steadfast in her resistance.

"I daresay that is why you and Charles are friends. He is as light-headed as I am. Feel free to invite us over whenever you and your father are at loggerheads. We'll bring the twins and turn the house wrong side out. Elizabeth is the only sensible one among us."

Jonathan could feel the distance she kept between them, and resignedly, he said, "It is not likely that my father and I will be sharing the same household any time soon." Changing the subject, he added, "I had supposed you would be married by now and helping your mother bring out Elizabeth. Is there a special suitor waiting for you when your mourning ends?"

Diana solemnly contemplated screaming at him, beating her fists against the starched linen of his broad chest until he awakened, but smiled coolly, instead.

"I've had suitors enough, thank you. As I've told you before, marriage never seemed worth the effort."

She turned to walk away, but gritting his teeth, Jon-

athan halted her with his words. "None of them to
your taste is that it, Janey? All too tame, perhaps?"

Diana swung back around and smiled sweetly. "You
think I've had no offers? There was old man Thomp-
son, I suppose. He was quite wealthy and stuck his
spoon in the wall only a year after he married the
sixteen-year-old who finally consented to be his bride.
I could be a wealthy widow today. Or if you think it
is tameness I dislike, I'll have you know Lord Ashley
asked for my hand just last spring. I suppose he
thought my loose tongue covered a multitude of sins
and we would suit."

"Ashley?" Jonathan's eyebrows shot up to his hair-
line. "The man's a rogue through and through. Whatever was your father thinking to entertain him?"

"Perhaps he was thinking I had enough sense to
know a rake when I see one. Anyway, Ashley's married now, too. I hear his new wife is already expecting
an heir and is currently enjoying her freedom while he
dallies with his latest courtesan. But forgive me, I
should not mention such subjects." Diana's tone grew
more acerbic as she spoke. "I should entertain you
with my other prospects. One is quite the gentleman
and my mother is holding out fond hopes we will make
a match of it. He is unfailingly polite, unlike some
men I know. He has a considerable fortune, I am told.
He is well-favored and quite persistent in his attentions. I am sure any woman would be delighted to be
the object of his affections."

Jonathan tried desperately to fathom the meaning
behind her acid words. He knew Diana well enough
to know she was angry, but he could not quite believe
she was angry with him. There could only be one reason she could be angry at him, and after this listing of
admirers, he could not imagine she was peeved with
his lackluster courtship. She could scarcely have
known he was gone.

"So what is the delay in announcing your nuptials?

Surely you'll not allow such a catch to escape?" His temper was more for himself than for her. It was his own fault that this had come to pass. He could not have expected it be otherwise. Without any prospects, he could scarcely expect her to wait for him.

Diana couldn't continue to take out her bitterness on Jonathan. He had come home from a long, painful war, weary at heart and soul, to be faced by a cold father and little future. It was Christmas, and she could afford to be generous with her love for just a little while, just not enough to let him suspect. She gave him a wry smile offering a truce.

"We have no interests in common. The only topic we have we can discuss together is the weather. Can you imagine saying 'It is raining out today, dear,' and having exhausted all conversation for the remainder of the day?"

Jonathan choked back a laugh of relief. Wickedly, he inquired, "Surely it cannot be so bad as that? After you were married, he would have to bring up a new subject or two, I daresay. What would he say . . ." he hesitated and modified his original thought somewhat, "if he wanted to kiss you?"

Diana understood that tell-tale hesitation. She had not followed at her brother's heels and eavesdropped on his conversations without learning a few things, but Jonathan persisted in being a gentleman. She gave him the reply his question deserved.

"I should imagine he would say, 'It's Saturday night, dear. Shall we?'" Then, not stopping to watch Jonathan's reaction to that conceit, Diana marched off to prepare herself for church. If Jonathan remained here much longer, she would have need of a prayer or two.

She heard his laughter behind her and smiled. It was good to have him home. She wouldn't wish him to leave too quickly, despite everything.

They came in from the quiet, dark snow, the sounds of the joyous choir still ringing in their ears, greetings of "Merry Christmas" still on their tongues, smiles on their faces. Despite his bandaged hand, Jonathan gallantly removed Diana's pelisse as the others removed theirs. The foyer filled with coats and scarves and stamping feet as they tried to shake the chill from their bones.

The yule log had been left to burn merrily, and they naturally gravitated toward the drawing room. Elizabeth and Marie led the way, and their outburst of giggles gave fair warning of mischief ahead. With a worried frown, Mrs. Carrington hastened after them.

Diana glanced suspiciously at Charles's grin, but he shrugged nonchalantly and gestured for her to proceed him. Then he made a point of seeing that Jonathan followed her through the doorway.

Diana gasped as she saw the silver-and-gold-beribboned mistletoe dangling from the center of the kissing bough. It was more elaborate than any attempt her father had ever made and it glistened in the firelight, swaying teasingly with the draft from the hall. Marie placed herself beneath it, studiously contemplating its brilliance with an innocent air.

Elizabeth looked at Diana, then glanced furtively at the man behind her. Jonathan was admiring the bauble without expression, but he did not appear eager to sample the forbidden pleasures offered under the protective auspices of the garland as she had hoped. Charles, to everyone's surprise, quickly took advantage of the poised beauty beneath the berried leaves. Skirting around Diana and Jonathan, he quickly caught Marie's hand and lifted it to his lips.

The loud cough behind them reminded Diana of why her usually reckless brother had limited himself to such circumspect behavior. Gently taking Jonathan's arm so as to include him in the conversation, she turned to Mr. and Mrs. Drummond as they entered.

"It appears Father Christmas or some mischievous

elves arrived while we were out. I do not remember
half so many gifts hanging among the garlands when
we left.''

The frown on Mr. Drummond's face faded as he
noted Charles properly escorting Marie from her improper position. However, the sight of his son dutifully keeping Diana from the compromising mistletoe
brought an irritated tic to the corner of his mouth.
Why this should be so, he could not fathom, and he
attempted some measure of humor.

''Well, let us investigate, shall we?'' He nodded to
where Charles was already reaching up among the
branches to bring down a package addressed to his
mother.

''I concur.'' With some formality but a trace of a
smile playing along his lips, Jonathan steered Diana
toward the garlands where Charles had already begun
to reach for a package addressed to Marie. It was
Christmas, and he intended to reward himself with the
gift of knowledge, even if knowing the answer hurt
more than the shrapnel in his leg.

Diana knew her brother had only followed the custom set by their father of tying tiny surprise packages
to the greenery, but she could not help a slight flutter
of anticipation as Jonathan purposely guided her toward the low-hanging branch where he and Freddie
had snitched the apples. The Drummond family had
been with them enough Christmases to join in the game
also, but it could scarcely be expected that Jonathan
would have had time to purchase any gifts.

Still, while everyone else was merrily tearing into
their surprises, Jonathan reached among the evergreens and pulled out a poorly wrapped and oddly
shaped parcel addressed to Diana. His expression as
he handed it to her was guarded.

''I have no roses as a reminder, and I'm not at all
certain that my gift is appropriate any longer, but if it
still lies where I left it four years ago, I would like

you to have it anyway. If it has already been found and discarded then I understand that, too. I only want all your Christmases to be happy ones.''

Jonathan's words were spoken so low none could hear except Diana, but the blush rising to her cheeks revealed enough to those who cared to observe. As Diana tore open her package, Charles distracted the others by discovering more surprises hidden in the evergreens, and the contents of his sister's package went unnoticed by all but the giver and receiver.

Diana held the key in the palm of her hand and stared up into Jonathan's dark face, desperately striving to keep the hope welling up inside her from showing. ''The attic key? However did you . . .'' Then noting the tension behind his stiff stance, she continued hurriedly, ''Shall we try it? Do you think anyone will come look for us if we do?''

''We shall be home free before they find us.'' Using the words of the child's game they had once played, Jonathan caught her elbow and escorted her hurriedly from the room.

Although their departure was noted, none interfered. Even Mr. Drummond kept his opinion to himself. It was Christmas, and the joy of this day needed to be shared, if only for a little while. The consequences of their yesterdays would be acted upon on the morrow. Even consequences have holidays.

With relief, Jonathan saw Diana needed no explanations of the palty gift hidden in the evergreens for her. He had not come prepared for the welcome he had found here, and the only fitting gift he knew either rested somewhere in the attic above or had already been rejected. He had taken his chances when he clumsily wrapped that key with one hand. Now his heart rested in his throat as Diana unerringly turned up the attic stairway.

He carried only the lamp from the bottom of the stairs, and it threw incongruous shadows over the walls as Diana bent to insert the key in the door. With the sudden anticipation of two children about to engage in mischief, they kept their voices to whispers as they rattled the lock.

"I feel like the twins must whenever they're about something they shouldn't be." The latch clicked and Diana gingerly pushed against the door.

"That's because you were always forbidden to hide up here and you always did, anyway," Jonathan reminded her. "I'm surprised the two of them aren't on our heels or in the midst of the company below. Their nanny must have given them laudanum."

Diana giggled. "At the very least. Ugh. I've just walked into a spider web. Shouldn't we have saved this expedition for All Hallow's Eve?"

"No." Jonathan's reply was almost curt as he lifted the lamp and led the way to keep her from encountering any more unpleasant surprises. "It has waited too long as it is."

Diana sent him a searching glance, but in the shadows from the lamp she could scarcely discern his face and certainly not his thoughts. He had changed his coat and cravat to attend services, and the elegant figure he cut in the dusty shadows of the attic brought a smile to her lips. Had she been permitted, she would have blurted out the words "I love you" just because of that anxious frown between his eyes right now. She had never stopped loving him, of course. She couldn't imagine why she had thought she ever would. He was as much a part of her heart and soul as the air she breathed. She didn't know what nonsense had brought him up here in the middle of the night while all else drank punch in the warmth below, but she would have followed him into darkest Africa had he asked.

"There it is." Jonathan pushed an old trunk out of the way so Diana could maneuver her skirts around it with a minimum of damage to the hem on the dust-coated floor. He set the lamp upon the scarred old secretary and turned to take Diana's hand.

"Did you ever once think to open this after I left?" He watched her face quizzically as she stared at the battered remains of their childish hiding place. In the lamplight her eyes glowed with a mysterious softness that sent his heart plunging from his throat to his stomach when she lifted her head to answer him.

"You hadn't been home in months. You ran off to join the cavalry instead of coming home for Christmas. I thought you were gone forever. I put it aside as I did my childish toys." She could have said she had put the desk aside with her childish dreams, that she couldn't bear the heartbreak of seeing that empty chamber and knowing there would never be another message waiting for her again. But she was not so outspoken as to reveal thoughts she had never said to herself. She turned from the intensity of his stare to trace her fingers through the thick dust upon the burnt surface.

"Open it now, Janey, one last time. Please, for me?"

Startled by the urgency of his tone, she sent him a darting glance, then turned to do as told. The charred drawer moved with difficulty, and Jonathan had to help her. But he stood aside as she reached behind the drawer to spring open the secret panel. They had thought themselves so clever when they found that hiding place when she was less than the twins' age. Now it squeaked open with less vigor than before, but two pairs of eyes studied it with the same excitement as then.

Diana's fingers searched the small chamber, quickly discovering the package hidden from sight. Her exclamation of surprise brought a smile of mixed relief and joy to Jonathan's lips. So she had not known it was there. That removed one heavy burden, although it opened the way for further pain. Still, the knowledge that she had not deliberately rejected him all those years ago was all he had asked. And now he had it.

"Come, let us take it below where it is warmer. We can open it there without sneezing."

Diana's fingers closing tightly around the gay ribbons of the package, and she said nothing, only nodding in agreement at his suggestion. She didn't dare hope too much, but her fingers trembled as she felt Jonathan take her arm. She didn't want to leave the darkness. She wanted to stay here with Jonathan's hand at her back, his long frame close to hers, pretending this was their world and the problems below did not exist.

But she followed him obediently, closing the attic door and locking it without conscious thought while Jonathan stood patiently behind her. As they descended the stairs the light from the wall sconces illuminated the narrow passage more adequately than the dark attic. She could see the brownness of long fingers closing around hers as he brought her to a halt at the bottom of the stairs, and they took their childhood seats on the stairs.

"I have no right to ask you to open that package any longer. I gave up that right when I left my home against my father's wishes. But for what we once had, I would like you to have it. Open it here, Diana. I would not wish to embarrass you by declaring my feelings in public."

Those words gave her the courage she needed, and Diana raised her gaze to meet his. At the sight of the warmth in those gray eyes, she opened her lips to speak but could find nothing to say. Jonathan touched a gentle finger to her chin to close them.

"Open it, Diana. I cannot say more until you do."

With shaking fingers she ripped the bright wrappings off the oblong box. She was surprised it had fit in the secret compartment, but then, the hiding place must once have been meant for letters. The package

was too thick to be a simple missive, but the right
length for one.

A thick vellum letter fell into Diana'a lap as she
unsealed the package, and from between the pages, a
fragile golden ring fell. Diana made a soft exclamation
of surprise and gently lifted the ring, but before she
could look to Jonathan for explanations, a scream rang
out from below, shattering the fragile bonds of anticipation drawing them together.

"Fire!" That panic-stricken cry destroyed any further thought. Even so, Diana carefully continued to
clutch her treasures when Jonathan helped her to her
feet. They both ran down the corridor toward the front
stairs where more cries and shouts echoed upward.
Diana's heart took on a frantic beat as she smelled the
smoke. Fire in the old wood and heavy draperies of
the drawing room would spread with terrifying swiftness. If not stopped at once, it could not be stopped
at all.

They entered the large room into a scene of chaos.
The twins, thoroughly chilled from the hiding place
they had taken in the window seats when the company
had returned from church sooner than they expected,
had taken the first opportunity to escape. When everyone wandered into the dining room to sample the fru-
menty Cook had brought in, they had crept from their
frozen seats. But the temptation of the gifts dangling
in the kissing bough had been stronger than the dis-
comfort of the cold or danger of getting caught. While
everyone dined festively in the other room, they had
stacked one chair atop another in an attempt to reach
the elusive garland.

The result confronted Jonathan and Diana as they
dashed into the drawing room. Freddie dangled precariously from the chandelier he had grabbed when
one loop of the garland came undone. The candles that
came tumbling down with the evergreens had ignited
the ribbons wrapped about the garland and the litter

left on the floor from the unwrapping of gifts. Flames now danced across the carpet, fed by the drafts along the floor, while Mr. Drummond and Charles stamped ineffectively at the tiny fires trailing dangerously closer to the older draperies and giving off clouds of smoke. The women milled frantically beneath the dangling child, ignoring the fire perilously close to their long skirts as they tried to bring the terrified boy down before he fell into the flames below.

Frankie, crying, carried the tea pot from the table to douse the flames closest to his brother when Jonathan jumped across the burning debris to grab it from him.

"Go fill the punch bowl with snow!" he yelled at the terrified child. "Charles, the coal scuttle! Anything else you can think of!"

Goudge tottered into the room with a bucket of water from the kitchen and nearly tripped and spilled it before Diana grabbed it from his hands to throw on the largest fire.

Understanding Jonathan's meaning immediately, Charles and Mr. Drummond scooped up the largest containers they could find and dashed outside for snow. Not only was it closer at hand and more abundant than the water from the old plumbing in the distant kitchen, but it would smother the flames more effectively.

Standing in the puddle Diana had created with Goudge's bucket of water, Jonathan reached up to grasp Freddie by his trouser waistband. "Steady on, old fellow. I've got you. Now let go."

With only one hand to grasp him by, Jonathan had to put all his strength in his one good arm as the terrified little boy released his grip on the fragile chandelier. With a shout from the others, he managed to swing Freddie down into the arms of his mother.

By this time, sleepy maids had joined them with all the pots and pans from the kitchen and mounds of snow lay melting all over the drawing room. The stench of burned carpet filled the air, and half of the kissing bough hung bedraggled and scorched to the floor, trailing smoking ribbons and bruised apples. With the flames finally doused, the company slowed their frantic activity to survey the damage.

Jonathan smiled with tired relief as he found Diana still clutching the crumpled letter and presumably the ring, although the objects were now wrapped around the bucket handle along with her hand. Sensing his gaze, she looked up, then blushing, she glanced down again at the mess she had made of his careful missive. She could tell by the look in his eyes what the letter contained, but she wished desperately for time to read the words.

"Good show, Drummond. Now I know how your troops made it through all those battles." Charles wrapped a weary arm around his friend's shoulder and gazed about him. "Now admit it. We never caused this much trouble. The twins have us whipped."

"At least this is the kind of war you can fight in relative comfort." Jonathan shrugged off the praise, his gaze never leaving Diana. She seemed bewildered and alone and he wanted to go to her again, but she had not yet given him the right to do so. His heart ached as she set down the bucket and carefully smoothed his letter between her fingers.

"You are too modest, son." Mr. Drummond stepped into the breach.

The twins' voices could be heard overhead protesting as Mrs. Carrington led them back to the nursery. Mrs. Drummond was on the point of ushering Elizabeth and Marie off to their rooms to remove their wet clothing, yet she hesitated at the proud but embarrassed sound of her husband's voice. Hope rose in her eyes as he approached Jonathan with his hand held out.

"You thought more quickly than any of us. You

would be a valuable asset on the battlefield, or anywhere else you chose to apply your efforts.''

Recognizing this as the only apology he would ever
receive for all those long years of agonizing silence,
Jonathan accepted his father's hand in his undamaged
left one. ''I learned that trick in service, sir. You would
have thought of it soon enough. I thank you for the
kind words, though.''

Smiling, Mrs. Drummond hastened the younger
girls away, but Diana remained behind. It was her future they were deciding with these hesitant overtures
of forgiveness. She had a right to stay. Almost absently, she slipped the lovely ring on her finger while
she listened to the battle of wills.

Jonathan saw her gesture and a wide smile brought
his browned face to life. Instead of the cold, formal
man accepting his father's stilted apology, he became
a boy again, a boy filled with life, laughter, and love.
The change startled everyone in the room but Diana,
who smiled back.

''You will have to forgive me, Father. There is the
matter of an unopened Christmas gift that the excitement interrupted.'' To his father's amazement, he
stepped away from the all-male circle to stand before
Diana. He lifted the hand wearing the ring and met
her smiling eyes with hope. ''You have not read the
letter yet,'' he reminded her.

''I trust it includes some explanation of your abrupt
departure,'' she answered solemnly, a teasing twinkle
in her eye belying her tone.

''That, among other things. I asked your father's
permission before I wrote it, of course.''

''Papa? You spoke to Papa?'' That knowledge
brought tears swiftly to her eyes as she gazed at him
in astonishment.

''His reply is in the letter, Janey. I wrote him from
Oxford. He did not know I intended to leave, but his
letter gave us his blessings. It was one of the happiest

days of my life. I did not know it was to be my last for a long time.''

"I didn't know, Johnny." She lifted her eyes to his and read the love and steadiness there. "He said nothing to me.''

Charles came up behind his sister and grabbed the letter from her hand. "You mean to say there is a letter from my father in here? A kind of posthumous blessing, as it were?''

Instead of being annoyed at the interruption, Jonathan grinned. "Relieving you of the responsibility, old fellow. All I need is the lady's word. Now give it back and go away, if you would be so kind.''

Mr. Drummond harrumphed from where he had been left standing across the room. All heads turned in his direction.

"It seems to me, if you're entertaining ideas of taking a bride, that you will need some prospect of financial security to offer the lady. I know of a promising position if you are willing to take direction from an obstinate old man.''

Jonathan tore his gaze away from the glowing promise in brown eyes long enough to meet his father's look. "I am willing to learn from a man with more experience, sir, if he will have me.''

"He'll have you all right, and with open arms." Embarrassing himself with this display of emotion, Mr. Drummond gestured curtly at Charles. "Come, Carrington. If we harbor any hopes of getting these two off our hands, we'd better turn in. I don't think the carpet will suffer more if it waits until morning.''

Grinning, Charles returned the letter to his sister, bussed her on the cheek, shook Jonathan's hand, and gesturing at the maid and butler hovering in the doorway, dismissed everyone but the lovers from the room. Quite pleased with himself, he grabbed up the bottle of brandy and guided his distinguished guest to the study for one last drink of celebration.

Jonathan and Diana scarcely noticed their departure.

Smiling, Jonathan lifted her fingers to his lips and admired the lovely color in her cheeks. He could not mistake the love he found in those clear, bright eyes, but he would have no mistake this time. Not daring to let himself hope more, he pressed the letter upon her.

"Read it, Diana. I do not think I can stand the suspense any longer."

Nodding, she unfolded the vellum pages carefully. For four years her happiness had been stored away in a secret hiding place. Four years were long enough. She read swiftly, starting with her father's letter to his best friend's son. The words of praise and caution brought tears to her eyes, and by the time she read his approval at the end of the letter, she was openly weeping. Jonathan had not needed this letter to speak his case, but his judgment that Diana would not accept him without her father's approval had been a right one. That it came now, after his death, was an unhappy but fortuitous instance. Her tears blotted the pages as she carefully tucked them away for later perusal.

Jonathan's youthful letter, on the other hand, brimmed with life and hope and dreams. He explained his father's opposition to his only son's desires to serve his country, and his own decision to buy a commission rather than return to the comfortable life of his father's house. Then he spoke of the life and the love he wished them to share if she would wait. The ring was to be her signal that she was prepared to set all others aside in favor of him. He did not expect her to make the decision soon or even quickly, but only to mention her decision to wear the ring when she wrote to Charles.

It was a young man's letter, full of nonsense and dreams, but the man standing before her now waited with the same eagerness and anxiety as the youth who had written it. The scar upon his forehead whitened with concentration as he watched her for some clue of her feelings, and the tension in his taut frame told her of the importance of her reply.

Eyes streaming with tears, Diana lifted the letter bearing Jonathan's loving farewell and kissed it as she would have done had she discovered it four years ago. Then twisting the ring upon her finger, she gazed longingly into his handsome face.

"Four years I waited for this letter. Four years I could have been wearing this ring. Do you think we can make up the lost time somehow?"

"It won't be easy, but I'll try. I love you, Diana. If I promise to find other topics besides the weather, will you marry me?"

A small smile of dazzling delight began to form on her lips. "You have four years of letter writing to catch up on. Do you think you can do it by the time my year of mourning is ended if I tell you now how much I love you and how much I have missed you?"

"I can move mountains and learn to deal with Frankie and Freddie if you'll just show me how much you mean those words." Jonathan moved daringly closer, sliding his arm around her waist as he reached to set the bulky letter aside.

"Jonathan!" Startled by his sudden brash behavior, Diana brought her hands to his chest to hold him off.

He smiled, glanced briefly up to the sparkling ribbons of the mistletoe still dangling among the remaining greenery overhead, and returned the heat of his gaze to her pinkened cheeks. "I caught you under the kissing bough, my love. You can't refuse."

"So I can't." Acknowledging defeat gladly, Diana slid her arms about Jonathan's neck and felt the warm pressure of his lips against hers and melted into the strong embrace she had only been allowed to dream of for so many years.

In the hallway, peering through the crack between the doors, two young girls giggled with delight at the sight of their brother and sister embracing beneath the mistletoe.

Caught up in the romance of the moment, they failed to note the shadow sneaking up from behind, dangling a piece of greenery, until the branch hung over their heads. A whispered "Surprise!" caused them to glance in tandem at the mistletoe, and squealing, they bolted wildly for the stairs.

Elizabeth's protesting cry of "Charles!" as she ran up the stairs made no impact on the pair in the drawing room. While the others raced madly through the upper halls, the happy couple laid more sedate plans for the future, all of them spoken through the magic of kisses, with the permission of the kissing bough above.

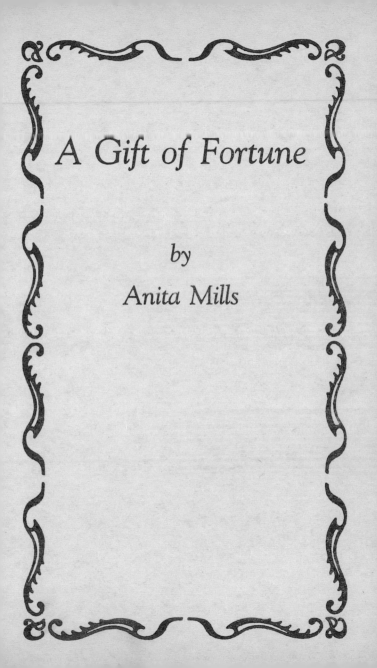

A Gift of Fortune

by

Anita Mills

The heavier snow did not augur well for any of them. The three women in the mail coach bound for York stared uneasily out into the blinding snow, each anxious to be home before Christmas. For Susannah Byrnes, it was more than a hope—it was an imperative, for the young widow had already expended all but a few shillings of her meager resources to book passage for herself, her small daughter, and her late husband's great-aunt at the very dear sum of six guineas apiece. That, coupled with the added cost of lodging and meals along the way, had left her proverbial pockets to let, and it was by no means certain they'd reach York ere nightfall.

Across from her, Aunt Letty kept her face fixed determinedly on the window, ignoring the rather garishly dressed young woman beside her. "Molly Hill, as she calls herself, is not the sort of female whose acquaintance one ought to encourage," she'd sniffed at the first stop outside London. " 'Tis as plain as a pikestaff what *she* is, and I cannot like our being thrown into company with her! I cannot think what the mails are about, letting a female of that stamp among decent women!" It had been almost comical to hear her say it, her indignation making her shake with such feeling that the feathers on her huge hat bobbed.

But Susannah felt a certain sympathy for the rouged

and painted female, suspecting that beneath the over-dressing and the excessive artifice the poor girl was as vulnerable as she herself. Despite the silk dress, the fur-trimmed pelisse, and the satin ribbons that trailed from a hat that rivaled Letty's, Molly betrayed a wistfulness that was not lost on Susannah. But she had to admit that Molly also exhibited a disconcerting familiarity with every man they encountered from the lowest ostler to the gentlemen travelers at each and every inn.

A gust of wind buffeted the coach, swaying it from side to side. Susannah carefully wiped the fogged window beside her with her handkerchief to peer again into the swirling storm, hoping the driver and coacheys could see better than she could. They must be frozen to their seats, she reflected soberly, and she did not see how they stood it.

Even as she thought of them, the coach slowed further, sending her already low spirits plummeting deeper. Despite the advertisements that promised ''ten miles per hour'' or better, she doubted they were going one third that. Hampered by fog in Northampton, rain and sleet out of Leicester and Nottingham, and the blinding snow since Sheffield, they were already running eleven hours late. This was one day that no one would set his watch by the *Tallyho*.

They were all tired beyond bearing from being cramped into the passenger compartment the better part of three days, but she had to admit that Katie had made the journey much better than expected. It could not be easy for a five-year-old to sit hours on end with naught but finger games and rhyming exercises to occupy her. She reached down to stroke the silky red-gold hair that spread across her knee. Even in sleep, the child looked so like much Charles. There was no question that she was a Byrnes through and through.

Sweet Katie, accepting what she could not have with good grace, wearing clothes that were little better than

those given for alms, making do for much of the trip
with little more than tea and toast to augment their
one true meal each day, the child seldom whined or
complained. A sense of bitterness stole over Susannah
as she studied her daughter's face. Born Katherine
Elizabeth Mary Byrnes in lawful wedlock, she ought
to have had everything the Byrnes fortune could have
provided, but she'd been ignored by Charles's family
from her birth.

When she got home—if she ever did—Susannah was
going to burn the hateful letter that had sent them all
hurrying to London. The old man had died, his solic-
itor had written, and as mother to one of the heirs,
could she come? She ought to have known better, but
Letty would have it that Charles' father had relented
at last, that he meant to do something for Katie. Poor
Letty, scatterbrained soul that she was, felt terrible
now for having urged the disastrous journey.

The will had not even mentioned the aunt who'd
supported Charles in his runaway marriage, and the
bequest to Katie did not bear thinking. As his final
punishment to them, the old man had left his youngest
granddaughter only two thousand pounds—on condition that she never see her mother again. God forgive
her, but Susannah had actually considered relinquish-
ing her daughter to a better life—until Charles's brother
had referred to Katie as "my brother's misbegotten
brat" in the child's presence. No, they'd starve together before she'd see her flesh and blood raised on
sufferance in his house.

"It ain't right—it ain't—for th' storm to spoil me
homecomin'," Molly Hill complained to the window.
"Not when I was wantin' t' show me mum I'd pros-
pered." Her voice caught and a tear trickled down her
cheek, streaking her reddened cheek. "It ain't right—
me first Christmas with her since I went to Lunnon.
Been ten years since I been home."

Impulsively, Susannah leaned over her sleeping

daughter to touch the woman's arm. "Your mother will be glad enough to see you whenever you are come, I am certain of it."

Molly looked up suspiciously, then seeing only kindness in Susannah's face, she managed a watery smile. " 'Tis a real lady you are, Mrs. Byrnes, to say that." She looked down to where Susannah's hand lay against the bright, almost gaudy silk of her own dress, and saw the worn fabric of Susannah's cloak. "Guess it ain't clothes that make the Quality. Aye—Mum's got to want to see her girl, ain't she?"

"Whenever you get there."

The girl turned away as she sat back. "Thing is—she thinks 'tis a lady's maid I've been being."

Despite Letty's thoroughly disapproving frown, Susannah shook her head. "She'll still be glad to see you."

"I don't know, but it ain't as like I was coming home without a full purse, you know," Molly mused half to herself. Then her chin jutted upward almost defiantly. "But I mean to be respectable—get meself a husband maybe—and a babe of me own to be christened in church. I-I ain't giving it away neither." Her reddened eyes traveled to the sleeping child. " 'Tis blessed you are, Mrs. Byrnes."

Before the woman's words were out of her mouth, the carriage slid suddenly sideways, throwing them about, and despite the shouts of the driver to the frightened horses, the coach went into the ditch. The axle, when it broke, sounded like a shot. They teetered, then fell over, coming to rest on the door.

Awakened by the wreck, Katie screamed in terror, then buried her head in Susannah's cloak, clinging to her convulsively. Realizing they'd survived, the women began gingerly disentangling themselves from each other. Above them, peering through the other door, one of the coacheys called down, "Yer all right, missus? Lor' lummee, but we tupped 'er o'er right quick.

But me'n Will's goin' ter pull yer out, so don't be a-frettin' yersels.''

"My poor hat—'tis ruined!" Letty wailed, pulling it out from beneath her. "And I shall never have another like it—I know it!" Tears welled in her faded eyes as she inspected her crushed bonnet. " 'Tis my vanity, I know, but—"

"Ohhhhhhh," Molly groaned, rubbing her hip where she'd hit it against the side of the coach. "At least it ain't me head. And if you'd cease the blubberin' on your bib, you could have mine," she told the old woman. "It ain't hurt none, and I can get me another."

Affronted, Letty lapsed into an aggrieved silence, pretending she had not heard the offer. But Molly would not leave it at that. She held up her own overwhelming bonnet. "See—ain't a louse on it."

Katie, who'd realized they were in no danger, peeped out from her mother's skirts. "I think it beautiful, Aunt Letty, but if you do not want it—"

Thankfully, the coacheys pried the door open just then, and reached hands to the little girl, and the women forgot about the hat. It was a precarious escape through the door above them, but they managed to climb out, sliding to the safety of the ground. Mr. Sims, the driver, bemoaned the lack of a blanket for the little girl, who blinked against the brightness of the swirling snow. Apologizing all the while, the poor man chafed cold hands and stomped to warm himself.

"Fourteen year on th' road, mum, and naught a spill ere now," he told them. "But not to worrit, mum, fer Jem's gone fer help. It ain't the post house, but there be the Red Stag up ahead 'bout a mile or so, I'd 'spect.''

Behind her, she heard one of the coacheys ask Molly Hill if she were injured. "Just me arse," the woman replied. As Susannah turned around, the fellow flashed

Molly a knowing grin. "Put yer out o' yer business, did it?"

"Moll's pensioned herself off, anyways," was her retort. "And don't you be a-standin' there like a sap-skull when there's females as is gettin' cold—else I mean to complain about the service, you hear?"

The grin faded as the coachey shook his head. "Couldn't make th' time in th' snow, but it ain't lost yet. Jem'll come back wi' a cart mebbe t' take yer t' th' Stag, and termorrit's mail'll take yer up ter York, I'll be bound."

"Tomorrow!" Molly fairly howled. "Nay—ye'll take us today! Me mum's a-waiting for me!" She appealed to Susannah. "Tell him—tell him we got to get to York ere Christmas, Mrs. Byrnes."

"Mama, I'm so hungry," Katie complained, shivering against her. "I cannot wait to supper."

"I know, dearest," Susannah soothed her helplessly. A despair greater than any she remembered since the word came of Charles's death had come nearly four years earlier washed over her. She and Katie and poor Letty were stranded at the side of the road without so much as the cost of a good meal left between them. And she did not have to be prescient to know that no one was going to get to York this day.

"Oh, dear," the elderly lady fretted beside her, "what now, my love? Oh, I should never have wished to come, and how I know it. We cannot—"

"No, we cannot," Susannah cut in tiredly as she hugged her daughter more tightly. "And I am afraid that in this instance, we shall have to rely on the Almighty. My own resources are, alas, at an end."

"You've had quite enough, don't you think?"

Before the disheveled young man knew what he meant to do, Justin Marshfield reached across the seat to wrest the silver-chased flask from his hands. "I say, but—" His befuddled protest was lost in the howl of the wind as the door opened a crack and the bottle disappeared into the storm that buffeted the elegant carriage. He blinked in disbelief, then his face screwed itself into the pucker of a thwarted child.

"Why'd you do that? Itsh not right . . ." But there was such disgust in the other man's face that he paused, finishing defensively with, "Jush swanted to chase the—the cold, thash all. You ain't my keeper, you know."

"You are utterly foxed, Bevis." His cousin enunciated the words distinctly, coldly. "And I'll not have you shoot the cat in my equippage, thank you."

"On the hoity-toity, ain't you? Who ashed you to take Bev-Bevis Thorndike up, anyway? You got no right to in-interfere, Jushtin—no right a-tall!"

It was an argument they'd had ever since Bevis had awakened from an earlier stupor to discover himself bundled off for York. For a moment, the marquess considered repeating an earlier answer, but it would have fallen on deaf ears. Instead, he turned his attention to the storm outside. By the looks of it, they'd not much more than reach Leeds for the night.

But Bevis, angered by the loss of his brandy, persisted. "You ain't nothing but a cold, queer fish, Jushtin. You got no right—"

"Cut line, coz!" Fed up, Justin leaned forward again, so close that his dark eyes swam before his young cousin. "Must I remind you again that the cent per cents can be deuced nasty when you cannot pay? And as titular head of this family, 'tis to me they all seem to apply."

"They'd a-waited—got expes-exspectashuns," Bevis mumbled, dropping his gaze to avoid the censure in those almost black eyes. "Besides, it ain't—"

"None of my affair?" Justin finished with deceptive softness. "Believe me, if it weren't for your mother, I should have washed my hands of you years ago instead of playing nursemaid to a sot at Christmas."

Bevis glared briefly, then lapsed into a sullen silence as his cousin settled back against the luxurious wine velvet squabs. It *was* none of Justin's affair, he repeated silently. He wasn't a green 'un just come to London from the country—he knew what he was about. His losses had just been a trifle heavy, that was all. And he could not help it if a scheming little adventuress had seen fit to send some rather indiscreet letters to the wealthy Marquess of Lydesdale when he couldn't pay. Dame Fortune had been deuced clutch-fisted at the tables, but his luck would turn.

"It ain't like you never been dished up yourself neither," he muttered under his breath.

Justin pushed his beaver hat forward until it tilted over his dark locks and shaded his face from the blinding whiteness of the snow. In no mood to reason with the young fool, he closed his eyes and feigned the sleep that had eluded him much of the way. What good did it do to try to impart the wisdom of one's own experience anyway? "Dished up" was scarce the way to phrase what he'd been through nearly nine years before.

"Ash I recall the story—"

"Even you are not so foxed that you would wish to rake old coals," Justin interrupted softly. "As you have so often remarked, I have a devilish temper, Bev. I should not try me today."

The young man blenched visibly and lapsed again into silence, turning to stare at the swirling snow. "I could have come about," he said finally.

"No."

"M'mother ain't goin' to be plea-pleashunt," he grumbled. "Don't see why she asht you to interfere."

"As your trustee, I expect she considered me her best ally in the matter," Justin answered dryly. "She hoped I could be depended on to buy you out again."

"Wouldn't hurt you—rich as Croesus, ain't you?"

"I don't like to spend my gold on scheming females, Bev. Having paid for my own follies, I see no reason to pay for yours."

At the thought of his homecoming, Bevis turned his face into the velvet-covered seat and pulled his cloak up over his head for warmth, wishing for all the world that he still had his flask. But it did no good to appeal further to Lydesdale—the fellow *was* a cold one, so cold it was difficult to imagine half the stories told of him.

From beneath lowered lids, Justin watched him, feeling suddenly rather old for his thirty-one years. Poor Bevis. He was not without sympathy for him, no matter what the young fool seemed to think. And he meant to try reason again, after his cousin had had time to recover from the effects of overindulgence. He'd have a better time of it then, he expected, for despite his resentment now, a sober Bevis was usually the best of fellows, more often than not full of good intentions. It was drink that made him foolish, drink that made him a bellicose boor. He just needed to face the fact that what he regarded as his salad days was more like to be his ruin if he failed to mend his ways. Justin knew—he'd had to live with his own terrible mistake, unable to escape the consequences of what he himself had done, and his lesson had been a bitter one.

As his cousin began to snore, Justin gave a harsh, self-deprecating little laugh. Aye, in his own way, he'd been a greater fool than Bevis even, and there would be those to laugh at his attempt to save the young man. There would be those who would say it was like the damned redeeming the doomed. And with that lowering thought, he wondered if he ought to have refused his aunt's plea out of hand.

Without warning, his driver reined in sharply, and for a moment, it appeared as though the carriage would skid into the ditch. It slid briefly, fishtailing around, then came to a halt on the road. Bevis went to the floor like an eel slipping from the fish counter, without rousing.

"What the devil?"

One of the two coachmen jumped down from the box and thrust his head through the door. Ruddy-faced from the cold, he announced breathlessly, "Trouble on the road, my lord—I'm to tell you there's a mail coach in the ditch."

"Can we pass it?"

"Aye, but—"

"We are late, Mr. Tompkins!" Justin snapped irritably. "And I've not slept for two days."

"Aye, but there's passengers in the roadway, my lord—there's females and a little 'un."

He started to tell his coachman that it was no concern of his, but then he saw them. Mother and child were huddled together, shivering in the cold, and next to them was an old woman who looked terribly frail. His eyes took in the shabbiness of their clothes, marking them for perhaps a family of workers returning to Leeds. He glanced from them to Molly Hill and his face hardened. A doxy by the looks of her, and probably a cheap one at that. But it didn't matter—he couldn't leave anyone there to freeze even if he wished to do so. He leaned down to pull the carriage rug from behind Bevis, then jumped down to approach them, telling Tompkins in an undervoice as he passed, "See if you can get Mr. Thorndike back onto the seat, will you? By the looks of it, we are going to be crowded up."

"The Lord provides," Letty told Susannah as he stepped down. Her eyes widened when she noted the crested door panel of his maroon and black lacquered carriage. "Oh, my."

"Gor!" Molly gasped. "We are found by a real swell, ain't we?"

He stopped in front of Susannah. Kneeling to provide warmth to Katie, she'd not noticed anything more than the fact that someone had come to aid them. But when she looked up, he was standing over her, holding out the patterned carriage rug, looking as though he'd descended through the malestrom of whirling snow like a Greek god come down from Olympus.

"I am rather pressed," he told her abruptly, "but if you will bundle the child into my carriage, I can take all of you as far as the first inn."

Two thoughts crossed Susannah's mind almost simultaneously—that he was incredibly handsome and that she must seem a veritable dowd. His black eyes were impersonal, his manner brusque, but he was nonetheless salvation from the cold. She nodded. "Our thanks, sir."

"Lydesdale."

Recognition dawned instantly, followed by a barely concealed curiosity. It had been some years now since she'd heard of him, but she could still recall the scandal. Letty's sharp intake of breath told her that Charles's great-aunt remembered also. She stepped lightly on the old woman's foot in warning.

"Gor!" Molly repeated again. "Lydesdale! Wait until I tell me mum that!"

"The snow's deep, madam, and there's ice beneath it—can you carry the child?"

"Yes." She hoisted Katie up on her hip as he clumsily threw the blanket over her. She stumbled slightly as she sank nearly a foot into a snowdrift. He muttered something and reached for the little girl. "No—we are all right, my lord," she protested.

"Tompkins!"

"Aye, my lord?"

"Get the other two. As for you, infant, let go of your mother that she may walk," he told Katie. Her blue eyes appeared enormous as she considered him, then much to Susannah's surprise, she leaned toward him. It was Susannah who viewed him skeptically. "I have never been known to molest the infantry," he assured her tersely. He shouldered the child easily, waiting until she got a good grip on one of the capes of his greatcoat, then he offered Susannah his hand. "Just hang on to me if you cannot see."

His grip was firm and oddly reassuring despite the coldness of his manner. And when she slipped in the icy carriage rut, he steadied her with fingers that felt as strong as iron.

Bevis Thorndike roused long enough to cast a reproachful look as he was squeezed against the side, then lapsed again into a stupor. Molly elbowed herself a place and then invited Letty to sit beside her, noting, "If Mrs. Byrnes holds the tyke, there's enough room for her on the other side, don't ye know? Lud, ain't it grand?" she asked rhetorically, looking around her at the maroon velvet, the gleaming mahogany, and the polished brass fittings.

Katie, handed up to Susannah, sat on her lap. "Will we get to eat soon, Mama?"

"I don't know, love."

"But I'm *famished,* Mama," she complained again, "truly I am."

Lydesdale heaved himself into the seat beside them. "I'd make you known to Bevis Thorndike, but he's not feeling quite the thing," he offered in explanation as Letty eyed his cousin curiously.

Molly, thinking he wanted an introduction, smiled archly. "Molly Hill—goin' to spend Christmas in York with me mum, your honor."

Startled, but not to be outdone, Letty blinked, then held out her thin, veined hand. "Letitia Byrnes—Miss Byrnes of the Byrnes of Haverhill." Then, self-conscious beneath the surprised lift of his eyebrow, she looked down at her worn pelisse. "Not that we enjoy much discourse anymore, of course, but—"

"I doubt his lordship is concerned with us beyond the next inn," Susannah cut in quickly, afraid that Letty meant to embark on a lengthy explanation. Realizing how impolite this must sound, she turned to the man beside her. "I am Susannah Byrnes, sir, and you have met my daughter, Katherine, who much prefers to be addressed as Katie."

"Katie."

The child gazed back, then scooted closer to her mother, suddenly shy. Where the carriage rug didn't cover her head, he could see she had bright, pretty hair, and despite the much-worn clothing he'd noted earlier, she lacked the pale, pinched appearance of the poor. Her cornflower blue eyes betrayed a hint of mischief, teasing from the safety of her mother's side. She was going to be a beauty and a baggage, if he could mark one.

They'd surprised him, but not enough to make him wonder more than momentarily how a Byrnes of Haverhill found herself in such straightened circumstances. It was immaterial anyway—an hour hence he could forget he'd met them. He settled back into a corner and moved his hat forward to cover the upper half of his face, discouraging any attempts at further conversation, leaving them to wonder at his singular lack of address.

It didn't matter to Susannah—she had enough to worry about as she contemplated what she could tell the innkeeper. If she had to offer to cook the meal herself, she meant to see her daughter fed.

Due to the deep snow that blanketed the thick layer of ice on the road, progress had been slow, and it had taken the elegant equippage nearly an hour to traverse the single mile, straining Lydesdale's temper even further. By the looks of it, none of them would be pressing on even as far as Leeds that day. The Red Stag appeared deserted when they arrived, but persistent pounding by the marquess's coachman finally brought forth a reluctant innkeeper and his wife.

" 'Tis closed we are,'' she insisted. "Sent home the maids for Christmas e'en.''

"There's been no travelers last night or t'day,'' her husband explained. "No sense payin' fer what ain't needed.''

"Th' road's impassable,'' the coachey protested, "and my lord's in need of a bed.''

"Ye'll have t' go t' Leeds.''

Justin moved forward, frowning. "I am Lydesdale, and I shall require beds for myself, Mr. Thorndike, my driver, and two coachmen.'' He half-turned to indicate the women who were stepping down from his carriage. "And also you behold four females taken up from the wreck of the *Tallyho* also, one of whom is but a small child. They are cold and exhausted. I refuse to travel one furlong further packed into my coach like ants in a hill.''

"The mail coach's down?'' the innkeeper asked, momentarily diverted. Then he shook his head. " 'Tis sorry I am, your lordship, but we ain't ready fer custom t'day.''

But his wife pulled him back, hissing loud enough for all to hear, " 'Tis Lydesdale, Bennett, me fool— he'll pay a pretty penny, I'll warrant! Ye can send t' th' village on foot fer Meg t' cook.''

"Promised 'er Christmas t' home just this mornin',' '' he reminded her.

"Aye, but ye can tell 'er ye'll pay double fer th' day.'' When he did not appear convinced, she tugged at his sleeve. "Bennett, 'tis Lydesdale,'' she repeated as though he were a simpleton.

"Aye,'' he nodded grudgingly. "And it ain't as we was goin' anywheres, I s'pose.''

When they turned back to Justin, the woman was smiling that obsequious simper reserved for the very rich. " 'Tis fortunate ye are, milord, for we'll have th' pots goin' in a trice.''

"Thank you.'' He sighed, knowing full well he was

about to be royally robbed for the privilege of staying at an inn he should not think of patronizing on another day. "Tompkins, assist Miss Byrnes and the others, will you?"

Once inside, he surveyed the taproom and the small parlor, wondering if perhaps he ought not to have tried for Leeds anyway. The place was cramped and dingy, the furniture left over from another, distant time, and everywhere there was an air of decay. Mrs. Bennett followed his critical gaze apologizing, "It ain't what yer lordship's used to, I'll grant ye, but since th' road's been improved, most of 'em goes to Leeds, ye know."

"How much?"

"Fer ye and t'other gentleman?" She eyed him shrewdly, then smiled again. "Pound apiece, I'd say— and th' same fer th' meals. Yer coacheys can share a bed fer ten shillings," she offered quickly as his eyebrow lifted. "Aye—and porridge fer 'em at a shilling a bowl."

Had the accommodations been more attractive, he wouldn't have minded the price, but the woman's attitude rankled. "I trust the sheets are clean," he muttered tersely.

"Aye."

"Very well."

"And th' females as is with yer lordship?"

"You'll have to ask them."

Susannah, who'd heard the extortionate prices, felt her stomach knot. She was about to humiliate herself before the elegant marquess and she knew it. And Katie, who'd been so good for so long, fretted now.

"When can we eat, Mama?"

"Soon, dearest, but you must help Aunt Letty first."

"But I want to eat *now!*" the child wailed. "My tum *hurts*, Mama!"

"I know it does, but you have to look to Letty," Susannah repeated firmly.

Bevis Thorndike, who'd wakened when the cold

snow hit him, leaned heavily between Lydesdale's coachmen. ''Feed th' brat,'' he mumbled thickly. ''Don't want t' listen t' that.''

Mrs. Bennett, noting the shabbiness of Susannah's and Katie's clothing, held out her hand, palm up. ''A pound apiece fer them as gets a bed t' themselves—and I'll be takin' it now.''

''With meals?'' Susannah asked faintly. ''Surely for my daughter . . .''

''Meals is more,'' the woman maintained. ''Unless ye want th' porridge wi' his lordship's men.''

''Mama, I don't want porridge!'' Katie pleaded.

For a moment, Susannah considered asking how much if they slept on the chairs in the taproom, but she knew it was hopeless. ''I have not the money,'' she admitted tiredly. ''But if you will let me assist you, I am not above earning my bread, Mrs. Bennett.'' Her chin came up as Molly Hill's dropped. ''I assure you that I can cook, clean, and empty chamberpots adequately.''

''No!'' Letty cried out. ''Surely . . .'' Her thin hands tugged at the brooch she wore to close her cloak. ''Surely she will take this, and perhaps—''

''I cannot let you, aunt,'' Susannah interrupted her firmly. ''I should prefer to do the work.''

The marquess, who'd turned to tell Tompkins to carry Bevis up the stairs, felt goaded. ''There is no need for enacting me a Cheltenham tragedy, Mrs. Byrnes,'' he snapped. ''Mrs. Bennett, you will add her shot to mine.''

''Ye'll be payin' fer all of 'em, yer lordship?''

''Yes.'' He swung around to face Susannah. '' 'Tis what you hoped for, isn't it?'' he gibed. ''Or are you really such an empty-headed widgeon that you'd drag a child the length of the country without so much as enough to feed her?''

''I . . .'' The color which had drained from her face at Mrs. Bennett's prices, returned tenfold as the blood pounded in her temples. Oh, how she wished for a proper setdown. Instead, she clenched her hands against her cloak. "I think I should prefer to work, sir."

"Nay, but you'll not," Molly Hill spoke up. She produced her bulging reticule and dug into it, pulling out a thick wad of bank notes. "You ought to swing on the nubbin' cheat for robbing us, and well you know it," she told Mrs. Bennett. "Here—for me and them." With a contemptuous look at the marquess, she counted out ten pounds. "And we don't want no porridge neither." Turning to Susannah, she nodded. "You was nice, talking to me in the coach, Mrs. Byrnes. Oh, don't think I don't know that if we was to meet in the general way of things, you'd be expected not to see me, but that don't matter." Her gaze dropped to Katie. "And 'tis Christmas, ain't it? I want the tyke to have a real feast." She reached out to touch the little girl's hair. "Looks like an angel, don't she? Got her own halo and all."

A lump formed in Susannah's throat, threatening her composure. "Thank you, Miss Hill."

"Molly. And it ain't enough to signify—I'm glad for the company, anyways." She backed away from them and looked at the innkeeper's wife. "Don't be standing there like a gapeseed—I want to see me room."

The woman thrust the ten pounds into the pockets she had tied from her waist. "Aye, and supper'll be coming at six."

"Mama . . ."

"But I'll see the child gets cheese and bread when I come down," she conceded. "And Mr. Bennett'll find a little chocolate fer 'er. The rest o' ye'll get hot punch. As fer ye," she addressed Letty, "ye'd best lie down. If ye'll come up wi' me, I'll show ye t' yer chamber too."

"Aunt Letty, take Katie with you, will you? Go on, love—you must help her up," Susannah directed the little girl. The child hesitated, sighing, then trod obediently after the old woman.

Justin waited until they'd disappeared up the stairs. "Mrs. Byrnes—"

"I must thank you for the carriage ride, sir," she cut in coldly, not wanting to hear anything further he might say. "Now, if you will pardon me, I think I shall seek a cup of punch."

"On your high ropes, eh?"

She spun around angrily. "Did I apply to you, my lord? I think I did not! I would not presume to expect an exalted personage such as yourself to be concerned with the likes of us, and certainly—"

"Mrs. Byrnes, 'twas not my intent—"

"It must be quite flattering to be pandered to—to have a name that produces everything you wish," she went on rashly. "The great Marquess of Lydesdale! As I seem to recall, you have no more right to be high in the instep than I have!"

Her words hung between them. For a long moment, he stared at her, then without saying anything further, he walked away, leaving her to stand there. The look in his dark eyes had been almost haunted, and she felt suddenly ashamed of her outburst.

"Wait."

He stopped in the doorway of the taproom, but did not turn around. As angry as she had been, she knew she'd been wrong to bring up the scandal, for if she remembered it right, the fault was not entirely his, and her own sense of justice demanded she apologize.

"I ask your pardon, my lord."

His broad shoulders shrugged beneath his caped greatcoat. "Why should you? You've said nothing that is not the truth, have you?"

"I should not have spoken of what I did not know."

"I am a man grown and do not wound easily, Mrs. Byrnes."

"We all wound if we are mortal, sir." There seemed

to be nothing more to say, so she merely repeated, "I still ask your pardon."

He swung around finally to face her across the open foyer. "I was not that kind either."

"No, but that does not excuse me, I think."

For the first time since he'd taken the mail coach passengers up, he managed a rueful smile. "On the contrary, Mrs. Byrnes, I think we are even. But no doubt we are both disappointed to be here at all. I daresay that you and your daughter must regret missing Christmas with your husband."

"My husband is dead, my lord."

It was as though he could see the sadness that passed over her face. "I am sorry."

"Thank you." She started for the taproom also, then thought perhaps he would think she meant to push the acquaintance. "Until supper, sir."

He noted her hesitation and stood back from the doorway. "I thought 'twas your intent to warm yourself with some of the punch."

"That was . . ."

"Before I decided to have some also? Mrs. Byrnes, you must not let your dislike of me keep you from sharing the taproom with me."

"Oh, no, but . . ."

9"If you like, I shall sit across the room." His dark eyes seemed almost black. "Despite what you may or may not have heard of me, I don't molest widows either."

"Punch's ready, your lordship!" the innkeeper called out. "Made hot to warm the blood!"

"After you, Mrs. Byrnes—I don't know about you, of course, but my blood could stand warming." His eyes still on her, he removed the greatcoat, handing it to one of his coachmen. "Tompkins, take Mrs. Byrnes' cloak, will you?"

"Aye, my lord. I'll put it in th' hall fer ye," the fellow told her. "We got t' see t' th' horses, anyway."

She was terribly conscious of the wrinkled and faded condition of the dress she wore, but there was no help for that. She shrugged out of the woolen cloak, revealing a blue gown that had been cut down with each successive fashion until it was about as plain a garment as she'd seen. His eyes traveled over her briefly, making her feel as plain as the dress.

It was obvious to him that she practiced the most shocking economies. For having been wed to a Byrnes of Haverhill, she did not appear to have shared in any of the wealth. But despite the awful dress, she was more than passably pretty.

"Yer punch, yer lordship." Bennett carried the steaming cup to him.

" 'Twould seem a shame to stare across the room at one another, don't you think?" Lydesdale asked her. Before she could answer, he'd turned back to the innkeeper. "I believe Mrs. Byrnes wishes one also."

"Aye, my lord."

As soon as she was given her cup, the marquess nodded toward a small table. "I should prefer to sit, but custom dictates that you must go first, madam—unless you cannot bear company." Not waiting for her to demur, he steered her by the elbow to the table. Taking the seat opposite her, he leaned back almost lazily against the wall and took the first sip of the wine punch. "How old is the child?" he asked conversationally.

"Five."

"You do not look old enough to be her mother, you know."

"I am six and twenty, my lord," she answered simply. "And well past the bloom of youth."

"Remarkably preserved, I should say then. She doesn't favor you much, does she?"

"No—she looks much as Charles did."

"You only have the one?"

She hesitated, thinking it highly improper to discuss

her life with a man she'd just encountered, but she
supposed he was just attempting conversation. "No—
yes—that is, she had a brother," she answered quietly.
"He succumbed to a fever while we were in Spain.
He would have been seven now." She'd looked away
toward the fire, affording him a fine view of her profile.

Aside from a slightly long nose, she would have
been beautiful. Her hair, a light, almost golden brown,
was pulled back from her face into a coiled braid at
her neck, but where tendrils escaped, they curled,
softening the severity of the style. But it was her hazel
eyes, more green than brown or blue, that intrigued
him. They made him forget the faded gown.

"Was it the war?"

"What?" As he'd just asked about the child, she
was momentarily at a loss. "You mean Charles?"

"Your husband."

She nodded. "It was Salamanca—he fell in the first
action."

"And you were there?"

"I was there when they brought him in."

"I am sorry."

"I think my greatest regret is that he cannot see
Katie grow," she added slowly, meeting his eyes. "He
would have been quite proud of her, I think."

There was an undefinable something that drew him,
the sadness perhaps, for most of the women he'd met
were far too selfish to waste themselves pining for lost
loves. Her next words jarred him as her chin came up
almost defiantly.

"But we shall survive, of course, whether anyone
expects us to do so or not."

"I'd always heard the Byrneses were rather plump
in the pocket."

"They are, but Charles was not." Not having any
wish to discuss her husband or his family further with

him, she changed the subject quite obviously. "I do hope your friend feels more the thing before supper."

"Bevis is my cousin, Mrs. Byrnes. Unlike one's friends or lovers, one cannot choose one's relatives." He drank deeply of the warm wine. "More's the pity to that."

"What a cynic you are, my lord," she chided.

He appeared to consider the matter. "I suppose I am," he conceded. Draining his cup, he rose abruptly. "Much as I dislike the notion, I'd best see to him. Your servant, Mrs. Byrnes."

What a strange man he was, to be sure, she mused as she watched him go. Tall, dark, broodingly handsome—but then he was Lydesdale, after all. Perhaps it was the old scandal that made him distant—or perhaps it was the fact that she recalled it which merely made him seem that way, she decided fairly as she took a sip of the punch. She'd but met him and already she could see that there was more than one side to the notorious marquess—that he could be quite aloof, disagreeable even, and yet still act honorably. Well, it mattered not a jot what she thought of him, anyway, for he'd be gone on the morrow, she reminded herself. She sighed, supposing she was no better than anyone else when it came to speculating about the rich and infamous. Still, it was as close as she'd ever come to a man who'd killed someone in a duel.

The child was sitting on the steps, playing with a huge, ugly calico cat when he came down. He guessed she'd eaten, for she giggled merrily while she fed the creature leftover bits of her nuncheon. Her red-gold head was bent so that she did not see him.

" 'Tis the mice rather than the cat that gets the cheese, you know."

She looked up then. "He didn't like the bread or chocolate," she offered in explanation. "Do you not think him beautiful?"

The marquis eyed the big calico skeptically, but the little girl's enthusiasm kept him from being brutally truthful. "Actually, I think it probably a female, for I am told the spotted ones are almost always girl cats."

"Oh."

"And Mrs. Bennett probably prefers it to eat mice." Katie rubbed the area between the creature's ears and was rewarded with a resonant purr. "I wish I had one, you know," she admitted wistfully. "I was going to ask Mama if I might get a kitten for Christmas, but Aunt Letty said I must not vex her just now." She sighed as the big cat rolled over playfully and butted its head against her hand. "Cats like me, you see, and I was used to have one before we went to Spain."

Despite her small stature, it was difficult to believe the child was but five, for she spoke so solemnly and her blue eyes were so sober. A child, he was certain, ought to be full of mischief and pranks. He'd meant merely to speak politely and go on, but instead he found himself bending over to scratch the ugly animal's head. It immediately batted at his watch chain, causing the little girl to giggle again.

"He likes you, I think."

"I suspect 'tis a fickle creature."

She studied the cat for a moment, cocking her head until her long, red-gold hair almost touched the floor, and he was struck by what a pretty little girl she was. "No," she decided finally, "I think he knows whom to like."

"If you had this, I doubt it would give me a passing glance. Here . . ." He disengaged the cat's claws from it and removed the fob chain from his vest, holding his watch up so that the bright gold seal bearing the Lydesdale coat of arms dangled at the other end. As the cat leaped and danced beneath the swinging bangle, Justin transferred his watch to Katie's hand. "Now, Miss Katherine, 'tis your turn to tease the creature." He sank down onto the step beside her and moved her arm to keep the chain just out of the cat's reach. "But you must let it win every now and again to be fair. Otherwise, 'twill tire of the game," he advised.

"Do you think my mama would let me have a kitten?" she asked as the calico pounced on the chain. "I told Aunt Letty that I should feed it."

"I am afraid that I do not know your mama well enough to answer that, infant."

"Aunt Letty says 'twould eat too much. And I am not an infant, sir—I am five years old last summer."

"Your pardon, then, but five seems quite young to me."

She nodded. "But then you are very old, I expect."

The corner of his mouth twitched. "Well, I am not quite in my dotage. I should have some years left, I think."

"Are you a catch?"

"I beg your pardon?"

"Aunt Letty says Mama must cease mourning Papa and find herself a catch ere we starve." She pulled the chain up, causing the cat to roll backward off the step, and instantly she was contrite. "Oh!" Very carefully, she bent over to pick the animal up, cradling it against her, nuzzling its head with her cheek. "I should never harm you," she murmured against its fur. "If you were mine, I should call you something pretty rather than Old Patch," she told it. Her eyes met his again. "Well, are you?"

"No."

" 'Tis a pity, for then I shall be in the basket." She sat the cat down carefully and held out the chain to it again. "I dislike Mr. Brandon, you see, but Aunt Letty says there is no help for it, 'cause he's the only man apt to offer for Mama. And he doesn't like me either."

"I should think that a matter for your mama to decide."

She shook her head gravely while continuing to tease

the animal with his chain. "Aunt Letty says she will take him, and I must not throw a spoke in the wheel if he asks her."

"Perhaps she won't, you know."

Her small hands dropped to her faded dress, smoothing it. "No," she decided glumly. "Aunt Letty says fifty pounds a year won't keep the roof over the roost."

" 'Twould seem that Aunt Letty says overmuch to a child," he muttered dryly.

" 'Tis what she says about me," she confided. "She says that Mama ought to teach me to hold my tongue." Her eyes met his again. "But Mama says I have years to learn to be a lady."

"Katie!"

The child gave a guilty start at the sound of the old woman's voice, then she held out his watch chain. "Thank you, sir—I must go. Mama relies on me to care for Aunt Letty, you know."

"Wait!" Before she could rise, he reached out to touch her shoulder. Drawing her hand back, he produced a shiny coin. "Miss Katherine Byrnes," he announced solemnly, "I believe you have grown a golden guinea in your hair."

She stared for a moment, then touched the coin gingerly. "But I . . ." Her other hand crept to her hair as though to see if there might be another. "Are you funning with me, sir?" she asked suspiciously.

"Word of a Marshfield, I am not."

"Is it truly mine?"

"Well, I did not grow it, so I—"

"Katie!"

"Maybe Mama will let me buy food for a kitten," she whispered as Letitia Byrnes came to the top of the stairs. "Good day, sir."

Katie passed a disheveled Bevis Thorndike on the steps as she ran up. He looked from her to his cousin, sneering. "Never thought you was into almsgiving, coz."

Justin shrugged and rose, dusting off his immaculate buff kerseymere pantaloons. " 'Tis Christmas, Bev." He reattached the watch, appearing absorbed in the task.

Bevis, who still nursed a devil of a head, saw the cat and winced. "Egad, but 'tis the ugliest creature I've ever seen."

"Beauty is in the eye of the beholder—or so I am told, Bev."

His cousin shook his head, then regretted it. "Got to have a hair of the dog," he muttered, passing his hand over his face.

"No."

"Dash it, Justin, but you ain't my keeper! Just need a finger to waggle," he added defiantly. "It ain't your affair, is it?" He brushed past him on the stairs.

The marquess dropped his watch back in his pocket and smoothed his vest. "I am not paying for you to fall under the table, Bev."

The other man's chin quivered and his pale eyes swam. For a moment, Justin thought he meant to cry. "You know I ain't got no money, coz," he whined.

"Eat something—I'll pay for that," Justin told him brutally.

When Bevis realized he was serious, he struck out nastily. "Coming it too strong, ain't you? Time was when you was known to tip over the perch yourself, you know! Aye, and now butter don't melt in your mouth—like you wasn't worse'n me! At least I never—"

"Begging your lordship's pardon, but I saw what you did, and 'twas good of you to do it," Molly Hill spoke from the taproom door.

Bevis' eyes traveled over her insolently, lingering between her neck and her waist suggestively. "Thought you said 'twas only three of 'em and the brat—daresay you was wanting to keep this morsel for yourself, coz.''

Lifting her chin higher and ignoring him, Molly continued to address the marquess. ''Been thinking, I have, and it don't look as though we'll be leavin' on the morrow even—seems to me we ought to have Christmas for the tyke, you know, and Mrs. Byrnes ain't got the money.'' When Lydesdale did not immediately rebuff her, she plunged ahead. ''Well, it don't seem right not to do something—and Mrs. Bennett's willing to let us have a celebration here.''

''The doxy's gouging you!'' Bevis snorted in disbelief. ''You ain't going—''

''Oh, I ain't wantin' his money,'' Mollie interrupted him. ''I was just wantin' t' make it seem like Christmas.'' She looked at Bevis Thorndike scornfully. ''I got me own gold, which as I was hearing it is something you cannot say for yourself now, can you?''

''What sort of celebration?'' Lydesdale asked.

''Well . . .'' For once, Molly's gaze dropped and her voice, which was usually rather loud, faded low. ''It don't seem right for me to read it, so's I was thinking mayhap you could read out of the Good Book, you know—about there was no room at the inn like. And then I'd see as the Bennett woman stuffed a goose and fixed a pudding, don't you see?'' She fingered the bright silk of her dress. ''I thought perhaps to give Mrs. Byrnes something for the little girl.''

But Bevis was still digesting the thought of his cousin reading aloud from the Bible. *''What?''* he howled. '' 'Tis Lydesdale, you fool! He ain't churchy a-tall!'' He turned to Justin, snorting. ''Woman's daft, ain't she? Next thing, she'll be saying we ought to put on a demned tableau—and wantin' you to play Joseph to her Mary!''

Lydesdale's expression went cold. '' 'Tis enough, Bev!'' he snapped.

"Oh, I don't mind him, my lord," Molly hastened to assure him. "Been seein' swells like him for years."

"I ought to make you eat porridge," he muttered to Bevis. To Molly, he suggested, "Perhaps you ought to ask Mrs. Byrnes to read. I'm not at all certain I should do the thing right."

"Been to Oxford, ain't you?" she countered. "Tell you what, you think on it, my lord. It ain't until day after tomorrow, anyways."

Mrs. Bennett, emerging from the taproom, saw Molly with the two gentlemen and frowned. "A word with ye, Missus Hill—or whatever 'tis yer be calling yerself," she ordered crisply. Molly reddened slightly, but stepped toward the back of the hall with her. Justin heard the innkeeper's wife hiss, " 'Tis a respectable place me'n Bennett runs, me girl, and don't yer be fergettin' it." Stung, Molly retorted, "I mean t' be as respectable as you, ma'am." Obviously angry, she flounced past them huffily and climbed the stairs with the dignity of a Siddons.

"Yer pardon, yer lordship, but if the doxy's botherin' ye—"

"Not at all."

"But she has 'er gold, ye see, and I'd not be a-turnin' a dog out in this," she continued apologetically until she realized he did not mean to complain. "Aye, well, if she comes too familiar wi' ye, I'll put a bee in her bonnet."

"Lord Lydesdale." He looked up to see Susannah Byrnes coming down the steps toward him, and she was holding something in her hand, frowning. "May I have a private word with you, if you please." She sounded much like one of his old governesses. Bevis gave her a knowing look, much as he'd done to Molly, but she appeared not to note it. "Perhaps the front parlor—I cannot think it occupied, given the lack of custom."

"Of course. Your pardon, Bev, Mrs. Bennett."

He hastened to open the door to the small, shabby parlor for Susannah, and she brushed past him. Her back was as rigid as Molly's had been moments earlier. Without preamble, she held out the guinea he'd given the little girl. "I believe this is yours, sir."

Not wanting Bevis to overhear, he closed the door. "No."

"I will not have Katie accepting money from strangers, Lord Lydesdale, and—" She stopped suddenly. "No? But I thought Katie said . . ."

" 'Tis Christmas, Mrs. Byrnes."

"Then you did give it to her," she accused. "And we cannot keep it."

"Oh, for Lud's sake! You cannot be serious, madam, 'tis but one guinea! I should give ten times that to the lowest tweeny in the house—or to an ostler even!"

"I cannot have her thinking money grows on her head, Lord Lydesdale. While 'tis nothing to you, sir, to Katie a guinea is a significant amount!" She held it out again. "Thank you, my lord, but we cannot keep it."

"No." His jaw worked as he sought to control his temper. "The child has little enough as it is, madam. I meant her to have it for Christmas."

"You do not even know us, sir."

"I don't have to know you to see that the child needs everything, Mrs. Byrnes. She's a taking little thing with a head on her shoulders, you know. She ought to have a governess—and a few of the other things girls have."

She glared at him. "How dare you—how dare you?" she sputtered when she found her voice. "We manage, thank you, without the interference of wealthy lords who think they can tell those not so fortunate how to go on."

"She is a Byrnes of the Byrneses of Haverhill—or so I have been told. Dash it, but where are they? The rest of the Byrneses, I mean?"

"That, sir, is none of your affair!"

"Do they know how the child is kept?" he countered. "Do they know she is dressed worse than my lowest tenant? Do they know you cannot even feed the child?"

She flushed to the roots of her hair. "Yes, but that is not anything to you either, my lord. We are not, after all, your pensioners." Her chin came up and her eyes met his defiantly. "Your guinea, sir." When he still made no move to take it, she reached for his hand and pressed it into his open palm. "Good day, my lord."

His hand closed over hers, holding it. "Don't you think you ought to ask Katie what she would do with it?" he inquired. "Or do you care?"

Her anger faded to self-consciousness as his fingers gripped hers. The accusation in his black eyes made her uncomfortable. "I must ask you to unhand me, my lord," she managed evenly.

Suddenly aware that he'd behaved rather boorishly, he released her and stepped back. She let the gold coin fall to the floor between them. Turning quickly, she started for the door.

"She wants a cat, you know, but the old woman has convinced her 'tis hopeless to ask," he told her.

"A cat?"

"Yes, but it costs too much to feed, or some such rot."

"She never said that—she is far too young to understand such things."

He had the satisfaction of seeing her stop. Walking to face her, he stepped between her and the closed door. "Fifty pounds a year does not keep the roof over the roost, does it?" Her eyes widened as they met his. "You must cease mourning and find yourself a catch— am I right? And Mr. Brandon appears to be your best hope," he added, this time more gently.

"Wherever did you hear that?" she asked faintly.

"Perhaps children understand a great deal more than any of us think."

"Aunt Letty." She sighed, looking down to her clasped hands. "You must not believe everything you have heard, my lord. Apparently Katie has overheard a great deal of nonsense."

It was as though the spirit had faded from her face, leaving it drained, and he was sorry for having told her. " 'Tis Christmas, Mrs. Byrnes, and none of us wants to be in this godforsaken hovel. Come—let us not quarrel while we are here." He walked back and picked up the coin. Straightening up, he held it out to her. "God willing, two days hence we will all have gone to our own homes, but for now, there *is* Christmas coming, you know. 'Tis a holiday for children, or so I have always thought. Take this and let your daughter buy herself something with it." He moved closer, still proffering the guinea. "It made me feel kind to give it to her, Mrs. Byrnes, and lud knows but I am seldom kind."

There was a strange, almost sad appeal in those dark eyes that moved her more than his words. Nodding silently, she took the coin. Her throat hurt as he walked past her.

"Thank you," she choked out in a near whisper. "Sometimes I am so concerned with myself that I forget to think of my daughter."

"Don't take Brandon, ma'am—I have it on the strictest authority that the child dislikes him."

"Mr. Brandon is not your concern," she retorted.

After he left, she stood there, feeling like the veriest fool for quite some time, wondering how she could have failed to note what she and Letty had done to her daughter. Instead of the bright, cheerful five-year-old she should have been, Katie worried too much, and it was their fault.

When she finally left the parlor, Lydesdale was nowhere in sight, but Mr. Thorndike and Molly Hill were still in the foyer. "It don't take much to make 'er happy, sir," Molly was wheedling. "Surely—"

"Don't ask me to do anything for the brat—it ain't mine," he retorted. " 'Course if you was to be a little nicer to me, I might think on the matter." He leaned forward, leering at the swell of Molly's breasts. "What's the matter, you ain't had Quality before?"

" 'Tis a respectable female I mean to be, Mr. Thorndike," the woman told him coldly. "Now if you ain't wantin' to help, I don't mean to talk with you."

"Respectable?" He gave a short, derisive laugh. "Coming it too strong, Moll, old girl." He closed in on her as she leaned away from his strong, stale brandy-breath. "Might as well entertain ourselves and forget the brat."

"Mr. Thorndike, you are disgusting!" Susannah caught at his sleeve as he made a final lunge for Molly. "You may call yourself Quality, sir, but you certainly cannot call yourself a gentleman."

The other woman bobbed beneath his arm and slipped by Susannah. "My thanks, Mrs. Byrnes—his kind don't know the meaning of no."

"What a reformer you would make, Mrs. Byrnes."

Both women looked up guiltily at the sardonic inflection of the marquess's voice. He stood in the taproom doorway holding a glass of wine, and for a moment Susannah thought he meant to amuse himself at her expense.

"You heard—and you did nothing?" she demanded indignantly.

"I rather thought you tended the matter admirably. But," he added, a faint smile quirking the corners of his mouth, "I feel it incumbent to tell you that Bevis Thorndike is considered a catch." The smile broadened, reaching his nearly black eyes. "Ah, yes— Cousin Bev will be a wealthy, wealthy young man when he reaches his twenty-fifth year, providing, of course, that I don't throttle him first."

Goaded, she could think of nothing suitable to say, and incredibly she heard herself answer, "Really? Perhaps then I was mistaken in his character. Rich men, I am told, must be forgiven these little lapses in behavior. But then, being a rich marquess, I expect you already know that, do you not?"

"Mama?" came a small, quavery voice from above. "Did he tell you he found it?"

Despite the fact that she thought she detected a gleam of triumph in those dark eyes, Susannah looked upward and nodded. "Ah—yes, as a matter of fact, he did, and I can see I was quite mistaken, dearest." She began climbing the steps, the coin clutched in her hand. "And since 'tis a *magical* guinea, Katherine Elizabeth Mary Byrnes, 'tis all yours. You may spend it as you see fit."

"Damn!" Justin muttered succinctly.

The rest of the party was already at supper when he entered the room, and by the looks of it, Bevis had managed to wheedle a bottle from somewhere. It did not take his cousin's practiced eye more than one look to discover that he was already more than half-foxed. Unlike earlier, when he was coming off a rather nasty drunk, Bevis was still in passably pleasant spirits. Justin sincerely hoped he remained that way, but had little hope of it.

Everyone had managed a change of clothing, but he could not say that it was an improvement for the Byrneses. He moved to the end of the table to take a seat opposite Susannah. She looked up briefly, then returned her attention to the table service before her, rubbing at a spot on her knife with her napkin. It took no great powers of perception to tell that she was quite subdued. Beside her, Letitia Byrnes chattered incessantly, not noting that no one paid much attention.

"Lud, but 'tis Lydesdale. Susannah, 'tis Lydesdale. Katie, you must not lean over the table, my love. Dear

Mr. Thorndike, but I vow I thought the snow should have ended by now, did you not also? Mr. Bennett says he's not witnessed such a storm in forty years—there has not been a carriage past since we arrived, you know.''

"Aunt Letty—''

"Hush, Katie. 'Tis not proper for a child to speak at table. Indeed, but if we were truly fashionable, you should not be present at all.''

Bevis rolled his eyes as though he'd had quite enough of the elderly lady's chatter, but said nothing. Instead, he toyed with his empty glass, drawing a pattern in the liquid that had spilled over the side of it.

Justin eased his tired body into his chair, smiling across the table at Susannah. She rewarded him with a look of long-suffering. "Well, Mrs. Byrnes, 'twould seem we shall be fed passably,'' he offered politely.

"Yes.''

Letty nodded happily. "A joint of mutton, a capon apiece, beans and potatoes, cheese and preserves, hot buns, and wine from their own berries—not to mention calf's foot jelly flavored with sherry and cream for dessert—what more could we wish for, I ask you?''

Bevis eyed the table contemptuously. "A great deal more, I think. The deuced keeper's so cheese-paring that he don't break out the Madeira or the brandy,'' he complained. "Says 'tis rum or gin—and I'll be demned if those are to a gentleman's taste!''

"I am sure you will manage to swallow it anyway,'' Justin observed dryly.

"Well, now that you are here, we may eat, in any event. Mrs. Byrnes would have it that we needed you to carve the joint—told her you were cow-handed with a blade, but she don't believe it.'' Bevis thrust his plate forward. "If the rest of 'em ain't hungry, you can start with me.''

Ignoring him, Justin sliced off thick pieces of mutton onto the platter as Susannah collected the plates from the others. Deliberately, he began serving Letty Byrnes, Susannah, Molly, and Katie first.

"Could understand the ladies," Bevis grumbled with a wave toward Molly Hill, "but when it comes to her afore me, 'tis outside of enough."

"Mr. Thorndike—"

"It don't bother me, ma'am," Molly hastened to assure Susannah. "I just remember where it comes from."

The young man rose and walked to the window to stare out into the darkness. "How the deuce can it still be snowing? 'Tis as though we are buried. Bennett!"

"Aye, sir?" the landlord answered, hurrying in from the back room.

"Changed m'mind—I'll take the rum." Bevis turned back to where Justin frowned. "Don't mind him—m'cousin's forgot how t' drink right. Give the home-made stuff t' the ladies—and t' Lydesdale." He laughed as though he'd said something funny. "He don't care what he drinks anymore."

"You've had enough, Bev."

Bennett returned immediately with the bottle, which Bevis snatched from his hand. Swinging it defiantly until some of the rum sloshed out, he walked back to sit down beside his cousin. "Got to have consolation for being lost in the provinces, don't you know? Ain't nothing to do here, anyways, is there? I ain't given to talking to brats, nor old females neither. And Old Moll ain't friendly anymore—or so she would have me believe." He poured himself a glass, overfilling it, then bent over to drink from the rim.

Briefly, Justin considered making an issue of the matter, then decided that he would only ruin the meal for the rest of them. If he were fortunate, Bevis would merely drown himself in the rum and fall into a stupor. Later he could take him to task for his behavior, but now he'd let it pass in the name of peace.

Despite Letty Byrnes's pleasure in the food, it was

a meager repast by his standards, and definitely not anything to linger over. He finished serving, and everyone fell to eating relatively silently. Bevis for the most part ignored the plate before him, merely tasting of it between gulps of his rum. Katie, having had quite a day, yawned sleepily throughout the meal, until Susannah, satisfied that she had consumed enough, sent her up to bed. The old woman pleaded fatigue also, leaving the other two females to partake of the homemade wine and sweet biscuits served after dinner.

Justin, who'd meant to seek his bed early, found himself accompanying them into the small parlor, where a cozy fire had been laid. The yellow light from the outside lantern gave proof through the thick windowpanes that it still snowed. He pulled a chair up to the settee where Molly and Susannah sat near the blazing hearth.

"Have you given thought to the tyke's Christmas?" Molly asked suddenly.

"Yes," Susannah answered simply.

Justin was startled to hear Molly say, "Me n' the marquess was thinking of havin' a wee celebration. Some singing and readin' from the Good Book—so's she'd know it was Christmas, don't you think? It don't cost nothing and it might lift spirits a trifle."

"Well, I . . ."

Molly turned to him, shaking her head. "And if you wasn't wantin' to read, I'd do it, but I'd as lief not, you know. It ain't that I cannot, but I ain't the best—besides, it don't seem right."

"I am sure he cannot possibly object."

He didn't want to tell two females that he didn't consider himself any more fit than Molly to read Scripture, that in his way, he was a greater sinner than she. He started to demur, but the appeal in Susannah's eyes stopped him. Instead, he shrugged as though it did not matter.

"All right."

Satisfied, Molly addressed Susannah. "If you ain't got anything for little Katie, I'll be bound as I can pry something out of the Bennett woman. Butter don't melt in her mouth when she sees the color of me gold."

"Oh—no! That is, I have already tended the matter, but I thank you for the kindness of your offer."

"Well, I know it ain't easy, you being a widow and all, and I got nobody but me mum." Molly's eyes misted and for a moment, she closed them to hide the tears. "And I ain't seeing her until after, anyways," she finished. "Might as well make a tyke happy, don't you think?"

She wiped at her eyes with the back of her hand, prompting Susannah to reach out and clasp the one that remained in her lap. "You are a kind woman, Miss Hill."

"No, I ain't," Molly sniffed. "I always wanted a girl of me own, you know, and yours is such a taking little thing. Well, I mean to see she don't mind being here on the holiday." She fished into the knitted reticule that hung from her wrist until she found the wad of bank notes again. "Here, you buy 'er something from you, you hear? See if that woman ain't got a trinket t' take Katie's eye," she went on, producing one of the notes. "Ten pound ought to buy something real fine."

Susannah flushed in embarrassment. Shaking her head, she pushed the money away. "I thank you, truly I do, but we simply cannot accept such a sum. Besides, I am already making a gift myself."

That it equalled one-tenth of her income was not lost on Justin, and he could not have blamed her for taking the money. He lifted an eyebrow at her refusal, but said nothing.

Bevis, who'd chosen to remain at the table over his bottle, appeared in the doorway, reeling from the effects of far too much rum. "Ain't no fun partyin' by myshelf," he muttered thickly. He staggered over to

Molly. "C'mon—make a little party t' ourshelves—whadda you shay?"

"You are dead foxed, Bev," Justin told him coldly. "Go to bed."

"Told you onesht—ain't my keeper. C'mon, Moll, lesh shee your—" As his fingers touched the neck of Molly's gown, Lydesdale caught him from behind. He staggered, nearly dragging both of them down. "Whaddy'a do that for? Jus wanna shee . . ." Pulling away from Justin, he caught at the arm of the settee for balance and righted himself in front of Susannah. "What about you, Mishus Byrnes? Th' Widow Byrnes wanna share shome rum upshtairs?"

This time, when Justin caught his arms, he held on, pulling him back. "I think you had best beg pardon ere I take you up to bed."

"Ain't—oush! What'd you do that for? I ain't a babe t' be bundled off t' bed, you know. Can go up myshelf when I wanna." He dipped his head slightly to Susannah as Justin's hand applied painful pressure to his arm. "Pardon, mishus—guessh Bevish Th-Thorndike ain't t' yer taste, eh?" Twisting back against the marquess, he muttered, "Ain't gonna 'pologize t' no doxy, Jushtin—ain't. Don't want your help neither."

Justin waited until he'd gotten Bevis to the doorway before he released him. "Tompkins!" he called out in the direction of the common room, "put Mr. Thorndike to bed!"

The coachey appeared promptly and shouldered Bevis's weight. "Aye, my lord."

Turning back to Susannah and Molly, Justin was about to offer an apology for his cousin's drunkenness, when Bevis lashed out. "May be a sot, but at least I ain't killed nobody. I ain't never been accused of murd'ring a fellow."

The marquess winced visibly, then recovered enough to offer, "I am terribly sorry, Mrs. Byrnes, Miss Hill,

for Mr. Thorndike's miserable manners. Good night.''
His shoulders seemed to slump as he turned away.

"Wait!"

It was Susannah who'd spoken, and she didn't know
why she'd done it, but it seemed unbearably sad for
him to leave them like that. Molly glanced at her
knowingly and rose quickly. " 'Tis tired I am also,"
she murmured as she slipped past him, "but it seems
a shame t' waste the rest of the bottle. You and Mrs.
Byrnes is welcome to share it.''

"Please, I should like that, I think,'' Susannah told
him quietly. Then feeling quite forward and foolish,
she added lamely, "If Letty is not asleep, she will talk
when I go up—and I am not precisely in the mood for
it just now.''

She was still seated, her hands folded neatly in her
lap, and as he turned back to refuse, he was struck by
how very calm she seemed. "You cannot wish for my
company, madam,'' he protested.

"Well, I cannot think you would want to listen to
Mr. Thorndike any more than I should like to hear
Letty.''

"No.''

Suddenly self-conscious at the way he was looking
at her, she reached for the wine bottle and was about
to refill his glass when Bennett stuck his head through
the door. "Got hot punch to warm yer lordship—take
the cold out o' yer bones.''

"I don't . . .'' Justin hesitated, then capitulated. It
was, after all, still early, and he knew if he faced Bevis
just then, he'd be tempted to choke the life out of him.
"All right. And bring a cup for Mrs. Byrnes also.''

What he brought was a steaming bowl filled almost
to the brim. It smelled of apples and cinnamon and
nutmeg, with slices of the fruit and sticks of the spice
floating in it. Justin dipped out a cup for Susannah and
handed it to her.

"Be careful lest you burn your mouth.''

She sipped and tears came to her eyes. But after the initial shock, she had to concede it was quite good. Warmth diffused through her, making the crackling fire almost unnecessary. He carried his own cup back to sit down across from her, watching her as he drank. For quite a long time, both stared into the violet and orange and gold flames, without speaking.

"Why didn't you take Molly's money?" he asked finally.

Her chin came up. "I am not anyone's pensioner, my lord. Besides, whether she realizes it or not, she will have need of it herself."

"*Do* you have something for your daughter?"

"Of course."

"She wants a cat, you know."

"I doubt Mrs. Bennett would wish to part with her mouser, my lord. Otherwise, I should ask her." Her hazel eyes met his momentarily. "I shall be certain to find one when I get home."

"I shall feel the veriest fool reading from Molly's Good Book, you know," he ventured.

"Would you prefer that I did it?"

"Yes." He sighed and turned his face back to the fire. "But she asked me."

"And you think you are unworthy," she hazarded. "Really, my lord, but I think—"

"I know I am, Mrs. Byrnes."

"You must not let drunken words plague you, sir."

"The truth, whatever its source, is still the truth," he responded. Then, not wanting to let her see too much, he reached for her empty cup. "Here—let me get you another."

The second cup was even mellower than the first, she supposed because it had cooled a little. She found herself drinking deeply of the spicy mixture. Setting it aside, she pursued the matter. "I do not think you a murderer, my lord. I thought 'twas decided in your favor."

"It was." He swallowed half of his punch before he could bring himself to say anything more. "But they did not have the right of it, Mrs. Byrnes. 'Twas ruled self-defense, you know, but I still regret having shot him."

"As I expect I should have also."

He considered her curiously, but she was quite serious. Her eyes betrayed a sympathy he'd not expected to find. The thought crossed his mind that he was becoming more than a little bosky, but he didn't care. "It seems like a long while ago sometimes, other times 'tis like yesterday," he mused, his voice low.

"Was she very beautiful?"

"Thantis? Very—and quite ugly underneath."

"But you were so young then, weren't you? I mean, I was not above sixteen when I heard the tale. And as I recall it, there were those who thought the fault was hers."

"She didn't want the scandal of a divorce, she said, but I know now she didn't want to lose his money. Thantis Harcourt, my dear Mrs. Byrnes, is mercenary to the core. I was but the means to an end."

"Then how can you punish yourself so?"

"It was I who killed him for her. Oh, he was the indignant, jealous husband, all right, but I was a fool who thought I was the only lover. As the one challenged, I chose pistols, knowing he was a better swordsman." He drained the rest of the cup. A self-deprecating little laugh escaped him as he set it on the table beside him. "What a fool a man can be, Mrs. Byrnes—while I met him at Smithfield, she was running off to France with someone else. If there is any consolation at all in the sorry affair, Mrs. Byrnes, 'tis that I had not yet come into my inheritance, else she'd have kept me in her clutches."

"Well, while I do not condone such liaisons, my lord, I cannot think you were entirely to blame."

"I should have deloped."

"And let him put a ball into you? Do not be ridiculous, sir! Then you would have merely made it even easier for her, wouldn't you?"

He knew he was foxed, for she made it sound sensible. He passed a hand over his face, trying to clear his thoughts. "It was easy enough as it was," he muttered bitterly. "I faced the inquest, and by the time it was over, I heard she'd wed Bricklin."

"It must have wounded you very deeply." Without thinking, she refilled his cup. "It is so very difficult to lose someone one loves, even when one can halfway expect it. In your case, I daresay 'twas doubly so, for you could not have known what she was."

"I discovered I did not love her, which makes the whole affair even more sordid," he admitted. "But enough of me," he decided abruptly. "What of you?"

She swirled the punch, staring into the bits of cinnamon and nutmeg that floated in the cup. "I loved Charles Byrnes enough to agree to a runaway marriage."

"Then you have your regrets also."

"No, not for that." Her words came slowly, softly. "We were quite happy, always so, in fact, but his family did not forgive him for ignoring their wishes in the matter. I was respectable enough, but not an heiress, you see. My papa was a mere country vicar with four girls to fire off, so I was unworthy of a Byrnes of Haverhill." She managed a small, wry smile. "If I have any regrets at all, they are for what I cost him— and for his death, of course."

"But after the child, surely—"

" 'Tis why I am come from London, my lord. I was summoned when Sir William died, and thinking he had relented on his deathbed, Letty persuaded me to go for Katie's sake."

"And, of course, he had not," he murmured.

"Not at all," she recalled, betraying her own bitterness. " 'Twas his final revenge, I think. Oh, he left

two thousand pounds for Katie, but only if I left her—
and God forgive me, but I considered doing so. I had
taken her to Sir John Byrnes—Charles's brother—and
was going to remove myself from her life even. But he
could not desist from calling her 'Charles's misbegotten brat,' you see. I did not think the money was worth
that.''

"No, of course not," he agreed.

"I think it hurt Letty more than Katie and me," she
added, "for she had such hopes of it when the letter
came. I just wish Sir William could have forgiven her
at least.''

"She was his sister?''

"Actually, she was his aunt. And when Charles and
I wed, she supported us with her competence, but
Charles's venture into trade did not prosper." She finished her now-cooled punch. " 'Twas why he became
a soldier, and we followed the drum.''

"What about Brandon?" he heard himself ask her.

She appeared befuddled by the sudden turn in conversation, then frowned. "Mr. Brandon, you mean? I
expect he means to come up to scratch one day." Rising unsteadily, she discovered the room swam around
her. "What a maudlin pair we are, speaking of such
unpleasant things, my lord, when 'tis Christmas.''

"Are you going to take him?''

Had she not been so comfortably fuzzy from the
wine, she would probably have thought it was none of
his affair. As it was, she answered, "I am not certain—I suppose that depends a great deal on Katie, and
whether I think I can make him a good wife. But I
don't want to think about that just now.''

"I take it you mean to desert me, Mrs. Byrnes?''

"Either that or disgrace myself," she admitted hon-
estly. "I fear the punch has left me rather giddy.''

"Do you need help up the stairs?''

"No—not yet. Good night, my lord.''

"Good night then.''

She paused when she reached the door and looked back. "You are wrong about Mr. Thorndike, you know. I see nothing of you in him—nor of him in you."

"If he were not in his cups, I daresay he would be far easier to like than me," he countered.

After she left, he stretched his tall frame, extending his feet toward the fire. He'd been wrong about her at first—she was far more than passably pretty. In a different way, she was almost as lovely as Thantis, but with an important exception—she had a heart. And he was certain that Mr. Brandon, wherever he was, did not deserve her.

When Susannah opened the door to her room, she was surprised to discover Molly Hill in her bed. The woman sat up sleepily as the door closed, mumbling, "Hope you don't mind it, ma'am, but 'tis colder in here—thought the little girl ought to be where there ain't a draft."

"You gave us your room?" Susannah asked incredulously. "Molly, you should have kept the best chamber. You are paying for it."

"It don't make no difference to me, ma'am—I been in worse places than this. Go on—out with you."

"And Letty?"

"She didn't want to sleep in me room—guess she thinks I got something she might get. Anyways, she's down the hall—next to Mr. Thorndike." Molly plumped a pillow and turned over to cradle it. "You know, Lydesdale ain't a bad fellow. Surprising, ain't it? What with him being a marquess and all, I mean. But you'd best be gettin' to bed rather'n talking to me. I don't doubt but what Katie's gettin' up early—wants to tease the cat or something."

"Good night, Miss Hill—Molly."

The embers from an earlier blaze gave a faint orange light to the other bedchamber. Susannah sat on the side of the bed away from her sleeping daughter and removed her shoes and stockings. She was tired, giddy from the punch, and yet strangely awake, wondering why a man like Lydesdale had bothered to ask about Mr. Brandon. Idle curiosity, she supposed, but nonetheless she was gratified to have him know that she was not entirely without resources. But why had she said she might take Johnny Brandon? That was a whisker, and she knew it. There was not a chance that she'd wed a man who not only did not like small creatures, but also seemed to think children were no more than a nuisance. However, it didn't matter what she'd told the marquess, she rationalized, for once they were gone from the Red Stag, she'd not be likely to ever see him again anyway.

She unpinned her hair and finished undressing down to her chemise before she slid between the cold covers, shivering. It did one absolutely no good whatsoever to think of a man like Lydesdale, she told herself severely, trying to put him from her mind. But she felt for him—if there ever was proof that great wealth did not necessarily make for happiness, he was that. How terribly haunted he was by what she could only consider a tragic folly of youth. Why could he not see that he was a very different man now? Stretching out toward the bedside table, she raised up and blew out the candle she'd carried up from the hallway.

It was some time before she slept, and then only fitfully, troubled by nightmares of ruin. She was going to lose her small house to Charles's brother, an utter absurdity in fact, but in the netherworld of the mind, it became startlingly real. And they were coming for Katie, saying that she could not take care of her own daughter. Hands were pulling the child away.

With a jolt, she came awake to the feel of someone stroking her hair against her shoulder, and suddenly she realized she and Katie were not alone. She rolled over and sat up screaming.

"Aiiiiieeeeeeeeeeee!"

"C'mon, Moll—just wanna have a good tumble," Bevis Thorndike mumbled as he lunged after her, pushing her back into the deep featherbed.

Wet kisses, heavy with the smell of rum and sour wine, sent a wave of nausea through her. She scratched and clawed, struggling from beneath him, trying to avoid his mouth. Next to her, Katie scrambled out of the bed and ran for the door, shouting, "Help my mama—please! There's somebody in our chamber!"

Taking advantage of Bevis's surprise, Susannah managed to push him off, and he fell heavily onto the floor. Shaking, she grasped the heavy candlestick from the bedside and stood over him, ready to strike. "How—how *dare* you, Mr. Thorndike?" she demanded awfully.

Justin Marshfield, Letty Byrnes, Molly Hill, and nearly everyone else came running. Lydesdale burst into the room carrying a pistol, followed by the innkeeper with a lantern. It was possibly the most humiliating moment of Susannah's life, but she was too angry to care. Brandishing the candlestick, she threatened, "Stay there else I shall part your hair crosswise! And believe me, I should like nothing more than to do it!"

The others stopped, staring at the sight of the lovely widow, her hair streaming about her shoulders, her body barely covered with her thin chemise, her arm upraised like an avenging goddess. Caught, Bevis glared at her as his hand felt the blood on his cheek where she'd scratched him.

"What'd you do that for?" Then— "You ain't Molly!"

"Your powers of perception overwhelm me, sir," she retorted acidly. Heedless of her appearance, her bosom heaving from her earlier exertion, she turned to the others. "This man attempted to ravish me!"

"No—didn't!" Bevis quailed at the sight of the gun in Lydesdale's hand. " 'Twas Molly—thought she was the other one, Jushtin—it ain't like you wassh to think," he pleaded.

"Mrs. Byrnes, we run a respectable house," Mrs. Bennett announced coldly, pushing past her staring husband.

"And I am a respectable female!" Susannah snapped back. "If you would complain, I suggest you look to your other custom!"

Letty, thinking the woman meant to turn them out into the stormy night, drew herself up to her full four feet eleven inches and faced Mrs. Bennett. " 'Tis to a Byrnes of the Haverhill Byrneses you would speak, madam, and we do not intend to suffer an insult in this house!"

"Aye, and I am the Princess Charlotte, I s'pose."

"There is no question Mrs. Byrnes is a respectable female, is there, Mrs. Bennett?" Justin asked meaningfully. " 'Twould appear she has been attacked by Mr. Thorndike."

Surprised to see her distinguished guest supporting a nobody against his own cousin, the woman backed down, muttering, "Just the same, we don't keep that kind of house, ye hear?" To Susannah, she apologized grudgingly, "Guess it ain't yer fault, ma'am."

"Admit it, Mr. Thorndike," Susannah demanded of the cowering Bevis.

"You will, of course, do the right thing," Justin told him with menacing softness.

"Dash it, Justin!"

"Bev . . ."

Casting a baleful look at the pistol, Bevis pulled himself up at the side of the bed, then turned his attention to Susannah. Telling himself that she was in truth a fine-looking woman, he swallowed visibly and nodded, suddenly almost sober.

"I ain't above admitting a mishtake, ma'am."

"Paltry, Bev."

"And I should of coursh rectify the inshult. I know

you ain't a loose female.'' The slur was almost gone from his speech, replaced by utter resignation. "Proud to marry you,'' he finished in a voice that clearly indicated otherwise. "Honored, in fact. There!'' He glared at his cousin. "I done it—got witnesses even. Old Bev's getting leg-shackled to the Widow Byrnes! You all heard it, didn't you?''

Her anger gone in the face of the ridiculousness of the situation, Susannah almost felt sorry for him. "No.''

"No?'' Letty almost cried. "Susannah, you—''

"Yes, I can, Aunt Letty.'' Setting down the candlestick, she faced Bevis Thorndike. "While I am conscious of the signal honor you do me, sir, I am afraid I must decline. I suggest you seek your own bed until you can think more clearly. And if I were you, I should avoid rum forever.''

It took a moment for her meaning to sink in, and then the young man brightened visibly. "I say, good of you, Mrs. Byrnes! Justin, she don't want to marry me—you hear it? Fine female, fine female—damme if she ain't.''

"A woman of remarkable sense,'' Lydesdale agreed. "And you ought to follow her advise.'' To Susannah, he said, "Again I must ask your pardon for my cousin, Mrs. Byrnes.''

Disappointed, everyone began filing out. Molly pressed her hand, telling her, " 'Tis sorry I am for what happened.''

"You cannot be blamed for it, my dear. Indeed, 'twas a kindness to give us your bed,'' Susannah reassured her.

"He's a bad man,'' Katie chimed in. "A real bad man.''

"No, merely a foxed one, dearest. Men in their cups are often confused, I think.''

She waited until only Lydesdale and Katie remained. "Did you really think me that desperate, my lord?"

A smile played at the corners of his mouth and lit his dark eyes. "Actually, Mrs. Byrnes, I only meant for him to apologize rather abjectly. It would not have hurt to have made him grovel a little for your forgiveness, you know."

"I considered it, but then what if he'd been perverse enough to hold me to it?"

"You'd be a very rich woman when he turns twenty-five. Mrs. Byrnes, you have just whistled a bloody fortune down the wind."

"Do not be absurd, my lord. Were I to wed on such a weak pretense, the marriage would be a sham—and that I could not bear. Having loved once, I have a fair notion of what I want in a husband, sir, and unfortunately, I am unready to rear a child several years younger than myself."

"But think of what you could have done to secure your daughter's happiness."

"I hope I shall be able to teach her that there is more to life than money, my lord. I'd have her know that honor and truth and love are to be valued much more highly."

"The romantical Mrs. Byrnes," he teased as his eyes strayed to her shift.

Suddenly realizing the picture she must present, she clasped her arms across her breasts as though she were cold. "Katie and I have had a rather eventful day, my lord. Good night."

When he got back to Bevis's chamber, he found his cousin sitting in a chair, staring as though he'd looked into the pits of hell and escaped. "Very near thing," he muttered. "What was you thinking of—what if she'd said yes? I'd a been in front of the parson as soon ash the snow thawed, coz, and you'dda made me a family man in one lick. Wife and brat at the same time."

Before Justin could stop him, Bevis reached for a half-empty bottle. "Ain't no wonder they call it ruin." He flung it at the fireplace, where it broke and spilled. The coals ignited, sending a swoosh of flames shooting briefly into the room, then disappearing without catching anything.

"You could have done a lot worse."

"Woman's twenty-five if she's got a day on her—and the old woman'd have me in Bedlam in a week. Besides, she ain't got no money, how'd yoush think I'd come about, I ash you? I got another year and more until you let me touch my blunt." He looked up through bloodshot eyes. "If you was wantin' to help her, you'd offer for her next time." He giggled as though he'd discovered a jest. "Be rich, wouldn't it—the hoity-toity Marquess of Lydesdale and the Widow Byrnes—*on-dit* of the *ton* for years."

"I suppose I could do a lot worse, too."

Bevis rocked back in his chair and nearly lost his balance. "Thought you wasn't a marryin' man, Jushtin—know you said so—heard you even."

"I don't know what I am," Lydesdale admitted.

"Mar—Marquess of Lydesdale," his cousin pronounced solemnly, "thash what you are." He ran his fingers through his touseled locks, raking them. "Got a devil of a head already."

"Good night, Bev."

"I ain't swearin' off the stuff for good, you know."

Later, lying in his own bed, Justin Marshfield stared into the darkness pensively for a long time. The last thing he remembered before he slept was the sight of Susannah Byrnes standing over Bevis, disheveled and thoroughly enchanting in that thin shift of hers, holding the candlestick like a weapon. A remarkable woman, the Widow Byrnes. And a damned fine-looking one, too.

" 'Tis still snowing," Letitia Byrnes greeted the marquess when he came down to breakfast. "I vow that I have lived in the north country for years and never seen the like. Do you take sugar with your coffee, my lord?'' she asked, pushing the sugar block and cleaver at him. "You would have thought that an inn should have it broken up, wouldn't you? Daresay you shall just have to hack at it as I have done.''

He took the seat across from her and broke off a piece of the loaf. Taking the tong, he dropped it into his cup and waited for her to pour his coffee. "I do not see Mrs. Byrnes or her daughter about yet,'' he observed casually.

"Susannah's been up for hours, and poor Katie is fagged to death, so she is still abed.'' She leaned across the table and lowered her voice conspiratorially. "Susannah is at work in the back room.''

He threw down his napkin and rose angrily. "If she was in such straits, she should have told me last night. I'll not see a gentlewoman reduced to earning her bread.''

"Oh—no!'' Then, realizing the interest he was expressing in Susannah, she played her cards close, so to speak, and added slyly, "But she thinks you a stranger, don't you see? I mean, you are but just met, after all.''

It was odd, but he didn't think of Susannah Byrnes as a stranger at all. "Where is she?'' he asked grimly.

"But I just told you,'' Letty replied mildly. "In the back room.''

"Tell Mrs. Bennett to set another place for her.''

He strode purposefully toward the closed door at the back of the dining room, fully expecting to see Susannah toiling over the butter churn or kneading bread with her hands. Instead, when he threw open the door, he found her bent over some sort of needlework. She looked up in surprise.

"Katie isn't with you, is she?'' she asked, whisking her work behind her back.

"No. Listen, my girl, if you are so dished up you

have to work back here, I'll cover for you. And if you were too proud to ask me, why the devil didn't you take Molly's money?''

"What? But I—''

"What has that Bennett woman got you doing, anyway?'' he demanded, reaching behind her. "Give it over.''

"I beg your pardon.''

"Come on—I mean to give it back to her. There is no need for you to labor at a common inn.'' His hand closed on hers behind her back.

"If you unravel my work, I shall—well, I don't know what I will do precisely, but I have not the time to do it over,'' she protested in alarm.

He started to pull, then realized he had a hand full of wool. "What the deuce?''

"Unhand me and I'll show you, though I cannot think you would consider my poor work very good.'' As he stepped back, she produced a ball of yarn and what appeared to be a knitted pouch.

"Egad—what is it?''

"Is it that bad?'' She eyed it skeptically and sighed. " 'Tis supposed to be a mitten for Katie, you know, and I was hiding from her while I made it. 'Twill look better when the thumb is attached, I should expect.'' She held it up for him to see it better. "I am not especially fond of the color, but 'twas all that Letty could get of Mrs. Bennett.''

"Actually, now that you tell me what it is, I can quite see it. And I am certain that Miss Katherine Byrnes will be the only young female in the pew with red mittens,'' he offered gallantly.

"Now I *know* you are funning with me, my lord.''

"Not at all. But don't you think you ought to join Aunt Letty and me for breakfast?'' he asked pointedly.

"I have to work while Katie sleeps.''

"And leave me to the mercy of Aunt Letty? I should think not, Mrs. Byrnes.'' This time, he very carefully disengaged her fingers from the half-finished mitten. "Tell you what—I am not above entertaining the infant for an hour or so later."

"Surely Aunt Letty cannot be that vexatious."

"Well, we have already exhausted the weather and the sorry state of the sugar before I have had my first cup of coffee, and I take leave to tell you I am deuced short-tempered early in the morning anyway."

"Oh."

"Besides, I like the infant. We'll play with Old Patch or something. And I assure you that I am quite as bored as she is, with the exception of your company, that is."

"Is that its name?" she asked faintly, not wanting to acknowledge that he could find her interesting in the least. "How very unoriginal."

"You would expect the Bennetts to perhaps call it Calpurnia or Antigone?"

"No, I suppose not."

"Come on—Aunt Letty is having another place made up for you," he coaxed. "And I am not above breaking up your sugar for you."

She stashed Katie's present behind a flour barrel and stood up. "Well, it *is* rather chill in here, so I suppose it will not hurt to warm up a trifle." Her hazel eyes took on an unholy light. "But I take leave to warn you—I knit quite slowly, my lord. You may find yourself with Katie all day."

"Maybe I'll take her and Bev out to play in the snow—they are about of an age by mind if not years."

"How is he, by the by?"

"Chastened." He held the door open for her. "He feels as though he has escaped quite narrowly from the jaws of parson's mousetrap, and he is not unconscious of how he got there. It will not last, of course, but he's sworn off the bottle for a few days."

"How ridiculous! He must surely have known he is not the sort of man I'd marry."

"Ah, yes—Mr. Brandon."

She opened her mouth to tell him she wouldn't have Mr. Brandon either, but then thought better of it. "There is nothing wrong with Mr. Brandon, precisely."

"If that is the best you can say of him, you ought to forget the notion, if you want my opinion of it."

"I don't believe I asked you."

A surge of hope sent Letty's spirits soaring when she saw them come out together. She bobbed her head quickly to hide the smile she could not quite suppress, and felt quite satisfied with herself. Let him think she was a shatterbrained old rambler, she knew what she was about—had from the first time she'd laid her eyes on him. Aye, the Marquess of Lydesdale was about as fine a catch as she'd ever been privileged to see. And good as Charles had been to all of them, it was time for Susannah to get on with her life for Katie's sake.

By evening, it was difficult to tell whether he'd exhausted Katie or she him. They'd played cards, built a snow fort, pelted the ailing Bevis with snowballs (and been pelted in return) until they were all but frozen, then sipped chocolate before the fire—and that had accounted for but half the day. The rest they'd spent under Molly Hill's insistent direction, decorating the front parlor for Christmas with bits of pasteboard cut into stars and painted. "For the Star of Bethlehem, don't you know?" Molly'd explained. And Bevis, more sober than he'd been for days, was almost pleasant, going so far as to string ribbons across the room to hold the stars with remarkable equanimity.

The snow had stopped some time after noon, and a crew of workmen was already busy in an attempt to clear the roadway. By the looks of things, the mail would run in a day or two, probably right after Christmas, whisking Susannah Byrnes and her little daughter out of Justin Marshfield's life as precipitously as they'd come into it. And he sensed he was going to miss them.

"You ought to wish on the Christmas star," Molly told the child, "for 'tis sometimes quite magical."

Katie eyed the large one that Mr. Thorndike was tying up in the center of the room. " 'Tis but pasteboard," she scoffed.

"But 'tis Christmas Eve, and who's to say what might happen then?" Molly countered.

Katie waited until she thought no one watched her, then, squeezing her eyes tightly shut, she wished quite fervently. Her lips moved silently, but there was no mistaking what she wanted. Lydesdale was quite certain she'd said the word *kitten* several times.

Susannah emerged at midafternoon to place a small package on the mantel in the front parlor, then busied herself helping finish the rather garish decorations. And as dusk settled over the silent snow, they sat down to a substantial meal. Despite the warning looks cast her way by Aunt Letty, Katie would not be stilled. With the universal eagerness of English children on Christmas Eve, she chattered on, rivaling the old woman herself.

"You are a prattle," Bevis told her pointedly. "Did your nurse never teach you to be still?"

"I never had a nurse," she shot back, unrepentant. Then, seeing her mother frown, she sighed. "But Mama did."

"You ought to listen to your mama then." But despite his words, he was smiling.

"Here now—'tis Christmastime, sir," Molly protested. "Let the tyke enjoy it."

The little girl turned to Justin. "Do you think a wish is more like to be granted because 'tis Christmas?" she asked him suddenly.

There was such hope in those bright blue eyes that he was loathe to dash it. Despite the shake of Susan-

nah's head, he too smiled at her daughter. "I should
think so—yes, quite definitely."

Katie leaned around the old woman to address Bevis. "And what do you think, Mr. Thorndike?"

For a moment, that gentleman thought he might
choke on a bite of meat, but even he was not proof to
the appeal in the child's eyes. "I'd listen to Lydesdale,
if 'twas me. I ain't seen no miracles myself, you
understand," he added, squirming under Susannah's
disbelieving frown. "Stands to reason—I mean, well—
dash it, ain't anything impossible, you know."

"See, Mama," Katie crowed in triumph, "I told
you 'twould happen!"

"You forget yourself, Katherine," Letty spoke
dampeningly, "particularly because 'tis Christmas,
you must remember that miracles come from God."

The child's face turned quite solemn for a moment,
then brightened again. "Then I know I shall get my
wish, for God loves me, does he not?"

Later, when the table was cleared and the small
group was repairing to the decorated parlor, Susannah
hissed at Lydesdale as she passed him, "You wretch—
she will think my poor mittens but meager compen-
sation for her lack of a kitten!"

And Bevis could not quite suppress a grin at his
discomfiture. "God, coz? I did not know you had his
acquaintance. What do you mean to do when Katie
discovers you and Moll have hoaxed her?"

"Even poor children need dreams, Bev," Justin retorted.

"Maybe you can bribe Bennett to part with the ugly
mouser. But I hope you can do it, old fellow—it ain't
right to dash her hopes."

"Just leave one candle for Lydesdale," they heard
Molly tell Bennett. "The rest of us can sit in the dark
t' listen."

"Ah, yes—the Good Book—I should not miss this

for the world, coz,'' Bevis teased. ''Lay you a monkey you ain't recited since you was a schoolboy.''

Justin shook his head. ''You'd win.''

There was no help for it then. By the time he'd joined them, everyone was waiting expectantly for him. The room was in deep shadows, illuminated only by the flickering yellow light of the blazing fire and the single candle placed beside his chair. As he sat down, Molly produced a worn Bible.

''Opened it to St. Luke, my lord, but if you don't like it, I can find—''

''No, this is fine.''

The candlelight danced across the pages, making the words move. Feeling very much the fool, he looked around him. Susannah sat quite still, her fine profile outlined by the firelight, and he was startled yet again to find her beautiful despite her lack of jewels or finery. She had a indefinable something, a certain charm and character that a fortune could not buy. His eyes traveled to where Letitia Byrnes was expectantly silent, waiting, and Katie sat cross-legged on the floor, her faded skirt spread over her knees to make a hollow bed for the old calico cat. The chimney draft blew the star above Molly Hill's bent head. Bevis leaned forward from his seat to push the candle nearer so he could see the print on the page.

Justin cleared his throat and began to read, haltingly at first, and then in a clear, strong voice. ''And it came to pass in those days, that there went out a decree from Caesar Augustus, that all the world should be taxed. And this taxing was first done when Cyrenius was governor of Syria. And all went to be taxed, everyone into his own city . . .''

It was not a long passage, quite the contrary in fact—only some twenty verses, telling a story he'd taken for granted most of his life—but there was something to the reading of it in that hushed room, where the only sound other than his voice was the popping of logs in the fire, that gave him pause. When he finished, he laid Molly's Good Book on the table next to the candle.

The woman wiped her rouged cheek, smearing it. "Kean couldn't have done it finer, my lord."

"That, Katie, is why we have Christmas," Letty told the little girl. "Anything else should merely enhance that blessing."

Bennett brought in a steaming bowl of punch and some chocolate for Katie. And Mrs. Bennett lit the rest of the candles. The mood, which had been quite solemn, turned festive as Susannah filled the cups. Bevis Thorndike's smile faded as he stared moodily into his for some time, then he set it down. He'd be hanged if he'd be a lout on Christmas and make a bloody fool of himself again. And he knew if he stayed, he'd want to drink every last drop in the bowl.

"I ain't thirsty. Thing is, still got a head—think I might put it to bed."

"Well, if that don't—Mr. Thorndike, 'tis Christmas," the old woman protested.

"Hush, Aunt Letty. Good night, Mr. Thorndike," Susannah told him. "And a happy Christmas to you, sir."

"Can you sing, Mrs. Byrnes?" Justin inquired suddenly.

"Well, I . . ."

"If I can recite, you dashed well ought to be able to sing," he coaxed. "I'd do it myself, but I am a trifle flat."

"What do you want to hear?"

"The old carols."

"Yes, Mama, do," Katie pleaded.

"Being a trifle flat does not excuse anyone," Susannah declared meaningfully. "I am not above making a fool of myself, my lord, but I refuse to do it alone."

As Bevis went up the stairs, he heard the cacophony of voices raised in Luther's Christmas hymn. If they didn't escape from the Red Stag soon, he reflected gloomily, he was going to turn into a Methodist.

Much later, when Lydesdale finally came up, Bevis was waiting for him. Still fully clothed, he sat in one of the two straight-backed chairs drawn close to the small fire. At first, Justin thought he'd been drinking alone, but when he spoke, Bevis's voice was more sober than his.

"What are we going to do about the damned cat?" he asked bluntly. "Dash it, but Katie Byrnes is going to expect to see one in the morning, ain't she? And I ain't going to want to listen when she don't get it. Beside, it ain't right—she ain't got nothing, Justin."

"What do you propose to do about it?" Lydesdale asked quietly.

"Well, I ain't praying over it, if that was what you was meaning," Bevis retorted. "Only one thing to do—got to get her one."

"Bev . . ."

"Well, what d'you think?"

"I think there's a foot of snow on the ground—and 'tis late and dark out."

"Dash it, but we as much as promised her one!" Bevis reminded him forcefully. "What's she supposed to think—that Bevis Thorndike and the Marquess of Lydesdale is liars? And it ain't as if we can't do it—crawled out the window once at Oxford under Old Frawley's nose in worse weather'n this, coz. Besides, every tenant has cats, don't you know? Just got to find one, that's all."

A grin spread across Justin's face, chasing the years away. "Oh, I mean to see she gets one, all right."

"Then let us get the coats—I ain't meanin' to stay out all night."

"I rather thought we'd go at first light." As he watched his cousin's face fall, he shook his head. "Bev, I don't think any farmer is going to want to get out of a warm bed to sell me a cat tonight."

"Oh—hadn't thought of that, of course," Bevis conceded. "Guess they all retire with the sun, don't they?"

"But since you are determined, I mean to see you are up at first light."

"Well—"

"First light, Bev," Justin repeated firmly.

There was no sign of the marquess or his cousin when Katie crept downstairs early. Confident of discovering her kitten, she moved from room to room, calling "Kitty—come, kitty," softly. There was a scratching at the storeroom door, but when she opened it, it was only Old Patch. Disappointed, she sank down on the back stairs, heedless of the calico that rubbed against her knee.

"Here now, it ain't right ter be glum on Chris'mus, ye know," Mrs. Bennett chided her.

"But I wished for a kitten!" Katie wailed. "On a magical star even! They lied to me, Mrs. Bennett—they did!"

"Who did that?"

"Lydesdale and Molly—and everyone!"

"Well, the marquess ain't here and neither is Mr. Thorndike, but I'd task 'em with it, I would."

"Katie!"

" 'Tis yer mum. Ye know, if I was ye, I don't think I'd worrit her over it. Seems t' me, she's been good enough ter ye."

The calico cat climbed onto her lap and insistently butted its head against her chin. Sighing, she scratched its head. "Mayhap," she conceded.

"Katie!"

"Go on wi' ye—and don't be making a Friday face t'day."

Katie sat through breakfast, trying to hide her disappointment, while Letty rattled on about the packages on the mantel. It didn't matter—she was certain none of them held what she wanted. Finally, when they saw she didn't mean to eat more than a piece of bread with jam, they produced the presents.

"But there's three," Letty observed in confusion. "Here's mine and yours, Susannah, but what's this one?" She held up a small, folded piece of paper.

" 'Tis for Mama." Katie brightened visibly as she took it from the old woman. Holding it out to her mother, she waited expectantly for Susannah to open it.

"Oh, but I . . ." The guinea fell into Susannah's hand and lay, bright and shiny, in her palm. She started to protest, but her daughter was smiling. "Why, thank you, Katie."

"Buy something pretty with it."

"I shall. But you have not opened yours, dearest."

The package was wrapped in folded newsprint, and as she felt along it, she could tell it was soft. She opened it carefully to discover bright red mittens. "Where is Lydesdale, do you think?" she asked, trying them on.

"Don't you like them?"

"Of course I like them—they are the very thing for the snow," she answered dutifully.

"And here is mine. And if you are as ungracious to me as to your mama, I'll have half a mind to take it back."

It was a small tortoise-framed mirror that she recognized as Aunt Letty's own. "Thank you." She held it up to catch the light, then stared at her reflection. "May I be excused, Mama?"

After she'd left to go upstairs, Letty turned to Susannah. "You would think she disliked what she got, wouldn't you? Perhaps we should have—"

"No. She liked them quite well, actually, but practical things cannot compare with a kitten today." She looked up the stairs. "If Lydesdale were here, I should cheerfully throttle him."

"But don't you like him, Susannah?" Letty wanted to know.

"Of course I like him!" she admitted crossly. "But what is that to do with anything, anyway? He ought not to have misled Katie."

The door burst open in the foyer behind them, admitting a blast of cold air. Lydesdale and Mr. Thorndike came in, stamping the snow from their boots. Both had extremely red faces and appeared quite chilled to the marrow.

"Is Katie up yet?"

"Of course she is up!" Susannah snapped. " 'Tis Christmas, isn't it? She got up early to find her Christmas cat! Now, if you will excuse me, I mean to console her."

She was halfway up the stairs when she heard the insistent mewing. "What . . . ?" Turning around, she saw the marquess lifting a black furball from beneath his caped greatcoat. "Oh—my!"

"Told you we should've gone last night," Bevis murmured reproachfully.

Lydesdale smoothed the long fur and held the squirming creature out to Susannah. "It might be better if you took him with you, don't you think?" He climbed the steps after her. "Here. I take leave to warn you that there is nothing wrong with its lungs— or its claws."

To demonstrate, the kitten displayed an alarming array of sharp projections from its paws. "I suspect 'tis scared, don't you?" Cradling the soft little animal against her shoulder, she made soothing sounds. Then she noted Lydesdale's coat. "Are those chicken feathers?" she asked curiously.

"Of course they are! You do not think I merely found him beside the road, do you? Oh no. When I finally encountered a farmer who had one, he told me to choose my own."

Bevis grinned openly now. "Ought to have seen

him, Mrs. Byrnes—the old mother cat had the litter in the henhouse, underneath the roosts."

"Oh, dear," she murmured, trying not to smile.

"Yes. You see, Mrs. Byrnes, spring is the season for kittens, or so I am told. Now, if you will pardon me, I mean to go back to bed—I got up deuced early this morning."

She nuzzled the soft, black fur, listening to the low, steady purr. "It seems that I must thank you yet again, my lord." She started to finish her climb up the stairs.

"Tell Katie I shall expect an extraordinary name for her magical cat, will you?"

"And tell her 'tis a fellow," Bevis added. "Might make a difference what she calls it, you know."

Lord Lydesdale came down early to breakfast the day after what he could only describe as an extraordinary Christmas to discover that Letitia Byrnes awaited him. His first thought was that it was simply too early to listen to her incessant prattle, but before he could retreat, she'd seen him. She smiled brightly and gestured to the chair across from her expectantly.

"Good morning, Lydesdale," she murmured as she reached to poor him a cup of steaming coffee. "I had Bennett crush the sugar for you this time. Told him if he was ever to expect to gain your custom, he'd best look to his service," she confided, "and since he don't see a marquess very often, he was quite pleased to oblige. Not that I should expect you to frequent the Red Stag, of course," she added truthfully.

"Thank you."

"I suppose Susannah thanked you for the cat, didn't she? We wasn't expecting it, you know, but I must say 'twas exceedingly kind of you, my lord." She passed the cup to him, then busied herself buttering a piece of toast. "A fellow rode over from the posting house to tell us the mail would come by at a quarter past noon, so Susannah is packing just now."

He felt as though he'd just been dashed with cold water. "I'd thought they'd wait until all the roads were cleared."

"Well, I had hoped they would have," she admitted regretfully, "but they do not mean to do so. The mails, it seems, are determined to be worthy of their charter."

It did not seem right that she and the child were leaving, not when they'd brought him the most peace and pleasure he'd discovered in years. Turning his head to stare soberly into the cheery fire, he felt as though he were about to lose something quite valuable.

"She is quite a remarkable woman," he said finally, more to himself than to Letty Byrnes.

"Susannah? Oh, my, yes, she is certainly that. How she manages to care for all of us since dear Charles . . ." She paused to dab at her eyes with her napkin as he turned back to her. "Well, I am sure I do not know how she can go on, but she does, and it cannot be an easy thing for her, you know. But she endures a flighty creature like me with a great deal of fortitude, I think, and she is a good mother to Katie."

"Yes."

"But she ought not to be alone in this life, and so I tell her. If only she and Mr. Brandon would make a match of it. He is so very . . ." She groped for words to describe the absent suitor, then finished rather lamely, ". . . so very solid, you see."

"You mean stolid," he ventured hopefully.

"Well, he is that, I suppose, but no, I meant rather that he is a man of some substance, which is what Susannah needs, of course, else how is she to provide for Katie? 'Tis all very well to teach the child at home now, but—well, I ask you, is it quite fitting that a Byrnes of the Haverhill Byrneses shall most likely never have a come-out?"

"Katie seems a trifle young to have to worry about that," he responded drily.

Toying with the spoon in his untouched coffee, he tried to sound quite casual as he asked, "So she is contemplating another marriage, I presume?"

Her faded eyes narrowed shrewdly, something he was too preoccupied to note. "Well, it would be a very good thing if she were, don't you agree? And certainly Mr. Brandon meets most of her requirements."

"Most?"

She sighed expressively and nodded. "The ones most females would consider of paramount importance, anyway."

"But not quite all?"

"Oh, dear, did I say that? Foolish me!"

"Miss Byrnes, I believe that plainspeaking on the matter might serve us both. Is she going to take Brandon, do you think?"

" 'Tis difficult to say," she admitted. "In the ordinary way of things, I should not think so, but our circumstances have gone quite beyond the ordinary, you know. I think if she loved him—and if he showed a degree of consideration for Katie—she would. But . . ." She carefully bit off a piece of toast and masticated it thoroughly, leaving him hanging for the next word. Swallowing finally, she washed it down with her coffee, then carefully blotted her mouth with her napkin. "Now, where was I? Oh, yes—Mr. Brandon. Well, I expect ere the year is out, everything will be outweighed by need, don't you see? And he does want her, after all, which is something that cannot be discounted. Far too many of those who call themselves gentlemen have quite something else in mind when they discover her utter lack of fortune. Mr. Brandon, however, is certain to offer marriage—said so to me, in fact."

"But Katie is the sticking point?"

She nodded. "He had great hopes she would be left

in London, but I daresay he will overcome his disappointment and offer anyway.''

He felt a small surge of triumph. ''Then he will possibly rethink the matter.''

''Oh, I shouldn't expect so. I should rather think he means to send her off to school immediately upon the marriage.''

The image of the small child being bundled away from Susannah was a painful one. It would be far better for Katie to have a competent governess, he was certain. When he looked up from his cup, he met Letty Brynes' pale eyes quite soberly.

''I like Katie very much,'' he said quietly. ''And I should like to take care of Susannah, I think. But I cannot think that a reasonable female would believe I have thrown my cap over the windmill in two days' time.''

''Well, I daresay that 'twould take a dozen visits to Almacks to achieve the degree of intimacy thrust on us here,'' she pointed out carefully.

''Far more than that.''

''And yet gentlemen are expected to come up to scratch on merest acquaintance sometimes.''

''And live to regret their rashness.''

''Well, then, at least you have seen Susannah as she truly is, Lord Lydesdale.''

It was, he suspected, the nudge he needed.

At a quarter after ten, he came down again, and even the child on the stairs knew he was dressed for traveling. She bent so low that her bright curls touched the step, as she whispered to the animal. When she looked up again at Lydesdale, her expression was unusually grave.

''He wants to know if we shall ever see you again?'' she asked in a small voice. ''He'll miss you, you know.''

Justin dropped down beside her and scratched the

black, furry head. "Tell him not to worry so much, infant." Moving his hand to her shoulder, he squeezed it. "Tell him 'tis a certainty."

"When?"

"Soon."

"Katie—oh." Susannah stood quite still when she saw him. Then, recovering, she nodded to the little girl. "I think Letty wishes help with Forty's basket."

Sighing, Katie picked up her cat carefully and trod dutifully upstairs. At the landing, she turned back. "Forty and I both shall miss you, sir."

"Do not depend on it, infant." As she disappeared around the balustrade, he raised an eyebrow. "Forty?"

"Didn't she tell you? She finally settled on a name for him this morning."

"The last I heard, she was vacillating between Black Jack and Lord Byron."

"Well, Letty was quite scandalized with Byron, of course, and the new name came to Katie quite suddenly. Considering herself quite lucky to have him, she has decided to call him Fortune."

She took in his greatcoat and knew they'd reached the end of what she would always remember as a wonderful adventure. Holding out her hand, she told him sincerely, "I am deeply indebted to you, my lord, for your kindness to Katie. I own I had not expected it of you."

His black eyes gleamed wickedly as he lifted her hand to his lips. "Dear Susannah, I shall not be fobbed off so easily. I have taken great pains and endured much to discover your direction from Aunt Letty. Indeed, if you should not dislike it excessively, I should like to pay a call after the New Year—to see how Forty goes on, of course," he added with a perfectly straight face.

"I have not a doubt in the world that Forty will welcome you, my lord."

Despite the plainness of her gown, she was in unusually fine looks this morning, having left more of her softly curling hair to frame her upturned face. He felt an incredible urge to kiss her and make a declaration on the spot. But he didn't want her to think him a here-and-thereian. Instead, he merely answered, "Good."

"Er—I believe you still have my hand, my lord."

The instant she said it, she felt the veriest fool, for the feel of his strong fingers was most reassuring. And the warmth in his eyes almost curled her toes.

"Oh—yes."

He dropped her hand and took out his watch, flipping open the cover. "Well, it grows late, Susannah, and Bevis is already warming his feet on a hot brick in my carriage. Good day, my dear." But he made no move to leave, lingering instead almost hesitatingly. Finally, he blurted out, "Don't take Brandon, Susannah—I have it on authority that he does not like Katie."

"What . . . ?"

"And I hasten to assure you that I do."

"But . . ."

"Oh, I know 'tis precipitous. I'd not have thought it possible that Justin Marshfield should discover a treasure in a place like the Red Stag, but I think I have, you know."

His dark eyes seemed almost black, but they were so very intent, as though he had to know what she thought of him. Like all females, she wanted to hear more.

"Well, I—"

"Oh, I should not expect an answer now, my dear. All I ask is the chance to court you as you deserve. Katie and Fortune aside, will you welcome me, Susannah?"

She considered all the wiles of her youth and decided they would not serve. Instead, she found herself meeting those dark eyes, and despite the rapid beating of her heart, she managed to answer simply, "Yes. Yes, I will—I shall make you most welcome, my lord."

"You know rubies would become you, Susannah," he observed suddenly. "And with proper gowns, you would make me the envy of every buck of the *ton*—provided you are of a like mind, of course."

Despite her reputation for being quite sensible, Susannah found herself touching her hair and blushing like a chit just out of the schoolroom. "Well, I—that is, garnets—oh, this is ridiculous, my lord, and . . ."

"Paltry, my dear—'tis rubies for marriage."

This time, he did lean forward, taking advantage of her confusion, and quite lightly brushed her lips. His warm breath, where it caressed her skin, sent an exquisite shiver through her.

"Until the New Year, Susannah," he whispered softly. "And tell Mr. Brandon you have discovered a man who likes Katie."

She stood there, rooted to the floor in the foyer, long after he left. It was ridiculous to think that a man like the Marquess of Lydesdale could possibly wish to continue his acquaintance with a poverty-stricken widow. Her hand crept to touch her lips as she remembered the way he'd looked at her.

"Do not be standing there gathering wool," Letty told her tartly as she came down. "Mr. Bennett has the portmanteau, and Mrs. Bennett is preparing a nuncheon to take along, but Forty positively refuses to stay in his basket. And Miss Hill is no help at all," she added with feeling, "for she says that we shall all take turns holding the creature." She stopped before she reached Susannah. "Are you quite all right, my dear?"

"Yes. Yes, I think I am." A slow, almost dreamy smile curved her mouth as she recalled everything the marquess had said when he left. Then, recovering, she looked up at Letty, and was unable to contain her happiness. "Oh, Aunt Letty—'tis not only Katie who receives a gift of fortune! Lydesdale is coming to see us in York!"

"Well, I knew he would," Letty answered mildly. "Bringing rubies, too, I expect."

The Star of
Bethlehem

by

Mary Balogh

"I've lost the Star of Bethlehem," she told him bluntly when he came to her room at her maid's bidding.
There was some sullenness in her tone, some stub-
bornness, and something else in addition to both,
perhaps.

He stood just inside the door of her bedchamber,
his feet apart, his hands clasped behind him, staring
at her, showing little emotion.

"You have lost the Star of Bethlehem," he repeated.
"Where, Estelle? You were wearing it last night."

"I still have the ring," she said with a noncha-
lance that was at variance with her fidgeting hands.
She noticed the latter, and deliberately and casually
brushed at the folds of her morning wrap in order to
give her hands something to do. "But the diamond is
gone."

"Was it missing last night when we came home?"
he asked, his eyes narrowing on her. Having assured
herself that her wrap fell in becoming folds, she was
now retying the satin bow at her throat. She looked as
if she cared not one whit about her loss.

"I would have mentioned it if I had noticed, would
I not?" she said disdainfully. "I really don't know,
Allan. All I do know is that it is missing now." She
shrugged.

"It probably came loose when you hurled the ring

at my head last night,'' he said coolly. ''Did you look at it when you picked it up again?''

She regarded him with raised chin and eyes that matched his tone. Only the heightened color of her cheeks suggested the existence of some emotion. ''Yes, I did,'' she said. ''This morning. The star was gone. And there is no point in looking about you as if you expect it to pop up at you. Annie and I have been on our knees for half an hour looking for it. It simply is not here. It must have fallen out before we came home.''

''I was standing at the foot of the bed when you threw it,'' he said. ''You missed me, of course. The ring passed to the left of me, I believe.''

''To the right,'' she said. ''I found it at the far side of the bed.''

''To the right, then,'' he said irritably. ''If I were to say that you threw it up into the air, you would probably say that you threw it under the floorboards.''

''Don't be ridiculous!'' she said coldly.

''The diamond probably landed on the bed,'' he said.

''What a brilliant suggestion!'' She looked at him with something bordering on contempt. ''Both Annie and I had similar inspiration. We have had all the bed-clothes off the bed. It is not there. It is not in this room, Allan.''

She reached into the pocket of her wrap and with-drew a ring, which she handed to him rather unnecessarily. There was certainly no doubt of the fact that the diamond was missing.

The Earl of Lisle took it on the palm of his hand and looked down at it—a wide gold band with a circlet of dark sapphires and an empty hole in the middle where the diamond had nestled. The Star of Bethlehem, she had called it—her eyes glowing like sister stars, her cheeks flushed, her lips parted—when he had given her the ring two years before on the occasion of their betrothal.

"Look, my lord," she had said—she had not called him by his given name until he had asked her to on their wedding night a few minutes after he had finished consummating their marriage. "Look, my lord, it is a bright star in a dark sky. And this is Christmas. The birthday of Christ. The beginning of all that is wonderful. The beginning for us. How auspicious that you have given me the Star of Bethlehem for our betrothal."

He had smiled at her—beautiful, dark-haired, dark-eyed, vivacious Estelle, the bride his parents had picked out for him, though his father had died a year before and unwittingly caused a delay in the betrothal. And holding her hand, the ring on her finger, he had allowed himself to fall all the way in love with her, though he had thought that at the age of thirty there was no room in his life for such deep sentiment. He had agreed to marry her because marriage was the thing to do at his age and in his position, and because marrying Estelle made him the envy of numerous gentleman—married and single alike—in London. She would be a dazzling ornament for his home and his life.

It would have been better if he had kept it so, if he had not done anything as foolish as falling in love with her. Perhaps they would have had a workable relationship if he had not done that. Perhaps after almost two years of marriage they would have grown comfortable together.

"Well," he said, looking down at the ring in his hand and carefully keeping both his face and voice expressionless, "it is no great loss, is it, Estelle? It was merely a diamond. Merely money, of which I have an abundance." He tossed the ring up, caught it, and closed his hand around it. "A mere bauble. Put it away." He held it out to her again.

286 *Mary Balogh*

Her chin lifted an inch as she took it from him. "I am sorry to have taken your time," she said, "but I thought you should know. I would not have had you find out at some future time and think that I had been afraid to tell you."

His lips formed into something of a sneer. "We both know that you could not possibly fear my ill opinion, don't we?" he said. "I am merely the man who pays the bills and makes all respectable in your life. Perhaps the diamond fell into the pocket or the neckcloth of Martindale last evening. You spent enough time in his company. You must ask him next time you see him. Later today, perhaps?"

She ignored his last words. "Or about the person of Lord Peterson or Mr. Hayward or Sir Caspar Rhodes," she said. "I danced with them all last evening, and enticed them all into anterooms for secret dalliance." Her chin was high, her voice heavy with sarcasm.

"I believe we said—or rather yelled—all that needs to be expressed about your behavior at the Eastman ball—or your lack of behavior—last night," he said. "I choose not to reopen the quarrel, Estelle. But I have thought further about what I said heatedly then. And I repeat it now when my temper is down. When Christmas is over and your parents return to the country, I believe it will be as well for you to return with them for a visit."

"Banishment?" she said. "Is that not a little gothic, Allan?"

"We need some time apart," he said. "Although for the past few months we have seen each other only when necessary, we have still contrived to quarrel with tedious frequency. We need a month or two in which to rethink our relationship."

"How about a lifetime or two?" she said.

"If necessary." He looked at her steadily from cold blue eyes. Beautiful, headstrong Estelle. Incurably

flirtatious. Not caring the snap of a finger for him beyond the fact that he had had it in his power to make
her the Countess of Lisle and to finance her whims for
the rest of a pampered life, despite the occasional flar-
ing of hot passion that always had him wondering
when it was all over and she lay sleeping in his arms
if she had ever gifted other men with such favors.
And always hating himself for such unfounded suspicions.

She shivered suddenly. "It is so cold in here," she
said petulantly. "How can we be without fires in December? It is quite unreasonable."

"You are the one being unreasonable," he said.
"You might be in the morning room now or in the
library, where there are fires. You might have slept in
a bedchamber where there was a fire. Chimneys have
to be swept occasionally if they are not to catch fire.
Half the house yesterday; the other half today. It is not
such a great inconvenience, is it?"

"It should be done in the summertime," she said.

"During the summer you said it could wait until the
winter when we would be going into the country," he
reminded her. "And then you had this whim about
having Christmas here this year with both our families. Well, I have given you your way about that,
Estelle—as usual. But the chimneys have been smoking. They must be cleaned before our guests arrive
next week. By tomorrow all will be set to rights
again."

"I hate it when you talk to me in that voice," she
said, "as if I were a little child of defective understanding."

"You hate it when I talk to you in any voice," he
said. "And sometimes you behave like a child of defective understanding."

"Thank you," she said, opening her hand and looking down at the ring. "I wish to get dressed, Allan,
and go in search of a room with a warm fire. I am

grateful that you have seen fit not to beat me over the loss of the diamond.''

''Estelle!'' All his carefully suppressed anger boiled to the surface and exploded in the one word.

She tossed her head up and glared across at him with dark and hostile eyes. He strode from the room without another word.

Estelle returned her gaze to the ring in the palm of her hand. The back of her nose and throat all the way down to her chest were a raw ache. The diamond was gone. It was all ruined. All of it. Two years was not such a very long time, but it seemed like another Estelle who had watched as he slid the ring onto her finger and rested her hand on his so that she could see it.

It had been Christmas, and she had been caught up in the usual euphoric feelings of love and goodwill, and the unrealistic conviction that every day could be Christmas if everyone would just try hard enough. She had looked at the diamond and the sapphires, and they had seemed like a bright symbol of hope. Hope that the arranged marriage she had agreed to because Mama and Papa had thought it such a splendid opportunity for her would be a happy marriage. Hope that the tall, golden-haired, unsmiling, rather austere figure of her betrothed would turn out to be a man she could like and be comfortable with—perhaps even love.

The ring had been the Star of Bethlehem to her from the start and without any effort of thought. And he had smiled one of his rare smiles when she had looked up at him and named the ring that. Looking into his blue eyes at that moment, she had thought that perhap he would grow fond of her. She had thought that perhaps he would kiss her. He had not, though he had raised her hand to his lips and kissed both it and the ring.

He had not kissed her mouth at all before their marriage. But he had kissed her afterward on their wedding night in their marriage bed. And he had made a tender and a beautiful and an almost painless experience out of what she had anticipated with some fright.

She had thought . . . She had hoped . . .

But it did not matter. The only really tender and passionate moments of their marriage had happened in her bed. Always actions of the body. Never words.

They had not really grown close. He never revealed much of himself to her. And she shared only trivialities with him. They never really talked.

They were lovers only in fits and starts. Sometimes wild passion for three or four nights in a row. And then perhaps weeks of nothing in between.

She had never conceived. Not, at least . . . But she was not at all sure.

The only thing consistent in their relationship was the quarrels. Almost always over her behavior toward other gentlemen. His accusations had been unjust at first. It was in her nature to be smiling and friendly, flirtatious even. She had meant nothing by it. All her loyalty had been given to her new husband. She had been hurt and bewildered by his disapproval. But in the last year, she had begun to flirt quite deliberately. Never enough to deceive the gentleman concerned. No one except Allan had ever been offered her lips or any other part of her body except her hand. And never even one small corner of her heart. But she had taken an almost fiendish glee in noting her husband's expression across a crowded drawing room or ballroom, and anticipating the wild rages they would both let loose when they came home.

Sometimes after the quarrels he would retire to his room, slamming the door that connected their dressing rooms behind him. Sometimes they would end up together in her bed, the heat of anger turned to the heat of sexual passion.

The night before had not been one of those latter occasions. She had dragged the Star of Bethlehem from her finger and hurled it at his head and screeched something to the effect that since the ring had become meaningless, he might have it back and welcome to it. And he had yelled something about its being less likely to scratch the cheeks of her lovers if she were not wearing it. And he had stalked out, leaving the door vibrating on its hinges.

And now she really was without the ring. No, worse. She had the shell of it left, just as the shell of her marriage still remained. The star was gone—from the ring and from her marriage.

She was taken by surprise when a loud and painful hiccup of a sob broke the silence of the room, and even more surprised when she realized that the sound had come from her. But it was a wonderful balm to her self-pity, she found. She allowed herself the rare indulgence of an extended and noisy cry.

It was all his fault. Nasty, unfeeling, sneering, cold, jealous monster! She hated him. She did not care that the ring was ruined. What did she care for his ring? Or for him? Or for their marriage? She would be delighted go home with Mama and Papa when Christmas was over. She would stay with them, surrounded by all the peace and familiarity of her childhood home. She would forget about the turmoil and nightmare of the past two years. She would forget about Allan.

"Allan."

The name was spoken on a wail. She looked down at the ring and sniffed wetly and noisily.

"Allan."

She drew back her arm suddenly and hurled the ring with all her strength across the room. She heard it tinkle as it hit something, but she did not go in pursuit of it. She rushed into her dressing room and slammed the door firmly behind her.

* * *

Two minutes passed after the slamming of the door before there came a rustling from the direction of the cold chimney followed by a quiet plop and the appearance of a tiny, ragged, soot-smeared figure among the ashes. After looking cautiously around and stooping for a moment to grub about among the ashes, it stepped gingerly out into the room and revealed itself as a child.

The chimney sweep's boy looked briefly down at the diamond in his hand, a jewel he had mistaken for a shard of glass until he had overheard the conversation of the man and woman. His eyes darted about the room, taking in the door through which the woman had disappeared, and close to which she must have been standing while she was crying and when he had heard the tinkling sound.

She must have thrown the ring they had been talking about. It was just the sort of thing women did when they were in a temper.

His mind tried to narrow the search by guessing in which direction she would have thrown the ring from that particular door. But his wits really did not need sharpening, he saw as soon as he turned his eyes in the direction that seemed most likely. It was lying on the carpet in the open, the light from the window sparkling off the gold band.

What queer coves these rich people were, giving up the search for the diamond after only half an hour, if the woman was to be believed—and the man had not even searched at all. And throwing a gold band set full of precious stones across a room and leaving it lying there on the floor for anyone to take.

The child darted across the room, scooped up the ring, and pulled a dirty rag from somewhere about his person. He stopped when he had one foot back among the ashes, and tied his two treasures securely inside the rag. He must get back to old Thomas. The sweep would be hopping mad by now, and the old excuse of getting lost among the maze of chimneys had been used only three days before.

However, the child thought with a philosophy born of necessity, today's haul would probably be worth every stinging stroke of old Thomas's hand. As long as he did not use his belt. Even the costliest jewel did not seem quite consolation enough for the strappings he sometimes got from the sweep's belt.

The boy had both feet in the grate and was about to pull himself up into the darkness and soot of the chimney when the door through which the lady had disappeared opened abruptly again. He started to cry pitifully.

Estelle, now clad in a morning dress of fine white wool, even though her hair was still about her shoulders in a dark cloud, stopped in amazement.

The child wailed and scrubbed his clenched fists at his eyes.

"What is it?" she said, hurrying across the room to the fireplace and stooping down to have a better look at the apparition standing there. "You must be the chimney sweep's boy. Oh, you poor child."

The last words were spoken after she had had a good look at the grimy, skeletal frame of the child and the indescribable filth of his person and of his rags. Hair of indeterminate color stood up from his head in stiff and matted spikes. Two muddy tracks flowed from his eyes to his chin. He looked as if he were no older than five or six.

"It's dark up there," he wailed. "I can't breathe."

"You shouldn't be climbing chimneys," she said. "You are just a baby."

The child sniffed wetly and breathed out on a shuddering sob. "I got lost," he said. "It's dark up there."

"Oh, you poor child." Estelle reached out a hand to touch him, hesitated, and took hold of one thin arm. "Step out here. The ashes will cut your poor feet."

The boy started to cry in noisy earnest again. "He'll—thrash—me," he got out on three separate sobs. "I got lost."

"He will not thrash you," Estelle said indignantly, taking hold of the child's other arm with her free hand and helping him step out onto the carpet. He was skin and bones, she thought in some horror. He was just a frightened, half starved little baby. "He will certainly not thrash you. I shall see to that. What is your name?"

"N-Nicky, missus," the boy said, and he hung his head and wrapped one skinny leg about the other and sniffed loudly.

"Nicky," she said, and she reached up and tried to smooth down the hair on top of his head. But it was stiff with dirt. "Nicky, when did you last eat?"

The child began to wail.

"Have you eaten today?" she asked.

He shuffled his shoulders back and forth and swayed on his one leg. He muttered something.

"What?" she said gently. She was down on her knees looking into his face. "Have you eaten?"

"I don't know, missus," he said, his chin buried on his thin chest. And he rubbed the back of his hand over his wet nose.

"Did your master not give you anything to eat this morning?" she asked.

"I ain't to get fat," he said, and the wails grew to a new crescendo. "I'm so hungry."

"Oh, you poor, poor child." There were tears in Estelle's eyes. "Does your mama know that you are kept half-starved? Have you told her?"

"I ain't got no maw." His sobs occupied the child for several seconds. "I got took from the orphinige, missus."

"Oh, Nicky." Estelle laid one gentle hand against his cheek, only half noticing how dirty her hand was already.

"He'll belt me for sure." The child scratched the back of one leg with the heel of the other foot and scrubbed at his eyes again with his fists. "I got lost. It's dark and I can't get me breath up there."

"He will not hurt you. You have my word on it." Estelle straightened up and crossed the room to the bell pull to summon her maid. "Sit down on the floor, Nicky. I shall see that you have some food inside you if nothing else. Does he beat you often?"

The child heaved one leftover sob as he sat down cross-legged on the carpet. "No more nor three or four times a day when I'm good," he said. "But I keep getting lost."

"Three or four times a day!" she said, and turned to instruct her maid to sit with the child for a few minutes. "I will be back, Nicky, and you shall have some food. I promise."

Annie looked at the apparition in some disbelief as her mistress disappeared from the room. She sat on the edge of the bed a good twenty feet away from him, and gathered her skirts close about her as if she were afraid that they would brush against a mote of soot floating about in his vicinity.

Estelle swept down the marble stairway to the hall below, her chin high, her jaw set in a firm line. At one glance from her eyes, a footman scurried across the tiles and threw open the doors of his lordship's study without even knocking first. His mistress swept past him and glared at her husband's man of business, who had the misfortune to be closeted with the earl at that particular moment.

"Can I be of service to you, my dear?" his lordship asked, as both men jumped to their feet.

"I wish to speak with you," she said, continuing her progress across the room until she stood at the window, gazing out at the gray, wintry street beyond. She did not even listen to the hurried leavetaking that the visitor took.

"Was that necessary, Estelle?" her husband's quiet voice asked as the doors of the study closed. "Porter is a busy man and has taken the time to come half across town at my request this morning. Such men have to work for a living. They ought not to be subject to the whims of the aristocracy."

She turned from the window. She ignored his cold reproof. "Allan," she said, "there is a child in my bedchamber. A thin, dirty, frightened, and hungry child."

He frowned. "The sweep's climbing boy?" he said. "But what is he doing there? He has no business being in any room where his master or one of our servants is not. I am sorry. I shall see to it. It will not happen again."

"He is frightened," she said. "The chimneys are dark and he cannot breathe. He gets lost up there. And then he is whipped when he gets back to the sweep."

He took a few steps toward her, his hands clasped behind his back. "They do not have an enviable lot," he said. "Poor little urchins."

"He is like a scarecrow," she said. "He cannot remember if he has eaten today. But he is not allowed to eat too much for fear he will get fat."

"They get stuck in the chimneys if they are too fat," he said, "or too big."

"He gets beaten three or four times a day, Allan," she said. "He does not have a mother or father to protect him. He comes from an orphanage."

He looked at her, his brows drawn together in a frown. "You ought not to be subjected to such painful realities," he said. "I shall have a word with Stebbins, Estelle. It will not happen again. And I shall see to it that the child is not chastised this time. I'm sorry. You are upset." He crossed the room to stand a couple of feet in front of her.

She looked up at him. "He is a baby, Allan," she said. "A frightened, starving little baby."

He lifted a hand to rest his fingertips against her cheek. "I will have a word with the sweep myself," he said. "Something will be done, I promise."

She caught at his hand and nestled her cheek against his palm. "You will do something?" she asked, her dark eyes pleading with him. "You will? You promise? Allan—" her voice became thin and high-pitched— "he is just a little baby."

"Is he still in your room?" he asked.

"Yes," she said. "I have promised him food."

"Have some taken to him, then," he said. "And keep him there for a while. I will come to you there."

"You will?" Her eyes were bright with tears, and she turned her head in order to kiss his wrist. "Thank you, Allan. Oh, thank you."

He held the door of the study open for her, his face as stern and impassive as usual, and summoned a footman with the lift of an eyebrow. He sent the man running in search of the butler and the chimney sweep.

A little more than half an hour later the Earl of Lisle was standing in his wife's bedchamber, his hands clasped behind his back, looking down at a tiny bundle of rags and bones huddled over a plate that held nothing except two perfectly clean chicken bones and a few crumbs of bread. The bundle looked up at him with wide and wary eyes. The countess's eyes were also wide, and questioning.

"You are Nicholas?" his lordship asked.

"Nicky, guv'nor," the child said in a high piping voice.

"Well, Nicky," the earl said, looking steadily down at him. "And how would you like to stay here and not have to climb chimneys ever again?"

The boy stared, open-mouthed. The countess clasped her hands to her bosom and continued to stare silently at her husband.

"I have talked with Mr. Thomas," the earl said, "and made arrangements with him. And I have instructed Mrs. Ainsford, the housekeeper, to find employment for you belowstairs. You will live here and be adequately fed and clothed. And you will continue to have employment with me for as long as you wish provided you do the work assigned to you. You will never be whipped."

He paused and looked down at the boy, who continued to stare up at him open-mouthed.

"Do you have anything to say?" he asked.

"No more chimbleys?" the child asked.

"No more chimneys."

Nicky's jaw dropped again.

"Does this please you?" the earl asked. "Would you like to be a part of this household?"

"Cor blimey, guv'nor," the boy said.

Which words the earl interpreted as cautious assent. He assigned his new servant to the tender care of the housekeeper, who was waiting outside the door and who considered that her position in the household was an exalted one enough that she could permit herself a cluck of the tongue and a look tossed at the ceiling before she took the little ragamuffin by the hand and marched him down the back stairs to the kitchen and the large tin bathtub that two maids had been instructed to fill with steaming water.

Estelle smiled dazzlingly at her husband and hurried after them. Her white dress, he noticed, standing and watching her go, his hands still clasped behind his back, was smudged with dirt in several places.

She looked more beautiful even than usual.

Estelle was lying in her husband's arms, feeling relaxed and drowsy, but not wanting to give in to sleep. It had been a happy and an exciting day and she was reluctant to let it go.

The best part of it was that Allan had come to her

after she had gone to bed, for the first time in two weeks. He had said nothing—he almost never did on such occasions—but he had made slow love to her, his hands and his mouth gentle and arousing, his body coaxing her response and waiting for it. They were good in bed together. They always had been, right back to that first time, when she had been nervous and quite ignorant of what she was to do. Even when there was anger between them, there was always passion too. But too often there was the anger, and it always left a bitterness when the body's cravings had been satiated.

It was best of all when there was no anger. And when he held her afterward and did not immediately return to his own room. She liked to fall asleep in his arms, the warmth and the smell of him lulling her.

Except that she did not want to fall asleep tonight. Not yet.

"Allan," she whispered hesitantly. They almost never talked when they were in bed. And very rarely when they were out of it, except when they were yelling at each other.

"Yes?" His voice sounded almost tense.

"Thank you," she said. "Thank you for what you did for Nicky. I think he will be happy here, don't you? You have taken him out of hell and brought him into heaven."

"Our home heaven?" he said quietly, jarring her mood slightly. "But he will be safe here, Estelle, and warm and well fed. It is all we can do."

"He has a new home in time for Christmas," she said. "Poor little orphan child. He must be so very happy, Allan, and grateful to you."

"He has merely exchanged one servitude for another," he said. "But at least he will not be mistreated here."

"What did you say to the sweep?" she asked. "Did you threaten him with jail?"

"He was doing nothing that every other sweep in

the country is not doing," he said. "The problem does not end with the rescue of the boy, Estelle. I merely bought him for twice his apprenticeship fee. The man made a handsome profit."

"Oh, Allan!" Her hand spread across his chest over the fabric of his nightshirt. "The poor little boys."

She felt him swallow. "Some members of the House are concerned over the matter," he said, "and over the whole question of child labor. I shall speak with them, find out more, perhaps even speak in the House myself."

"Will you?" She burrowed her head more deeply into the warmth of his shoulder. She wanted to find his mouth in the darkness. But she only ever had the courage to do that when he had aroused passion in her.

"In the meantime," he said, "you can console yourself with the thought that at least your little Nicky has a warm and soft bed for the night and a full stomach."

And then a wonderful thing happened. Something that had never happened before in almost two years of marriage. He turned his head and kissed her, long minutes after their lovemaking was over, and turned onto his side and stroked the hair back from her face with gentle fingers. And before another minute had passed, she knew that he was going to come to her again.

She fell asleep almost immediately after it was over. It was not until later in the night when she had awoken and nestled closer to the sleeping form of her husband, who was still beside her, that reality took away some of the magic of the previous day. He had done a wonderful thing for Nicky, she thought. They would be able to watch him grow into a healthy and carefree childhood, long after this particular Christmas was past.

They would be able to watch him? *He* would, perhaps. Allan would. But would she? She was to be banished to Papa's home after Christmas for a stay that would surely extend itself beyond weeks into months. Perhaps even years. Perhaps forever. Perhaps she would only ever see Allan again on brief visits, for form's sake.

He was sending her away. So that they might rethink their relationship, he had said. So that he might end their marriage to all intents and purposes. He didn't want her anymore. He did not want their marriage to continue. And even if he was forced to continue their marriage to some degree, even if her suspicion and hardly admitted hope proved right, it would be an empty thing, only a third person holding them together.

And there was that other thing. That thing that she had not allowed to come between her and her joy the previous day. The missing ring. Not just the diamond, but the whole ring. She had hunted for it until she had felt almost sick enough to vomit. But she had not found it. Or told Allan about its disappearance. She had repressed her panic and the terrible sense of loss that had threatened to overwhelm her.

Where could it have gone? Had it been swept up by the maids? She had even thought briefly of Nicky, but had shaken the thought off immediately. It had just disappeared, as the diamond had.

Christmas was coming, and there would be no Star of Bethlehem for her. No joy or love or hope.

But she would not think such depressing and self-pitying thoughts. She settled her cheek more comfortably against her husband's broad shoulder and rested a hand on his warm arm. And she deliberately thought back on the brighter part of the previous day. She smiled.

Nicky not wanting to be parted from his filthy rags and bursting into pitiful wailings when Mrs. Ainsford snatched away the rag of a handkerchief he clutched even after he had relinquished all else. He had a curl of his mother's hair in the little bundle, he had claimed, and a seashell that someone had given him at the orphanage. All his worldy possessions. Mrs. Ainsford had given the rag back to him and another clean one to use instead. But the child had not unpacked his treasures to their interested gaze.

Estelle smiled again, listened for a few moments to the deep and even breathing of the man beside her, and turned her head to kiss his shoulder before allowing herself to slip back into sleep.

The earl had not slept for a while after making love to his wife for the second time. He ought not to have come. Relations between them had been strained enough for several months, and the bitter quarrel of the night before had brought matters to a crisis. He had made the decision that they should live apart, at least for a time. They must keep up the charade over Christmas, of course, for the sake of her family and his own. But the pretense did not at least have to extend to the bedchamber.

There was no harmony between them—none—except in what passed between them in silence between the sheets of her bed. He had often wanted to try to extend that harmony into other aspects of their life by talking to her in the aftermath of passion, when they would perhaps feel more kindly disposed to each other than at any other time.

But he had never done so. He was no good at talking. He had always been afraid to talk to Estelle, afraid that he would not be able to convey his inner self to her. He had chosen to keep himself closed to her rather than try to communicate and know himself a failure. He had always been mortally afraid of having his love thrown back in his face. Better that she did not know. And so he had contented himself with giving his love only the one outlet. Only the physical.

But he should not have come tonight. The events of the day had created the illusion of closeness between them. And so he had come to her, and she had received him with something more than the usual passion, which he knew himself capable of arousing. There had been an eagerness in her, a tenderness almost. A gratitude for what he had done for her little climbing boy.

He should not have come. How would he do without her after she had left with her parents after Christmas?

How would he live without her?

What would he give her as a Christmas gift? It must be something very special, something that would perhaps tell her, as he could never do, that despite everything he cared.

Some jewels perhaps? Something to dazzle her?

He smiled bitterly into the darkness as Estelle made low noises in her sleep and burrowed more closely into his warmth. Something to remind her that she had a wealthy husband. More baubles for her to lose or to cast aside with that look of disdain that she was so expert at when he was angry with her for some reason.

Like that ring. He stared upward at the dark canopy over his head. The Star of Bethlehem. The ring that had told him as soon as he slid it onto her finger two years before that she was the jewel of his life, the star of his life. It was not a bauble. Not merely a symbol of wealth.

It was a symbol of his love, of his great hope for what their marriage might have been.

If he could replace the diamond . . .

Where had she put the ring? It had probably been tossed into a drawer somewhere. It should not be hard to find. He could probably find it with ease if he waited for her to go out and then searched her rooms.

He would have the diamond replaced for her. She had been careless about its loss. It had not really mattered to her. She had told him about it merely to avoid a scolding if he had discovered it for himself at a later date.

But surely if he could put it on her finger again this Christmas, whole again, the Star of Bethlehem new again, as Christmas was always new even more than eighteen hundred years after the first one, then it would mean something to her.

Perhaps she would be pleased. And perhaps in the months to come, when she had not seen him for a while, when the bitterness of their quarrels had faded, she would look at it and realize that he had put more than his money into the gift.

He turned his head and kissed his sleeping wife with warm tenderness just above the ear. There was an excitement in him that would surely make if difficult to get to sleep.

Estelle had been happy about Nicky. He remembered the look she had given him as she left this very room after Mrs. Ainsford and the child—a bright and sparkling look all focused on him. The sort of look he had dreamed of inspiring before he married her. Before he knew himself quite incapable of drawing to himself those looks that she bestowed so willingly on other men. Before he realized that he would find himself quite incapable of communicating with her.

He would bask in the memory. And the child had been saved from a brutal life. That poor little skeletal baby, who was probably sleeping peacefully at that very moment in another part of the house, as babies ought.

At that precise moment the former climbing boy, whom his new master thought to be peacefully asleep, was sitting cross-legged on the floor of a room in quite another part of London—a dingy, dirty attic room that was sparsely furnished and strewn with rags and stale remnants of food and empty jugs.

"I tell you, Mags," he was saying in his piping voice, which nevertheless did not sound as pathetic as it had sounded in the countess's bedchamber the previous day, "I took me life in me 'ands comin' 'ere in these togs." He indicated the white shirt and breeches, obviously of an expensive cut and equally obviously part of a suit of livery belonging to some grand house. "But there weren't nothin' else. They burned all me other things."

The Mags referred to shook with silent laughter. "I scarce knew you, young Nick," he said. "I always thought you 'ad black hair."

The child touched his soft fair hair. "Such a scrubbin' you never did 'ear tell of," he said in some disgust. "I thought she'd rub me skin away for sure."

"So yer can't be up to the old lark no more," Mags said, the laughter passing as silently as it had come.

"Naw." Nicky scratched his head from old habit. "Thought she was bein' a blessed angel, she did, that woman. And 'im standin' there arskin' me if I wanted to stay at their 'ouse. Exceptin' I couldn't say no. I would've given an 'ole farthin' to 'ave seen old Thomas's face." He giggled, sounding for a moment very much like the baby the Earl and Countess of Lisle had taken him for. He was in reality almost eleven years old.

"This might be better," Mags said, rubbing his hands together thoughtfully. "You can go 'round the 'ouse at leisure, young Nick, and lift a fork 'ere and a jeweled pin there. P'raps they'll take you to other 'ouses, and yer can 'ave a snoop around them too."

"It'll be almost too easy," Nicky said, rubbing the side of his nose with one finger. His voice was contemptuous. "They're a soft touch if ever I seen one, Mags."

"Got anythin' for me tonight?" Mags asked.

The child shifted position and scratched his rump. "Naw," he said after a few moments' consideration. "Nothin' tonight, Mags. Next time."

"It weren't hardly worth comin', then, were it?" the older man said, his narrowed eyes on the child.

"Just wanted yer to know that me fairy godmother come," the child said, leaping lightly to his feet. "Did yer give the money to me maw for that thimble I brought you last week?"

" 'Tweren't worth much," Mags said quickly. "But yes. Yer maw got her food money." He laughed silently again. "And yer sister got 'er vittles to grow on. Another two or three years, young Nick, and yer maw'll be rich with the two of yer."

"I got to go," the child said. And he climbed down the stairs from the attic and went out into the street, where for the first time in his life he had something to fear. His appearance made him fair game for attack. Only the filthy stream of curses he had been quite capable of producing had discouraged one pair of tough-looking urchins when he had been on his way to Mags's attic.

And unexpectedly he still had something to protect on his way back home. He still had the ring and the diamond pressed between the band of his breeches and his skin, although the main reason for his night's outing had been to deliver them to Mags for payment. One of his better hauls. But he had not given them up. That woman, whom he had been told he must call "your ladyship," had bawled like a baby after the man had left her, and flung the ring across the room.

And she had had food brought to him, and had sat and watched him eat it, and smiled at him. And she was the one who had told the big sour-faced, big-bosomed woman to give him back his bundle—the bundle that held her ring and diamond, and who had stooped down and kissed him on the cheek before he got dumped in that hot water up to the neck and scrubbed raw.

She was pretty. Silly of course, and not a brain in her brainbox—calling him a baby, indeed, and believing his story about the orphanage and about his mother's lock of hair! But very pretty. Well, he would keep her ring for a day or two and sell it to Mags the next time he came. He would have more things by then, though not much. The reason he had never been caught was probably that he had never been greedy. He had learned his lesson well from Mags. He had never taken more than one thing from each house, and never anything that he had thought would be sorely missed.

Nicky darted in his bare feet along a dark street in the shadows of the buildings and cursed his clean hair and skin, which would make him more noticeable, and his clothes, which would be like a red flag to a bull if the wrong people were to spot him on these particular streets.

The bed was empty beside Estelle when she woke up the following morning. She felt only a fleeting disappointment. After all, he never had stayed until morning. And if he had been there, there would have been an awkwardness between them. What would they say to each other, how would they look at each other if they awoke in bed together in the daylight? And remembered the hot passion they had shared before they had fallen asleep.

When she met him downstairs—in the breakfast room perhaps, or later in some other part of the house—he would be, as always, his immaculate, taciturn, rather severe self again. It would be easy to look at him then. He would seem like a different man from the one whose hands and mouth and body had created their magic on her during the darkness of the night.

It was a good thing that he was not there this morning. The night had had its double dose of lovemaking and silent tenderness. At least she could imagine it was tenderness until she saw him again and knew him incapable of such a very human emotion.

Estelle threw back the bedclothes even though Annie had not yet arrived and even though the fire was all but extinguished in the fireplace. She shivered and stood very still, wondering if she really felt nausea or if she was merely willing the feeling on herself. She shrugged, and resumed the futile search for her ring. She had combed through every inch of the room the day before, more than once. It was not to be found.

What she should do was repeat what she had done the day before. She should send for Allan before she had time to think and tell him the truth. If he ripped up at her, if he yelled at her, or—worse—if he turned cold and looked at her with frozen blue eyes and thinned lips, then she would think of some suitably cutting retort. And she need not fear him. He had never beaten her, and she did not think she could ever do anything bad enough that he would.

And what could he do that he had not already done? He had already decided to banish her. There was nothing he could do worse than that. Nothing.

"Oh, my lady," Annie said a few minutes later, coming into the room with her morning chocolate and finding her standing in the corner of the room where she had thrown the ring, "you will catch your death."

Estelle glanced down at herself and realized that she had not even put on a wrap over her nightgown. She shivered. And looked at her maid and opened her mouth to tell the girl to go summon his lordship.

"It is rather cold in here," she said instead. "Will you have some coals sent up immediately, Annie?"

The girl curtsied and disappeared from the room.

And Estelle knew immediately that the moment had been lost. In the second that had elapsed between the opening of her mouth and the speaking of the words about coal being brought for the fire, she had turned coward.

It had been easy the morning before to have Allan called and to tell him about the missing diamond. She had still been smarting from the accusations he had hurled at her the night before, and the sentence he had

passed on her. She had derived a perverse sort of pleasure from telling him of the ruin of his first gift to her.

This morning it was different. This morning she
could remember his kindness to a little child. And his
gentle tenderness to her the night before. And she
could hope that perhaps it would be repeated that night
if nothing happened during the day to arouse the hos-
tility that always lurked just below the surface of their
relationship—except when it boiled up above the surface, that was.

This morning she was a coward. This morning she
could not tell him.

She had arranged to go shopping with her friend
Isabella Lawrence. There were all sorts of Christmas
gifts to be purchased before their house guests began
to arrive to take up all her time. There was Allan's gift
to be chosen, and she did not know what she would
get him. She did have one gift for him already, of
course. She had persuaded Lord Humber, that elderly
miser, to part with a silver snuffbox Allan had admired months before, and she had kept it as a Christmas gift. But that had been a long time ago. And Lord
Humber had refused to take anything but a token payment. Besides, she had given him a snuffbox the year
before too. She wanted something else, something very
special. But what did one buy for a man who had everything? Still, she would enjoy the morning despite
the problem. Isabella could always cheer her up with
her bright chatter and incessant gossiping.

She ate her breakfast in lone state, her husband having already removed to his study, Stebbins told her.
She did not know whether to be glad or sorry.

But there was one thing she had to do before going
out. She had Annie bring Nicky to her dressing room.

She smiled at him when he stood inside the door,
his chin tucked against his chest, one leg wrapping
itself around the other. He was clean and dressed

smartly in the livery of the house. But he was still, of course, pathetically thin and endearingly small.

"Good morning, Nicky," she said.

He muttered something into the front of his coat.

She crossed the room in a rush, stooped down in front of him and set her hands on his thin shoulders. "Did you have a good breakfast?" she asked. "And did you sleep well?"

"Yes, missus," he said. "I mean . . ."

"That is all right," she said, lifting a hand to smooth back his hair. "You do look splendid. Such shiny blond hair. Are you happy, Nicky, now that you have a real home of your own?"

"Yes, missus," he said, sniffing and drawing his cuff across his nose.

"Nicky," she said, "I lost a ring yesterday. In my bedchamber. You did not see it there when you came down the chimney, I suppose?"

The child returned his foot to the floor and scratched the back of his leg with his other heel.

"No, of course you did not," she said, putting her arms about his thin little body and hugging him warmly. "Oh, Nicky, his lordship gave me the ring when we were betrothed. And now I have lost it. It was without question my most precious possession. Like the lock of your mama's hair is to you. And the seashell." She sighed. "But no matter. Something else very precious came into my life yesterday. Even more precious perhaps because it is living." She smiled at his bowed head and kissed his cheek. "You came into my life, dear. I want you to be happy here. I want you to grow up happy and healthy. There will never be any more chimneys, I promise you. His lordship would not allow it."

Nicky rubbed his chin back and forth on his chest and rocked dangerously on his one leg.

"Annie is waiting outside for you," Estelle said. "She will take you back to the kitchen, and Mrs.

Ainsford will find you jobs to do. But nothing too hard, I assure you. Run along now. I shall buy you a present for Christmas while I am out. And I will not add 'if you are good.' I shall give you a gift even if you are not good. Everyone should have a Christmas gift whether he deserves it or not.''

Nicky looked up at her for the first time, with eyes that seemed far too large for his pale thin face. Then his hand found the door knob and opened the door. He darted out to join the waiting maid.

Estelle tied the strings of her bonnet beneath her chin and knew what she was going to buy for her husband for Christmas. It was not really a gift for him, she supposed. But it would do. It would be the best she could do, and perhaps after she had gone away into her banishment he would understand why she had chosen to give him such a strange gift. Perhaps—oh, just perhaps—her exile would not last a lifetime.

The Earl of Lisle felt very guilty. He had often accused his wife of flirting, the basis of very hard evidence he had seen with his own eyes. He had a few times accused her of doing more than flirt. She had always hotly denied the charges, though she had usually ended the arguments with a toss of the head and that look of disdain and the comment that he might believe what he pleased. And who, apart from him, would blame her anyway for taking a lover, when she was tied for the rest of a lifetime to such a husband?

He had never looked for evidence. And it was not because he was afraid of what he might discover. Rather it was out of a deep conviction that even though he was her husband, he did not own her. Although in the eyes of the law she was his possession, he would never look on her as such. She was Estelle. His wife. The woman he had secretly loved since before his marriage to her. And if she chose to flirt with other men, if she chose to be unfaithful to him with one or more of those men, then he would rant and rave and perhaps put her away from him forever. But he would never spy on her, never publicly accuse her, never publicly disown her.

He would endure if he must, as dozens of wives were expected to endure when their husbands chose to take mistresses. ˙

It was with the greatest of unease, then, that he searched his wife's rooms after she had left on her shopping trip with Isabella Lawrence. He was looking for the ring. He was terrified of finding something else. Something that he did not want to find. Something that would incriminate her and destroy him.

He found nothing. Nothing to confirm some of his worst suspicions. And not the ring either. Wherever she had put it, it certainly was not in either her bedchamber or her dressing room.

It seemed to him, as he wandered through into his own dressing room, that he must now abandon the plan that had so delighted him the night before. But not necessarily so, he thought after a while. The diamond would have been new anyway. Why not the whole ring? Why not have the whole thing copied for her? A wholly new gift.

A wholly new love offering.

The trouble was, of course, that he would have to describe the ring very exactly to a jeweler in order that it could be duplicated. He had bought the ring for her two years before. He had put it on her hand. He had looked at it there, with mingled pride and love and despair, a thousand times and more. And yet he found that he could not be clear in his mind whether there had been eight sapphires or nine. And exactly how wide had the gold band been?

He tried sketching the ring, but he had never been much of an artist.

He would have to do the best he could. After all, it

was not as if he were going to try to pretend to her
that it was the original ring.

The idea of the gift excited him again. Perhaps he
would even be able to explain to her when he gave it.
Explain why he had done it, what the ring meant to
him. What she meant to him.

Perhaps. Perhaps if he did so she would look at him
in incomprehension. Or with that look of disdain.

Or perhaps—just perhaps—with a look similar to the
one she had given him the day before after he had told
the little climbing boy that he would be staying with
them.

He would go immediately, he decided. The ring
would have to be made specially. And there was less
than two weeks left before Christmas. He must go
without delay.

He decided on eight sapphires when the moment
came to give directions to the jeweler he had chosen.
And he picked out a diamond that looked to him almost identical to the Star of Bethlehem. And left the
shop on Oxford Street feeling pleased with the morning's work and filled with a cautious hope for the future. Christmas was coming. Who would not feel
hopeful at such a season of the year?

But his mood was short-lived. As he walked past
the bow windows of a confectioner's shop, he turned
his head absently to look inside and saw his wife sitting at a table there with Lady Lawrence. And with
Lord Martindale and Sir Cyril Porchester. Estelle's
face was flushed and animated. She was laughing, as
were they all.

She did not see him. He walked on past.

Estelle, inside the confectioner's shop, stopped
laughing and shook her head at the plate of cakes that
Sir Cyril offered to her. "What a perfectly horrid thing
to say," she said to Lord Martindale, her eyes still
dancing with merriment. "As if I would buy Allan an
expensive gift and have the bill sent to him."

"There are plenty of wives who do just that, my dear Lady Lisle," he said.

"I save my money for Christmas," she said, "so that I can buy whatever I want without having to run to Allan."

"But you still refuse to tell us what you are going to buy him, the lucky man?" Sir Cyril asked.

"Absolutely," she said, bright-eyed and smiling. "I have not even told Isabella. It is to be a surprise. For Allan alone."

Lord Martindale helped himself to another cake. "One would like to know what Lisle has done to deserve such devotion, would one not, Porchester?"

Estelle patted him lightly on the arm. "He married me," she said, and looked at Lady Lawrence and laughed gaily.

"Oh, unfair, ma'am," Lord Martindale said. "Since he has already done so, you see, the rest of us poor mortals are unable to compete."

"We could find some excuse to slap a glove in his face and shoot him," Sir Cyril said.

They all laughed.

"But I should not like that at all," Estelle said. "I would be an inconsolable widow for the rest of my life, I warn you."

"In that case," Sir Cyril said with a mock sigh, getting to his feet and circling the table in order to pull out Lady Lawrence's chair, "I suppose we might as well allow Lisle to live. Lucky devil!"

When they were all outside the shop, the gentlemen bowed and took their leave, and Estelle promised to meet Lady Lawrence at the library as soon as she had completed her errand. She did not want her friend to come into the jeweler's shop with her—a different jeweler from the one her husband had visited half an hour before.

She was very excited. Surely he would understand

when he saw it, even though strictly speaking it would
not seem like a gift for him.

She had the advantage over the earl. She remembered quite clearly that there had been nine sapphires.
And she was able to tell the jeweler exactly how wide
the gold band was to be made. She took a long time
picking out a diamond, and did so eventually only because she must do so unless the whole idea was to be
abandoned, for none of them looked quite like the Star
of Bethlehem.

But it did not matter. She was not going to try to
deceive Allan. There was no question of trying to pass
off this new ring as the lost one. She would give it to
him only because she wanted him to know that the
betrothal ring had been important enough to her that
she would spend almost all she had on replacing it.
She wanted him to know that there was still the hope
in her that she had worn on her finger for two years.

The hope that one day he would come to love her as
she loved him.

She was going to ask him to keep the ring until she
came home to stay. Perhaps he would understand that
she wanted that day to come.

Perhaps.

But she would want him to have it anyway.

She hurried along the street in the direction of the
library a short while later, her cheeks still flushed, her
eyes still bright. Everyone around her seemed to be
loaded down with parcels. Everyone looked happy and
smiled back at her.

What a wonderful time of year Christmas was. If
only every day could be Christmas!

The Earl of Lisle was sitting in one corner of his
darkened town carriage, his wife in the other. Heavy
velvet curtains were drawn across the windows, it being late at night. Estelle's gaze was necessarily con-
fined within the carriage, then. But she did not need

to see out. Her gaze was fixed on an imaginary scene
of some magnificence.

" 'For unto us a child is born,' " she sang quietly
to herself. " 'Unto us a son is given; unto us a son is
given.' " She looked across to her husband's darkened
face. "Or is it 'a child is born' twice and 'a son is
given' once?" she asked. "But no matter. Mr. Handel's *Messiah* must be the most glorious music ever
composed, don't you agree, Allan?"

"Very splendid," he agreed. "But I am surprised
you heard any of it, Estelle. You did so much talking." He had meant the words to be teasing, but he
never found it easy to lighten the tone of his voice.

"But only before the music began and during the
interval," she said. "Oh, come now, Allan, you must
admit it is true. I did not chatter through the music.
How could I have done so when I was so enthralled?
And how could I have sat silent between times when
we were in company with friends? They would have
thought I was sickening for something."

Her eyes fixed on the upholstery of the seat opposite
her, and soon she was singing softly again. " 'There
were shepherds abiding in the field, Keeping watch
over their flocks by night.' " She hummed the orches-
tra's part.

The earl watched her broodingly. He could not see
her clearly in the darkness, but he would wager that
her cheeks still glowed and that her eyes still shone.
As they had done through dinner at the Mayfields',
through the performance of Handel's *Messiah* they had
attended in company with six friends, and through late
evening tea and cards at the Bellamys'.

She was so looking forward to Christmas, she had
told everyone who had been willing to listen—and everyone was always willing to listen to Estelle, it
seemed. The first that she and her husband had spent
at their own home. And her mama and papa were coming and her married brother with his wife and two

children, and her unmarried brother. And her husband's mother and his two sisters with their families. And two aunts and a few cousins. One more week and they would begin to arrive.

She had been pleased when he had agreed a couple of months before to stay in London and host the family Christmas that year. But she had not bubbled over so with high spirits to him. He could not seem to inspire such brightness in her.

"I spent a fortune this morning, Allan," she said to him now, turning her head in his direction. And he could tell from her voice that she was still bubbling, though she had only him for audience. "I bought so many presents that Jasper looked dubious when I staggered along to the coach. I think he wondered how we were to get all the parcels inside." She laughed.

"Did you enjoy yourself?" he asked.

"I love Christmas," she said. "I live like the world's worst miser from summer on just so that I can be extravagant at Christmas. I think I enjoy choosing gifts more than I like receiving them. I bought Nicky a little silver watch for his pocket. Such a dear little child's thing. You should just see it." She giggled. "I suppose he cannot tell time. I will have to teach him."

"Did you buy such lavish gifts for the other servants?" he asked.

"Oh, of course not." She laughed again. "I would have to live like a beggar for five years. But I did buy them all something, Allan. And they will not mind my giving Nicky something special, will they? He is just a child, and has doubtless never had a gift in his life. Except for his sea-shell, of course."

"Did you meet anyone you knew?" he asked.

"I was with Isabella," she said. "We nodded to a few acquaintances." There was the smallest of hesitations. "No one special."

"Martindale is not special?" he asked quietly. "Or Porchester?"

There was a small pause again. "Someone told you," she said. "We met them on Oxford Street and they invited us for tea and cakes. I was glad to sit down for half an hour. My feet were sore."

"Were they?" he said. "You did not look as if you were in pain."

She looked sharply at him. "You saw us," she said. "You were there, Allan. Why did you not come inside?"

"And break up the party?" he said. "And make odd numbers? I am more of a sport than that, Estelle."

"Oh," she cried, "you are cross. You think that I was doing something I ought not to have been doing. It is quite unexceptionable for two married ladies to take tea with two gentlemen friends at a public confectioner's. It is too bad of you to imply that it was some clandestine meeting."

His voice was cold. "One wonders why you decided not to tell me about it if it was so unexceptionable," he said.

"Oh!" she said, exasperated. "For just this reason, Allan. For just this reason. I knew you would read into it something that just was not there. It was easier not to tell you at all. And now I have put myself in the wrong. But if you will spy on me, then I suppose you must expect sometimes to be disappointed. Though when I think about that last statement, I don't suppose you were disappointed. Unless it was over the fact that it was not just me and one of the gentlemen. That would have suited you better, would it not?"

"One is hardly spying on one's wife by walking along Oxford Street in the middle of the day," he said.

"Then why did you ask me those questions?" she said. "In the hope that I would lie or suppress the truth? Why did you not simply remark that you had seen me with Isabella and Lord Martindale and Sir Cyril?"

"I should not have had to either ask or make the comment," he said. "If it was all so innocent, Estelle, you would have come home and told me about the afternoon and your encounters. You find it very easy to talk to all our friends and acquaintances, it seems. You never stop talking when we are out. Yet you have very little to say to me. How can I escape the conclusion sometimes that you have something to hide?"

"What nonsense you speak!" she said. "I have been talking to you tonight, have I not? I talked to you about the concert and you remarked that I had chattered too much. I told you about my Christmas gifts and you suggested that I had spent too much on Nicky. Do you think I enjoy such conversation? Do you think I enjoy always being at fault? I don't think I am capable of any goodness in your eyes."

"There is no need to yell," he said. "We are in a small space and I am not deaf."

"I am not yelling!" she said. "Oh, yes I am, and I yell because I choose to do so. And if you were not so odious and so determined to put me in the wrong, you would yell too. I know you have lost your temper. You speak quietly only so that I will lose mine more."

"You are a child!" he said coldly. "You have never grown up, Estelle. That is your trouble."

"Oh!" she said. And then with a loudly indrawn breath, "I would rather be a child than a marble statue. At least a child has feelings. You have none, do you? Except a fanatical attachment to propriety. You would like a little mouse of a wife to mince along at your side, quiet and obedient and adding to your consequence. You have no human feelings whatsoever. You are incapable of having any."

"We had best be quiet," he said. "We neither of us have anything to say except what will most surely wound the other. Be quiet, Estelle."

"Oh, yes, lord and master," she said, her voice

suddenly matching his in both volume and temperature. "Certainly, sir. Beg pardon for being alive to disturb you, my lord. Console yourself that you will have to put up with me for only another few weeks. Then I will be gone with Mama and Papa."

"Something to be looked forward to with eager anticipation," he said.

"Yes," she said.

They sat side by side for the remainder of the journey home in frigid silence.

Estelle had to keep swallowing against the lump in her throat. It had been another lovely day, though she had seen very little of her husband until the evening, when they had been in company. She had so hoped that they could get to the end of the day without trouble. She had hoped that he would come back to her that night so they might recapture the tenderness of the night before. And they had come so close.

She took his hand as he helped her from the carriage, and tilted her chin up at such an angle that he would know her unappeased. His jaw was set hard and his eyes were cold, she saw in one disdainful glance up at him.

He unlocked the door and stood aside to allow her to precede him into the hallway. Although the coachman had been necessarily kept up very late indeed, all the other servants were in bed. The Earl of Lisle refused to keep them up after midnight when he was perfectly capable of turning a key in a lock. He had explained his strange theories to his butler three years before, on his acquisition of the title and the town house.

Estelle waited in cold silence while he took her cloak and laid it on a hallstand, and picked up a branch of lit candles. But before she could reach out a hand to place on his sleeve so that he might escort her to her room, he set a warning hand on her arm and stood very still, in a listening attitude.

Estelle looked at him questioningly. He handed her the candlestick slowly and without a word, his eyes on a marble statue that stood to one side of the staircase, between the library and his study. A hand gesture told her that she was to stay exactly where she was. He moved silently toward the statue.

A child's treble wailing broke the silence before the earl reached his destination. The sounds of a child whose heart was breaking.

"What are you doing here?" the earl asked, stopping beside the statue and looking down. His voice was not ungentle.

Estelle hurried across the tiles to his side. Nicky was standing between the statue and the wall, his fists pressed to his eyes, one bare foot scratching the other leg through his breeches.

"I was thirsty," he said through his sobs. "I got lost."

The earl stooped down on his haunches. "You wanted a drink of water?" he asked. "Did you not go down the back stairs to the kitchen? How do you come to be here?"

The sobs sounded as if they were tearing the child's chest in two. "I got lost," he said eventually.

"Nicky." The earl reached out a hand and pushed back the boy's hair from his forehead. "Why did you hide?"

"I got scared," the boy said. "Are you goin' ter beat me?" His fists were still pressed to his eyes.

"I told you yesterday that you would not be beaten here, did I not?" the earl said.

Estelle went down on her knees and set the candlestick on the tiled floor. "You are in a strange house and you are frightened," she said. "Poor little Nicky. But you are quite safe, you know, and we are not cross with you." She took the thin huddled shoulders in her hands and drew the child against her. She patted his back gently while his sobs gradually subsided. She glanced across at her husband. He was still stooped down beside her.

The sobs were succeeded by a noisy and prolonged yawn. The earl and his countess found themselves smiling with some amusement into each other's eyes.

"Come on," Estelle said, "we will take you back to your bed, and you shall have your drink."

"I'll take him, Estelle," the earl said, and he stood up, scooping the small child into his arms as he did so. Nicky yawned again.

She picked up the candlestick and preceded them down the stone stairs to the kitchen for a cup of water and up the back stairs to the servants' quarters and the little room that she had been to once the day before. She helped a yawning Nicky off with his shirt and on with his nightshirt while her husband removed the child's breeches.

She smoothed back his hair when he was lying in his bed, looking sleepily up at her. "Sleep now, Nicky," she said softly. "You are quite safe here and must not be afraid of his lordship and me or of anyone else in the house. Good night." She stooped down and kissed him on the cheek.

"Bring a cup to bed with you at nights," the earl said, glancing to the washstand and its full jug of water. "And no more wanderings, Nicky. Go to sleep now. And there must be no more fear of beatings either." He touched the backs of two fingers to the child's cheek, and his lips twitched when a loud yawn was his only answer.

Nicky soon was asleep, even though the yawning stopped abruptly when his door closed softly behind his new master and mistress. He clasped his hands behind his head and stared rather glumly at the ceiling. Mags would kill him if he didn't show up with something within the next few days. More to the point, there would be no money for his mother.

But he was, after all, only ten years old. And the

hour was something after two in the morning. Sleep overtook him. She smelled like a garden, he thought as he drifted off. Or as he imagined a garden would smell. A really soft touch, of course, as was the governor, for all his stern looks. But she smelled like a garden for all that.

The Earl of Lisle had taken the candlestick from his wife's hand. He held it high to light their way back to the main part of the house and their own rooms.

Estelle turned to face him when they entered her dressing room. Her eyes were soft and luminous, he saw. They had lost their cold disdain.

"Oh, Allan," she said, "how my heart goes out to that child. Poor little orphan, with no one to love him and hug him and tuck him into his bed at night."

"You were doing quite well a few minutes ago," he said.

There were tears in her eyes. "He is so thin," she said. "And he was so frightened. Thank you for being gentle with him, Allan. He did not expect you to be."

"I would not imagine he knows a great deal about gentleness or kindness," he said.

"He should not be working," she said. "He should be playing. He should be carefree."

He smiled. "Children cannot play all the time," he said. "Even children of our class have their lessons to do. Mrs. Ainsford will not overwork him. If you fear it, you must have a word with her tomorrow."

"Yes," she said. "I will. How old do you think he is, Allan? He did not know when I asked him."

"I think a little older than he looks," he said. "I will see what I can do, Estelle. I need to make a few inquiries."

Her face brightened. She smiled up at him. "For Nicky?" she said. "You will do something for him? Will you, Allan?"

He nodded and touched her cheek lightly with his knuckles as he had touched the child's a few minutes before. "Good night," he said softly, before taking one of the candles and going into his own dressing room. He shut the door quietly behind him.

Estelle looked at the closed door before beginning to undress herself rather than summon her maid from sleep. She wished fleetingly that she had apologized for calling him a marble statue. He was not. He did have feelings. They had shown in his dealings with Nicky. But what was the point of apologizing? If she could not call him that in all truth, there were a hundred other nasty things she would call him when next he angered her. And his own words and suspicions were unpardonable.

She climbed into bed ten minutes later and tried not to think of the night before. Soon enough she would have to accustom herself to doing without altogether. She needed to sleep anyway. It was very late.

But even before she had found a totally comfortable position in which to lie and quieted her mind for sleep, the door of her dressing room opened and closed and she knew that after all she was not to be alone. Not for a while anyway.

And as soon as he climbed into the bed beside her and touched her face with one hand so that his mouth could find hers in the darkness, she knew that he had not come to her in anger. She put one arm about his strongly muscled chest and opened her mouth to his seeking tongue.

During the week before their guests began to arrive and the Christmas celebrations could begin in earnest, Estelle kept herself happily busy with preparations. Not that there was a great deal for her to do beyond a little extra shopping. She was not the one who cleaned the house from top to bottom or warmed the extra bedrooms and changed their bed linen and generally readied them for the reception of their temporary occupants. She was not the one who would cook and bake all the mounds of extra food.

But she did confer with Mrs. Ainsford about the allocation of rooms and with the cook on the organization of meals. And she insisted, the day before her parents were to arrive and her husband's mother, and a few of the other relatives, on decorating the drawing room herself with mounds of holly and crepe streamers and bows and a bunch of mistletoe.

The earl was called in to help, and it was generally he who was to risk having all his fingers pricked to the bone, he complained, handling the holly and placing it and replacing it while Estelle stood in the middle of the room, one finger to her chin, directing its exact placement.

But there was not a great deal of rancor in his complaints. There had been no more quarrels since the night of the concert. And Estelle seemed to be happy to be at home, aglow with the anticipation of Christmas. She smiled at him frequently. And he basked in her smiles, pretending to himself that it was he and not the festive season that had aroused them.

"Oh, poor Allan," she said with a laugh after one particularly loud exclamation of protest as he pricked his finger on a holly leaf. "Do you think you will survive? I will kiss it better if you come over here."

"I am being a martyr in a good cause," he said, not looking over his shoulder to note her blush as she realized what she had said.

The mistletoe had to be moved three times before it was in a place that satisfied her. Not over the doorway, she decided on second thoughts, or everyone would get mortally tired of kissing everyone else, and Allan's cousin Alma, who was seventeen with all the giddiness of her age, would be forever in and out of the room. And not over the pianoforte, or only the musical people would ever be kissed.

"This is just right," she said, standing beneath its

final resting place to one side of the fireplace. "Perfect." She smiled at her husband, and he half smiled back, his hands clasped behind his back. But he did not kiss her.

She made some excuse to see Nicky every day. Mrs. Ainsford would despair of ever training him to be a proper servant, the earl warned her at breakfast one morning when the child had come into the room to bring him his paper, if she persisted in putting her arm about his shoulders whenever he appeared, whispering into his ear, and kissing him on the cheek. And the poor housekeeper would doubtless have an apoplexy if she knew that her mistress was taking a cup of chocolate to the child's room each night after he was in bed.

But he did not forbid her to do either of those things. For entirely selfish reasons, he admitted to himself. Estelle was happy with the child in the house, and somehow her happiness extended to him, as if he were solely responsible for saving the little climbing boy from a life of drudgery. She smiled at him; her eyes shone at him; she gave him tenderness as well as passion at night.

The Earl of Lisle was not entirely idle as far as his new servant was concerned, though. He had learned during his interview with the chimney sweep, of course, that Nicky was no orphan, but that there was a mother at least and perhaps a father, and probably also some brothers and sisters somewhere in the slums of London. The mother had paid to have the boy apprenticed. The sweep had shrugged when questioned on that point. Someone had probably given her the money. He did not know who, and why should he care?

The mother had not come to protest the ending of the apprenticeship. Neither had anyone else. His lordship had not tried to penetrate the mystery further. He had decided not to question the child, not to confront him with his lie. Not that first lie, anyway. But the

second? Had Estelle really believed that the boy had
been in search of a drink and had got lost? Yes, doubtless she had. She had seen only a thin and weeping
orphan, alone in the dark.

The earl had still not done anything about the matter
five days after the incident. But on the fifth day he
entered his study in the middle of the morning to find
Nicky close to his desk, his eyes wide and startled.

"Good morning, Nicky," he said, closing the door
behind him.

"I brought the post," the boy said in his piping
voice, indicating the small pile on the desk and making his way to the door.

Lord Lisle did not stand aside. His eyes scanned the
desk top. His hands were behind his back. "Where is
it, Nicky?" he asked eventually.

"What?" The eyes looked innocently back into his.

"The top of the inkwell," the earl said. "The _silver_
top." He held out one hand palm-up.

The child looked at the hand and up into the steady
eyes of his master. He lifted one closed fist slowly and
set the missing top in the earl's outstretched hand. "I
was just lookin' at it," he said.

"And clutched it in your and when I came in?"

"I was scared," the child said, and dropped his
head on his chest. He began to cry.

Lord Lisle strolled over to his desk and sat in the
chair behind it. "Come here, Nicky," he said.

The boy came and stood before the desk. His sobs
were painful to hear.

"Here," the earl directed. "Come and stand in front
of me."

The child came.

The earl held out a handkerchief. "Dry your eyes
and blow your nose," he said. "And no more crying.
Do you understand me? Men do not cry—except under
very exceptional circumstances."

The boy obeyed.

"Now," the earl said, taking the crumpled hand-kerchief and laying it on one corner of the desk, "look at me, Nicky." The boy lifted his eyes to his master's chin. "I want you to tell me the truth. It must be the truth, if you please. You meant to take the inkwell top?"

"I didn't think you'd miss it," the boy said after a pause.

"Have you taken anything else since you have been here?"

"No." Nicky lifted his eyes imploringly to the earl's and shook his head. "I ain't took nothin' else."

"But you meant to a few nights ago when we found you outside this door?"

His lordship's eyes advised the truth. Nicky hung his head. "Nothin' big," he said. "Nothin' you'd miss."

"What do you do with what you steal, Nicky?" the earl asked.

"I ain't never stole nothin' before," the child whispered.

A firm hand came beneath his chin and lifted it.

"What do you do with what you steal, Nicky?"

The boy swallowed against the strong hand. "Sell it," he said.

"You must have a lot of money hidden away some-where then," the earl said. "In that little bundle of yours, perhaps?"

Nicky shook his head. "I ain't got no money," he said.

The earl looked into the frightened eyes and frowned. "The man you sell to," he said, "is he the same man who apprenticed you to the sweep?"

The eyes grew rounder. The child nodded.

"Who gets the money?" the earl asked.

There was no answer for a while. "Someone," the boy whispered eventually.

"Your mother, Nicky?"

"Maw's dead," the boy said quickly. "I was in the orphinige."

The earl's tone was persistent, though not ungentle. "Your mother, Nicky?" he asked again.

The eyes, which were too old for the face, looked back into his. "Paw left," the child said. "Maw 'ad me an' Elsie to feed. 'E said we would all 'ave plenty if I done it."

The earl removed his hand from the child's chin at last. He leaned back in his chair and steepled his fingers against his mouth. The boy stood before him, his head hanging low, one foot scuffing rhythmically against the carpet.

"Nicky," Lord Lisle said at last, "I will need to know this man's name and where he may be found."

The boy shook his head slowly.

The earl sighed. "Your mother's direction, then," he said. "She will perhaps be worried about you. I will need to communicate with her. You will tell me where she may be found. Not now. A little later, perhaps. I want to ask you something. Will you look at me?"

Nicky did so at last.

"Do you like her ladyship?" the earl asked.

The child nodded. And since some words seemed to be required of him in response, he said, "She's pretty." And when his master still did not say anything, "She smells pretty."

"Would you want her to know that I found you with the silver top in your hand?" the earl asked.

The child shook his head.

"Neither would I," the earl said. "We are in entire agreement on that. What do you think she would do if she knew?"

Nicky swallowed. "She would cry," he said.

"Yes, she would," the earl agreed gently. "Very hard and very bitterly. She will not be told about this, Nicky. But if it were to happen again, perhaps she

would have to know. Perhaps she would be the one to
discover you. I don't want that to happen. Her ladyship
is more important to me than anyone or anything else
in this life. Do you know what a promise is?''

The child nodded.

"Do you keep your promises?''

Another nod.

"Are you able to look me in the eye and promise
me that you will never steal again, no matter how small
the object and no matter how little it will be missed?''
Lord Lisle looked gravely and steadily back into the
child's eyes when he looked up.

Another nod.

"In words, Nicky, if you please.''

"Yes, guv'nor,'' he whispered.

"Good man. You may leave now.'' But before the
child could turn to go, the earl set a hand on his head
and shook it slightly. "I am not angry with you,'' he
said. "And you must remember that we are now in a
conspiracy together to make her ladyship happy.''

He removed his hand, and the child whisked himself
from the room without further ado. Lord Lisle stared
at the door for a long while.

Estelle was not entirely pleased with the ring when
she returned to the jeweler's to fetch it. It was very
beautiful, of course, but she did not think she would
have called it the Star of Bethlehem if this had been
the one Allan had put on her finger. The diamond no
longer looked like a star in a night sky. She did not
know why. It was surely no larger or no smaller than
the other had been, and yet it looked more prominent.
It did not nestle among the sapphires.

But no matter. She had not expected it to look the
same, anyway. There could be no real substitute for
the original ring. This one would serve its purpose—
perhaps. She took it home and packed it away with
the rest of her gifts.

The following day the guests would begin to arrive. She would see her parents for the first time in six months. She had missed them. And everyone else would be coming, too, either on the same day or within the few days following. And Christmas would begin.

She was going to enjoy it more than any other Christmas in her life. It might be her last with Allan. The last during which they would be truly husband and wife, anyway. And though panic grabbed at her stomach when she thought of what must happen when the holiday was over and Mama and Papa began to talk about returning home, she would not think of that. She wanted a Christmas to remember.

The Earl of Lisle was no better pleased with his ring. He knew as soon as he saw it that the original must have had nine sapphires. The arrangement of eight just did not look right. They did not look like a night sky with a single star shining from it.

But it did not matter. Nothing could look quite like the Star of Bethlehem, and this ring was lovely. Perhaps she would know that it was not meant to be a substitute, but something wholly new. Perhaps. He wrapped the little velvet box and carried it about with him wherever he went.

Nicky, in the meanwhile, was feeling somewhat uncomfortable, for several reasons. There was the whole question, for example, of what Mags would do with him if he could get his hands about his throat. And what his new master would do with him if he caught him thieving again. Nicky had the uncomfortable feeling that it would not be a whipping, which would be easy to bear. The governor would force him to look into his eyes for a start, and that would be worse than a beating. He was proving to be not such a soft touch after all.

Then, of course, there was his mother. And Elsie. Were they starving? Was Mags bothering them? He knew what Mags did to help girls to a living. But Elsie was not old enough yet. Nicky did not know what he would do short of abandoning his family to their fate. Nothing had been said about any money in this new position of his. Plenty of clothes and food, yes, and very light work. But no money.

There was, of course, the shiny shilling the lady had given him the first night she came to him with a cup of chocolate. Nicky had never seen so much money all in once. But he couldn't give that to his mother. He needed it for something else.

And that brought him to the nastiest problem of all. That ring and that diamond almost burned a hole in his stomach every day, pressed between the band of his breeches and his skin as they always were. He couldn't sell them to Mags now. It would seem like breaking his promise, though the things were already stolen when he had been forced to look into his master's eyes and make the promise, and though he had never thought of keeping a promise before.

And he couldn't put them back in the lady's room, though he had thought of doing so. Because she would tell the governor and he would know the truth. He was a real sharper, he was. And he would not whip or even scold. He would look with those eyes. He might even put a hand on his head again and make him squirm with guilt.

There was only one thing he could think of doing. And that would mean leaving his room again during the night, and the house, after the lady had brought him his chocolate and kissed him and allowed him to breathe in the scent of her. And the governor might catch him and look at him. And the stupid clothes he would be forced to wear would draw ruffians like bees to a honey pot. And Ned Chandler might refuse to help him at the end of it all and might not believe where he had got the things and what he meant to do with them.

Nicky sighed. Sometimes life was very hard. Sometimes he wished he were all grown up already so that he would know without any difficulty at all what was what. And he was getting used to a warm and comfortable bed and to a full night's sleep. He did not particularly want to be prancing about the meaner streets of London at an hour when no one would ever hear of him again if he were nabbed.

Ned Chandler had been a jeweler of sorts at one time. He still had the tools of his trade and still mended trinkets for anyone who came to ask and dropped a few coins his way. Nicky, as a very small child, had often crept into the man's hovel and sat cross-legged and open-mouthed on the floor watching him when he was busy.

It was doubtful that Chandler had ever held in his hands a gold ring of such quality set with nine sapphires of such dark luster, and a diamond that must be worth a fortune in itself.

"Where did you get these 'ere, lad?" he asked in the middle of one particular night, not at all pleased at having been dragged from his slumbers and his two serviceable blankets. He held the ring in one hand, the diamond in the other.

"It belongs to my guv'nor's missus," the child said. "I'm 'avin' it mended for 'er. She sent me. She sent a shillin'."

"A shillin'?" The former jeweler frowned. "And sent yer in the middle of the night, did she?"

Nicky nodded.

"Did you steal these 'ere?" Chandler asked grimly. "I'll whip the skin off yer backside if you did."

Nicky began to cry. His tears were perhaps somewhat more genuine than was usual with him. "She's pretty," he said, "an' she smells like a garden, an' she brings me choc'lut when I'm in bed. An' I'm 'avin' it mended for 'er."

"But she didn't send yer, lad." It was a statement, not a question.

Nicky shook his head. "It's to be a surprise," he said. "Honest, Mr. Chandler. She lost the di'mond, an' she cried, an' I found it. I'm 'avin' it mended for 'er. I'll give you a shillin'."

"I'll do it," Ned Chandler said with sudden decision, looking ferociously down at the tiny child from beneath bushy eyebrows with a gaze that reminded Nicky uncomfortably of the earl. "But if I 'ear tell of a lady wot 'ad a ring stole, Nick lad, I'll find yer and whip yer backside. Understood?"

"Yes." Nicky watched in silent concentration as the jeweler's tools were unwrapped from an old rag and the diamond replaced in the ring.

"You can keep yer shillin'," the man said, tousling the boy's hair when the mended ring had been carefully restored to its hiding place. "And you make sure to give that ring back, lad. Don't you be tempted to keep it, or I'll be after yer, mind."

"Take the money," the boy said, holding out his treasure, "or it won't be my present. Please?"

The man chuckled suddenly. "Well," he said. "I'll take it, 'cos it shows me yer must be honest. Off with yer then, lad. Be careful on your way back."

Nicky grinned cheekily at him and was gone.

Christmas Eve. It had always been Estelle's favorite day of the season. It was on Christmas Day, of course, that the gifts were opened and that one feasted and sat around all day enjoying the company of one's family. But there had always been something magical about Christmas Eve.

On Christmas Eve there was all the anticipation of Christmas.

And this year was to be no exception. There was all the hustle and bustle of the servants and all the tantalizing smells coming from the kitchen, that of the mince pies being the most predominant. And there was Alma pretending to forget a dozen times during the day that the mistletoe was hanging in that particular spot, and standing beneath it. Especially when Estelle's unmarried brother, Rodney, happened to be in the room.

And there was Papa working everyone's excitement to fever pitch, as he did every year, with hints dropped about the presents, hints that stopped just short of telling one exactly what the gift was. And Mama sitting with her needlepoint having a comfortable coze with Allan's mother. And the children rushing about getting under everyone's feet, and their parents threatening halfheartedly to banish them to the nursery even if it was Christmas.

And the men playing billiards. And the girls whispering and giggling. And Papa tickling any child who was unwise enough to come within arm's length of him. And Allan relaxed and smiling, playing the genial host. And Nicky following the tea tray into the drawing room with a plate of cakes and pastries, looking fit enough to eat himself, and the pleased way he puffed out his chest when Estelle caught his eye and smiled and winked at him.

And the group of carolers who came to the door before the family went to church and were invited inside the hall and stood there and sang, their cheeks rosy from the cold outside, their lanterns still lit and in their hands. And the noisy and cheerful exchange of season's greetings before they left again.

And the quiet splendor of the church service after the hectic day. And the Christmas music. And the Bible readings. And Bethlehem. And the star. And the birth of the baby, the birth of Christ.

And suddenly the meaning of it all, the quiet and breathless moment in the middle of all the noisy festivities surrounding it.

The birth of Christ.

Estelle was seated beside her husband, their arms

almost touching. She looked at him, and he looked back. And they smiled at each other.

The drawing room was noisy again when they went back home, even though the children had been put to bed before they went to church. But finally the adults too began to yawn and make their way upstairs. After all, someone said, it would be a terrible tragedy if they were too tired to enjoy the goose the next day.

Estelle smiled rather regretfully at her husband when they were alone together. "It's going so quickly," she said. "One more day and it will all be over."

"But there are always more Christmases," he said.

"Yes." Her smile did not brighten.

"Are you tired, Estelle?" he asked.

She shrugged. "Mm," she said. "But I don't want the day to end. It has been lovely, Allan, hasn't it?"

"Come and sit down," he said, seating himself on a love seat. "I want to tell you about Nicky."

"About Nicky?" She frowned. And Allan wanted to talk to her?

One of his arms was draped along the back of the love seat, though he did not touch her when she sat down beside her. "I have been making some plans for him," he said. "I spoke with him in my study this morning. He seemed quite agreeable."

"Plans?" Estelle looked wary. "You are not going to send him away, Allan? Not another apprenticeship? Oh, please, no. He is too young."

"He is going to live with his mother and his sister," he said.

She looked her incomprehension.

"I am glad to say the orphanage was a fabrication," he said. "To win your sympathy, I do believe."

"He lied to me?" she said. "He has a family?"

"I am afraid he became the victim of a villainous character," he told her gently. "Someone who was willing to set him up in life, buy his apprenticeship to a chimney sweep in exchange for stolen items from the houses that a climbing boy would have access to.''

Estelle's eyes were wide with horror. She did not even notice her husband take one of her hands in his.

''I told him I would not tell you,'' he said. ''But I have decided to do so, knowing that you will not blame Nicky or think the worse of him. I caught him at it a week ago, Estelle, though I already had my suspicions.''

She bit her upper lip. There were tears in her eyes.

''The money from his stolen goods—or some fraction of it—was going to the upkeep of his mother and sister,'' he said. ''It seems the father took himself off some time ago.''

''Oh, the poor baby,'' she whispered.

''I have spoken with the mother.'' He was massaging her hand, which had turned cold, in both of his. ''I had her brought here yesterday. I had from her the name of the villain who has been exploiting the child in this way and have passed it on with some pertinent information to the appropriate authorities. Enough of that. To cut a long story short, the mother has agreed that she would consider life in a country cottage as washerwoman to our house as little short of heaven. Nicky confessed this morning to a lifelong ambition to own a horse. I have suggested that he may enjoy working in our stables—when he is not at school, of course. Somehow he was not nearly so enthusiastic about the idea of school.''

''So he is to live on your estate with his mother?'' she asked.

''Yes.'' He raised her hand to his lips, and this time she did notice as she saw it there and felt his lips warm against her fingers. ''Do you think it a good solution, Estelle? Are you pleased?'' He looked almost anxious.

''And you did all this without a word to me?'' she

asked in some wonder. "You did it to save me some pain, Allan? Did you do it for me?"

His smile was a little twisted. "I must confess to a certain fondness for the little imp," he said. "But yes, Estelle. I thought it might make you happy. Does it?"

"Yes." She leaped to her feet in some agitation and stood quite unwittingly beneath the mistletoe.

He said nothing for a few moments, but he got to his feet eventually and came to stand behind her. He set his hands on her shoulders. "Now this is an invitation impossible to resist," he said, lowering his head and kissing the back of her neck.

She turned quickly and stared at him in some amazement. He had never—ever—held her or kissed her outside her bed. She had not even quite realized that he was so tall and that he would feel thus against her—strong and warm and very safe.

He lowered his head, and his mouth came down open on hers.

And how could a kiss when one was standing and fully clothed and in a public room that might possibly be entered by someone else at any moment seem every bit as erotic as any of the kisses they had shared in bed, when his hands were beneath her nightgown against her naked flesh and when his body was in intimate embrace with hers?

But it was so. She felt an aching weakness spiral downward from her throat to her knees.

When he removed his mouth from hers, it was only to set his forehead against her own and gaze downward at her lips.

"I want to give you your gift tonight," he said. "Now. I want to do it privately. No one else would understand. May I?"

Her senses were swimming, but she smiled at him. "I feel the same way about mine to you," she said. "Yes, now, tonight, Allan. Just the two of us." She ran across the room to where they had all piled their gifts and came back to him with a small parcel in her hands. He had removed his from a pocket.

"Open mine first," he said, and he watched her face as she did so. They were both still standing, very close together, underneath the mistletoe. "It is not the original," he said quickly as she opened the velvet box. "It is not nearly as lovely. There were nine sapphires, were there not? I could not remember, but these do not look right. But I want you to have it anyway. Will you, Estelle? Will you wear it?" He took it from the box and slid it onto her nerveless finger.

"Allan!" she whispered. "But why?"

He was not sure he could explain. He had never been good with words. Especially with her. "You called it the Star of Bethlehem," he said. "I always loved that name, because it suggested Christmas and love and peace and hope. All the things I have ever wanted for you. And with you. I felt I could only tell you with the ring. Never in words. Until now."

He laughed softly. "It must be the mistletoe. I am not the man for you, Estelle. You are so beautiful, so full of life. So—glittering! I have always envied those other men and wanted to be like them. And I have been horribly jealous and tried to make your life a misery. But I have not meant to. And after Christmas you can go away with your parents, and no one will know that we are separated. There will be no stigma on your name. But you will be free of my taciturn and morose presence." He smiled fleetingly. "My marble-statue self. But perhaps the ring will help you to remember me a little more kindly. Will it?"

"Allan!" She whispered his name. And looked down at the ring on her finger, the ring that was not the Star of Bethlehem, but that she knew would be just as precious to her. And she noticed the parcel lying forgotten in her hands. She held it out to him. "Open yours."

He was disappointed that she said no more. He tried

to keep his hands from trembling as he opened her gift.

He stood smiling down at the silver snuffbox with its turquoise studded lid a moment later. "It is the very one I could not persuade Humber to sell me," he said. "You succeeded, Estelle? You remembered that I wanted it for my collection? Thank you, my dear. I will always treasure it."

But she was looking anxiously into his eyes. "Open it," she said. "There is something else inside. It is not really a present. I mean, it is not for you. It fits me. But I lost the other—yes, I did, Allan. I lost it all, though I have been afraid to tell you. But I wanted you to have this so that you would know that I did not do so carelessly."

He lifted the lid of the snuffbox and stood staring down at a diamond ring set with nine sapphires. He looked up at her, his eyes wide and questioning.

"I didn't mean to lose it," she said. "I have broken my heart over it, Allan. It was my most treasured possession. Because it was your first gift to me, and because at the time I thought it was a symbol of what our marriage would be. And because I spoiled that hope by going about a great deal with my friends when I might have stayed with you and by flirting quite deliberately with other men when you were so quiet and never told me that I meant anything to you. Because I wanted you to know that my behavior has never shown my true sentiments. Those other men have meant nothing whatsoever to me. I have never allowed any of them to touch more than my fingers. You are the only person—the only one, Allan—who occupies the center of my world. The only one I can't bear to think of spending my life without.

"Because I wanted you to keep the ring when you send me away after Christmas, so that perhaps you will come to know that I love you and only you. And so that perhaps you will want to bring me home again some day and put it on my finger again.'' She flashed him a nervous smile. "I have given it to you, you see, in the hope that you will give it back to me one day. Now is that not the perfect gift?''

He lifted the ring from the snuffbox, slipped the box into a pocket, and took her right hand in his. He slid the ring onto her third finger and looked up into her face. ''Perfect,'' he said. ''Now you have two gifts and I have one. I do not need to keep the ring for even one minute, you see, Estelle.''

The look in his eyes paralyzed her and held her speechless.

''It is the most wonderful gift I have ever had,'' he said. ''It is yourself you are giving me, is it not, Estelle?''

She nodded mutely.

''Come, then,'' he said. ''Give me your second and most precious gift.''

She moved into his arms and laid one cheek against his broad shoulder. She closed her eyes and relaxed all her weight against him.

''Do you understand that my gift is identical to yours in all ways?'' he murmured against her ear.

''Yes.'' She did not open her eyes or raise her head. She lifted her hand to touch his cheek with the backs of her fingers. ''Except that your ring has only eight sapphires.''

He laughed softly.

''You love me, Allan?'' She closed her eyes even more tightly.

''I always have,'' he said. ''I knew it the moment I put the Star of Bethlehem on your finger two years ago. I am not good at showing it, am I?''

She raised her head suddenly and gazed into his eyes. ''How is it possible,'' she said, ''for two people to be married for almost two years and live close to each other all that time and really not know each other at all?''

He smiled ruefully. "It is rather frightening, is it not?" he said. "But think of what a wonderful time we have ahead of us, Estelle. I have so much to tell you if I can find the words. And there is so much I want to know about you."

"I may find too many words," she said. "You know that I can't be stopped once I start, Allan."

"But always to other people before," he said. "Very rarely to me, because you must have thought that I did not want to hear. Oh, Estelle." He hugged her to him and rocked her.

Her arms were wrapped about his chest. She held up her two hands behind his back and giggled suddenly. "I love my two presents," she said. "One on each hand. But I love the third present even more, Allan. The one I hold in my arms."

"This was an inspired choice of location for mistletoe," he said, kissing her again. "Perhaps we should take it upstairs with us, Estelle, and hang it over the bed."

She flushed as she smiled back at him. "We have never needed any there," she said.

He took her right hand in his, smiled down in some amusement at his Christmas present, which he had placed there, and drew her in the direction of the door and the stairs and—for the first time in their married life—his own bedchamber.

The servants had been called into the drawing room to receive their Christmas gifts, the cook first as she flatly refused to abandon her kitchen for longer than five minutes at the very most.

The Earl of Lisle allowed his wife to distribute the presents, contenting himself with shaking each servant's hand warmly and conversing briefly with each. He wondered if he was looking quite as glowingly happy as Estelle was looking this morning. But he doubted it. No one was capable of glowing quite like her.

Anyway, it was against his nature to show his feelings on the outside. He doubtless looked as humorless and taciturn as ever, he reflected somewhat ruefully, making a special effort to smile at one of the scullery maids, who clearly did not quite know where to put herself when it became clear that she was expected to place her hand into that of her employer, whom she rarely saw.

But, the earl thought, startling the girl by asking if she had quite recovered from the chill that had kept her in her bed for two days the week before and so showing her that he knew very well who she was, it was impossible—quite impossible—for Estelle to be feeling any happier than he was feeling. He hoped that she was *as* happy as he, but she could not be more so.

For he knew that the glow and the sparkle in her that had caused all attention to be focused on her since she had appeared in the breakfast room before they all adjourned to the drawing room to open their gifts—he knew that he had been the cause of it all. She glowed because he loved her and had told her so and shown her so all through what had remained of the night when they had gone to bed.

Indeed, it was amazing that she was not yawning and that she did not have dark rings beneath her eyes to tell the world that she had scarce had one wink of sleep all night. When they had not been making love, they had been talking. They had both tried to cram a lifetime of thoughts and feelings and experiences into one short night of shared confidences. And when they had paused for breath, then they had used even more breath in making love to each other and continuing their conversation in the form of love murmurings and unremembered nonsense.

It seemed that the only time they had nodded off to sleep had been just before his valet had come into his room from the dressing room, as he always did, to pull back the curtains from the windows. It was fortunate that the time of year was such that the earl had covered Estelle up to the neck with blankets, because she did not have a stitch on beneath the covers any more than he did.

Poor Higgins had frozen to the spot when he had glanced to the bed and seen his master only barely conscious, his cheek resting on a riot of tumbled dark curls. The poor man had literally backed out of the room. Estelle, fortunately, had slept through the encounter until he woke her with his kisses a few minutes later. And he had gazed in amusement and wonder at the blush that had colored her face and neck—after two years of marriage.

Estelle had just given Nicky his present and, child that he was, he had to open it right there. She sat down close to where he stood, one arm about his thin waist, heedless of the presence of all her guests and many of the other servants. She looked into his face with a smile and watched his look of wide-eyed wonder and his dropped jaw as he saw his watch for the first time.

She laughed with delight. "It is a watch for you, Nicky," she said, "so that you will always know what time of day it is. Do you know how to tell time?"

"No, missus," he said in his treble voice, his eyes on his new treasure.

"Then I shall teach you," she said, hugging him and kissing his cheek. "And when you move to the country with your mama and your sister, you will know when it is time to come to the stables to groom the horses, and when it is time to go home from school. Happy Christmas, sweetheart."

He traced the silver frame of the watch with one finger, as if he were not quite sure that it was real.

"His lordship and I will be going into the country after Christmas too," she said. "We will meet your mama and your sister. What is her name?"

"Elsie," he said, and then added hastily, "missus."

"You will want to run along," she said, kissing his cheek again. "I hear that one of the footmen is to accompany you and carry a basket of food to your mama and then go back for you tonight. Do have a lovely day."

"But he don't need to come for me," the child said with some spirit. "I know the way."

Estelle smiled, and the earl held out his hand gravely. "Happy Christmas, Nicky," he said. "Her ladyship and I are very happy that you have come to us."

The child forced his eyes up to the dreaded ones of his master, but he saw nothing but a twinkling kindness there. He turned to leave, but at the last moment whisked a crumpled rag out from the band of his breeches and almost shoved it into Estelle's hands.

"For you," he said, and was gone from the room before she could react at all.

"Oh, Allan, he has given me his seashell," she said to her husband in some distress before being caught up again in the noise and bustle of the morning.

An hour passed before there was a lull enough that the Earl of Lisle could take his wife by the hand and suggest into her ear that they disappear for half an hour. She picked up the half-forgotten rag as they were leaving the room.

"I wished you a happy Christmas very early this morning under the mistletoe," he said with a smile when the study door was safely closed behind them, "and early this morning after I had quite finished waking you. But I feel the need to say it again. Happy Christmas, Estelle." He lifted her hands one at a time to his lips, kissing first the ring he had given her, and then the one she had given him. "We have established an undying reputation for eccentricity, I believe, with two almost identical rings, one on each of your hands."

"They are identical in meaning too," she said, gripping his hands and stretching up to kiss him on the lips. "Allan, what am I to do with this seashell? He has treasured it so much."

"He really wanted to give it to you," he said. "Let's have a look at it, shall we?"

They both stood speechless a few moments later, their foreheads almost touching as they gazed down at the Star of Bethlehem nestled on her palm inside the rag. And then their foreheads did touch and Estelle closed her eyes.

"Oh," she said, after a lengthy silence during which neither of them seemed able to find quite the right words to say, "was there ever such a Christmas, Allan?"

"What I am wondering," he said in a voice that sounded surprisingly normal considering the emotion that had held them speechless, "is where we are to find another finger to put it on."

"I see how it is," she said, clasping ring and rag in one hand and lifting both arms up about his neck. She made no attempt to suggest a solution to the problem he had posed. "The wise men lost the star too for a while, but when they found it again, it was over Bethlehem, and they found also everything they had ever been looking for. Oh, Allan, that has happened to us too. It has, hasn't it? What would we have ever done if Nicky had not come into our lives?"

He did not answer her. He kissed her instead.

She giggled suddenly after he had lifted his head. "I have just had a thought," she said. "A thoroughly silly thought. Nicky came down a chimney and brought us a Christmas happier than any our dreams could have devised."

He laughed with her. "But I don't think even our wildest dreams could convey sainthood on Nicky," he said. "I don't think he can possibly be the real Saint Nicholas, Estelle. Would a real saint steal both a diamond and a ring, as Nicky of the sharp eyes obviously did, be smitten by a pretty lady who smells pretty, and have the ring mended by some devious means? I think it will be entirely better for my digestion if I don't investigate that last point too closely, though doubtless I will feel obliged to do just that tomorrow. The little imp. Perhaps he is Saint Nicholas after all. Now do you suppose we should go back upstairs to our guests?"

She hesitated and brushed at an imaginary speck of lint on his shoulder and passed a nervous tongue over her lips.

"What is it?" he asked.

She flushed and kept her eyes on his shoulder. "I have another gift for you," she said. "At least, I am not sure about it, though I am almost sure. And I suppose I should not offer it as a gift until I am certain. But by that time Christmas will be over. And it is such a very special Christmas that I have become greedy and want to make it even more so."

He laughed softly. "Suppose you give it to me," he said, "and let me decide if it is a worthy offering or not."

She raised her eyes to his and flushed a deeper shade. "I can't actually give it to you for a little more than seven months," she said. "That is, if I am right about it anyway. But I think I must be, Allan, because it has been almost a whole month now."

"Estelle?" He was whispering.

"I think it must be right," she said, wrapping her arms about his neck again, "because I am never late except perhaps by a day or two. And I think I have felt a little dizzy and nauseated some mornings when getting out of bed, though that could, of course, be wishful thinking. I think I am with child, Allan. I think so. After almost two years. Can it be true, do you think?"

He did not even attempt to answer her question. He caught her up in a hug that seemed designed to crush every bone in her body, and in the body of their child too. He pressed his face to her neck. Hers was hidden against his shoulder.

For the next several minutes it is doubtful that Estelle was the only one without dry eyes. It seemed that men did sometimes cry—in very exceptional circumstances.

About the Authors

Gayle Buck lives in Bandera, Texas. She won the *Romantic Times* Reviewers Choice Award for the Best New Regency Author in 1986 and for Best Regency Romance in 1987.

Edith Layton lives in Jericho, New York. She has won seven writing prizes and was recently elected to the *Romantic Times* Romance Writers Hall of Fame.

Patricia Rice lives in Mayfield, Kentucky. She won the 1988 *Romantic Times* Award for Best Historical Regency for *Indigo Moon*.

Anita Mills lives in Kansas City, Missouri. She won the *Romantic Times* Award for Best New Regency Author in 1987.

Mary Balogh, who lives in Kipling, Saskatchewan, won the *Romantic Times* Award for Best New Regency Writer in 1985, and the Waldenbooks Award for Bestselling Short Historical in 1986 for *The First Snowdrop*.

HISTORICAL ROMANCE –

—send in the coupon below—

To get your FREE historical romance and start saving, fill out the coupon below and mail it today. As soon as we receive it we'll send you your FREE book along with your first month's selections.